OXFORD WORLD'S CLASSICS

For over 100 years Oxford World's Classics have brought readers closer to the world's great literature. Now with over 700 titles—from the 4,000-year-old myths of Mesopotamia to the twentieth century's greatest novels—the series makes available lesser-known as well as celebrated writing.

The pocket-sized hardbacks of the early years contained introductions by Virginia Woolf, T. S. Eliot, Graham Greene, and other literary figures which enriched the experience of reading. Today the series is recognized for its fine scholarship and reliability in texts that span world literature, drama and poetry, religion, philosophy and politics. Each edition includes perceptive commentary and essential background information to meet the changing needs of readers.

OXFORD WORLD'S CLASSICS

HENRY JAMES

The American

Edited with an Introduction and Notes by
ADRIAN POOLE

Oxford New York
OXFORD UNIVERSITY PRESS
1999

OXFORD

UNIVERSITY PRESS

Great Clarendon Street, Oxford OX2 6DP

Oxford New York

Athens Auckland Bangkok Bogotá Buenos Aires Calcutta
Cape Town Chennai Dar es Salaam Delhi Florence Hong Kong Istanbul
Karachi Kuala Lumpur Madrid Melbourne Mexico City Mumbai
Nairobi Paris São Paulo Singapore Taipei Tokyo Toronto Warsaw

and associated companies in Berlin Ibadan

Oxford is a registered trade mark of Oxford University Press

Introduction, Select Bibliography, Explanatory Notes © Adrian Poole 1999
Chronology © Leon Edel 1983

First published as an Oxford World's Classics paperback 1999
Reissued 2009

British Library Cataloguing in Publication Data
Data available

Library of Congress Cataloging in Publication Data
James, Henry, 1843–1916.
The American / Henry James; edited with an introduction and notes
by Adrian Poole.
(Oxford world's classics)
Includes bibliographical references (p.   ).
1. Americans—France—Paris—Fiction.   2. Family—France—Paris
Fiction.   I. Poole, Adrian.   II. Title.   III. Series: Oxford
world's classics (Oxford University Press)
PS2116.A6   1999   813'.4—dc21   98-42570
ISBN 978-0-19-955520-8

1

Typeset by Best-set Typesetter Ltd., Hong Kong
Printed in Great Britain
by Clays Ltd, St Ives plc

CONTENTS

ACKNOWLEDGEMENTS

I am grateful to Jean Khalfa for advice about the French words and phrases in the novel, to Jean Gooder, Richard Gooder, and Philip Horne for helpful suggestions about some of the Explanatory Notes, and to Tony Tanner for the instructive pleasures of the James seminar we taught together for a number of years, in which this novel was always our point of departure.

INTRODUCTION

*Readers who do not wish to learn details of the plot will prefer to
treat the Introduction as an Epilogue*

'I take possession of the old world—I inhale it—I appropriate it!' So
James crowed to his folks back home on arrival in Europe in Novem-
ber 1875.[1] He paused in London—'the same old big black
London'—but his destination was Paris, the city of Art and Culture,
and more particularly the city of Balzac, the novelist whom he would
later describe as 'the father of us all'.[2] It was also the lodging of
Turgenev, the living novelist he most admired, and through him
James would find an introduction to Balzac's successors, the circle of
'realists' gathered round Gustave Flaubert, including Daudet,
Edmond de Goncourt, Maupassant, and Zola. What a dream, surely,
for an aspiring writer in his thirty-third year. And yet Paris held him
for merely a twelvemonth. By Christmas 1876 he was settled in the
big, black London that would be his home for twenty years and his
base for the rest of his life. Looking back on his year in Paris shortly
after, he reflected: 'I saw . . . that I should be an eternal outsider.'[3]

The novel he wrote during his year in France is at one level a
complex personal romance. The American of the title, Christopher
Newman, arrives in Paris all set to appropriate the old world, but the
climax of his story finds him up against a blank wall behind which
the object of his desire is irretrievably confined. As James later
recalled the germ of the story in his Preface, he had thought of 'the
situation, in another country and an aristocratic society, of some
robust but insidiously beguiled and betrayed, some cruelly wronged,
compatriot', the victim of 'persons pretending to represent the
highest possible civilisation and to be of an order in every way superior to his own' (p. 4). It was an old story, of American innocence

---

[1] *Henry James Letters*, ed. Leon Edel, vol. ii: *1875–1883* (London, 1978). Hereafter
referred to as *Letters*, ii.
[2] 'The Lesson of Balzac' (1905), in *Literary Criticism*, vol. ii: *French Writers, Other
European Writers, the Prefaces to the New York Edition*, ed. Leon Edel with the assistance
of Mark Wilson (New York, 1984). Hereafter referred to as *LC*, ii.
[3] *The Complete Notebooks of Henry James*, ed. Leon Edel and Lyall H. Powers (New
York, 1987), 217.

Introduction

confronting European sophistication. James had told it once already in *Roderick Hudson* (1875), and he would tell it again, with all sorts of ingenious variations, in *The Portrait of a Lady* (1881), *The Reverberator* (1888, an overt reworking of *The American*), *The Wings of the Dove* (1902), *The Ambassadors* (1903), and *The Golden Bowl* (1904). The twist for James always inhered in the question of what the victims would do when the truth of their injury dawned. Would they take revenge? If so, exactly how? And if not, what would they take in its place? What compensation or redress more virtuous or more subtle than brute denunciation, all the uproar and violence of a public fiasco?

In this respect Christopher Newman is the prototype of many subsequent Jamesian figures. What seized James was the thought of him poised on the brink of vengeance, and then—'he would simply turn, at the supreme moment, away' (p. 4). It is the most characteristic of Jamesian movements, though it can mean many different things. Newman turns away twice, once from the prospect of possessing his desire, then again from the prospect of punishing those who have robbed him of it. He loses the woman he desires, but he also relinquishes the desire itself to hold the others in his masterful grip, both the loved and the hated. Why *does* he turn away from revenge? James makes some suggestions—'Christian charity or unregenerate good nature' (1879), 'Christian charity or mere human weakness of will' (1907). But he will not pass judgement: 'what it was, in the background of his spirit—I don't pretend to say' (p. 359). Nor does he pretend to say what Newman may gain from his whole ordeal as he turns away to the future.

The reader should know that between 1879 and 1907 a good deal happens to Newman and his novel. These dates refer respectively to the texts of the first English edition (Macmillan) and of the New York Edition (Scribner). For this latter, James revised the novel very extensively, and an account of this process, including some detailed comparisons between the early and late versions, is provided in Appendix 2.

So there are certain parallels between Newman's 'failure' in Paris and James's own. Through Newman's assault on the old world James could imagine the drama of initiation that eternally fascinated him. What does it take to get inside the walls of the city or fortress or palace? How thick are these walls and who guards their gates and is there a password? Whose is that face at the window? What if you get in but then lose yourself in the labyrinth and cannot get out again or simply can't breathe? At the heart of the darkness inside, will you find a treasure or beauty or love or secret, one worth risking all you have, all you are for? Romantic questions no doubt, but ones that James and his fiction keep asking—unlike his French contemporaries, as he felt, the realists who knew in advance that the quest for hidden value or meaning or truth was in vain. The novel that occupied him throughout his year in France would be his way of turning away from them and their world, even of avenging himself on them.

And yet the hero of *The American*—and the word 'hero' is not inappropriate, however ironically qualified—is about as unlike James as he could be. Christopher Newman sets foot in Paris with all the money he needs and more, keen to possess and appropriate, though not necessarily to inhale. Possess what, exactly? Newman is conscious that he lacks something which he believes old Europe can provide. Call it 'culture', perhaps: 'I don't come up to my own standard of culture', he confesses to his confidante Mrs Tristram. Less self-assured in 1907 than thirty years earlier, Newman tells her he has the 'instincts' if not 'the forms of a high old civilisation' (p. 45). What he needs, he supposes, must take the form of a woman, 'a pure pearl', 'the best article in the market' (pp. 47, 48). Mrs Tristram is happy to play fairy godmother and proposes a princess, Claire de Cintré, née de Bellegarde, the beauty well guarded by her stiff patrician kinsfolk, her old mother the Marquise, and her elder brother Urbain. Newman is spurred by their opposition to his suit, not least because he cannot quite grasp what it is they have against him. He is a good-natured fellow and he cannot believe that deep down, beneath the difference of language and culture and manners and history, everyone else isn't like him. He woos the imprisoned beauty with his dollars and inches, but just as he seems on the point of triumph, the villains realize that they cannot after all stomach his manners and origins, or his lack of them. There is no good nature in their culture after all, not one little bit. At which point one kind of romance gives way to another, and the dream turns black.

Meanwhile Newman's creator was almost certainly not in search of a wife in Paris. There was Henrietta Reubell, he told his brother William, for instance:

extremely ugly, but with something very frank, intelligent and agreeable about her. If I wanted to desire to marry an ugly Parisian-American, with money and *toutes les élégances*, and a very considerable capacity for development if transported into a favoring medium, Miss R would be a very good objective. But I don't—*j'en suis à 1000 lieues*. (*Letters*, ii. 42)

Instead she became a good friend (and the model for Miss Barrace in *The Ambassadors*). The nearest anyone has ever got to suggesting a real-life model for Claire de Cintré is the novelist and woman of letters, Marie-Thérèse Solms, who wrote under the name of 'Mme Bentzon'.[4] There are some intriguing parallels between the unhappy circumstances and experience of James's heroine and those of Mme Bentzon—and her own fictionalized account of these in her novel *Une vie manquée* (1874). But there is no urgency to suppose that James himself got entangled with Mme Bentzon in person: they may never even have met. All James ever needed was the merest hint of a story, as his wonderful *Notebooks* attest.

If we are looking for real-life models, there is firmer evidence for the impact of a Russian painter called Paul Joukowsky (as James spelt it, though today it would be 'Zhukovski'). Just after disowning the prospect of romance with Miss Reubell, James confessed to his brother William that with Joukowsky he had 'quite sworn an eternal friendship' (*Letters*, ii. 42). We do not know how far James's feelings for this man went,[5] but it seems clear that the friendship contributed to the one in the novel between Newman and Valentin de Bellegarde, Claire's younger brother. When he came to revise the novel it is notable how much the older James intensified the relationship between the two men (see Appendix 2, pp. 379–83). It would be too simple to mark a difference between Newman and James by saying that one desires Claire and the other desires Valentin, for Newman is powerfully drawn both to brother and sister. Yet if one may think of novelists sometimes competing with their own central characters, one may say that James never dreams of himself as a rival with Newman for Claire. This helps to explain the flimsiness of her pres-

---

[4] See Jean Perrot, 'Un Amour de James', *Revue de littérature comparée*, 57 (1983), 275–94; Sheldon M. Novick, *Henry James: The Young Master* (New York, 1996).

[5] Sheldon M. Novick proposes that James is recalling his own emotional state when Bernard Longueville, in the novel *Confidence* (1879), discovers that he is in love, in what is clearly the same Normandy resort of Étretat James visited and described in August 1876.

ence, which James himself laments in his Preface, and the surreptitiously telling impression she makes on Tom Tristram of 'a great white doll of a woman' (p. 52). Valentin is a different matter.

Nor were James's own pockets brimming over with Newman's kind of fantasy money. This was why he began the novel so promptly on arrival in Paris. To underline the urgency, he received a stinging rebuke from his mother for drawing too heavily on his father's credit en route, at a time when the family finances were rocked by the economic climate back home (*Letters*, ii. 18–19). Of course plenty of James's protagonists are blessed and cursed with the fortune he didn't have himself, from Rowland Mallett and Isabel Archer to Milly Theale and Maggie Verver. Like Newman many of them confront Europe for the first time, whereas for James by 1876 Europe was scarcely a novelty, however full of new and renewable delights. He had spent his childhood and youth shuttling between the old world and the new: the young Jameses thought of themselves as 'hotel children'. In *A Small Boy and Others* (1913) he recalls that Paris was the scene of his earliest memory, and in any case 'some relative or other, some member of our circle, was always either "there" ("there" being of course generally Europe, but particularly and pointedly Paris) or going there or coming back from there'.[6]

What makes Newman so different both from James's other American innocents abroad and from their experienced author is that he has made the fortune all by himself—and from 'business'. James confessed, on behalf of the family, that 'we all formed together quite a monstrous exception: business in a world of business was the thing we most agreed (differ as we might on minor issues) in knowing nothing about.'[7] What is more, Newman is a Westerner from the newest margin of the new world, California—not a son of the old East, like James and his family (and the Revd Babcock). Then again Newman has fought in the Civil War, as Henry (and his elder brother William) had not. Newman is simply more unlike James than any other protagonist in his full-length fiction, with the exception of Basil Ransom in *The Bostonians* (1886), who has also fought in the Civil War, though on the losing side. Christopher Newman sports his auspiciously adventurous name at least as candidly as the hero of the later novel whose names connote royalty and deliverance, the

---

[6] *Henry James: Autobiography*, ed. Frederick W. Dupee (London, 1956), 33.
[7] *Autobiography*, 35.

readiness of a man to pay a 'king's ransom' to save an imprisoned princess. The early James briskly assures us that Newman is 'physically, a fine man' (1879); in 1907 this swells to admiration for 'the general easy magnificence of his manhood' (p. 18). The later Valentin echoes this when he congratulates Newman for being 'in the flower of your magnificent manhood' (p. 101). A real man then, and perhaps a man of the future, thoroughly deserving, at least at first glance, to be called 'the superlative American' (p. 18)—as one might say *americanissimo*. This is the fate from which James tries to save him.

Saving people and things is always a prime motive in James, both for his fictional figures and for the writer himself, and in *The American* it applies at all sorts of level. Within the novel Newman thinks of himself as a would-be redeemer. Of Claire de Cintré of course, the imprisoned beauty, but also of her vagrant counterpart, the perilously liberated Noémie Nioche, who catches his attention in the opening scene in the Louvre. If the statuesque Claire needs to be released then the loose Noémie needs to be locked up—in marriage with a decent young man of her own class to keep her in place. Noémie knows she needs a saviour but this is not what she has in mind. (Valentin makes an ironic reference at one point to Perseus and Andromeda.) Newman thinks his money might help to save her, though she must pretend to work for it. Being a new man, he can ignore her sexual attractions (as the unregenerate Valentin cannot).

This is because Newman is more concerned to save her bedraggled father, as he himself affirms. But why? We are told that 'the old man's decent forlornness appealed to his democratic instincts' (p. 57). The 'forlornness' here associates M. Nioche with the 'forlorn aristocracies' of which James speaks in his Preface with a certain emphasis (p. 13). It is only the decent bits of the old world that Newman democratically wants to save, and there must be a decent father somewhere. M. Nioche is the only candidate. A good father is what Newman forlornly wants to make of the hapless and feckless old man. Democratic or not, his instincts rightly tell him that Noémie is dangerous.

There is no good father to be found at the Bellegardes', but only the stony usurpers, the old Marquise and her elder son. Newman assures the beautiful woman he tries to prise from their grasp, though he stutters revealingly over it, that with him she will be ' "as safe—as safe"—and even in his ardour he hesitated for a comparison—"as safe," he said with a kind of simple solemnity, "as in your father's arms"' (p. 188). But there is another child of the house worth saving, Claire's brother Valentin, the aimless, dissolute, charming young patrician who will die in a meaningless duel of honour. He too speaks of the sense of 'safety' Newman gives him (p. 101). Like his sister, Valentin is largely but not wholly in thrall to the values and manners of his caste, the best of which he truly upholds, the worst of which he cannot slough off, a potential defector not immune to Newman's temptations. Valentin's delicate moustache produces a quietly delicate joke about his resembling a 'page in a romance' (p. 99). And his name—Newman sounds it as 'Valentine'—associates him not only with the saint popularly identified with 'Love', but also with the George Sand romance of that title, which James declared in an essay of 1877 to have 'an irresistible charm' (*LC* ii. 722).[8] If only the romantic young brother and sister could be rescued from their diabolic elder kinsfolk, then perhaps the House of Bellegarde might be saved after all, decayed and superannuated emblem that it is of the Old World itself. As Valentin says: 'a visit like Mr Newman's is just what it wants and has never had. It's a rare chance all round' (p. 92).

But who will save Newman? He has helpers of course, two godmothers in particular, though both are somewhat ambivalent figures. For all the difference in their names, one all poetry the other all prose, Mrs Tristram and Mrs Bread are both embroiled in romance. Mrs Tristram fantasizes about a great Western Barbarian swooping down on a corrupt old world and carrying off the last fair princess. Mrs Bread obliges with its counterpart, a familiar archaic nightmare about the persecution and sacrifice of a beautiful maiden. Each in their different ways inflames Newman's desire for the most blatant forms of triumph or revenge. This is not what he needs to be saved.

The only time men of business really crossed James's path was when they got mixed up with art and artists—publishers, for instance. But writers could themselves be men of business. The great, if eternally perplexing, example was Balzac. In the French writer, James said, there was a 'monstrous duality'. He was 'a man of business doubled with an artist' (*LC* ii. 96). They struggled together, these twin brothers, the man of business threatening to suffocate the artist, the artist striving to save the man of business.

---

[8] Patricia Thomson emphasizes that George Sand was 'a significant part of James's consciousness for over fifty years' (*George Sand and the Victorians* (London, 1977), 216).

Newman is 'the man of business' desperately in need of an artist twin brother. This role is shared between Valentin, James himself, and the reader.

The redeemable elements in the man of business can be glimpsed in the opening scene at the Louvre. We are given a few positive details about his appearance—his nose is 'bold', his eye is 'a clear, cold grey', and so on—but these impinge on us much less than the sense of a certain open-endedness, irresolution, and indefinition. The words and phrases that lodge in our minds are 'blankness', 'full of contradictory suggestions', 'you could find in it almost anything you looked for', 'sufficiently promising', 'undefined and mysterious boundaries' (pp. 18–19). These might be the sort of qualities associated with a country or society or nation full of natural resources awaiting development.

What is he doing in the Louvre? He is being a dutiful tourist looking at all the pictures singled out in the guidebook. We observe him taking 'serene possession', not of a picture that especially captures his imagination, but of a 'commodious ottoman' on which he can stretch out his legs (p. 17). Our first glimpse of him suggests a man not notably susceptible to artistic impressions. Indeed we are soon told that he is 'rather baffled on the aesthetic question', and it is not at all clear that this bafflement is ever dispelled. Nor is it clear that Newman ever suffers more than a passing irritation from his bewilderment, if that. When he makes his summer tour we are told that he 'believed serenely that Europe was made for him and not he for Europe' (p. 72), and that he often gazed 'with culpable serenity at inferior productions' (p. 73). It is as if he waits to see if some organ or faculty will blossom in himself—and James and the reader wait with him—but it never quite does. The nearest thing to it is a passage introduced by the narrator's tortuous thought that 'there is sometimes nothing like the imagination of those people who have none'. He goes on to record Newman feeling 'before some lonely, sad-towered church or some angular image of one who had rendered civic service in an unknown past . . . a singular deep commotion' (p. 74).

In this respect Newman is a bit of a disappointment. To Paris itself he is remarkably unresponsive. 'The complex Parisian world about him seemed a very simple affair; it was an immense, surprising spectacle, but it neither inflamed his imagination nor irritated his curiosity' (p. 42). Looking back in the Preface, James lamented that there was not much of Paris in the novel; he had himself been too on the spot and pressed for time, whereas impressions are always more sharply rendered at leisure, from a distance. As if in recompense he now recalls his own susceptibility at the time of writing to the sounds and sights of the city, 'the particular light Parisian click of the small cab-horse on the clear asphalt', and the 'martial clatter' of a troop of cuirassiers, 'the hard music of whose hoofs so directly and thrillingly appealed' (p. 7). These are the sensual thrills poor Newman never enjoys. His author would 'hang over' the window-bar, his favourite position in any great city, but Newman is never allowed to do so himself, though he does get to sit with Mrs Tristram on her balcony. He is never impressed in return by what James calls the city's 'immense overhanging presence'. It is a disappointment for which James will seek reparation through Lambert Strether, the protagonist of his later and greater Parisian novel, *The Ambassadors*.

But it would be wrong to think of Newman as a lost cause. It is not serenity that has sent him to Europe but the shock of an awakening in a New York cab, which comes on him 'as abruptly as an old wound that begins to ache' (p. 36). Newman may be at a loss before works of art and incurious about the sights and sounds of a great city, but he is much more responsive to drama and story. In that opening scene in the Louvre it is not the paintings on the walls that interest him but the performance of the fetching little copyist. Now *she* has potential, his instincts tell him, for all sorts of things. Modern critics often roundly chastise Newman for all sorts of obtuseness, prejudice, and chauvinism (see Appendix 2, pp. 368–9). But if he *is* redeemable it is because he is curious about, and has the instincts if not the forms for understanding, the dramas and stories he gets entangled with. For this he is not always now given credit. This is what draws Valentin to him and vice versa in what is the novel's real living encounter. They are curious about each other, about the sheer difference of their lives, their temperaments, their desires. Newman wants Valentin's sister, but he also wants to see what wanting her will make happen.

The wound that has started to ache in him is the need to be the spectator and perhaps reader of his own story: 'I sat watching it as if it were a play at the theatre' (pp. 36–7). When he hears Mrs

Tristram's stories about the Bellegardes' victimizing of Claire, his reaction is that 'It's like something in a regular old play' (p. 87). Valentin confirms that Claire's first arranged marriage was 'a first act for a melodrama' (p. 114: in 1879 it was 'a chapter for a novel'). The social gatherings at the Bellegardes' seem to Newman all theatre: 'He felt as if he were at the play and as if his own speaking would be an interruption; sometimes he wished he had a book to follow the dialogue; he half expected to see a woman in a white cap and pink ribbons come and offer him one for two francs' (p. 108). He is uncertain whether he is on stage or in the audience, or even quite what the play is. He has some instincts for theatre, even if he has none for the visual arts, but to develop them he needs to do more reading. Alas, we are told, 'He had never read a page of printed romance' (p. 41). If only he could have read some really good novels (like this one). They might have fortified and subtilized the powers of analysis he needs to survive on this foreign stage in a drama he does not understand. Claire makes him think of reading, but he is simply a novice: 'he had opened a book and the first lines held his attention' (p. 89). Does he ever get past the first lines? Valentin warns him—a sentence added in 1907—that they are a strange family: 'We're fit for a museum or a Balzac novel' (p. 120). To survive in the world of this novel it is not Baedeker he needs but Balzac. But Newman, we know, hasn't read any Balzac, any more than he has read Laclos's *Les Liaisons dangereuses*, an odd volume of which he is handed, 'as a help to wakefulness', by the clever doctor in the Swiss Inn where Valentin lies dying (p. 265).

Romance? Melodrama? Balzac novel? Comedy of manners? Tragedy? Black farce? Like Newman's eye, you can find in this novel almost anything you look for. As Newman waits for Valentin to die, we are told: 'The day had, in its regulated gloom, the length of some interminable classic tragedy' (p. 269). This sentence itself lengthened before it reached its final form in 1907; thirty years earlier it had simply read: 'The day seemed terribly long.' When Mrs Bread finally spills the dark family secret to Newman, she pauses at the climax: 'and, for her listener, the most expert story-teller couldn't have been more thrilling. Newman made almost the motion of turning the page of a "detective story"' (p. 307). When Newman makes his way to the convent in the Avenue de Messine in which Claire has taken refuge, the unreality of it makes him think that 'it was like a page torn out of some superannuated unreadable book' (p. 323).

From its very origins *The American* flaunted its own generic inde-
terminacy. Peter Brooks suggests an important line of thought about
its 'turn' from social comedy to melodrama, and more largely about
the general affiliation of James's fiction to melodrama. The novel can
be understood, Brooks contends, as 'an allegory of James's uncertain
choices among different available forms of "the novelistic" '.[9] Yet it
is doubtful that James was ever as uncertain as this suggests. Even in
the early version there are plenty of clues about reading and writing.
These are liberally scattered to excite the reader's sense of the tale's
own artfulness, of the possible directions in which it might go, of the
genres into which it might settle but fails to. When James came to
revise the text he multiplied and embellished the clues that were
already there, but he also gave Newman himself a much quicker ear
for them. Philip Horne justly concludes: 'The revision of the novel's
expression takes Newman's point of view and grants him the intelligence of its own flexibility, bringing our experience of reading sympathetically close to Newman's reading of experience.'[10] Perhaps in
the intervening years Newman *has* after all inhaled some Balzac. As
he says to Mrs Tristram—and it is a thought that had not occurred
to him in 1877—'there are so many twists and turns over here'
(p. 46).

Brooks puts the case that James is here conducting a dialogue with
Balzac and there is much to be said for this. One might also say that
the novel tries to save Balzac by rewriting him. Not that Balzac is the
only novelist in James's mind or sights. In *Roderick Hudson* he had
gone to Italy specifically to rewrite Hawthorne's *The Marble Faun*.
But in *The American* the fictional models and influences are more
various. The candidates include Edmond About's *Tolla*, Balzac's
Le Père Goriot, Mme Bentzon's *Une vie manquée*, Dumas *fils*' play
L'Étrangère, and Turgenev's *A Nest of Gentlefolk* (or *Lisa*, as it is
often known in English).[11] Around this time James was actively

[9] Peter Brooks, 'The Turn of *The American*', in Martha Banta (ed.), *New Essays on The American* (Cambridge, 1987), 47; see also Brooks, *The Melodramatic Imagination: Balzac, Henry James, Melodrama, and the Mode of Excess* (New Haven, 1976).
[10] Philip Horne, *Henry James and Revision: The New York Edition* (Oxford, 1990), 174.
[11] In Select Bibliography see Novick pp. 55–6, 324 (for About), Brooks and Stowe (for Balzac), Perrot (for Mme Bentzon), Cargill (for Dumas *fils*), and Edel, Kelley, and Lerner (for Turgenev). For the possible influence of George Sand on the 'turn' of the novel to melodrama—rather than Balzac, as Brooks proposes—see Kelley, supported by Thomson.

rehearsing in public his thoughts about other writers, especially those gathered in the volume *French Novelists and Poets* (1878). Between 1874 and 1879 he wrote important essays on all the five major novelists with whom his own creative identity and practice were most closely involved: Turgenev (1874), Flaubert (1874, 1876), Balzac (1875, 1878), George Eliot (1876), and Hawthorne (1879).[12]

It is particularly significant that the first of James's five essays on Balzac should have appeared in print at exactly the moment he arrived in Paris (in *Galaxy*, December 1875). Though they span nearly forty years the keynote of his admiration remains largely unchanged. It is above all vigour, force, energy that Balzac displays, James says in 1875: 'incomparable power'. Behind his figures 'we feel a certain heroic pressure that drives them home to our credence' (*LC* ii. 53); or again, in 1905, Balzac 'was always astride of his imagination, always charging, with his heavy, his heroic lance in rest, at every object that sprang up in his path' (*LC* ii. 124). The French writer seems the epitome of forces conventionally thought of as male—all aggression, acquisition, penetration, excess, 'the appetite of an ogre' (p. 93). Of Balzac's relations to his own characters James finds himself saying, 'He gets, for further intensity, into the very skin of his *jeunes mariées*' (p. 114). Or again, 'what he liked was absolutely to get into the constituted consciousness, into all the clothes, gloves and whatever else, into the very skin and bones, of the habited, featured, coloured, articulated form of life that he desired to present' (p. 132). There would be something monstrous about such a total appropriation—'the very skin and bones'—if it failed to leave its creatures infused with a life of their own. But here is the paradox of this quasi-divine force, as James hails it in 'The Lesson of Balzac' (1905), that it issues in 'the liberty of the subject' (*LC* ii. 133). Balzac's is the love of a creator for his creatures: 'The love, as we call it, the joy in their communicated and exhibited movement, in their standing on their feet and going of themselves and acting out their characters . . . It was by loving them . . . that he knew them; it was not by knowing them that he loved' (*LC* ii. 132).

A miraculous idea, yet it was not one which commanded James's own deepest loyalties, nor reflected his own creative practice. The

---

[12] See Tony Tanner, *Henry James and the Art of Nonfiction* (Athens, Ga., 1995), ch. 2: 'Henry James and the Art of Criticism'.

paradox he discerns in Balzac remains after all deeply unstable; the divine love is never certainly purged of the shadow of diabolic possession. There is a revealing passage in the Preface to this novel, written not so long after 'The Lesson of Balzac'. James is thinking of his own authorial relation to Newman, and he finds himself reflecting: 'A beautiful infatuation this, always, I think, the intensity of the creative effort to get into the skin of the creature; the act of personal possession of one being by another at its completest' (p. 14). This is obviously a memory of Balzac, or his own idea of Balzac. But note that this is an 'infatuation', however beautiful, and infatuation is not love. James is indulging himself for a moment, and he knows it. Just prior to this he has been speaking of the way Newman holds the novel together: 'for the interest of everything is all that it is *his* vision, *his* conception, *his* interpretation: at the window of his wide, quite sufficiently wide, consciousness we are seated, from that admirable position we "assist"' (p. 14).[13] One notes the slight defensiveness in that description of Newman's consciousness as 'wide, quite sufficiently wide', which leaves open the question of its depth. But in itself the metaphor of the window is a telling one, and it is truer to the ethics of James's own aesthetic than the fantasy about getting into someone else's skin which he goes on to borrow from Balzac. Looking out of a window is a relatively modest occupation of someone else's property, and distinctly more sociable. You can share the view with them.

When James expressed his reservations about Balzac—and he had plenty of them, though they diminish in volume as he grows older— it was the lack of windows and air about which he complained. In 1875 he said that 'The great general defect of his manner . . . is the absence of fresh air' (*LC* ii. 33); the reader 'longs for an open window' (*LC* ii. 37). The great merit of his work is its solidity, the 'close texture' of its material (*LC* ii. 73); everything is 'close-packed, pressed down' (*LC* ii. 92); 'the earth-scented facts of life, which the poet puts under his feet, he had put above his head' (*LC* ii. 82)—as if for all the world he were labouring underground. The gravitational pull is too strong, as it were; we yearn for some countervailing centrifugal force that will raise the spirit above the earth and into the air, a balloon perhaps. But is there any spirit left? There's a

[13] James is thinking of the French *assister à*, to attend (a play or spectacle).

menacing confinement and claustrophobia in Balzac's world, not enough room to breathe, an 'odd want of elbow-room' (*LC* ii. 93), the sense of a cage: 'The cage is simply the complicated but dreadfully definite French world that built itself so solidly in and roofed itself so impenetrably over him' (*LC* ii. 101). James had happier ways of imagining a Balzac building: at the other extreme he could think of a marvellous conjunction of museum, cathedral, and palace. But he could never entirely free himself of the fear that Balzac induced of being trapped and buried alive. Only Balzac could survive in the confines of his own world; other novelists, like James, couldn't hope to compete in building such structures.

From the moment our imagination plays at all, of course, and from the moment we try to catch and preserve the pictures it throws off, from that moment we too, in our comparatively feeble way, live vicariously—succeed in opening a series of dusky passages in which, with a more or less child-like ingenuity, we can romp to and fro. Our passages are mainly short and dark, however; we soon come to the end of them—dead walls, without resonance, in presence of which the candle goes out and the game stops, and we have only to retrace our steps. Balzac's luxury, as I call it, was in the extraordinary number and length of his radiating and ramifying corridors—the labyrinth in which he finally lost himself. (*LC* ii. 126–7)

In *The American* James brought his protagonist up against just such a wall, a 'pale, dead, discoloured wall' (p. 358). By comparison with Balzac's Rastignac in *Le Père Goriot*, Newman gets nowhere. But the dead wall also represents James's own sense of the Balzac novel as, for him, a dead end. Let Flaubert and his circle do it to death. James could see that if he were to salvage anything from Balzac and Paris and the French realist novel, he would need to find more air and more windows.

This is where Turgenev came to his rescue. And not only the admired novelist himself but the other Russian expatriates, such as Joukowski, in whose cosmopolitan company he felt himself so much more at home than with the parochial, self-obsessed French or the dull and incurious Americans. Turgenev he was delighted to find had been far from thoroughly Gallicized or Parisianized: 'he had, with that great tradition of ventilation of the Russian mind, windows open into distances which stretched far beyond the *banlieue*', James wrote in 1884 (*LC* ii. 1026). He had expressed his admiration for Turgenev ten years earlier, in an essay which made the Russian sound like a good model for an ambitious young American novelist. Tur-

genev, he said, 'gives us a peculiar sense of being out of harmony
with his native land—of his having what one may call a poet's quarrel
with it. He loves the old, and he is unable to see where the new is
drifting. American readers will peculiarly appreciate this state of
mind; if they had a native novelist of a larger pattern, it would probably be, in a degree, his own' (*LC* ii. 975). There was a drawback
here, for an American writer could scarcely expect to find enough of
'the old' in his native land to love (or to loathe). But then there was
an obvious solution. An American writer of a larger pattern could
preserve the terms of the poet's quarrel by seeking 'the old' elsewhere. This of course meant Europe.

Balzac might demonstrate 'incomparable power' but he lacked
'charm'. In his writing and world, 'Strength of purpose seems the
supremely admirable thing' (*LC* ii. 48). Turgenev by contrast was
drawn to failure, at least in his typical male figures such as Rudin or
Lavretski. Sooner or later a good native American would feel bound
to protest against the Russian's 'agglomerations of gloom', 'so many
ingenious condensations of melancholy', the implication of 'something essentially ridiculous in human nature, something indefeasibly
vain in human effort' (*LC* ii. 995). Surely, James protested, we should
at least try to be cheerful.

But if there was something premature about Turgenev's pes-
simism, James was none the less deeply drawn to it. Turgenev's work
as a whole says something like this to us, James declares, and the
eloquence of his summary vision suggests his readiness to identify
with it.

Life *is* in fact a battle. On this point optimists and pessimists agree. Evil
is insolent and strong; beauty enchanting but rare; goodness very apt to
be weak; folly very apt to be defiant; wickedness to carry the day; imbe-
ciles to be in great places, people of sense in small, and mankind generally, unhappy. But the world as it stands is no illusion, no phantasm, no
evil dream of a night; we wake up to it again for ever and ever; we can
neither forget it nor deny it nor dispense with it. We can welcome experience as it comes, and give it what it demands, in exchange for something
which it is idle to pause to call much or little so long as it contributes to
swell the volume of consciousness. In this there is mingled pain and
delight, but over the mysterious mixture there hovers a visible rule, that
bids us learn to will and seek to understand. So much as this we seem to
decipher between the lines of M. Turgénieff's minutely written chron-
icle. (*LC* ii. 998)

The swelling volume of consciousness: this is not what James thought one could find in the French realists. For this one must go to Turgenev—or, to look across the English Channel to the land in which he would shortly settle for good, the George Eliot whose *Daniel Deronda* James was avidly, critically reading, as it came out in parts through 1876. Just as he had marked his arrival in Paris with the appearance of a piece on Balzac, so his move to London would coincide with the publication of his dialogue essay, '*Daniel Deronda*: A Conversation', in the *Atlantic Monthly* for December 1876.

Turgenev's is a strong presence in *The American*, and it seems clear that James had in his head the novel known in English as *A Nest of Gentlefolk* or *Lisa* (after the main female character). The ending made a particularly deep impression on him. It is a scene in which the central male figure Lavretski visits the convent to which the young woman he loves has retreated, and catches the briefest glimpse of her. James comments, of the author, that 'He has found the moral interest, if we may make the distinction, deeper than its sentimental one; a pair of lovers accepting adversity seem to him more eloquent than a pair of lovers grasping at happiness' (*LC* ii. 981). This is close to the voice with which James was to defend the 'unhappy' ending to his own novel, in a well-known letter to his editor W. D. Howells:

We are each the product of circumstances and there are tall stone walls which fatally divide us. I have written my story from Newman's side of the wall, and I understand so well how Mme. de Cintré couldn't really scramble over from *her* side! If I had represented her as doing so I should have made a prettier ending, certainly; but I should have felt as if I were throwing a rather vulgar sop to readers who don't really know the world and who don't measure the merit of a novel by its correspondence to the same. . . . I don't think that 'tragedies' have the presumption against them as much as you appear to; and I see no logical reason why they shouldn't be as *long* as comedies. . . . I suspect it is the tragedies in life that arrest my attention more than the other things and say more to my imagination; . . . (*Letters*, ii. 104–5)

It was Turgenev, we may suppose, who helped James listen to his own imagination.

Finally there is the sense in which James may be thought to save his own novel when he came to revise it for the New York Edition. This was true of all the works he chose to gather into this ark. But *The American* needed *more* saving than any of the other full-length novels, even than the earlier *Roderick Hudson* or the shortly subsequent *Portrait of a Lady*, extensively revised as these were. As I have suggested, this was mainly because a greater distance separated him from his central character than in any other full-length fiction. Of the figures of speech he uses to think of his revisions the most favoured is that of 'retouching' (as a painter retouches a canvas).[14] Certainly Newman himself is massively retouched, in a generous effort to swell the 'volume of consciousness' that gathers through his ordeal (see Appendix 2, pp. 370–3). When James came to wonder in his Preface how he had saved the novel from the faults he now saw in it, it was, so he thought, through 'multiplying the fine touches by which Newman should live' (p. 15).

James has much to say here about his own ordeal as well as Newman's. Not just the experience of writing the novel in the first place, scaring and exhilarating as that was, against time, for its serial run in the *Atlantic Monthly*. It was also the experience of rereading it after all these years, and recognizing all the things he might have done otherwise and now could not alter—as well as those that he could. Like Newman himself, the revising James found himself in a given 'predicament', a 'cluster of circumstances', a 'situation', and even a 'trap'. He could not change the events of the plot, the actions and consequences. These he was stuck with. Most damaging of all— though the reader is by no means bound to agree—was the incredibility, as it seemed to him now, of the Bellegardes proving unable to swallow Newman's manners for the sake of his fortune. 'They would positively have jumped . . . at my rich and easy American, and not have "minded" in the least any drawback', he roundly affirms (p. 13). This fundamental falsity had, as he thought, made for all sorts of trouble. There was the rank implausibility of Newman going off on his own to the opera, for instance, just after he has been apparently accepted by the Bellegardes, instead of spending his time with Claire. There was an immovable difficulty about her and her motivation, he reflected. How exactly was she persuaded to go back on her word? 'The delicate clue to her conduct is never definitely placed' in the

---

[14] On 7 August 1905 James reassured the novelist Robert Herrick, who had protested in advance at the thought of the revisions: 'The retouching with any insistence will in fact bear but on one book (*The American*—on *R. Hudson* and the *P. of a Lady* very much less); . . .'. (*Henry James Letters*, ed. Leon Edel, vol. iv (Cambridge, Mass., 1984), 371).

reader's hand, he sighed (p. 15). In all sorts of respects, James bravely confessed, he realized now that he had 'been plotting arch-romance without knowing it' (p. 6).

This leads him to a famous formulation of the difference between 'realism' and 'romance', and shortly after, to this extraordinary metaphor for the activity of the 'romancer':

The balloon of experience is in fact of course tied to the earth, and under that necessity we swing, thanks to a rope of remarkable length, in the more or less commodious car of the imagination; but it is by the rope we know where we are, and from the moment that cable is cut we are at large and unrelated: we only swing apart from the globe—though remaining as exhilarated, naturally, as we like, especially when all goes well. The art of the romancer is, 'for the fun of it', insidiously to cut the cable, to cut it without our detecting him. (p. 12)

This makes the romancer all conscious of what he is up to. Yet this is exactly what the young James had *not* been, as he now confesses. He had cut the cable without realizing it. Logic might suggest that what he should now do, without being detected, was to mend the cable and secretly reattach it to the free-floating balloon. But it was too late for that.

Yet logic is beside the point where these volatile figures of speech are concerned. As James himself says, typically switching his metaphors, one can no more say for certain where realism ends and romance begins, than one can plant a milestone between north and south. The balloon that floats away represents a zenith of peril as Balzac's underground tomb marks a nadir, but the two extremes meet in another image for the danger to which James believes he has succumbed, when he speaks of 'the fine flower of Newman's experience blooming in a medium "cut off" and shut up to itself' (p. 15). To preserve Newman he thinks of himself as having had 'to exclude the outer air' (p. 16). One way or the other it becomes difficult to breathe, whether you are stuck in a bell-jar or floating up into the stratosphere. Being cut off and unrelated, that is the image of disaster.

The idea of threads and cables and ropes and clues was of the utmost importance to James. In the spring of 1876 he wrote from Paris to his father: 'The very slender thread of my few personal relations hangs on, without snapping, but it doesn't grow very stout' (*Letters*, ii. 37). It was not just the thread of his personal relations he had to ensure hung on without snapping. This was also the way he thought of his novel when he looked back in the Preface all those years later: 'It had to save as it could its own life, to keep tight hold of the tenuous silver thread' (p. 8). And again, as he thought of the way his novel might be thought to be saved, it was the 'thread' of 'Newman's own intimate experience all' (p. 12). It was this thread, if anything, that could compensate for the failure to provide the reader with the 'clue' of Claire's conduct, or even perhaps the cut cable itself that should still have tethered the balloon of experience.

In Paris young James was at large and unrelated. And he was anxious. He imagined a character similarly placed but entirely at ease with himself and the world, the very figure of romance itself as he later imagined it: 'liberated and disconnected', 'disengaged, disembroiled, disencumbered' (Preface, pp. 16, 12). They would keep each other company. Newman would begin to learn something of James's own and the rest of the world's discomfort, while James would breathe more easily for sharing his trouble. James ends his rueful, proud, remorseful Preface by thinking of himself as 'clinging to my hero as to a tall, protective, good-natured elder brother in a rough place' (p. 16). Paris in 1876 proved a rougher place than he had expected, for all its surface polish and brilliance.

But then the whole world was a rough place, as James would prove in fiction after fiction, brimming with pain and violence and darkness barely concealed by and sometimes erupting through its smooth and civilized surfaces. One may see in *The American* his first great effort to take and give readers, in the largest sense of the words, the rough with the smooth.

NOTE ON THE TEXT

The novel was first published in twelve instalments of the *Atlantic Monthly* (vols. 37–9) from June 1876 to May 1877. The divisions were as follows:

1	June 1876	Chapters 1–3
2	July 1876	Chapters 4–5
3	August 1876	Chapters 6–7
4	September 1876	Chapters 8–10
5	October 1876	Chapters 11–12
6	November 1876	Chapters 13–14
7	December 1876	Chapters 15–16
8	January 1877	Chapters 17–18
9	February 1877	Chapters 19–20
10	March 1877	Chapters 21–2
11	April 1877	Chapters 23–4
12	May 1877	Chapters 25–6

It was first published in volume form in May 1877 by the Boston firm of James R. Osgood and Co. Some eighty substantive variants from the serial version have been reported by James W. Tuttleton, but it is not clear how much of a hand James himself had in them.[1] English readers could have got their first glimpse of the novel from copies imported the following month by Trübner and Co., or an unauthorized edition by Ward, Lock, & Co., in December. The first authorized English edition was published by Macmillan and Co. in March 1879. A few years later the novel made up volumes vi and vii of the Macmillan Collective Edition of James's works (14 vols., 1883). James does not seem to have wished to tamper with the text at this stage.

It was a very different matter when he came to prepare the novel for the New York Edition of his works to be published in New York by Charles Scribner's Sons in 1907–9, and in London by Macmillan and Co. in 1908–9.[2] James worked on the 1883 Macmillan text to

[1] See the detailed 'Note on the Text' in his Norton Critical Edition of the novel (New York, 1978), 311–17.

[2] See the Memorandum James wrote to Scribner's on 30 July 1905, in *Henry James Letters*, ed. Leon Edel, vol. iv (Cambridge, Mass., 1984), 366–8.

produce a new version of the novel, significantly altered in texture if not in structure. James's own copy survives in the Houghton Library at Harvard, and a facsimile has been published by the Scolar Press (London, 1976). This shows in fascinating detail James's mind and hand at work in the process of revision, but it is important to realize that it does not represent the final state of the text. Further revisions took place between the Houghton MS leaving James's hands and the novel's appearance as vol. ii of the New York Edition in December 1907.

For a fuller discussion of differences between the two versions of the novel, early and late, see Appendix 2. The text of the novel printed here is that of the New York Edition of 1907.

SELECT BIBLIOGRAPHY

1. James's Writings

One way of thinking about the other novels to read in conjunction with *The American* would be simply to take a cue from James himself. Near the end of his life James received an enquiry from a 'delightful young man from Texas' who wanted to know from the horse's mouth which five novels he should read. James offered him two different lists. The first was comprised of *Roderick Hudson*, *The Portrait of a Lady*, *The Princess Casamassima*, *The Wings of the Dove*, and *The Golden Bowl*; the second of *The American*, *The Tragic Muse*, *The Wings of the Dove*, *The Ambassadors*, and *The Golden Bowl*. James cautioned that the second list was 'as it were, the more "advanced"' (letter of 14 September 1913, in *Letters*, ed. Leon Edel, vol. iv (Cambridge, Mass., 1984)). Another way would be to set *The American* alongside some of the other novels and tales that use a Parisian setting. Most pertinent, because of their additional thematic resemblances, are *The Reverberator* (1888) and *The Ambassadors* (1903); but there is also *The Princess Casamassima* (1886) and *The Tragic Muse* (1890), and amongst the tales, 'Madame de Mauves' (1874), 'The Pension Beaurepas' and 'A Bundle of Letters' (both 1879). One can also get a concerted sense of the fiction James was producing 'around' *The American* from the volume of tales which covers the years immediately before and after the time of its first writing in 1876: *The Tales of Henry James*, vol. iii, *1875–1879*, ed. Maqbool Aziz (Oxford, 1984). The stage version(s) of the novel (see Appendix 1) may be read in *The Complete Plays of Henry James*, ed. Leon Edel (New York, 1990).

Of James's non-fictional writings the following are particularly relevant: *French Poets and Novelists* (London, 1878), *A Little Tour in France* (London, 1884), *Parisian Sketches: Letters to the New York Tribune, 1875–1876*, ed. Leon Edel and Ilse Dusoir Lind (London, 1958). Some of James's correspondence for the year of the novel's first writing can be read in *Henry James Letters*, ed. Leon Edel, vol. ii, *1875–1883* (London, 1978). For James's collected reflections on the European writers important to his own ideas and practice—Balzac, Sand, Flaubert, Zola, Turgenev, and others—see *Literary Criticism*, vol. ii: *French Writers, Other European Writers, the Prefaces to the New York Edition*, ed. Leon Edel with the assistance of Mark Wilson (New York, 1984).

2. Biography

Leon Edel, *Henry James: The Conquest of London, 1870–1883*, vol. ii of *The Life of Henry James* (London, 1962).

Kenneth Graham, *Henry James: A Literary Life* (London, 1995).

Lyndall Gordon, *A Private Life of Henry James: Two Women and his Art* (London, 1998)

Fred Kaplan, *Henry James: The Imagination of Genius: A Biography* (New York, 1992).

Sheldon M. Novick, *Henry James: The Young Master* (New York, 1996).

3. Selected Criticism

Elizabeth Allen, *A Woman's Place in the Novels of Henry James* (London, 1984).

Charles R. Anderson, *Person, Place, and Thing in Henry James's Novels* (Durham, NC, 1977).

John V. Antush, 'The "Much Finer Complexity" of History in *The American*', *Journal of American Studies*, 6 (1972), 85–95.

Martha Banta (ed.), *New Essays on The American* (Cambridge, 1987).

Mutlu Blasing, 'Double Focus in *The American*', *Nineteenth Century Fiction*, 28 (1973), 74–84.

Peter Brooks, *The Melodramatic Imagination: Balzac, Henry James, Melodrama, and the Mode of Excess* (New Haven, 1976).

R. W. Butterfield, '*The American*', in John Goode (ed.), *The Air of Reality: New Essays on Henry James* (London, 1972).

Oscar Cargill, *The Novels of Henry James* (New York, 1961).

Edwin Sill Fussell, *The French Side of Henry James* (New York, 1990).

—— *The Catholic Side of Henry James* (Cambridge, 1993).

Roger Gard (ed.), *Henry James: The Critical Heritage* (London, 1968).

David Gervais, *Flaubert and Henry James: A Study in Contrasts* (London, 1978).

Royal A. Gettman, 'Henry James's Revision of *The American*', *American Literature*, 16 (1945), 279–95.

Eric Haralson, 'James's *The American*: A (New)man is Being Beaten', *American Literature*, 64 (1992), 475–95.

Michael Hobbs, 'Reading Newman Reading: Textuality and Possession in *The American*', *Henry James Review*, 12 (1992), 115–25.

Philip Horne, *Henry James and Revision: The New York Edition* (Oxford, 1990).

Cornelia Pulsifer Kelley, *The Early Development of Henry James* (Urbana, Ill., 1930).

Daniel Lerner, 'The Influence of Turgenev on Henry James', *The Slavonic Year-Book*, 20 (Dec. 1941), 28–54.

David McWhirter (ed.), *Henry James's New York Edition: The Construction of Authorship* (Stanford, Calif., 1996).

Lee Clark Mitchell, 'A Marriage of Opposites: Oxymorons, Ethics, and James's *The American*', *Henry James Review*, 19 (1998), 1–16.

Jean Perrot, 'Un Amour de James', *Revue de littérature comparée*, 57 (1983), 275–94.

Richard Poirier, *The Comic Sense of Henry James* (New York, 1960).

Constance Rourke, *Native American Humor: A Study of the National Character* (New York, 1931).

John Carlos Rowe, 'The Politics of the Uncanny in Henry James's *The American*', *Henry James Review*, 8 (1987), 79–90.

Lewis O. Saum, 'Henry James's Christopher Newman: "The American" as Westerner', *Henry James Review*, 15 (1994), 1–9.

William T. Stafford, 'The Ending of James's *The American*: A Defense of the Early Version', *Nineteenth Century Fiction*, 18 (1963), 86–9.

William W. Stowe, *Balzac, James, and the Realistic Novel* (Princeton, 1983).

Tony Tanner, *Henry James and the Art of Nonfiction* (Athens, Ga., 1995).

Patricia Thomson, *George Sand and the Victorians: Her Influence and Reputation in Nineteenth-Century England* (London, 1977).

Adeline R. Tintner, *The Museum World of Henry James* (Ann Arbor, Mich., 1986).

Cheryl B. Torsney, 'Translation and Transubstantiation in *The American*', *Henry James Review*, 17 (1996), 40–51.

James Tuttleton, 'Re-Reading *The American*: A Century Since', *Henry James Review*, 1 (1980), 139–53.

William Veeder, *Henry James—the Lessons of the Master: Popular Fiction and Personal Style in the Nineteenth Century* (Chicago, 1975).

Pierre A. Walker, *Reading Henry James in French Cultural Contexts* (DeKalb, Ill., 1995).

Viola Hopkins Winner, *Henry James and the Visual Arts* (Charlottesville, Va., 1970).

4. Further Reading in Oxford World's Classics

Honoré de Balzac, *Cousin Bette*, tr. and ed. Sylvia Raphael, introduction by David Bellos.

——*Père Goriot*, tr. and ed. A. J. Krailsheimer.

——*Eugenie Grandet*, tr. and ed. Sylvia Raphael, introduction by Christopher Prendergast.

Gustave Flaubert, *Madame Bovary*, tr. Gerard Hopkins and ed. Terence Cave.

——*A Sentimental Education*, tr. and ed. Douglas Parmée.

222 22 2 22 2 2 2 2 2 2 2 2 2 2 2 2 2 2 2 2 2 2 2

Henry James, *The Ambassadors*, ed. Christopher Butler.
—— *The Aspern Papers and Other Stories*, ed. Adrian Poole.
—— *Daisy Miller and Other Stories*, ed. Jean Gooder.
—— *The Europeans*, ed. Ian Campbell Ross.
—— *The Golden Bowl*, ed. Virginia Llewellyn Smith.
—— *The Portrait of a Lady*, ed. Nicola Bradbury.
—— *What Maisie Knew*, ed. Adrian Poole.
—— *The Wings of the Dove*, ed. Peter Brooks.
Guy de Maupassant, *A Day in the Country and Other Stories*, tr. and ed. David Coward.
Ivan Turgenev, *Fathers and Sons*, tr. and ed. Richard Freeborn.
—— *A Month in the Country*, tr. and ed. Richard Freeborn.
Émile Zola, *L'Assommoir*, tr. Margaret Mauldan, ed. Robert Lethbridge.
—— *Nana*, tr. and ed. Douglas Parmée.

A CHRONOLOGY OF HENRY JAMES
COMPILED BY LEON EDEL

1843   Born 15 April at No. 21 Washington Place, New York City.

1843–4   Taken abroad by parents to Paris and London: period of residence at Windsor.

1845–55   Childhood in Albany and New York.

1855–8   Attends schools in Geneva, London, Paris, and Boulogne-sur-mer and is privately tutored.

1858   James family settles in Newport, Rhode Island.

1859   At scientific school in Geneva. Studies German in Bonn.

1860   At school in Newport. Receives back injury on eve of Civil War while serving as volunteer fireman. Studies art briefly. Friendship with John La Farge.

1862–3   Spends term in Harvard Law School.

1864   Family settles in Boston and then in Cambridge. Early anonymous story and unsigned reviews published.

1865   First signed story published in *Atlantic Monthly*.

1869–70   Travels in England, France, and Italy. Death of his beloved cousin Minny Temple.

1870   Back in Cambridge, publishes first novel in *Atlantic*, *Watch and Ward*.

1872–4   Travels with sister Alice and aunt in Europe; writes impressionistic travel sketches for the *Nation*. Spends autumn in Paris and goes to Italy to write first large novel.

1874–5   On completion of *Roderick Hudson* tests New York City as residence; writes much literary journalism for *Nation*. First three books published: *Transatlantic Sketches*, A *Passionate Pilgrim* (tales), and *Roderick Hudson*.

1875–6   Goes to live in Paris. Meets Ivan Turgenev and through him Flaubert, Zola, Daudet, Maupassant, and Edmond de Goncourt. Writes *The American*.

1876–7   Moves to London and settles in 3 Bolton Street, Piccadilly. Revisits Paris, Florence, Rome.

1878   'Daisy Miller', published in London, establishes fame on both sides of the Atlantic. Publishes first volume of essays, *French Poets and Novelists*.

1879–82   *The Europeans, Washington Square, Confidence, The Portrait of a Lady.*

1882–3   Revisits Boston: first visit to Washington. Death of parents.

1884–6   Returns to London. Sister Alice comes to live near him. Fourteen-volume collection of novels and tales published. Writes *The Bostonians* and *The Princess Casamassima*, published in the following year.

1886   Moves to flat at 34 De Vere Gardens West.

1887   Sojourn in Italy, mainly Florence and Venice. 'The Aspern Papers', *The Reverberator*, 'A London Life'. Friendship with grand-niece of Fenimore Cooper—Constance Fenimore Woolson.

1888   *Partial Portraits* and several collections of tales.

1889–90   *The Tragic Muse.*

1890–1   Dramatizes *The American*, which has a short run. Writes four comedies, rejected by producers.

1892   Alice James dies in London.

1894   Miss Woolson commits suicide in Venice. James journeys to Italy and visits her grave in Rome.

1895   He is booed at first night of his play *Guy Domville*. Deeply depressed, he abandons the theatre.

1896–7   *The Spoils of Poynton, What Maisie Knew.*

1898   Takes long lease of Lamb House, in Rye, Sussex. *The Turn of the Screw* published.

1899–1900   *The Awkward Age, The Sacred Fount.* Friendship with Conrad and Wells.

1902–4   *The Ambassadors, The Wings of the Dove* and *The Golden Bowl.* Friendships with H. C. Andersen and Jocelyn Persse.

1905   Revisits USA after 20-year absence, lectures on Balzac and the speech of Americans.

1906–10   *The American Scene.* Edits selective and revised 'New York Edition' of his works in 24 volumes. Friendship with Hugh Walpole.

1910   Death of brother, William James.

1913   Sargent paints his portrait as 70th birthday gift from some 300 friends and admirers. Writes autobiographies, *A Small Boy and Others*, and *Notes of a Son and Brother.*

1914   *Notes on Novelists.* Visits wounded in hospitals.

1915   Becomes a British subject.

THE AMERICAN

PREFACE

'THE AMERICAN', which I had begun in Paris early in the winter of 1875–76, made its first appearance in 'The Atlantic Monthly' in June of the latter year and continued there, from month to month, till May of the next. It started on its course while much was still unwritten, and there again come back to me, with this remembrance, the frequent hauntings and alarms of that comparatively early time; the habit of wondering what would happen if anything *should* 'happen', if one should break one's arm by an accident or make a long illness or suffer, in body, mind, fortune, any other visitation involving a loss of time. The habit of apprehension became of course in some degree the habit of confidence that one would pull through, that, with opportunity enough, grave interruption never yet *had* descended, and that a special Providence, in short, despite the sad warning of Thackeray's 'Denis Duval' and of Mrs Gaskell's 'Wives and Daughters' (that of Stevenson's 'Weir of Hermiston'* was yet to come) watches over anxious novelists condemned to the economy of serialisation. I make myself out in memory as having at least for many months and in many places given my Providence much to do: so great a variety of scenes of labour, implying all so much renewal of application, glimmer out of the book as I now read it over. And yet as the faded interest of the whole episode becomes again mildly vivid what I seem most to recover is, in its pale spectrality, a degree of joy, an eagerness on behalf of my recital, that must recklessly enough have overridden anxieties of every sort, including any view of inherent difficulties.

I seem to recall no other like connexion in which the case was met, to my measure, by so fond a complacency, in which my subject can have appeared so apt to take care of itself. I see now that I might all the while have taken much better care of it; yet, as I had at the time no sense of neglecting it, neither acute nor rueful solicitude, I can but speculate all vainly to-day on the oddity of my composure. I ask myself indeed if, possibly, recognising after I was launched the danger of an inordinate leak—since the ship has truly a hole in its side more than sufficient to have sunk it—I may not have managed, as a counsel of mere despair, to stop my ears against the noise of waters and *pretend* to myself I was afloat; being indubitably, in any case, at sea, with no harbour of refuge till the end of my serial voyage. If I succeeded at all in that emulation (in another sphere) of the pursued ostrich I must have succeeded altogether; must have buried my head in the sand and there found beatitude. The explanation of my enjoyment of it, no doubt, is that I was more than commonly enamoured of my idea, and that I believed it, so trusted, so imaginatively fostered, not less capable of limping to its goal on three feet than on one. The lameness might be what it would: I clearly, for myself, felt the thing *go*—which is the most a dramatist can ever ask of his drama; and I shall here accordingly indulge myself in speaking first of how, superficially, it did so proceed; explaining then what I mean by its practical dependence on a miracle.

It had come to me, this happy, halting view of an interesting case, abruptly enough, some years before: I recall sharply the felicity of the first glimpse, though I forget the accident of thought that produced it. I recall that I was seated in an American 'horse-car' when I found myself, of a sudden, considering with enthusiasm, as the theme of a 'story', the situation, in another country and an aristocratic society, of some robust but insidiously beguiled and betrayed, some cruelly wronged, compatriot: the point being in especial that he should suffer at the hands of persons pretending to represent the highest possible civilisation and to be of an order in every way superior to his own. What would he 'do' in that predicament, how would he right himself, or how, failing a remedy, would he conduct himself under his wrong? This would be the question involved, and I remember well how, having entered the horse-car without a dream of it, I was presently to leave that vehicle in full possession of my answer. He would behave in the most interesting manner—it would all depend on that: stricken, smarting, sore, he would arrive at his just vindication and then would fail of all triumphantly and all vulgarly enjoying it. He would hold his revenge and cherish it and feel its sweetness, and then in the very act of forcing it home would sacrifice it in disgust. He would let them go, in short, his haughty contemners, even while feeling them, with joy, in his power, and he would obey, in so doing, one of the large and easy impulses *generally* characteristic of his type. He wouldn't 'forgive'—that would have, in the case, no application; he would simply turn, at the supreme moment, away, the bitterness of his personal loss yielding to the very force of his aversion. All he would have at the end would be therefore just the moral convenience, indeed the moral necessity, of his practical, but quite unappreciated, magnanimity; and one's last view of him would be that of a strong man indifferent to his strength and too wrapped in fine, too wrapped above all in *other* and intenser, reflexions for the assertion of his 'rights'. This last point was of the essence and constituted in fact the subject: there would be no subject at all, obviously,—or simply the commonest of the common,—if my gentleman should enjoy his advantage. I was charmed with my idea, which would take, however, much working out; and precisely because it had so much to give, I think, must I have dropped it for the time into the deep well of unconscious cerebration: not without the hope, doubtless, that it might eventually emerge from that reservoir, as one had already known the buried treasure to come to light, with a firm iridescent surface and a notable increase of weight.

This resurrection then took place in Paris, where I was at the moment living, and in December 1875; my good fortune being apparently that Paris had ever so promptly offered me, and with an immediate directness at which I now marvel (since I had come back there, after earlier visitations, but a few weeks before), everything that was needed to make my conception concrete. I seem again at this distant day to see it become so quickly and easily, quite as if filling itself with life in that air. The objectivity it had wanted it promptly put on, and if the questions had been, with the usual intensity, for my hero and his crisis—the whole formidable list, the who? the what? the where? the when? the why? the how?—they gathered their answers in the cold shadow of the Arc de Triomphe, for fine reasons, very much as if they had been plucking spring flowers for the weaving of a frolic garland. I saw from one day to another my particular cluster of circumstances, with the life of the splendid city playing up in it like a flashing fountain in a marble basin. The very splendour seemed somehow to witness and intervene; it was important for the effect of my friend's discomfiture that it should take place on a high and lighted stage, and that his original ambition, the project exposing him, should have sprung from beautiful and noble suggestions—those that, at certain hours and under certain impressions, we feel the many-tinted medium by the Seine irresistibly to communicate. It was all charmingly simple, this conception, and the current must have gushed, full and clear, to my imagination, from the moment Christopher Newman rose before me, on a perfect day of the divine Paris spring, in the great gilded Salon Carré of the Louvre. Under this strong contagion of the place he would, by the happiest of hazards, meet his old comrade, now initiated and domiciled; after which the rest would go of itself. If he was to be wronged he would be wronged with just that conspicuity, with his felicity at just that pitch and with the highest aggravation of the general effect of misery mocked at. Great and gilded the whole trap set, in fine, for his wary freshness and into which it would blunder upon its fate. I have, I confess, no memory of a disturbing doubt; once the man himself was imaged to me (and *that* germination is a process almost always untraceable) he must have walked into the situation as by taking a pass-key from his pocket.

But what then meanwhile would be the affront one would see him as most feeling? The affront of course done him as a lover; and yet not that done by his mistress herself, since injuries of this order are the stalest stuff of romance. I was not to have him jilted, any more than I was to have him successfully vindictive: both his wrong and his right would have been in

these cases of too vulgar a type. I doubtless even then felt that the conception of Paris as the consecrated scene of rash infatuations and bold bad
treacheries belongs, in the Anglo-Saxon imagination, to the infancy of art.
The right renovation of any such theme as *that* would place it in Boston
or at Cleveland, at Hartford or at Utica—give it some local connexion in
which we had not already had so much of it. No, I should make my heroine
herself, if heroine there was to be, an equal victim—just as Romeo was
not less the sport of fate for not having been interestedly sacrificed by
Juliet; and to this end I had but to imagine 'great people' again, imagine
my hero confronted and involved with them, and impute to them, with a
fine free hand, the arrogance and cruelty, the tortuous behaviour, in given
conditions, of which great people have been historically so often capable.
But as this was the light in which they were to show, so the essence of the
matter would be that he should at the right moment find them in his power,
and so the situation would reach its highest interest with the question of
his utilisation of that knowledge. It would be here, in the possession and
application of his power, that he would come out strong and would so
deeply appeal to our sympathy. Here above all it really was, however, that
my conception unfurled, with the best conscience in the world, the embla-
zoned flag of romance; which venerable ensign it had, though quite unwittingly, from the first and at every point sported in perfect good faith. I had
been plotting arch-romance without knowing it, just as I began to write it
that December day without recognising it and just as I all serenely and
blissfully pursued the process from month to month and from place to
place; just as I now, in short, reading the book over, find it yields me no
interest and no reward comparable to the fond perception of this truth.

The thing is consistently, consummately—and I would fain really make
bold to say charmingly—romantic; and all without intention, presumption, hesitation, contrition. The effect is equally undesigned and
unabashed, and I lose myself, at this late hour, I am bound to add, in
a certain sad envy of the free play of so much unchallenged instinct. One
would like to woo back such hours of fine precipitation. They represent
to the critical sense which the exercise of one's *whole* faculty has, with
time, so inevitably and so thoroughly waked up, the happiest season of surrender to the invoked muse and the projected fable: the season of images
so free and confident and ready that they brush questions aside and disport
themselves, like the artless schoolboys of Gray's beautiful Ode,* in all the
ecstasy of the ignorance attending them. The time doubtless comes soon
enough when questions, as I call them, rule the roost and when the little
victim, to adjust Gray's term again to the creature of frolic fancy, doesn't
dare propose a gambol till they have all (like a board of trustees discussing
a new outlay) sat on the possibly scandalous case. I somehow feel, accord-

ingly, that it was lucky to have sacrificed on this particular altar while one still could; though it is perhaps droll—in a yet higher degree—to have done so not simply because one was guileless, but even quite under the conviction, in a general way, that, since no 'rendering' of any object and no painting of any picture can take effect without some form of reference and control, so these guarantees could but reside in a high probity of observation. I must decidedly have supposed, all the while, that I was acutely observing—and with a blest absence of wonder at its being so easy. Let me certainly at present rejoice in that absence; for I ask myself how without it I could have written 'The American'.

Was it indeed meanwhile my excellent conscience that kept the charm as unbroken as it appears to me, in rich retrospect, to have remained?— or is it that I suffer the mere influence of remembered, of associated places and hours, all acute impressions, to palm itself off as the sign of a finer confidence than I could justly claim? It is a pleasure to perceive how again and again the shrunken depths of old work yet permit themselves to be sounded or—even if rather terrible the image—'dragged': the long pole of memory stirs and rummages the bottom, and we fish up such fragments and relics of the submerged life and the extinct consciousness as tempt us to piece them together. My windows looked into the Rue de Luxem- bourg—since then meagrely re-named Rue Cambon—and the particular light Parisian click of the small cab-horse on the clear asphalt, with its sharpness of detonation between the high houses, makes for the faded page to-day a sort of interlineation of sound. This sound rises to a martial clatter at the moment a troop of cuirassiers charges down the narrow street, each morning, to file, directly opposite my house, through the plain portal of the barracks occupying part of the vast domain attached in a rearward manner to one of the Ministères that front on the Place Vendôme; an expanse marked, along a considerable stretch of the street, by one of those high painted and administratively-placarded garden walls that form deep, vague, recurrent notes in the organic vastness of the city. I have but to re-read ten lines to recall my daily effort not to waste time in hanging over the window-bar for a sight of the cavalry the hard music of whose hoofs so directly and thrillingly appealed; an effort that inveter- ately failed—and a trivial circumstance now dignified, to my imagination, I may add, by the fact that the fruits of this weakness, the various items of the vivid picture, so constantly recaptured, must have been in them- selves suggestive and inspiring, must have been rich strains, in their way, of the great Paris harmony. I have ever, in general, found it difficult to write of places under too immediate an impression—the impression that prevents standing off and allows neither space nor time for perspective. The image has had for the most part to be dim if the reflexion was to be, as is proper for a reflexion, both sharp and quiet: one has a horror, I think, artistically, of agitated reflexions.

Perhaps that is why the novel, after all, was to achieve, as it went on, no great—certainly no very direct—transfusion of the immense overhanging presence. It had to save as it could its own life, to keep tight hold of the tenuous silver thread, the one hope for which was that it shouldn't be tangled or clipped. This earnest grasp of the silver thread was doubtless an easier business in other places—though as I remount the stream of composition I see it faintly coloured again: with the bright protection of the Normandy coast (I worked away a few weeks at Etretat*); with the stronger glow of southernmost France, breaking in during a stay at Bayonne;* then with the fine historic and other 'psychic' substance of Saint-Germain-en-Laye,* a purple patch of terraced October before returning to Paris. There comes after that the memory of a last brief intense invocation of the enclosing scene, of the pious effort to unwind my tangle, with a firm hand, in the very light (that light of high, narrow-ish French windows in old rooms, the light somehow, as one always feels, of 'style' itself) that had quickened my original vision. I was to pass over to London that autumn; which was a reason the more for considering the matter—the matter of Newman's final predicament—with due intensity: to let a loose end dangle over into alien air would so fix upon the whole, I strenuously felt, the dishonour of piecemeal composition. Therefore I strove to finish—first in a small dusky hotel of the Rive Gauche, where, though the windows again were high, the days were dim and the crepus-cular court, domestic, intimate, 'quaint', testified to ancient manners almost as if it had been that of Balzac's Maison Vauquer in 'Le Père Goriot':* and then once more in the Rue de Luxembourg, where a black-framed Empire portrait-medallion, suspended in the centre of each white panel of my almost noble old salon, made the coolest, discreetest, most measured decoration, and where, through casements open to the last mild-ness of the year, a belated Saint Martin's summer, the tale was taken up afresh by the charming light click and clatter, that sound as of the thin, quick, quite feminine surface-breathing of Paris, the shortest of rhythms for so huge an organism.

I shall not tell whether I did there bring my book to a close—and indeed I shrink, for myself, from putting the question to the test of memory. I follow it so far, the old urgent ingenious business, and then I lose sight of it: from which I infer—all exact recovery of the matter failing—that I did not in the event drag over the Channel a lengthening chain; which would have been detestable. I reduce to the absurd perhaps, however, by that small subjective issue, any undue measure of the interest of this insistent recovery of what I have called attendant facts. There always has been, for the valid work of art, a history—though mainly inviting, doubtless, but to the curious critic, for whom such things grow up and are formed very much in the manner of attaching young lives and characters, those conspicuous cases of happy development as to which evidence and anecdote are always in order. The development indeed must be certain to have been happy, the life sincere, the character fine: the work of art, to create or repay critical curiosity, must in short have been very 'valid' indeed. Yet there is on the other hand no mathematical measure of that importance—it may be a matter of widely-varying appreciation; and I am willing to grant, assuredly, that this interest, in a given relation, will nowhere so effectually kindle as on the artist's own part. And I am afraid that after all even his best excuse for it must remain the highly personal plea—the joy of living over, as a chapter of experience, the particular intellectual adventure. Here lurks an immense homage to the general privilege of the artist, to that constructive, that creative passion—portentous words, but they are convenient—the exercise of which finds so many an occasion for appearing to him the highest of human fortunes, the rarest boon of the gods. He values it, all sublimely and perhaps a little fatuously, for itself—as the great extension, great beyond all others, of experience and of consciousness; with the toil and trouble a mere sun-cast shadow that falls, shifts and vanishes, the result of his living in so large a light. On the constant nameless felicity of this Robert Louis Stevenson has, in an admirable passage* and as in so many other connexions, said the right word: that the partaker of the 'life of art' who repines at the absence of the rewards, as they are called, of the pursuit might surely be better occupied. Much rather should he endlessly wonder at his not having to pay half his substance for his luxurious immersion. He enjoys it, so to speak, without a tax; the effort of labour involved, the torment of expression, of which we have heard in our time so much, being after all but the last refinement of his privilege. It may leave him weary and worn; but how, after his fashion, he will have lived! As if one were to expect at once freedom and ease! That silly safety is but the sign of bondage and forfeiture. Who can imagine free selection—which is the beautiful, terrible *whole* of art—without free difficulty? This is the very franchise of the city and high ambition of the citizen. The vision of the difficulty, as one looks back, bathes one's course in a golden glow by which the very objects along the road are transfigured and glorified; so that one exhibits them to other eyes with an elation possibly presumptuous.

Since I accuse myself at all events of these complacencies I take advantage of them to repeat that I value, in my retrospect, nothing so much as the lively light on the romantic property of my subject that I had not expected to encounter. If in 'The American' I invoked the romantic

association without malice prepense, yet with a production of the romantic effect that is for myself unmistakable, the occasion is of the best
perhaps for penetrating a little the obscurity of that principle. By what art
or mystery, what craft of selection, omission or commission, does a given
picture of life appear to us to surround its theme, its figures and images,
with the air of romance while another picture close beside it may affect us
as steeping the whole matter in the element of reality? It is a question, no
doubt, on the painter's part, very much more of perceived effect, effect
after the fact, than of conscious design—though indeed I have ever failed
to see how a coherent picture of anything is producible save by a complex
of fine measurements. The cause of the deflexion, in one pronounced
sense or the other, must lie deep, however; so that for the most part we
recognise the character of our interest only after the particular magic, as
I say, has thoroughly operated—and then in truth but if we be a bit critically minded, if we find our pleasure, that is, in these intimate apprecia-
tions (for which, as I am well aware, ninety-nine readers in a hundred have
no use whatever). The determining condition would at any rate seem so
latent that one may well doubt if the full artistic consciousness ever
reaches it; leaving the matter thus a case, ever, not of an author's plotting
and planning and calculating, but just of his feeling and seeing, of his con-
ceiving, in a word, and of his thereby inevitably expressing himself, under
the influence of one value or the other. These values represent different
sorts and degrees of the communicable thrill, and I doubt if any novelist,
for instance, ever proposed to commit himself to one kind or the other
with as little mitigation as we are sometimes able to find for him. The
interest is greatest—the interest of his genius, I mean, and of his general
wealth—when he commits himself in both directions; not quite at the
same time or to the same effect, of course, but by some need of performing his whole possible revolution, by the law of some rich passion in him
for extremes.

Of the men of largest responding imagination before the human scene,
of Scott, of Balzac, even of the coarse, comprehensive, prodigious Zola,*
we feel, I think, that the deflexion toward either quarter has never taken
place; that neither the nature of the man's faculty nor the nature of his
experience has ever quite determined it. His current remains therefore
extraordinarily rich and mixed, washing us successively with the warm
wave of the near and familiar and the tonic shock, as may be, of the far
and strange. (In making which opposition I suggest not that the strange
and the far are at all necessarily romantic: they happen to be simply the
unknown, which is quite a different matter. The real represents to my perception the things we cannot possibly *not* know, sooner or later, in one way
or another; it being but one of the accidents of our hampered state, and

one of the incidents of their quantity and number, that particular instances have not yet come our way. The romantic stands, on the other hand, for the things that, with all the facilities in the world, all the wealth and all the courage and all the wit and all the adventure, we never *can* directly know; the things that can reach us only through the beautiful circuit and subterfuge of our thought and our desire.) There have been, I gather, many definitions of romance, as a matter indispensably of boats, or of caravans, or of tigers, or of 'historical characters', or of ghosts, or of forgers, or of detectives, or of beautiful wicked women, or of pistols and knives, but they appear for the most part reducible to the idea of the facing of danger, the acceptance of great risks for the fascination, the very love, of their uncertainty, the joy of success if possible and of battle in any case. This would be a fine formula if it bore examination; but it strikes me as weak and inadequate, as by no means covering the true ground and yet as landing us in strange confusions.

The panting pursuit of danger is the pursuit of life itself, in which danger awaits us possibly at every step and faces us at every turn; so that the dream of an intenser experience easily becomes rather some vision of a sublime security like that enjoyed on the flowery plains of heaven, where we may conceive ourselves proceeding in ecstasy from one prodigious phase and form of it to another. And if it be insisted that the measure of the type is then in the *appreciation* of danger—the sign of our projection of the real being the smallness of its dangers, and that of our projection of the romantic the hugeness, the mark of the distinction being in short, as they say of collars and gloves and shoes, the size and 'number' of the danger—this discrimination again surely fails, since it makes our difference not a difference of kind, which is what we want, but a difference only of degree, and subject by that condition to the indignity of a sliding scale and a shifting measure. There are immense and flagrant dangers that are but sordid and squalid ones, as we feel, tainting with their quality the very defiances they provoke; while there are common and covert ones, that 'look like nothing' and that can be but inwardly and occultly dealt with, which involve the sharpest hazards to life and honour and the highest instant decisions and intrepidities of action. It is an arbitrary stamp that keeps these latter prosaic and makes the former heroic; and yet I should still less subscribe to a mere 'subjective' division—I mean one that would place the difference wholly in the temper of the imperilled agent. It would be impossible to have a more romantic temper than Flaubert's Madame Bovary,* and yet nothing less resembles a romance than the record of her adventures. To classify it by that aspect—the definition of the spirit that happens to animate her—is like settling the question (as I have seen it witlessly settled) by the presence or absence of 'costume'. Where again then does costume begin or end?—save with the 'run' of one or another sort of play? We must reserve vague labels for artless mixtures.

The only *general* attribute of projected romance that I can see, the only one that fits all its cases, is the fact of the kind of experience with which it deals—experience liberated, so to speak; experience disengaged, disembroiled, disencumbered, exempt from the conditions that we usually know to attach to it and, if we wish so to put the matter, drag upon it, and operating in a medium which relieves it, in a particular interest, of the inconvenience of a *related*, a measurable state, a state subject to all our vulgar communities. The greatest intensity may so be arrived at evidently—when the sacrifice of community, of the 'related' sides of situations, has not been too rash. It must to this end not flagrantly betray itself; we must even be kept if possible, for our illusion, from suspecting any sacrifice at all. The balloon of experience is in fact of course tied to the earth, and under that necessity we swing, thanks to a rope of remarkable length, in the more or less commodious car of the imagination; but it is by the rope we know where we are, and from the moment that cable is cut we are at large and unrelated: we only swing apart from the globe—though remaining as exhilarated, naturally, as we like, especially when all goes well. The art of the romancer is, 'for the fun of it', insidiously to cut the cable, to cut it without our detecting him. What I have recognised then in 'The American', much to my surprise and after long years, is that the experience here represented is the disconnected and uncontrolled experience—uncontrolled by our general sense of 'the way things happen'—which romance alone more or less successfully palms off on us. It is a case of Newman's own intimate experience all, that being my subject, the thread of which, from beginning to end, is not once exchanged, however momentarily, for any other thread;* and the experience of others concerning us, and concerning him, only so far as it touches him and as he recognises, feels or divines it. There is our general sense of the way things happen—it abides with us indefeasibly, as readers of fiction, from the moment we demand that our fiction shall be intelligible; and there is our particular sense of the way they don't happen, which is liable to wake up unless reflexion and criticism, in us, have been skilfully and successfully drugged. There are drugs enough, clearly—it is all a question of applying them with tact; in which case the way things don't happen may be artfully made to pass for the way things do.

Amusing and even touching to me, I profess, at this time of day, the ingenuity (worthy, with whatever lapses, of a better cause) with which, on behalf of Newman's adventure, this hocus-pocus is attempted: the value of the instance not being diminished either, surely, by its having been attempted in such evident good faith. Yes, all is romantic to my actual vision here, and not least so, I hasten to add, the fabulous felicity of my candour. The way things happen is frankly not the way in which they are represented as having happened, in Paris, to my hero: the situation I had conceived only saddled me with that for want of my invention of something better. The great house of Bellegarde, in a word, would, I now feel, given the circumstances, given the *whole* of the ground, have comported itself in a manner as different as possible from the manner to which my narrative commits it; of which truth, moreover, I am by no means sure that, in spite of what I have called my serenity, I had not all the while an uneasy suspicion. I had dug in my path, alas, a hole into which I was destined to fall. I was so possessed of my idea that Newman should be ill-used—which was the essence of my subject—that I attached too scant an importance to its fashion of coming about. Almost any fashion would serve, I appear to have assumed, that would give me my main chance for him; a matter depending not so much on the particular trick played him as on the interesting face presented by him to *any* damnable trick. So where I part company with *terra-firma* is in making that projected, that performed outrage so much more showy, dramatically speaking, than sound. Had I patched it up to greater apparent soundness my own trick, artistically speaking, would have been played; I should have cut the cable without my reader's suspecting it. I doubtless at the time, I repeat, believed I had taken my precautions; but truly they should have been greater, to impart the air of truth to the attitude—that is first to the pomp and circumstance, and second to the queer falsity—of the Bellegardes.

They would positively have jumped then, the Bellegardes, at my rich and easy American, and not have 'minded' in the least any drawback—especially as, after all, given the pleasant palette from which I have painted him, there were few drawbacks to mind. My subject imposed on me a group of closely-allied persons animated by immense pretensions—which was all very well, which might be full of the promise of interest: only of interest felt most of all in the light of comedy and of irony. This, better understood, would have dwelt in the idea not in the least of their not finding Newman good enough for their alliance and thence being ready to sacrifice him, but in that of their taking with alacrity everything he could give them, only asking for more and more, and then adjusting their pretensions and their pride to it with all the comfort in life. Such accommodation of the theory of a noble indifference to the practice of a deep avidity is the real note of policy in forlorn aristocracies—and I meant of course that the Bellegardes should be virtually forlorn. The perversion of truth is by no means, I think, in the displayed acuteness of their remembrance of 'who' and 'what' they are, or at any rate take themselves for; since it is the misfortune of all insistence on 'worldly' advantages—and the

situation of such people bristles at the best (by which I mean under whatever invocation of a superficial simplicity) with emphasis, accent, assumption—to produce at times an effect of grossness. The picture of their
tergiversation, at all events, however it may originally have seemed to me
to hang together, has taken on this rococo appearance precisely because
their preferred course, a thousand times preferred, would have been to
haul him and his fortune into their boat under cover of night perhaps, in
any case as quietly and with as little bumping and splashing as possible,
and there accommodate him with the very safest and most convenient seat.
Given Newman, given the fact that the thing constitutes itself organic-
ally as *his* adventure, that too might very well be a situation and a subject:
only it wouldn't have been the theme of 'The American' as the book
stands, the theme to which I was from so early pledged. Since I had wanted
a 'wrong' this other turn might even have been arranged to give me *that*,
might even have been arranged to meet my requirement that somebody or
something should be 'in his power' so delightfully; and with the signal
effect, after all, of 'defining' everything. (It is as difficult, I said above, to
trace the dividing-line between the real and the romantic as to plant a milestone between north and south; but I am not sure an infallible sign of the
latter is not this rank vegetation of the 'power' of bad people that good
get into, or *vice versa*. It is so rarely, alas, into *our* power that any one gets!)

It is difficult for me to-day to believe that I had not, as my work went
on, *some* shade of the rueful sense of my affront to verisimilitude; yet I
catch the memory at least of no great sharpness, no true critical anguish,
of remorse: an anomaly the reason of which in fact now glimmers inter-
estingly out. My concern, as I saw it, was to make and to keep Newman
consistent; the picture of his consistency was all my undertaking, and the
memory of *that* infatuation perfectly abides with me. He was to be
the lighted figure, the others—even doubtless to an excessive degree the
woman who is made the agent of his discomfiture—were to be the
obscured; by which I should largely get the very effect most to be invoked,
that of a generous nature engaged with forces, with difficulties and
dangers, that it but half understands. If Newman was attaching enough,
I must have argued, his tangle would be sensible enough; for the interest
of everything is all that it is *his* vision, *his* conception, *his* interpretation:
at the window of his wide, quite sufficiently wide, consciousness we are
seated, from that admirable position we 'assist'. He therefore supremely
matters; all the rest matters only as he feels it, treats it, meets it. A beautiful infatuation this, always, I think, the intensity of the creative effort to
get into the skin of the creature; the act of personal possession of one
being by another at its completest—and with the high enhancement, ever,
that it is, by the same stroke, the effort of the artist to preserve for his

subject that unity, and for his use of it (in other words for the interest he desires to excite) that effect of a *centre*, which most economise its value. Its value is most discussable when that economy has most operated; the content and the 'importance' of a work of art are in fine wholly dependent on its *being* one: outside of which all prate of its representative character, its meaning and its bearing, its morality and humanity, are an impudent thing. Strong in that character, which is the condition of its really bearing witness at all, it is strong every way. So much remains true then on behalf of my instinct of multiplying the fine touches by which Newman should live and communicate life; and yet I still ask myself, I confess, what I can have made of 'life', in my picture, at such a juncture as the interval offered as elapsing between my hero's first accepted state and the nuptial rites that are to crown it. Nothing here is in truth 'offered'—everything is evaded, and the effect of this, I recognise, is of the oddest. His relation to Madame de Cintré takes a great stride, but the author appears to view that but as a signal for letting it severely alone.

I have been stupefied, in so thoroughly revising the book, to find, on turning a page, that the light in which he is presented immediately after Madame de Bellegarde has conspicuously introduced him to all her circle as her daughter's husband-to-be is that of an evening at the opera quite alone; as if he wouldn't surely spend his leisure, and especially those hours of it, with his intended. Instinctively, from that moment, one would have seen them intimately and, for one's interest, beautifully together; with some illustration of the beauty incumbent on the author. The truth was that at this point the author, all gracelessly, could but hold his breath and pass; lingering was too difficult—he had made for himself a crushing complication. Since Madame de Cintré was after all to 'back out' every touch in the picture of her apparent loyalty would add to her eventual shame. She had acted in clear good faith, but how could I give the *detail* of an attitude, on her part, of which the foundation was yet so weak? I preferred, as the minor evil, to shirk the attempt—at the cost evidently of a signal loss of 'charm'; and with this lady, altogether, I recognise, a light plank, too light a plank, is laid for the reader over a dark 'psychological' abyss. The delicate clue to her conduct is never definitely placed in his hand: I must have liked verily to think it *was* delicate and to flatter myself it was to be felt with finger-tips rather than heavily tugged at. Here then, at any rate, is the romantic *tout craché*—the fine flower of Newman's experience blooming in a medium 'cut off' and shut up to itself. I don't for a moment pronounce any spell proceeding from it necessarily the less workable, to a rejoicing ingenuity, for that; beguile the reader's suspicion of *his* being shut up, transform it for *him* into a positive illusion of the largest liberty, and the success will ever be proportionate to the chance. Only all this gave me,

I make out, a great deal to look to, and I was perhaps wrong in thinking that Newman by himself, and for any occasional extra inch or so I might smuggle into his measurements, would see me through my wood. Anything more liberated and disconnected, to repeat my terms, than his prompt general profession, before the Tristrams, of aspiring to a 'great' marriage, for example, could surely not well be imagined. I had to take that over with the rest of him and fit it in—I had indeed to exclude the outer air. Still, I find on re-perusal that I have been able to breathe at least in my aching void; so that, clinging to my hero as to a tall, protective, good-natured elder brother in a rough place, I leave the record to stand or fall by his more or less convincing image.

HENRY JAMES

I

On a brilliant day in May, of the year 1868,* a gentleman was reclining at his ease on the great circular divan which at that period occupied the centre of the Salon Carré,* in the Museum of the Louvre. This commodious ottoman has since been removed, to the extreme regret of all weak-kneed lovers of the fine arts; but our visitor had taken serene possession of its softest spot, and, with his head thrown back and his legs outstretched, was staring at Murillo's beautiful moon-borne Madonna* in deep enjoyment of his posture. He had removed his hat and flung down beside him a little red guide-book and an opera-glass. The day was warm; he was heated with walking, and he repeatedly, with vague weariness, passed his handkerchief over his forehead. And yet he was evidently not a man to whom fatigue was familiar; long, lean, and muscular, he suggested an intensity of unconscious resistance. His exertions on this particular day, however, had been of an unwonted sort, and he had often performed great physical feats that left him less jaded than his quiet stroll through the Louvre. He had looked out all the pictures to which an asterisk was affixed in those formidable pages of fine print in his Bädeker;* his attention had been strained and his eyes dazzled; he had sat down with an æsthetic headache. He had looked, moreover, not only at all the pictures, but at all the copies that were going forward around them in the hands of those innumerable young women in long aprons, on high stools, who devote themselves, in France, to the reproduction of masterpieces; and, if the truth must be told, he had often admired the copy much more than the original. His physiognomy would have sufficiently indicated that he was a shrewd and capable person, and in truth he had often sat up all night over a bristling bundle of accounts and heard the cock crow without a yawn. But Raphael and Titian and Rubens were a new kind of arithmetic, and they made him for the first time in his life wonder at his vaguenesses.

An observer with anything of an eye for local types would have had no difficulty in referring this candid connoisseur to the scene of his origin, and indeed such an observer might have made an ironic point of the almost ideal completeness with which he filled out the

mould of race. The gentleman on the divan was the superlative
American; to which affirmation of character he was partly helped by
the general easy magnificence of his manhood. He appeared to
possess that kind of health and strength which, when found in perfection, are the most impressive—the physical tone which the owner
does nothing to 'keep up'. If he was a muscular Christian* it was
quite without doctrine. If it was necessary to walk to a remote spot
he walked, but he had never known himself to 'exercise'. He had no
theory with regard to cold bathing or the use of Indian clubs; he was
neither an oarsman, a rifleman nor a fencer—he had never had time
for these amusements—and he was quite unaware that the saddle is
recommended for certain forms of indigestion. He was by inclination a temperate man; but he had supped the night before his visit
to the Louvre at the Café Anglais*—some one had told him it was
an experience not to be omitted—and he had slept none the less the
sleep of the just. His usual attitude and carriage had a liberal looseness, but when, under a special inspiration, he straightened himself
he looked a grenadier on parade. He had never tasted tobacco. He
had been assured—such things are said—that cigars are excellent for
the health, and he was quite capable of believing it; but he would no
more have thought of 'taking' one than of taking a dose of medicine.
His complexion was brown and the arch of his nose bold and
well-marked. His eye was of a clear, cold grey, and save for the abun-
dant droop of his moustache he spoke, as to cheek and chin, of the
joy of the matutinal steel. He had the flat jaw and the firm, dry neck
which are frequent in the American type; but the betrayal of native
conditions is a matter of expression even more than of feature, and
it was in this respect that our traveller's countenance was supremely
eloquent. The observer we have been supposing might, however, perfectly have measured its expressiveness and yet have been at a
loss for names and terms to fit it. It had that paucity of detail which
is yet not emptiness, that blankness which is not simplicity, that
look of being committed to nothing in particular, of standing in a
posture of general hospitality to the chances of life, of being very
much at one's own disposal, characteristic of American faces of the
clear strain. It was the eye, in this case, that chiefly told the story;
an eye in which the unacquainted and the expert were singularly
blended. It was full of contradictory suggestions; and though it was
by no means the glowing orb of a hero of romance you could find

in it almost anything you looked for. Frigid and yet friendly, frank yet cautious, shrewd yet credulous, positive yet sceptical, confident yet shy, extremely intelligent and extremely good-humoured, there was something vaguely defiant in its concessions and something profoundly reassuring in its reserve. The wide yet partly folded wings of this gentleman's moustache, with the two premature wrinkles in the cheek above it, and the fashion of his garments, in which an exposed shirt-front and a blue satin necktie of too light a shade played perhaps an obtrusive part, completed the elements of his identity. We have approached him perhaps at a not especially favourable moment; he is by no means sitting for his portrait. But listless as he lounges there, rather baffled on the æsthetic question and guilty of the damning fault (as we have lately discovered it to be) of confounding the aspect of the artist with that of his work (for he admires the squinting Madonna of the young lady with the hair that somehow also advertises 'art', because he thinks the young lady herself uncommonly taking), he is a sufficiently promising acquaintance. Decision, salubrity, jocosity, prosperity, seem to hover within his call; he is evidently a man of business, but the term appears to confess, for his particular benefit, to undefined and mysterious boundaries which invite the imagination to bestir itself.

As the little copyist proceeded with her task, her attention addressed to her admirer, from time to time, for reciprocity, one of its blankest, though not of its briefest, missives. The working-out of her scheme appeared to call, in her view, for a great deal of vivid by-play, a great standing off with folded arms and head dropping from side to side, stroking of a dimpled chin with a dimpled hand, sighing and frowning and patting of the foot, fumbling in disordered tresses for wandering hair-pins. These motions were accompanied by a far-straying glance, which tripped up, occasionally, as it were, on the tall arrested gentleman. At last he rose abruptly and, putting on his hat as if for emphasis of an austere intention, approached the young lady. He placed himself before her picture and looked at it for a time during which she pretended to be quite unconscious of his presence. Then, invoking her intelligence with the single word that constituted the strength of his French vocabulary, and holding up one finger in a manner that appeared to him to illuminate his meaning, '*Combien?*' he abruptly demanded.

The artist stared a moment, gave a small pout, shrugged her shoulders, put down her palette and brushes and stood rubbing her hands.

'How much?' said our friend in English, '*Combien?*'

'Monsieur wishes to buy it?' she asked in French.

'Very pretty. *Splendide. Combien?*' repeated the American.

'It pleases monsieur, my little picture? It's a very beautiful subject,' said the young lady.

'The Madonna, yes; I'm not a real Catholic, but I want to buy it. *Combien?* Figure it right there.' And he took a pencil from his pocket and showed her the fly-leaf of his guide-book. She stood looking at him and scratching her chin with the pencil. 'Isn't it for sale?' he asked. And as she still stood reflecting, probing him with eyes which, in spite of her desire to treat this avidity of patronage as a very old story, added to her flush of incredulity, he was afraid he had offended her. She was simply trying to look indifferent, wondering how far she might go. 'I haven't made a mistake—*pas insulté*, no?' her interlocutor continued. 'Don't you understand a little English?'

The young lady's aptitude for playing a part at short notice was remarkable. She fixed him with all her conscious perception and asked him if he spoke no French. Then '*Donnez!*' she said briefly, and took the open guide-book. In the upper corner of the fly-leaf she traced a number in a minute and extremely neat hand. On which she handed back the book and resumed her palette.

Our friend read the number: '2000 francs.' He said nothing for a time, but stood looking at the picture while the copyist began actively to dabble with her paint. 'For a copy, isn't that a good deal?' he inquired at last. '*Pas beaucoup?*'

She raised her eyes from her palette, scanned him from head to foot, and alighted with admirable sagacity upon exactly the right answer. 'Yes, it's a good deal. But my copy is extremely *soigné*. That's its value.'

The gentleman in whom we are interested understood no French, but I have said he was intelligent, and here is a good chance to prove it. He apprehended, by a natural instinct, the meaning of the young woman's phrase, and it gratified him to find her so honest. Beauty, therefore talent, rectitude; she combined everything! 'But you must finish it,' he said. '*Finish*, you know;' and he pointed to the unpainted hand of the figure.

'Oh, it shall be finished in perfection—in the perfection of perfections!' cried mademoiselle; and to confirm her promise she deposited a rosy blotch in the middle of the Madonna's cheek.

But the American frowned. 'Ah, too red, too red!' he objected. '*Her* complexion,' pointing to the Murillo, 'is more delicate.'

'Delicate? Oh it shall be delicate, monsieur; delicate as Sèvres *biscuit*.* I'm going to tone that down; I promise you it shall have a surface! And where will you allow us to send it to you? Your address.'

'My address? Oh yes!' And the gentleman drew a card from his pocket-book and wrote something on it. Then hesitating a moment: 'If I don't like it when it is finished, you know, I shall not be obliged to pay for it.'

The young lady seemed as good a guesser as himself. 'Oh, I'm very sure monsieur's not capricious!'

'Capricious?' And at this monsieur began to laugh. 'Oh no, I'm not capricious. I'm very faithful. I'm very constant. *Comprenez?*'

'Monsieur's constant; I understand perfectly. It's not the case of all the world. To recompense you, you shall have your picture on the first possible day; next week—as soon as it's dry, I'll take the card of monsieur.' And she took it and read his name: 'Christopher Newman.' Then she tried to repeat it aloud and laughed at her bad accent. 'Your English names are not *commodes* to say!'

'Well, mine's partly celebrated,' said Mr Newman, laughing too. 'Did you never hear of Christopher Columbus?'

'*Bien sûr!* He first showed Americans the way to Europe; a very great man. And is he your patron?'

'My patron?'

'Your patron saint, such as we all have.'

'Oh, exactly; my parents named me after him.'

'Monsieur is American then too?'

'Doesn't it stick right out?' monsieur enquired.

'And you mean to carry my dear little picture away over there?' She explained her phrase with a gesture.

'Oh, I mean to buy a great many pictures—*beaucoup, beaucoup*,' said Christopher Newman.

'The honour's not less for me,' the young lady answered, 'for I'm sure monsieur has a great deal of taste.'

'But you must give me your card,' Newman went on; 'your card, you know.'

The young lady looked severe an instant. 'My father will wait on you.'

But this time Mr Newman's powers of divination were at fault. 'Your card, your address,' he simply repeated.

'My address?' said mademoiselle. Then, with a little shrug: 'Happily for you, you're a stranger—of a distinction *qui se voit*. It's the first time I ever gave my card to a gentleman.' And, taking from her pocket a well-worn flat little wallet, she extracted from it a small glazed visiting-card and presented the latter to her client. It was neatly inscribed in pencil, with a great many flourishes, 'Mlle Noémie Nioche.'* But Mr Newman, unlike his companion, read the name with perfect gravity; all French names to him were equally *incommodes*.

'And precisely—how it happens!—here's my father; he has come to escort me home,' said Mademoiselle Noémie. 'He speaks English beautifully. He'll arrange with you.' And she turned to welcome a little old gentleman who came shuffling up and peering over his glasses at Newman.

M. Nioche wore a glossy wig, of an unnatural colour, which over-hung his little meek, white, vacant face, leaving it hardly more expressive than the unfeatured block upon which these articles are displayed in the barber's window. He was an exquisite image of shabby gentility. His scant, ill-made coat, desperately brushed, his darned gloves, his highly polished boots, his rusty, shapely hat, told the story of a person who had 'had losses' and who clung to the spirit of nice habits even though the letter had been hopelessly effaced. Among other things M. Nioche had lost courage. Adversity had not only deprived him of means, it had deprived him of confidence—so frightened him that he was going through his remnant of life on tiptoe, lest he should wake up afresh the hostile fates. If this strange gentleman should be saying anything improper to his daughter M. Nioche would entreat him huskily, as a particular favour, to forbear; but he would admit at the same time that he was very presumptuous to ask for particular favours.

'Monsieur has bought my picture,' said Mademoiselle Noémie. 'When it's finished you'll carry it to him in a cab.'

'In a cab!' cried M. Nioche; and he stared, in a bewildered way, as if he had seen the sun rising at midnight.

'Are you the young lady's father?' said Newman. 'I think she said you speak English.'

'Spick English—yes.' The old man slowly rubbed his hands. 'I'll bring it in a cab.'

'Say something then,' cried his daughter. 'Thank him a little—not too much.'

'A little, my daughter, a little?' he murmured in distress. 'How much?'

'Two thousand!' said Mademoiselle Noémie. 'Don't make a fuss or he'll take back his word.'

'Two thousand!' gasped the old man; and he began to fumble for his snuff-box. He looked at Newman from head to foot; he looked at his daughter and then at the picture. 'Take care you don't spoil it!' he cried almost sublimely.

'We must go home,' said Mademoiselle Noémie. 'This is a good day's work. Take care how you carry it!' And she began to put up her utensils.

'How can I thank you?' asked M. Nioche. 'My English is far from sufficing.'

'I wish I spoke French half so well,' said Newman good-naturedly. 'Your daughter too, you see, makes herself understood.'

'Oh sir!' and M. Nioche looked over his spectacles with tearful eyes, nodding out of his depths of sadness. 'She has had an education—*très-supérieure*! Nothing was spared. Lessons in pastel at ten francs the lesson, lessons in oil at twelve francs. I didn't look at the francs then. She's a serious worker.'

'Do I understand you to say that you've had a bad time?' asked Newman.

'A bad time? Oh sir, misfortunes—terrible!'

'Unsuccessful in business?'

'Very unsuccessful, sir.'

'Oh, never fear; you'll get on your legs again,' said Newman cheerily.

The old man cast his head to one side; he wore an expression of pain, as if this were an unfeeling jest: whereupon 'What is it he says?' Mademoiselle Noémie demanded.

M. Nioche took a pinch of snuff. 'He says I shall make my fortune again.'

'Perhaps he'll help you. And what else?'

'He says thou hast a great deal of head.'

'It's very possible. You believe it yourself, my father.'

'Believe it, my daughter? With this evidence!' And the old man turned afresh, in staring, wondering homage, to the audacious daub on the easel.

'Ask him then if he'd not like to learn French.'

'To learn French?'

'To take lessons.'

'To take lessons, my daughter? From thee?'

'From thee.'

'From me, my child? How should I give lessons?'

'*Pas de raisons!* Ask him immediately!' said Mademoiselle Noémie with soft shortness.

M. Nioche stood aghast, but under his daughter's eye he collected his wits and, doing his best to assume an agreeable smile, executed her commands. 'Would it please you to receive instruction in our beautiful language?' he brought out with an appealing quaver.

'To study French?' Newman was rather struck.

M. Nioche pressed his finger-tips together and slowly raised his shoulders. 'A little practice in conversation!'

'Practice, conversation—that's it!' murmured Mademoiselle Noémie, who had caught the words. 'The conversation of the best society.'

'Our French conversation is rather famous, you know,' M. Nioche ventured to continue. 'It's the genius of our nation.'

'But—except for your nation—isn't it almost impossible?' asked Newman very simply.

'Not to a man of *esprit* like monsieur, an admirer of beauty in every form!' And M. Nioche cast a significant glance at his daughter's Madonna.

'I can't fancy myself reeling off fluent French!' Newman protested. 'And yet I suppose the more things, the more names of things, a man knows, the better he can get round.'

'Monsieur expresses that very happily. The better he can get round. *Hélas, oui!*'

'I suppose it would help me a great deal, knocking about Paris, to be able to try at least to talk.'

'Ah, there are so many things monsieur must want to say: remarkable things, and proportionately difficult.'

'Everything I want to say is proportionately difficult. But you're in the habit of giving lessons?'

Poor M. Nioche was embarrassed; he smiled more appealingly. 'I'm not a regular professor,' he admitted. 'I can't *pourtant* tell him I've a diploma,' he said to his daughter.

'Tell him it's a very exceptional chance,' answered mademoiselle; 'an *homme du monde*—one perfect gentleman conversing with another. Remember what you are. Remember what you *have* been.'

'A teacher of languages in neither case! Much more *dans le temps* and much less to-day! And if he asks the price of the lessons?'

'He won't ask it,' said the girl.

'What he pleases, I may say?'

'Never! That's bad style.'

'But if he wants to know?'

Mademoiselle Noémie had put on her bonnet and was tying the ribbons. She smoothed them out, her shell-like little chin thrust forward. 'Ten francs,' she said quickly.

'Oh my daughter! I shall never dare.'

'Don't dare then! He won't ask till the end of the lessons, and you'll let me make out the bill.'

M. Nioche turned to the confiding foreigner again and stood rubbing his hands with his air of standing convicted of almost any counsel of despair. It never occurred to Newman to plead for a guarantee of his skill in imparting instruction; he supposed of course M. Nioche knew the language he so beautifully pronounced, and his brokenness of spring was quite the perfection of what the American, for vague reasons, had always associated with all elderly foreigners of the lesson-giving class. Newman had never reflected upon philological processes. His chief impression with regard to any mastery of those mysterious correlatives of his familiar English vocables which were current in this extraordinary city of Paris was that it would be simply a matter of calling sharply into play latent but dormant muscles and sinews. 'How did you learn so much English?' he asked of the old man.

'Oh, I could do things when I was young—before my miseries. I was wide awake then. My father was a great *commerçant*; he placed me for a year in a counting-house in England. Some of it stuck to me, but much I've forgotten!'

'How much French can I learn in about a month?'

'What does he say?' asked mademoiselle; and then when her father had explained: 'He'll speak like an angel!'

But the native integrity which had been vainly exerted to secure M. Nioche's commercial prosperity flickered up again. '*Dame*, monsieur!' he answered. 'All I can teach you!' And then, recovering himself at a sign from his daughter: 'I'll wait upon you at your hotel.'

'Oh yes, I should like to converse with elegance,' Newman went on, giving his friends the benefit of any vagueness. 'Hang me if I should ever have thought of it! I seemed to feel it too far off. But you've brought it quite near, and if you could catch on at all to our grand language—that of Shakespeare and Milton and Holy Writ— why shouldn't I catch on to yours?' His frank, friendly laugh drew the sting from the jest. 'Only, if we're going to converse, you know, you must think of something cheerful to converse about.'

'You're very good, sir; I'm overcome!' And M. Nioche threw up his hands. 'But you've cheerfulness and happiness for two!'

'Oh no,' said Newman more seriously. 'You must be bright and lively; that's part of the bargain.'

M. Nioche bowed with his hand on his heart. 'Very well sir; you've struck up a tune I could almost dance to!'

'Come and bring me my picture then; I'll pay you for it, and we'll talk about that. That will be a cheerful subject!'

Mademoiselle Noémie had collected her accessories and she gave the precious Madonna in charge to her father, who retreated backwards, out of sight, holding it at arm's length and reiterating his obeisances. The young lady gathered her mantle about her like a perfect Parisienne, and it was with the 'Au revoir, monsieur!' of a perfect Parisienne that she took leave of her patron.

II

THIS personage wandered back to the divan and seated himself, on the other side, in view of the great canvas on which Paul Veronese has spread, to swarm and glow there for ever, the marriage-feast of Cana of Galilee.* Weary as he was his spirit went out to the picture; it had an illusion for him; it satisfied his conception, which was strenuous, of what a splendid banquet should be. In the left-hand corner is a young woman with yellow tresses confined in a golden head-dress; she bends forward and listens, with the smile of a charming person at a dinner-party, to her festal neighbour. Newman detected her in the crowd, admired her and perceived that she too had her votive copyist—a young man whose genius, like that of Samson, might have been in his bristling hair. Suddenly he was aware of the prime throb of the mania of the 'collector'. He had taken the first step—why should he not go on? It was only twenty minutes before that he had bought the first picture of his life, and now he was already thinking of art-patronage as a pursuit that might float even so heavy a weight as himself. His reflexions quickened his good-humour and he was on the point of approaching the young man with another 'Combien?' Two or three facts in this relation are noticeable, although the logical chain that connects them may seem imperfect. He knew Mademoiselle Nioche had asked too much; he bore her no grudge for doing so, and he was determined to pay the young man exactly the proper sum. At this moment, however, his attention was attracted by a gentleman who had come from another part of the room and whose manner was that of a stranger to the gallery, though he was equipped neither with guide-book nor with opera-glass. He carried a white sun-umbrella lined with blue silk, and he strolled in front of the great picture, vaguely looking at it but much too near to see anything but the grain of the canvas. Opposite Christopher Newman he paused and turned, and then our friend, who had been observing him, had a chance to verify a suspicion roused by an imperfect view of his face. The result of the larger scrutiny was that he presently sprang to his feet, strode across the room and, with an outstretched hand, arrested this blank spectator. The gaping gentleman gaped afresh, but put out his hand at a venture. He was large, smooth and

pink, with the air of a successfully potted plant, and though his countenance, ornamented with a beautiful flaxen beard carefully divided
in the middle and brushed outward at the sides, was not remarkable
for intensity of expression, it was exclusive only in the degree of the
open door of an hotel—it would have been closed to the undesirable.
It was for Newman in fact as if at first he had been but invited to
'register'.

'Oh come, come,' he said, laughing; 'don't say now you don't know
me—if I've *not* got a white parasol!'

His tone penetrated; the other's face expanded to its fullest capacity and then broke into gladness. 'Why, Christopher Newman—I'll
be blowed! Where in the world—? Who would have thought? You've
carried out such extensive alterations.'

'Well, I guess you've not,' said Newman.

'Oh no, I hold together very much as I was. But when did you get
here?'

'Three days ago.'

'Then why didn't you let me know?'

'How was I to be aware—?'

'Why, I've been located here quite a while.'

'Yes, it's quite a while since we last met.'

'Well, it *feels* long—since the War.'

'It was in Saint Louis, at the outbreak. You were going for a
soldier,' Newman said.

'Oh no, not I. It was you. Have you forgotten?'

'You bring it unpleasantly back.'

'Then you did take your turn?'

'Oh yes, I took my turn. But that was nothing, I seem to feel, to
this turn.'

'How long then have you been in Europe?'

'Just seventeen days.'

'First time you've been?'

'Yes, quite immensely the first.'

Newman's friend had been looking him all over. 'Made your everlasting fortune?'

Our gentleman was silent a little, and then with a tranquil smile,
'Well, I've grubbed,' he answered.

'And come to buy Paris up? Paris *is* for sale, you know.'

'Well, I shall see what I can do about it. So they carry those parasols here—the men-folk?'

'Of course they do. They're great things, these parasols. They
understand detail out here.'

'Where do you buy them?'

'Anywhere, everywhere.'

'Well, Tristram, I'm glad to get hold of you. I guess you can tell
me a good deal. I suppose you know Paris pretty correctly,' Newman
pursued.

Mr Tristram's face took a rosy light. 'Well, I guess there are not
many men that can show me much. I'll take care of you.'

'It's a pity you were not here a few minutes ago. I've just bought
a picture. You might have put the thing through for me.'

'Bought a picture?' said Mr Tristram, looking vaguely round the
walls. 'Why, do they sell them?'

'I mean a copy.'

'Oh, I see. These'—and Mr Tristram nodded at the Titians and
Vandykes—'these, I suppose, are originals?'

'I hope so,' said Newman. 'I don't want a copy of a copy.'

'Ah,' his friend sagaciously returned, 'you can never tell. They
imitate, you know, so deucedly well. It's like the jewellers with their
false stones. Go into the Palais Royal* there; you see 'Imitation' on
half the windows. The law obliges them to stick it on, you know; but
you can't tell the things apart. To tell the truth,' Mr Tristram continued—and his grimace seemed a turn of the screw of discrimination—'I don't do so very much in pictures. They're one of the things
I leave to my wife.'

'Ah, you've acquired a wife?'

'Didn't I mention it? She's a very smart woman. You must come
right round. She's up there in the Avenue d'Iéna.'*

'So you're regularly fixed—house and children and all?'

'Yes; a tip-top house, and a couple of charming cubs.'

'Well,' sighed Christopher Newman, stretching his arms a little,
'you affect me with a queer feeling that I suppose to be envy.'

'Oh no, I don't,' answered Mr Tristram, giving him a little poke
with his parasol.

'I beg your pardon; you do.'

'Well, I shan't then, when—when—!'

'You don't certainly mean when I've seen your pleasant home?'

'When you've made *yours*, my boy. When you've seen Paris. You want to be in light marching order here.'

'Oh, I've skipped about in my shirt all my life, and I've had about enough of it.'

'Well, try it on the basis of Paris. That makes a new thing of it. How old may you be?'

'Forty-two and a half, I guess.'

'*C'est le bel âge*, as they say here.'

Newman reflected. 'Does that mean the age of the belly?'

'It means that a man shouldn't send away his plate till he has eaten his fill.'

'It comes to the same thing. I've just made arrangements, anyhow, to take lessons in the language.'

'Oh, you don't want any lessons. You'll pick it right up. I never required nor received any instruction.'

'You speak it then as easily as English?'

'Easier!' said Mr Tristram roundly. 'It's a splendid language. You can say all sorts of gay things in it.'

'But I suppose,' said Christopher Newman with an earnest desire for information, 'that you must be pretty gay to begin with.'

'Not a bit: that's just the beauty of it!'

The two friends, as they exchanged these remarks, which dropped from them without a pause, had remained standing where they met and leaning against the rail which protected the pictures. Mr Tristram at last declared that he was overcome with lassitude and should be happy to sit down. Newman recommended in the highest terms the great divan on which he had been lounging, and they prepared to seat themselves. 'This is a great place, isn't it?' he broke out with enthusiasm.

'Great place, great place. Finest thing in the world.' And then suddenly Mr Tristram hesitated and looked about. 'I suppose they won't let you smoke?'

Newman stared. 'Smoke? I'm sure I don't know. You know the regulations better than I.'

'I? I never was here before.'

'Never! all your six years?'

'I believe my wife dragged me here once when we first came to Paris, but I never found my way back.'

'But you say you know Paris so well!'

'I don't call this Paris!' cried Mr Tristram with assurance. 'Come; let's go over to the Palais Royal and have a smoke.'

'I don't smoke,' said Newman.

'What's that for?' Mr Tristram growled as he led his companion away. They passed through the glorious halls of the Louvre, down the staircases, along the cool, dim galleries of sculpture and out into the enormous court. Newman looked about him as he went, but made no comments; and it was only when they at last emerged into the open air that he said to his friend: 'It seems to me that in your place I'd have come here once a week.'

'Oh no, you wouldn't!' said Mr Tristram. 'You think so, but you wouldn't. You wouldn't have had time. You'd always mean to go, but you never *would* go. There's better fun than that here in Paris. Italy's the place to see pictures; wait till you get there. There you *have* to go; you can't do anything else. It's an awful country; you can't get a decent cigar. I don't know why I went into that place to-day. I was strolling along, rather hard up for amusement. I sort of took in the Louvre as I passed, and I thought I might go up and see what was going on. But if I hadn't found you there I should have felt rather sold. Hang it, I don't care for inanimate canvas or for cold marble beauty; I prefer the real thing!' And Mr Tristram tossed off this happy formula with an assurance which the numerous class of persons suffering from an overdose of prescribed taste might have envied him.

The two gentlemen proceeded along the Rue de Rivoli and into the Palais Royal, where they seated themselves at one of the little tables stationed at the door of the café which projects, or then projected, into the great open quadrangle. The place was filled with people, the fountains were spouting, a band was playing, clusters of chairs were gathered beneath all the lime-trees and buxom, white-capped nurses, seated along the benches, were offering to their infant charges the amplest facilities for nutrition. There was an easy, homely gaiety in the whole scene, and Christopher Newman felt it to be characteristically, richly Parisian.

'And, now,' began Mr Tristram when they had tasted the decoction he had caused to be served to them,—'now just give an account of yourself. What are your ideas, what are your plans, where have you come from and where are you going? In the first place, where are you hanging out?'

'At the Grand Hotel.'*

He put out all his lights. 'That won't do! You must change.'

'Change?' demanded Newman. 'Why, it's the finest hotel I ever was in.'

'You don't want a "fine" hotel; you want something small and quiet and superior, where your bell's answered and your personality recognised.'

'They keep running to see if I've rung before I've touched the bell,' said Newman, 'and as for my personality they're always bowing and scraping to it.'

'I suppose you're always tipping them. That's very bad style.'

'Always? By no means. A man brought me something yesterday and then stood loafing about in a beggarly manner. I offered him a chair and asked him if he'd sit down. Was that bad style?'

'I'll tell my wife!' Tristram simply answered.

'Tell the police if you like! He bolted right away, at any rate. The place quite fascinates me. Hang your "superior" if it bores me. I sat in the court of the Grand Hotel last night until two o'clock in the morning, watching the coming and going and the people knocking about.'

'You're easily pleased. But you can do as you choose—a man in your shoes. You've made a pile of money, hey?'

'I've made about enough.'

'Happy the man who can say that! But enough for what?'

'Enough to let up a while, to forget the whole question, to look about me, to see the world, to have a good time, to improve my mind and, if my hour strikes, to marry a wife.' Newman spoke slowly, with a quaint effect of dry detachment and with frequent pauses. This was his habitual mode of utterance, but it was especially marked in the words just recorded.

'Jupiter, there's an order!' cried Mr Tristram. 'Certainly all that takes money, especially the wife; unless indeed she gives it, as mine did. And what's the story? How have you done it?'

Newman had pushed his hat back from his forehead, folded his arms and stretched his legs. He listened to the music, he looked about him at the bustling crowd, at the plashing fountains, at the nurses and the babies. 'Well, I haven't done it by sitting round this way.'

Tristram considered him again, allowing a finer curiosity to measure his generous longitude and retrace the blurred lines of his resting face. 'What have you been in?'

'Oh, in more things than I care to remember.'

'I suppose you're a real live man, hey?'

Newman continued to look at the nurses and babies; they imparted to the scene a kind of primordial, pastoral simplicity. 'Yes,' he said at last, 'I guess I am.' And then in answer to his companion's enquiries he briefly exposed his record since their last meeting. It was, with intensity, a tale of the Western world, and it showed, in that bright alien air, very much as fine dessicated, articulated 'specimens', bleached, monstrous, probably unique, show in the high light of museums of natural history. It dealt with elements, incidents, enterprises, which it will be needless to introduce to the reader in detail; the deeps and the shallows, the ebb and the flow, of great financial tides. Newman had come out of the war with a brevet* of brigadier-general, an honour which in this case—without invidious comparisons—had lighted upon shoulders amply competent to carry it. But though he had proved he could handle his men, and still more the enemy's, with effect, when need was, he heartily disliked the business; his four years in the army had left him with a bitter sense of the waste of precious things—life and time and money and ingenuity and opportunity; and he had addressed himself to the pursuits of peace with passionate zest and energy. His 'interests', already mature, had meanwhile, however, waited for him, so that the capital at his disposal had ceased to be solely his whetted, knife-edged resolution and his lively perception of ends and means. Yet these were his real arms, and exertion and action as natural to him as respiration: a more completely healthy mortal had never trod the elastic soil of great States of his option. His experience moreover had been as wide as his capacity; necessity had in his fourteenth year taken him by his slim young shoulders and pushed him into the street to earn that night's supper. He had not earned it, but he had earned the next night's, and afterwards, whenever he had had none, it was because he had gone without to use the money for something else, a keener pleasure or a finer profit. He had turned his hand, with his brain in it, to many things; he had defied example and precedent and probability, had adventured almost to madness and escaped almost by miracles, drinking alike of the flat water, when not the rank poison, of failure, and of the strong wine of success.

A born experimentalist, he had always found something to enjoy in the direct pressure of fate even when it was as irritating as the haircloth shirt of the mediæval monk. At one time defeat had seemed inexorably his portion; ill-luck had become his selfish bed-fellow, and whatever he touched had turned to ashes out of which no gleaming particle could be raked. His most vivid conception of a supernatural element in the world's affairs had come to him once when he felt his head all too bullyingly pummelled; there seemed to him something stronger in life than his personal, intimate will. But the mysterious something could only be a demon as personal as himself, and he accordingly found himself in fine working opposition to this rival concern. He had known what it was to have utterly exhausted his credit, to be unable to raise a dollar and to find himself at nightfall in a strange city, without a penny to mitigate its strangeness. It was under these circumstances that he had made his entrance into San Francisco, the scene subsequently of his most victorious engagements. If he did not, like Dr Franklin in Philadelphia, march along the street munching a penny loaf* it was only because he had not the penny loaf necessary to the performance. In his darkest days he had had but one simple, practical impulse—the desire, as he would have phrased it, to conclude the affair. He had ended by concluding many, had at last buffeted his way into smooth waters, had begun and continued to add dollars to dollars. It must be rather nakedly owned that Newman's only proposal had been to effect that addition; what he had been placed in the world for was, to his own conception, simply to gouge a fortune, the bigger the better, out of its hard material. This idea completely filled his horizon and contented his imagination. Upon the uses of money, upon what one might do with a life into which one had succeeded in injecting the golden stream,* he had up to the eve of his fortieth year very scantly reflected. Life had been for him an open game, and he had played for high stakes. He had finally won and had carried off his winnings; and now what was he to do with them? He was a man to whom, sooner or later, the question was sure to present itself, and the answer to it belongs to our story. A vague sense that more answers were possible than his philosophy had hitherto dreamt of* had already taken possession of him, and it seemed softly and agreeably to deepen as he lounged in this rich corner of Paris with his friend.

'I must confess,' he presently went on, 'that I don't here at all feel my value. My remarkable talents seem of no use. It's as if I were as simple as a little child, and as if a little child might take me by the hand and lead me about.'

'Oh, I'll be your little child,' said Tristram jovially; 'I'll take you by the hand. Trust yourself to me.'

'I'm a grand good worker,' Newman continued, 'but I've come abroad to amuse myself; though I doubt if I very well know how.'

'Oh, that's easily learned.'

'Well, I may perhaps learn it, but I'm afraid I shall never do it by rote. I've the best will in the world about it, but my genius doesn't lie in that direction. Besides,' Newman pursued, 'I don't want to work at pleasure, any more than ever I played at work. I want to let myself, let everything go. I feel coarse and loose and I should like to spend six months as I am now, sitting under a tree and listening to a band. There's only one thing: I want to hear some first-class music.'

'First-class music and first-class pictures? Lord, what refined tastes! You've what my wife calls a rare mind. I haven't a bit. But we can find something better for you to do than to sit under a tree. To begin with, you must come to the club.'

'What club?'

'The Occidental. You'll see all the Americans there; all the best of them at least. Of course you play poker?'

'Oh, I say,' cried Newman, with energy, 'you're not going to lock me up in a club and stick me down at a card-table! I haven't come all this way for that.'

'What the deuce then *have* you come for? You were glad enough to play poker in Saint Louis, I recollect, when you cleaned me out.'

'I've come to see Europe, to get the best out of it I can. I want to see all the great things and do what the best people do.'

'The "best" people? Much obliged. You set me down then as one of the worst?'

Newman was sitting sidewise in his chair, his elbow on the back and his head leaning on his hand. Without moving he played a while at his companion his dry, guarded, half-inscrutable and yet altogether good-natured smile. 'Introduce me to your wife!'

Tristram bounced about on his seat. 'Upon my word I'll do nothing of the sort. She doesn't want any help to turn up her nose at me, nor do you either.'

'I don't turn up my nose at you, my dear fellow; nor at any one nor anything. I'm not proud, I assure you I'm not proud. That's why I'm willing to take example by the best.'

'Well, if I'm not the rose, as they say here, I've lived near it. I can show you some rare minds too. Do you know General Packard? Do you know C. P. Hatch? Do you know Miss Kitty Upjohn?'

'I shall be happy to make their acquaintance. I want to cultivate society.'

Tristram seemed restless and suspicious; he eyed his friend askance, and then, 'What are you up to, anyway?' he demanded. 'Are you going to write a heavy book?'

Christopher Newman twisted one end of his moustache in silence and finally made answer. 'One day, a couple of months ago, something very curious happened to me. I had come on to New York on some important business; it's too long and too low a story to tell you now—a question of getting in ahead of another party on a big transaction and on information that was all my own. This other party had once played off on me one of the clever meannesses the feeling of which works in a man like strong poison. I owed him a good one, the best one he was ever to have got in his life, and as his chance here—for he was after it, but on the wrong tip—would have been a remarkably sweet thing, a matter of half a million,* I saw my way to show him the weight of my hand. The good it was going to do me, you see, to feel it come down on him! I jumped into a hack and went about my business, and it was in this hack—this immortal historical hack—that the curious thing I speak of occurred. It was a hack like any other, only a trifle dirtier, with a greasy line along the top of the drab cushions, as if it had been used for a great many Irish funerals. It's possible I took a nap; I had been travelling all night and, though I was excited with my errand, I felt the want of sleep. At all events I woke up suddenly, from a sleep or from a kind of reverie, with the most extraordinary change of heart—a mortal disgust for the whole proposition. It came upon me like *that*!'—and he snapped his fingers—'as abruptly as an old wound that begins to ache. I couldn't tell the meaning of it; I only realised I had turned against myself worse than against the man I wanted to smash. The idea of *not* coming by that half-million in that particular way, of letting it utterly slide and scuttle and never hearing of it again, became the one thing to save my life from a sudden danger. And all this took place quite independently of my will, and I sat watching it as if it were a play at the theatre. I could feel it going on inside me. You may depend upon it that there are things going on inside us that we understand mighty little about.'

'Jupiter, you make my flesh creep!' cried Tristram. 'And while you sat in your hack watching the play, as you call it, the other man looked in and collared your half-million?'

'I haven't the least idea. I hope so, poor brute, but I never found out. We pulled up in front of the place I was going to in Wall Street, but I sat still in the carriage, and at last the driver scrambled down off his seat to see whether his hack hadn't turned into a hearse. I couldn't have got out any more than if I *had* been a corpse. What was the matter with me? Momentary brain-collapse, you'll say. What I wanted to get out of was Wall Street. I told the man to drive to the Brooklyn ferry and cross over. When we were over I told him to drive me out into the country.* As I had told him originally to drive for dear life down town, I suppose he thought I had lost my wits on the way. Perhaps I had, but in that case my sacrifice of them has become, in another way, my biggest stroke of business. I spent the morning looking at the first green leaves on Long Island. I had been so hot that it seemed as if I should never be cool enough again. As for the damned old money, I've enough, already, not to miss it—you see how that spoils my beauty. I seemed to feel a new man under my old skin; at all events I longed for a new world. When you want a thing so very badly you probably had better have it and see. I didn't understand my case in the least, but gave the poor beast the bridle and let him find his way. As soon as I could get out of harness I sailed for Europe. That's how I come to be sitting here.'

'You ought to have bought up that hack,' said Tristram; 'it isn't a safe vehicle to have about. And you've really wound up and sold out then? you've formally retired from business?'

'Well, I'm not at present transacting any—on any terms. There'll be plenty to be done again if I don't hold out, but I shall hold out as long as possible. I dare say, however, that a twelvemonth hence the uncanny operation will be repeated in the opposite sense and the pendulum swing back again. I shall be sitting in a gondola or on a dromedary, or on a cushion at the feet of Beauty, and all of a sudden I shall want to clear out. But for the present I'm perfectly free. I've even arranged that I'm to receive no business letters.'

'Oh, it's a real *caprice de prince*,' said Tristram. 'I back out; a poor devil like me can't help you to spend such very magnificent leisure as that. You should get introduced to the crowned heads.'

Newman considered a moment and then with all his candour, 'How does one do it?' he asked.

'Come, I like that!' cried Tristram. 'It shows you're in earnest.'

'Of course I'm in earnest. Didn't I say I wanted the best? I know the best can't be had for mere money, but I'm willing to take a good deal of trouble.'

'You're not too shrinking, hey?'

'I haven't the least idea—I must see. I want the biggest kind of entertainment a man can get. People, places, art, nature, everything! I want to see the tallest mountains, and the bluest lakes, and the finest pictures, and the handsomest churches, and the most celebrated men, and the most elegant women.'

'Settle down in Paris then. There are no mountains that I know of, higher than Montmartre, and the only lake's in the Bois de Boulogne* and not particularly blue. But there's everything else: plenty of pictures and churches, no end of celebrated men, and several elegant women.'

'But I can't settle down in Paris at this season, just as summer's coming on.'

'Oh, for the summer go right up to Trouville.'*

'And what may Trouville be?'

'Well, a sort of French Newport*—as near as they can come. All the Americans go.'

'Is it anywhere near the Alps?'

'About as near as Newport to the Rocky Mountains.'

'Oh, I want to see Mont Blanc,' said Newman, 'and Amsterdam, and the Rhine, and a lot of places. Venice in particular. I've grand ideas for Venice.'

'Ah,' said Mr Tristram, rising, 'I see I shall have to introduce you to my wife. She'll have grand ideas for *you*!'

III

HE performed that ceremony the following day, when, by appointment, Christopher Newman went to dine with him. Mr and Mrs Tristram lived behind one of those chalk-coloured façades which decorate with their pompous sameness the broad avenues distributed by Baron Haussmann* over the neighbourhood of the Arc de Triomphe. Their apartment was rich in the modern conveniences, and Tristram lost no time in calling his visitor's attention to their principal household treasures, the thick-scattered gas-lamps and the frequent furnace-holes. 'Whenever you feel homesick,' he said, 'you must come right up here. We'll stick you down before a register, under a good big burner, and—'

'And you'll soon get over your homesickness,' said Mrs Tristram.

Her husband stared; this lady often had a tone that defied any convenient test; he couldn't tell for his life to whom her irony might be directed. The truth is that circumstances had done much to cultivate in Mrs Tristram the need for any little intellectual luxury she could pick up by the way. Her taste on many points differed from that of her husband; and though she made frequent concessions to the dull small fact that he had married her it must be confessed that her reserves were not always muffled in pink gauze. They were founded upon the vague project of her some day affirming herself in her totality; to which end she was in advance getting herself together, building herself high, enquiring, in short, into her dimensions.

It should be added, without delay, to anticipate misconception, that if she was thus saving herself up it was yet not to cover the expense of any foreseen outlay of that finest part of her substance that was known to her tacitly as her power of passion. She had a very plain face and was entirely without illusions as to her appearance. She had taken its measure to a hair's breadth, she knew the worst and the best, she had accepted herself. It had not been indeed without a struggle. As a mere mortified maiden she had spent hours with her back to her mirror, crying her eyes out; and later she had, from desperation and bravado, adopted the habit of proclaiming herself the most ill-favoured of women, in order that she might—as in common politeness was inevitable—be contradicted and reassured.

It was since she had come to live in Europe that she had begun to take the matter philosophically. Her observation, acutely exercised here, had suggested to her that a woman's social service resides not in what she is but in what she appears, and that in the labyrinth of appearances she may always make others lose their clue if she only keeps her own. She had encountered so many women who pleased without beauty that she began to believe she had discovered her refuge. She had once heard an enthusiastic musician, out of patience with a gifted bungler, declare that a fine voice is really an obstacle to singing properly; and it occurred to her that it might perhaps be equally true that a beautiful face is an obstacle to the acquisition of charming manners. Mrs Tristram then undertook to persuade by grace, and she brought to the task no small ingenuity.

How well she would have succeeded I am unable to say; unfortunately she broke off in the middle. Her own excuse was the want of encouragement in her immediate circle. But she had presumably not a real genius for the charming art, or she would have pursued it for itself. The poor lady was after all incomplete. She fell back upon the harmonies of dress, which she thoroughly understood, and contented herself with playing in its lock that key to the making of impressions. She lived in Paris, which she pretended to detest, because it was only in Paris that one could find things to exactly suit one's complexion. Besides, out of Paris it was always more or less of a trouble to get ten-button gloves. When she railed at this serviceable city and you asked her where she would prefer to reside she returned some very unexpected answer. She would say in Copenhagen or in Barcelona; having, while making the tour of Europe, spent a couple of days at each of these places. On the whole, with her poetic furbelows* and her misshapen, intelligent little face, she was, when known, a figure to place, in the great gallery of the wistful, somewhere apart. She was naturally timid, and if she had been born a beauty she would (content with it) probably have taken no risks. At present she was both reckless and diffident; extremely reserved sometimes with her friends and strangely expansive with strangers. She overlooked her husband; overlooked him too much, for she had been perfectly at liberty not to marry him. She had been in love with a clever man who had eventually slighted her, and she had married a fool in the hope that the keener personage, reflecting on it, would conclude that she had had no appreciation of his keenness and that he had flattered her in thinking her touched. Restless, discontented, visionary, without personal ambitions but with a certain avidity of imagination, she was interesting from this sense she gave of her looking for her ideals by a lamp of strange and fitful flame. She was full—both for good and for ill—of beginnings that came to nothing; but she had nevertheless, morally, a spark of the sacred fire.

Newman was fond, in all circumstances, of the society of women; and now that he was out of his native element and deprived of his habitual interests he turned to it for compensation. He took a great fancy to Mrs Tristram; she frankly repaid it, and after their first meeting he passed a great many hours in her drawing-room. Two or three long talks had made them fast friends. Newman's manner with women was peculiar, and it required some diligence on a lady's part to discover that he admired her. He had no gallantry in the usual sense of the term; no compliments, no graces, no speeches. Fond enough of a large pleasantry in his dealings with men, he never found himself on a sofa beside a member of the softer sex without feeling that such situations appealed, like beautiful views, or celebrated operas, or fine portraits, or handsome 'sets' of the classics, or even elegant 'show' cemeteries, to his earnest side. He was not shy and, so far as awkwardness proceeds from a struggle with shyness, was not awkward: grave, attentive, submissive, often silent, he was simply swimming in a sort of rapture of respect. This emotion was not at all theoretic, it was not even in a high degree romantic; he had thought very little about the 'position' of women, and he was not familiar, either sympathetically or otherwise, with the image of a President in petticoats. His attitude was simply the flower of his general good-nature and a part of his instinctive and genuinely democratic assumption of every one's right to lead an easy life. If a shaggy pauper had a right to bed and board and wages and a vote, women, of course, who were weaker than paupers, and whose physical tissue was in itself an appeal, should be maintained, sentimentally, at the public expense. Newman was willing to be taxed for this purpose, largely, in proportion to his means. Moreover many of the common traditions with regard to women were with him fresh personal impressions. He had never read a page of printed romance.

He spent a great deal of time in listening to advice from Mrs Tristram; advice, it must be added, for which he had never asked. He would have been incapable of asking for it, inasmuch as he had no

perception of difficulties and consequently no curiosity about reme-
dies. The complex Parisian world about him seemed a very simple
affair; it was an immense, surprising spectacle, but it neither inflamed
his imagination nor irritated his curiosity. He kept his hands in his
pockets, looked on good-humouredly, desired to miss nothing important, observed a great many things in detail, and never reverted to
himself. Mrs Tristram's 'advice' was a part of the show and a more
entertaining element of her free criticism than any other. He enjoyed
her talking about *him*—it seemed a part of her beautiful culture; but
he never made an application of anything she said or remembered it
when he was away from her. For herself, she appropriated him: he
was the most interesting thing she had had to think about for many a
month. She wished to do something with him—she hardly knew
what. There was so much of him; he was so rich and robust, so easy,
friendly, well-disposed, that he kept her imagination constantly on
the alert. For the present the only thing she could do was to like him.
She told him he was beyond everything a child of nature, but she
repeated it so often that it could have been but a term of endearment.
She led him about with her, introduced him to fifty people, took
extreme satisfaction in her conquest. Newman accepted every proposal, shook hands universally and promiscuously, and seemed
equally unversed in trepidation and in 'cheek'. Tom Tristram complained of his wife's rapacity, declaring he could never have a clear
five minutes with his friend. If he had known how things were going
to turn out he never would have brought him to the Avenue d'Iéna.

The two men had formerly not been intimate, but Newman
recalled his earlier impression of his host and did Mrs Tristram, who
had by no means taken him into her confidence, but whose secret
he presently discovered, the justice to admit that her husband had
somehow found means to be degenerate without the iridescence of
decay.* People said he was very sociable, but this was as much a
matter of course as for a dipped sponge to expand; and it was a sociability affirmed, on its anecdotic side, too much at the expense of
those possible partakers who were not there to guard their interest
in it. He was patient at poker; he was infallible upon the names and
the other attributes of all the *cocottes*; his criticism of cookery, his
comparative view of the great 'years' of champagne, enjoyed the
authority of the last word. And then he was idle, spiritless, sensual,

snobbish. He irritated our friend by the tone of his allusions to their native country, and Newman was at a loss to understand wherein such a country, as a whole, could fall short of Mr Tristram's stomach. He had never been a very systematic patriot, but it vexed him to see the United States treated as little better than a vulgar smell in his friend's nostril, and he finally spoke up for them quite as if it had been Fourth of July, proclaiming that any American who ran them down ought to be carried home in irons and compelled to live in Boston—which for Newman was putting it very vindictively. Tristram was a comfortable man to snub; he bore no malice and he continued to insist on Newman's finishing his evenings at the Occidental Club. The latter dined several times in the Avenue d'Iéna, and his host always proposed an early adjournment to this institution. Mrs Tristram protested, declaring as promptly that her husband exhausted a low cunning in trying to displease her.

'Oh no, I never try, my love,' he answered; 'I know you loathe me quite enough when I take my chance.' But their visitor hated to see a married couple on these terms, and he was sure one or other of them must be very unhappy. Yet he knew it was not Tristram. The lady had a balcony before her windows, upon which, during the June evenings, she was fond of sitting, and Newman used frankly to say that he preferred the balcony to the club. It had a fringe of perfumed plants in tubs and enabled you to look up the broad street and see the Arch of Triumph vaguely massing its heroic sculptures in the summer starlight. Sometimes he kept his promise of following Mr Tristram in half an hour to the Occidental and sometimes forgot it. His companion asked him a great many questions about himself, but on this subject he was an indifferent talker. He was not 'subjective', though when he felt her interest sincere he made a real effort to meet it. He told her many things he had done, and regaled her with pictures of that 'nature' as the child of which he figured for her; she herself was from Philadelphia and, with her eight years in Paris, talked of herself as a languid Oriental. But some other person was always the hero of the tale, though by no means always to his advantage; and the states of Newman's own spirit were but scantily chronicled. She had an especial wish to know whether he had ever been in love—seriously, passionately—and, failing to gather any satisfaction from his allusions, at last closely pressed him. He hesitated a while,

but finally said 'Hang it then, no!' She declared that she was
delighted to hear it, as it confirmed her private conviction that he
was a man of no real feeling.

'Is that so?' he asked very gravely. 'But how do you recognise a
man of real feeling?'

'I can't make out,' said Mrs Tristram, 'whether you're very simple
or very deep.'

'I'm very deep. That's a fact.'

'I believe that if I were to tell you with a certain air that you're as
cold as a fish you would implicitly believe me.'

'A certain air?' Newman echoed. 'Well, try your air and see.'

'You'd believe me, but you wouldn't care,' said Mrs Tristram.

'You've got it all wrong. I should care immensely, but I shouldn't
believe you. The fact is I have never had time to "feel" things so very
beautifully. I've had to *do* them, had to make myself felt.'

'Oh, I can imagine indeed that you may have sometimes done that
tremendously.'

'Yes, there's no mistake about that.'

'When you're in one of your furies it can't be pleasant.'

'Ah, I don't have to get into a fury to do it.'

'I don't, nevertheless, see you always as you are now. You've *something* or other behind, beneath. You get harder or you get softer.
You're more displeased—or you're more pleased.'

'Well, a man of any sense doesn't lay his plans to be angry,' said
Newman, 'and it's in fact so long since I've been displeased that I've
quite forgotten it.'

'I don't believe,' she returned 'that you're never angry. A man
ought to be angry sometimes, and you're neither good enough nor
bad enough always to keep your temper.'

'I lose it perhaps every five years.'

'The time's coming round then,' said his hostess. 'Before I've
known you six months I shall see you in a magnificent rage.'

'Do you mean to put me into one?'

'I shouldn't be sorry. You take things too coolly. It quite exasper-
ates me. And then you're too happy. You've what must be the
most agreeable thing in the world—the consciousness of having
bought your pleasure beforehand, having paid for it in advance.
You've not a day of reckoning staring you in the face. Your reckon-
ings are over.'

'Well, I suppose I'm happy,' said Newman almost pensively.

'You've been odiously successful.'

'Successful in copper,' he recalled, 'but very mixed in other mining ventures. And I've had to take quite a back seat on oil.'

'It's very disagreeable to know how Americans have come by their money,' his companion sighed. 'Now, at all events, you've the world before you. You've only to enjoy.'

'Oh, I suppose I'm all right,' said Newman. 'Only I'm tired of having it thrown up at me. Besides, there are several drawbacks. I don't come up to my own standard of culture.'

'One doesn't expect it of you,' Mrs Tristram answered. Then in a moment: 'Besides, you do come up. You *are* up!'

'Well, I mean to have a good time, wherever I am,' said Newman. 'I find I take notice as I go, and I guess I shan't have missed much by the time I've done. I feel something under my ribs here,' he added in a moment, 'that I can't explain—a sort of strong yearning, a desire to stretch out and haul in.'

'Bravo!' Mrs Tristram cried; 'that's what I want to hear you say. You're the great Western Barbarian, stepping forth in his innocence and might, gazing a while at this poor corrupt old world and then swooping down on it.'

'Oh come,' Newman protested; 'I'm not an honest barbarian either, by a good deal. I'm a great fall-off from *him*. I've seen honest barbarians, I know what they are.'

'I don't mean you're a Comanche chief or that you wear a blanket and feathers. There are different shades.'

'I have the instincts—have them deeply—if I haven't the forms of a high old civilisation,' Newman went on. 'I stick to that. If you don't believe it I should like to prove it to you.'

Mrs Tristram was silent a while. 'I should like to make you prove it,' she said at last. 'I should like to put you in a difficult place.'

'Well, put me!' said Newman.

'Vous ne doutez de rien!' his companion rejoined.

'Oh,' he insisted, 'I've a very good opinion of myself.'

'I wish I could put it to the test. Give me time and I will.' And Mrs Tristram remained silent a minute, as if trying to keep her pledge. It didn't appear that evening that she succeeded; but as he was rising to take his leave she passed suddenly, as she was very apt to do, from the tone of ingenious banter to that of almost tremulous sympathy. 'Speaking seriously,' she said, 'I believe in you, Mr Newman. You flatter my latent patriotism.'

'Your latent—?'

'Deep within me the eagle shrieks, and I've known my heart at times to bristle with more feathers than my head. It would take too long to explain, and you probably wouldn't understand. Besides, you might take it—really you might take it—for a declaration. Yet it has nothing to do with you personally; the question is of what you almost unconsciously represent. Fortunately you don't know all that, or your conceit would increase insufferably.' And then as Newman stood wondering what this great quantity might be: 'Forgive all my meddlesome chatter and forget my advice. It's very silly in me to undertake to tell you what to do. When you're embarrassed do as you think best, and you'll do very well. When you're in a difficulty judge for yourself. Only let it then be all you.'

'I shall remember everything you've told me,' he made answer. 'There are so many twists and turns over here, so many forms and ceremonies—'

'Forms and ceremonies are what I mean of course.'

'Ah, but I don't want not to take account of them,' he declared. 'Haven't I as good a right as another? They don't scare me, and you needn't give me leave to ignore them. I want to know all about 'em.'

'That's not what I mean. I mean that you're to deal with them in your own way. Settle delicate questions by your own light. Cut the knot or untie it, as you choose.'

'Oh, if there's ever a big knot,' he returned—'and they all seem knots of ribbon over here—I shall simply pull it off and wear it!'

The next time he dined in the Avenue d'Iéna was a Sunday, a day on which Mr Tristram left the cards unshuffled, so that there was a trio in the evening on the balcony. The talk was of many things, and at last Mrs Tristram suddenly observed to their visitor that it was high time that he should take a wife.

'Listen to her: she has the *toupet*!' said Tristram, who on Sunday evenings was always a little peevish.

'I don't suppose you've made up your mind not to marry?' Mrs Tristram continued.

'Heaven forbid!' cried Newman. 'I'm quite viciously bent on it.'

'It's a very easy mistake,' said Tristram; 'and when it's made it's made.'

'Well then,' his wife went on, 'I suppose you don't mean to wait till you're fifty.'

'On the contrary, I'm in an almost indecent hurry.'

'One would never guess it. Do you expect a lady to come and propose to you?'

'No; I'm willing to put the case before her myself. I think a great deal about it.'

'Tell me some of your thoughts.'

'Well,' said Newman slowly, 'I want to marry about as well as you *can*.'

'"Well" in what sense?'

'In every sense. I shall be hard to suit.'

'You must remember that, as the French proverb puts it,* the finest girl in the world can give but what she has.'

'Since you ask me,' said Newman, let me be frank about it—I want quite awfully to marry. It's time, to begin with; before I know it I shall be forty-five. And then I'm lonely, and I really kind of pine for a mate. There are things for which I want help. But if I marry now, so long as I didn't do it in hot haste when I was twenty, I must do it, you see, with my eyes open. I want to set about it rather grandly. I not only want to make no mistakes, but I want to make a great hit. I want to take my pick. My wife must be a pure pearl. I've thought an immense deal about it.'

'Perhaps you think too much. The best thing's simply to fall in love.'

'When I find the woman who satisfies me I shall rise to the occasion. My wife shall be as satisfied as I shall.'

'You begin grandly enough,' said Mrs Tristram. 'There's a chance for the pure pearls!'

'You're not fair,' Newman presently broke out. 'You draw a fellow on and put him off his guard and then you gibe at him.'

'I assure you,' she answered, 'that I'm very serious. To prove it I make you a proposal. Should you like me, as they say here, to marry you?'

'To hunt up a wife for me?'

'She's already found. I'll bring you together.'

'Oh come,' said Tristram, 'we don't keep a *bureau de placement*. He'll think you want your commission.'

'Present me to a woman who comes up to my notion.' Newman declared, 'and I'll marry her to-morrow.'

'You've a strange tone about it, and I don't quite understand you. I didn't suppose you could be so cold-blooded.'

Newman was silent a while. 'Well, I want a great woman. I stick to that. That's one thing I *can* treat myself to, and if it's to be had I mean to have it. What else have I toiled and struggled for all these years? I've succeeded, and now what am I to do with my success? To make it perfect, as I see it, there must be a lovely being perched on the pile like some shining statue crowning some high monument. She must be as good as she's beautiful and as clever as she's good. I can give my wife many things, so I'm not afraid to ask certain others myself. She shall have everything a woman can desire; I shall not even object to her being too good for me. She may be cleverer and wiser than I can understand, and I shall only be the better pleased. I want, in a word, the best article in the market.'

'Why didn't you tell a fellow all this at the outset?' Tristram demanded. 'I've been trying so to make you fond of *me*!'

'It's remarkably interesting,' said Mrs Tristram. 'I like to see a man know his own mind.'

'I've known mine for a long time,' Newman went on. 'I made up my mind tolerably early in life that some rare creature all one's own is the best kind of property to hold. It's the greatest victory over circumstances. When I say rare I mean rare all through—grown as a rarity and recognised as one. It's a thing every man has an equal right to; he may get it if he *can* get it. He doesn't have to be born with certain faculties on purpose; he needs only to be—well, whatever he really *is*. Then he need only use his will, and such wits as he can muster, and go in.'

'It strikes me,' said Mrs Tristram, 'that your marriage is to be rather a matter of heartless pomp.'

'Well, it's certain,' Newman granted, 'that if people notice my wife and admire her I shall count it as part of my success.'

'After this,' cried Mrs Tristram, 'speak of any man's modesty!'

'But none of them will admire her so much as I.'

'You really have the imagination of greatness.'

He hesitated as if in fear of her mockery, but he kept it up, repeating his dry formula: 'I want the best thing going.'

'And I suppose you've already looked about you a good deal.'

'More or less, according to opportunity.'

'And you've seen nothing that has tempted you?'

'No,' said Newman half reluctantly, 'I'm bound to say in honesty that I've seen nothing that has come up to my idea.'

'You remind me of the heroes of the French romantic poets, Rolla and Fortunio* and all those other insatiable gentlemen for whom nothing in this world was handsome enough. But I see you're in earnest, and I *should* like to help you,' Mrs Tristram wound up.

'Who the deuce is it, darling, that you're going to palm off upon him?' her husband asked. 'We know a good many pretty girls, thank goodness, but nobody to be mentioned in *that* blazing light.'

'Have you any objections to a foreigner?' Mrs Tristram continued, addressing their friend, who had tilted back his chair and, with his feet on a bar of the balcony railing and his hands in his pockets, sat looking at the stars.

'No Irish need apply,' said Tristram.

Newman remained pensive. 'Just as a foreigner, no. I've no prejudices.'

'My dear fellow, you've no suspicions!' Tristram cried. 'You don't know what terrible customers these foreign women are; especially those grown, as you call it, for the use of millionaires. How should you like an expensive Circassian with a dagger in her baggy trousers?'*

Newman administered a vigorous slap to his knee. 'I'd marry a Patagonian if she pleased me.'

'We had better confine ourselves to Europe,' said Mrs Tristram. 'The only thing is then that the young person herself should square with your tremendous standard?'

'She's going to offer you an unappreciated governess!' Tristram groaned.

'Of course I won't deny that, other things being equal, I should like one of my own countrywomen best,' Newman pursued. 'We should speak the same language, and that would be a comfort. But I'm not afraid of any foreigner who's the best thing in her own country. Besides, I rather like the idea of taking in Europe too. It enlarges the field of selection. When you choose from a greater number you can bring your choice to a finer point.'

'Sardanapalus!'* Tristram sighed.

'Well, you've come to the right market,' Newman's hostess brought out after a pause. 'I happen to number among my friends the finest creature in the world. Neither more nor less. I don't say a

very charming person or a very estimable woman or a very great
beauty: I say simply the finest creature in the world.'

'I'm bound to say then,' cried Tristram, 'that you've kept very
quiet about her. Were you afraid of *me*?'

'You've seen her,' said his wife, 'but you've no perception of such
quality as Claire's.'

'Ah, her name's Claire? I give it up.'

'Does your friend wish to marry?' Newman asked.

'Not in the least. It's for you to make her change her mind. It won't
be easy; she has had one husband and he gave her a low opinion of
the species.'

'Oh, she's a widow then?'

'Are you already afraid? She was married at eighteen, by her
parents, in the French fashion, to a man with advantages of fortune,
but objectionable, detestable, on other grounds, and many years too
old. He had, however, the discretion to die a couple of years afterwards, and she's now twenty-eight.'

'So she's French?'

'French by her father, English by her mother. She's really more
English than French, and she speaks English as well as you or I—or
rather much better. She belongs, as they say here, to the very top of
the basket.* Her family, on each side, is of fabulous antiquity; her
mother's the daughter of an English Catholic peer. Her father's dead,
and since her widowhood she has lived with her mother and a
married brother. There's another brother, younger, who I believe is
rather amusing but quite impossible. They have an old hôtel in the
Rue de l'Université,* but their fortune's small and they make, for
economy's sake, a common household. When I was a girl of less than
fifteen I was put into a convent here for my education while my father
made the tour of Europe. It was a fatuous thing to do with me, but
it had the advantage that it made me acquainted with Claire de
Bellegarde.* She was younger than I, yet we became fast friends. I
took a tremendous fancy to her, and she returned my adoration so
far as she could. They kept such a tight rein on her that she could
do very little, and when I left the convent she had to give me up. I
was not of her *monde*; I'm not now either, but we sometimes meet.
They're terrible people—her *monde*; all mounted upon stilts a mile
high and with pedigrees long in proportion. It's the skim of the milk
of the old noblesse. Did you ever hear of such a prehistoric monster

as a Legitimist or an Ultramontane?* Go into Madame de Cintré's* drawing-room some afternoon at five o'clock and you'll see the best-preserved specimens. I say go, but no one is admitted—to intimacy—who can't show good cause in the form of a family tree.'

'And this is the lady you propose to me to marry?' asked Newman. 'A lady I can't even approach?'

'But you said just now that you recognised no reasons against you.'

Newman looked at Mrs Tristram a while, stroking his moustache. 'Is she a very great beauty?' he demanded.

She hung fire a little. 'No.'

'Oh then it's no use—!'

'She's not a very great beauty, but she's very, very beautiful; two quite different things. A beauty has no faults in her face; the face of a beautiful woman may have faults that only deepen its charm.'

'I remember Madame de Cintré now,' said Tristram. 'She's as plain as a copy in a copy-book—all round o's and uprights a little slanting. She just slants toward *us*. A man of your large appetite would swallow her down without tasting her.'

'In telling how little use *he* has for her my husband sufficiently describes her,' Mrs Tristram pursued.

'Is she good, is she clever?' Newman asked.

'She's perfect! I won't say more than that. When you're praising a person to another who's to know her, it's bad policy to go into details. I won't exaggerate, I simply recommend her. Among all the women I've known she stands alone; she's of a different clay.'

'I should like to see her,' said Newman simply.

'I'll try to manage it. The only way will be to invite her to dinner. I've never invited her before, and I'm not sure she'll be able to come. Her old feudal countess of a mother rules the family with an iron hand and allows her to have no friends but of her own choosing and to visit only in a certain sacred circle. But I can at least invite her.'

At this moment Mrs Tristram was interrupted; a servant stepped out upon the balcony and announced that there were visitors in the drawing-room. When she had gone in to receive her friends Tom Tristram approached his guest.

'Don't put your foot into *this*, my boy,' he said, puffing the last whiffs of his cigar. 'There's nothing in it!'

Newman eyed him with oblique penetration. 'You tell another story, eh?'

'I say simply that Madame de Cintré's a great white doll of a woman and that she cultivates quiet haughtiness.'

'Ah, she's *really* haughty, eh?'

'She looks at you as if you were so much thin air, and blows you away as easily.'

'She's *really* proud, eh?' Newman pursued with interest.

'Proud? As proud as they make 'em over here.'

'And not good-looking?'

Tristram shrugged his shoulders. 'She leaves me cold. She's as cold herself as a porcelain stove, and has about as much expression. But I must go in and amuse the company.'

Some time elapsed before Newman followed his friends into the drawing-room. When he at last joined them there he remained but a short time, and during this period sat perfectly silent, listening to a lady to whom Mrs Tristram had straightway introduced him and who treated him, without drawing breath, to the full force of an extraordinarily high-pitched voice. He could but gaze and attend. Presently he came to bid his hostess good-night. 'Who is that lady?'

'Miss Dora Finch. How do you like her?'

'Well, as I like the gong that sounds for dinner. She's good for a warning.'

'She's thought so sweet! Certainly you have ideas,' said Mrs Tristram.

He hung about, but at last, 'Don't forget about your friend,' he said, 'the lady of the proud people. Do make her come, and give me good notice.' And with this he departed.

Some days later he came back; it was in the afternoon. He found Mrs Tristram in her drawing-room and entertaining a visitor, a woman young and pretty and dressed in white. The two had risen and the visitor was apparently taking leave. After Newman had approached he received from Mrs Tristram, who had turned to her companion, a glance of the most vivid significance, which he was yet not immediately able to interpret. 'This is a good friend of ours, Mr Christopher Newman. I've spoken of you to him, and he has an extreme desire to make your acquaintance. If you had consented to come and dine I should have offered him an opportunity.'

The stranger presented her face with a still brightness of kindness. He was not embarrassed, for his unconscious equanimity was boundless; but as he became aware that this was the proud and beautiful Madame de Cintré, the finest creature in the world, the promised perfection, the proposed ideal, he made an instinctive movement to gather his wits together. Through the slight preoccupation it produced he had a sense of a longish fair face and of the look of a pair of eyes that were both intense and mild.

'I should have been most happy,' said Madame de Cintré. 'Unfortunately, as I have been telling Mrs Tristram, I go next week to the country.'

Newman had made a solemn bow. 'I'm very very sorry.'

'Paris is really getting too hot,' Madame de Cintré added, taking her friend's hand again in farewell.

Mrs Tristram seemed to have formed a sudden and somewhat venturesome resolution, and she smiled more gaily, as women do when they become more earnest. 'I want Mr Newman to know you,' she said, dropping her head on one side and looking at Madame de Cintré's bonnet-ribbons.

Christopher Newman stood gravely silent, and his native penetration admonished him. Mrs Tristram was determined to force her friend to address him a word of encouragement which should be more than one of the common formulas of politeness; and if she was prompted by charity it was by the charity that begins at home. Madame de Cintré was her dearest Claire and her especial admiration; but Madame de Cintré had found it impossible to dine with her and Madame de Cintré should for once be forced gently to render tribute to Mrs Tristram. 'It would give me great pleasure,' she said, looking at Mrs Tristram.

'That's a great deal,' cried the latter, 'for Madame de Cintré to say!'

'I'm very much obliged to you,' said Newman. 'Mrs Tristram can speak better for me than I can speak for myself.'

Madame de Cintré turned on him again her soft lustre. 'Are you for long in Paris?'

'We shall keep him,' said Mrs Tristram.

'But you're keeping *me*!' And Madame de Cintré disengaged her hand.

'A moment longer,' said Mrs Tristram.

Madame de Cintré looked at Newman again; this time without her smile. Her eyes lingered a little. 'Will you come and see me?'

Mrs Tristram kissed her at this; Newman acknowledged it more

formally, and she took her departure. Her hostess went with her to
the door, leaving Newman briefly alone. Presently she returned,
clasping her hands together and shaking them at him. 'It was a
fortunate chance. She had come to decline my invitation. You triumphed on the spot, making her ask you, at the end of three minutes,
to her house.'

'It was you who triumphed,' said Newman. 'You mustn't see too
much in her.'

Mrs Tristram stared. 'What do you mean?'

'She didn't strike me as so very proud. I should call her quite
timid.'

'I should call *you* quite deep! And what do you think of her face?'

'Well, I guess I like her face,' said Newman.

'I should think you might! May I guess, on my side, that you'll go
and see her?'

'To-morrow!' cried Newman.

'No, not to-morrow; next day. That will be Sunday; she leaves
Paris on Monday. If you don't see her it will at least be a beginning.'
And she gave him Madame de Cintré's address.

He walked across the Seine late in the summer afternoon and
made his way through those grey and silent streets of the Faubourg
Saint Germain whose houses present to the outer world a face as
impassive and as suggestive of the concentration of privacy within
as the blank walls of Eastern seraglios. Newman thought it a perverse, verily a 'mean' way for rich people to live; his ideal of grandeur
was a splendid façade, diffusing its brilliancy outward too, irradiat-
ing hospitality. The house to which he had been directed had a dark,
dusty, painted portal, which swung open in answer to his ring. It
admitted him into a wide, gravelled court, surrounded on three
sides with closed windows; here was a doorway facing the street,
approached by three steps and surmounted by a tent-like canopy.
The place was all in the shade; it answered to Newman's conception
of a convent. The portress couldn't say if Madame de Cintré were
visible; he would please to apply at the further door. He crossed
the court; a gentleman was sitting, bareheaded, on the steps of the
portico, in play with a beautiful pointer. He rose as Newman
approached, and, as he laid his hand on the bell, said, almost soci-
ably, in English, that he was ashamed a visitor should be kept waiting:
the servants were scattered; he himself had been ringing; he didn't

know what the deuce was in them. This gentleman was young; his English was excellent, his expression easy. Newman pronounced the name of Madame de Cintré.

'I dare say,' said the young man, 'that my sister will be visible. Come in, and if you'll give me your card I'll carry it to her myself.'

Newman had been accompanied on his present errand by a sentiment I will not say of defiance—a readiness for aggression or for defence, as either might prove needful—but rather of meditative, though quite undaunted and good-humoured suspicion. He took from his pocket, while he stood on the portico, a card upon which, under his name, he had written the words 'San Francisco', and while he presented it he looked warily at his interlocutor. His glance found quick reassurance; he liked the young man's face; it strongly resembled that of Madame de Cintré, whose brother he would clearly be. The young man, on his side, had made a rapid inspection of Newman's person. He had taken the card and was about to enter the house with it when another figure appeared on the threshold—an older man, of a fine presence, habited in evening-dress. He looked hard at Newman and Newman met his examination. 'Madame de Cintré,' the younger man repeated as an introduction of the visitor. The other took the card from his hand, read it in a sustained stare, looked again at Newman from head to foot, hesitated a moment and then said, gravely but urbanely: 'Madame de Cintré is not at home.'

The younger man made a gesture and turned to Newman. 'I'm very sorry, sir.'

Newman gave a friendly nod, to show that he bore him no malice, and retraced his steps. At the porter's lodge he stopped; the two men were still standing on the portico. 'Who may the gentleman with the dog be?' he asked of the old woman who reappeared. He had begun to learn French.

'That's Monsieur le Comte.'

'And the other?'

'That's Monsieur le Marquis.'

'A marquis?' said Christopher in English, which the old woman fortunately did not understand. 'Oh then he's not the major-domo!'*

IV

EARLY one morning, before he was dressed, a little old man was ushered into his apartment, followed by a youth in a blouse who carried a picture in a shining frame. Newman, among the distractions of Paris, had forgotten M. Nioche and his accomplished daughter; but this was an effective reminder.

'I was afraid you had given me up, sir,' M. Nioche confessed after many apologies and salutations. 'We have made you wait so many days. You accused us perhaps of a want of respectability, of bad faith, what do I know? But behold me at last! And behold also the pretty "Madonna". Place it on a chair, my friend, in a good light, so that monsieur may admire it.' And M. Nioche, addressing his companion, helped him to dispose the work of art.

It had been endued with a layer of varnish an inch thick, and its frame, of an elaborate pattern, was at least a foot wide. It glittered and twinkled in the morning light and looked to Newman's eyes wonderfully splendid and precious. He thought of it as a very happy purchase and felt rich in his acquisition. He stood taking it in complacently while he proceeded with his dressing, and M. Nioche, who had dismissed his own attendant, hovered near, smiling and rubbing his hands.

'It has wonderful *finesse*,' he critically pronounced. 'And here and there are marvellous touches; you probably perceive them, sir. It attracted great attention on the Boulevard as we came along. And then a gradation of tones! That's what it is really to know how to paint. I don't say it because I'm her father, sir; but as one man of taste addressing another I can't help observing that you've acquired an object of price. It's hard to produce such things and to have to part with them. If our means only allowed us the luxury of keeping it! I in fact may say, sir'—and M. Nioche showed a feebly insinuating gaiety—'I really may say that I envy you your privilege. You see,' he added in a moment, 'we've taken the liberty of offering you a frame. It increases by a trifle the value of the work and it will save you the annoyance—so great for a person of your delicacy—of going about to bargain at the shops.'

The language spoken by M. Nioche was a singular compound, which may not here be reproduced in its integrity. He had apparently once possessed a certain knowledge of English, and his accent was oddly tinged with old cockneyisms and vulgarisms, things quaint and familiar. But his learning had grown rusty with disuse and his vocabulary was defective and capricious. He had repaired it with large patches of French, with words anglicised by a process of his own, with native idioms literally translated. The result, in the form in which he in all humility presented it, would be scarcely comprehensible to the reader, so that I have ventured to attempt for it some approximate notation. Newman only half followed, but he was always amused, and the old man's decent forlornness appealed to his democratic instincts. The assumption of any inevitability in the depressed state always irritated his strong good-nature—it was almost the only thing that did so; and he felt the impulse to pass over it the dipped sponge of his own prosperity. Mademoiselle Noémie's parent, however, had apparently on this occasion been vigorously indoctrinated and showed a certain tremulous eagerness to cultivate unexpected opportunities.

'How much do I owe you then with the frame?' Newman asked.

'It will make in all three thousand francs,' said the old man, smiling agreeably but folding his hands in instinctive suppliance.

'Can you give me a receipt?'

'I've brought one,' said M. Nioche. 'I took the liberty of drawing it up in case monsieur should happen to desire to discharge his debt.' And he drew a paper from his pocket-book and presented it to his patron. The document, Newman judged, had the graces alike of penmanship and of style. He laid down the money, and M. Nioche dropped the napoleons* one by one, solemnly and lovingly, into an old leathern purse.

'And how's your young lady?' he proceeded. 'She made a great impression on me.'

'An impression? monsieur is very good. Monsieur finds her—?' the old man quavered.

'I find her remarkably pretty.'

'Alas, yes, she's very very pretty!'

'And what's the harm in her being so?'

M. Nioche fixed his eyes upon a spot in the carpet and shook his head. Then raising them to a more intimate intelligence: 'Monsieur knows what Paris is. Dangerous to beauty when beauty hasn't the sou.'

'Ah, but that's not the case with your daughter. Isn't she rich now?'

'We're rich—yes, for six months. But if my daughter were less attractive I should sleep none the worse.'

'You're afraid of the young men?'

'The young and the old!'

'She ought to get a husband.'

'Ah, monsieur, one doesn't get a husband for nothing. Her husband must take her as she is; I can't give her a *liard*. But the young men don't see with that eye.'

'Oh,' said Newman, 'her talent's in itself a good outfit.'

'*Heuh*, for that it needs first to be converted into specie!'*—and M. Nioche slapped his purse tenderly before he stowed it away. 'The miracle doesn't take place every day.'

'Well, your young men have very little grit; that's all I can say. They ought to pay for your daughter,' Newman said, 'and not ask money themselves.'

'Those are very noble ideas, monsieur; but what will you have? They're not the ideas of this country. We want to know where we are when we marry.'

'Well, how much will it take to show where your daughter is?' M. Nioche stared as if he wondered what might be coming next; but he promptly recovered himself, at a venture, and replied that he knew a very nice young man, employed by an insurance company, who would content himself with fifteen thousand francs. 'Let your daughter paint half a dozen pictures for me,' his benefactor then resumed, 'and you can offer him his figure.'

'Half a dozen pictures—his figure? Monsieur isn't speaking inconsiderately?'

'If she'll make me six or eight copies in the Louvre as pretty as that "Madonna", I'll pay her the same price,' said Newman.

Poor M. Nioche was speechless a moment, with amazement and gratitude; after which he seized Newman's hand and pressed it between his own ten fingers, gazing at him with watery eyes. 'As pretty as that? They shall be a thousand times prettier—they shall be perfect little loves. Ah, if I only knew how to paint myself, sir, so that I might lend a hand! What can I do to thank you? *Voyons!*'— and he pressed his forehead while he tried to think of something.

'Oh, you've thanked me enough,' said Newman.

'Ah, here it is, sir!' cried M. Nioche. 'To express my gratitude I'll charge you nothing for our lessons!'

'Our lessons? I had quite forgotten them. Listening to your English,' Newman laughed, 'is really quite a lesson in French.'

'Ah, I don't profess to teach English, certainly,' said M. Nioche. 'But for my own admirable tongue I'm still at your service.'

'Since you're here then we'll begin. This is a very good hour, I'm going to have my coffee. Come every morning at half-past nine and have yours with me'.

'Monsieur offers me my coffee also?' cried M. Nioche. 'Truly my *beaux jours* are coming back.'

'*Allons, enfants de la patrie,*' said Newman; 'let's begin! The coffee's ripping hot. How do you say that in French?'

Every day then, for the following three weeks, the minutely respectable figure of M. Nioche made its appearance, with a series of little enquiring and apologetic obeisances, among the aromatic fumes of Newman's morning beverage. I know not what progress he made; but, as he himself said, if he didn't learn a great deal, at least he didn't learn much harm. And it amused him; it gratified that irregularly sociable side of his nature which had always expressed itself in a relish for ungrammatical conversation and which often, even in his busy and preoccupied days, had made him sit on rail fences in the twilight of young Western towns and gossip scarce less than fraternally with humorous loafers and obscure fortune-seekers. He had notions, wherever he went, about talking with the natives; he had been assured, and his judgement approved the advice, that in travelling abroad it was an excellent thing to look into the life of the country. M. Nioche was very much of a native, and though his life might not be particularly worth looking into he was a palpable and smoothly-rounded unit in that 'stiff' sum of civilisation and sophistication which offered our hero so much easy entertainment and proposed so many curious problems to his idle but active mind. Newman had a theory that his intelligence was lying down, but at least it couldn't sleep. He was fond of statistics; he liked to know how things were done; it gratified him to learn what taxes were paid, what profits were gathered, what commercial habits prevailed, how the battle of life was fought. M. Nioche, as a reduced capitalist, was familiar with these considerations, and he formulated his information, which he was proud to be able to impart, in the neatest possible terms and with a pinch of snuff between finger and thumb. As a Frenchman—quite apart from Newman's napoleons—M. Nioche loved conversation, and even in his decay his urbanity had not declined. As a Frenchman too he could give a clear account of things, and—still as a Frenchman—when his knowledge was at fault he could supply its lapses with the most convenient and ingenious hypotheses. The small shrunken bourgeois rejoiced, ever, to have questions asked him, and he scraped together information by frugal processes, he took in his little greasy pocket-book notes of matters that might interest his munificent friend. He read old almanacks at the book-stalls on the quays and began to frequent another café, where more newspapers were taken and his post-prandial *demi-tasse* cost him a penny extra, and where he used to con the tattered sheets for curious anecdotes, freaks of nature and strange coincidences. He would relate with solemnity the next morning that a child of five years of age had lately died at Bordeaux, whose brain had been found to weigh sixty ounces—the brain of a Napoleon or a Washington! or that Madame X, *charcutière* in the Rue de Clichy,* had found in the wadding of an old petticoat the sum of three hundred and sixty francs, which she had lost five years before. He pronounced his words with great pomp and circumstance, and Newman assured him that his way of dealing with the French tongue was very superior to the bewildering chatter that he heard in other mouths. Upon this M. Nioche's accent became more flutelike than ever; he offered to read extracts from Lamartine* and protested that, although he did endeavour according to his feeble lights to cultivate authority of diction, monsieur, if he wanted the real thing, should go to the Comédie.*

Newman took an interest in the wondrous French thrift and conceived a lively admiration for Parisian economies. His own economic genius was so entirely for operations on a larger scale, and, to move at his ease, he needed so imperatively the sense of great risks and great prizes, that he found diversion akin to the watching of ants in the spectacle of fortunes made by the aggregation of copper coins and in the minute subdivision of labour and profit. He questioned M. Nioche about his own manner of life and felt a friendly mixture of compassion and respect for the mystery of these humilities. The worthy man told him how he and his daughter had at one period supported existence comfortably on the sum of fifteen sous *per diem*; recently, having succeeded in dragging ashore the last floating fragments of the wreck of his fortune, his budget had been a trifle more ample. But they still had to butter their bread very thin, and M. Nioche intimated with a sigh that his young companion didn't bring to this task the zealous co-operation that might have been desired. 'But what will you have? One is in the flower of youth, one is pretty, one needs new dresses and fresh gloves; one can't wear shabby gowns among the splendours of the Louvre.'

'Yet she must earn what will pay for her clothes,' Newman felt enlisted enough to suggest.

M. Nioche looked at him with weak, uncertain eyes. He would have liked to be able to say that his daughter's talents were appreciated and that her crooked little daubs commanded a market; but it seemed a scandal to abuse the credulity of this free-handed stranger, who, without a suspicion or a question, had admitted him to equal social rights. He compromised, he declared that while it was obvious that Mademoiselle Noémie's reproductions of the old masters had only to be seen to be coveted, the prices which, in consideration of their altogether peculiar degree of finish, she felt obliged to ask for them, had kept purchasers at a respectful distance. 'Poor little cherished one!' said M. Nioche with a sigh; 'it's almost a pity that her work's so perfect! It would be in her interest to be a bit of an impostor.'

'But if she has this spark of the flame,' Newman benevolently reasoned, 'why should you have those fears for her that you spoke of the other day?'

M. Nioche meditated; there was an inconsistency in his position; it made him particularly uncomfortable. Though he had no desire to destroy the goose with the golden eggs—Newman's benevolent confidence—he felt a weary need to speak out all his trouble. 'Ah, she has a spark of that flame, my dear sir, most assuredly. But, to tell you the truth, she has also more than a mere spark of another. She's a *franche coquette* if there ever was one. I'm sorry to say,' he added in a moment, shaking his head with a world of accepted melancholy, 'it was to come to her as straight as a letter in the post. Her poor mother had that sad vice.'

'Why, you weren't happy with your wife?' Newman almost incredulously asked.

M. Nioche gave half a dozen little backward jerks of his head. 'She was my heavy cross, monsieur!'

'She wasn't very good?'

'She was good for some things and some people, but not for a poor
man like me. She deceived me, under my nose, year after year. I was
too stupid, and the temptation was too great. But I found her out at
last. I've only been once in my life a man to be afraid of; I know it
very well: it was in that hour! Nevertheless I don't like to think of it.
I loved her—I can't tell you why nor how much. Oh, she was—if I
must say so—bad.'

'She's not living?'

'She's gone to her account.'

'Her influence on your daughter then,' said Newman encouragingly, 'is not to be feared.'

'She cared no more for her daughter than for the wind in the
chimney. But Noémie has no more use for bad examples than for
good. She's sufficient to herself. She's stronger than I.'

'She doesn't mind what you say?'

'There isn't much to mind, sir—I say so little. What's the use of
my saying anything? It would only irritate her and drive her to some
coup de tête. She's very clever, like her poor mother; she would waste
no time about it. As a child—when I was happy, or supposed I was—
she studied drawing and painting with first-class professors, and they
assured me she had the gift. I was delighted to believe it, and when
I went into society I used to carry her little water-colours with me
in a portfolio and hand them round to the company. I remember how
a lady once thought I was offering them for sale and that I took it
very ill. We don't know what we may come to! Then came my dark
days and my final rupture with Madame Nioche. Noémie had no
more twenty-franc lessons; but in the course of time, when she grew
older and it became highly expedient that she should do something
that would help to keep us alive, she bethought herself of her palette
and brushes. Some of our friends in the *quartier* pronounced the idea
fantastic: they recommended her to try bonnet-making, to get a
situation in a shop, or—if she was more ambitious—to advertise for
a place of *dame de compagnie*. She did advertise, and an old lady wrote
her a letter and bade her come and see her. The old lady liked her
and made her an offer of her living and six hundred francs a year;
but Noémie discovered that she passed her life in her arm-chair and
had only two visitors, her confessor and her nephew: the confessor
very strict, and the nephew a man of fifty, with a broken nose and a
government clerkship of two thousand francs. She threw her old lady

over, bought a paint-box, a canvas and a new dress, and went and set up her easel in the Louvre. There, in one place and another, she has passed the last two years; I can't say it has made us millionaires. But she tells me Rome wasn't built in a day, that she's making great progress, that I must leave her to her own devices. The fact is, without prejudice to her "gift", that she has no idea of burying herself alive. She likes to see the world and to be seen of the world. She says herself that she can't work in the dark. Her appearance itself holds up the lamp for others! Only I can't help worrying and trembling—I can't help wondering what may happen to her there all alone, day after day, amid that prowling of people from the ends of the earth. I can't be always at her side. I go with her in the morning, and I come to fetch her away, but she won't have me near her in the interval; she says I give on her nerves. As if it didn't give on mine to keep walking up and down outside! Ah, if anything were to happen to her!' cried M. Nioche, clenching his two fists and jerking back his head again portentously.

'Oh, I guess she'll come out all right,' his friend soothingly returned.

'I believe I should shoot her otherwise!' said the old man solemnly.

'Well, we'll marry her quick enough,' insisted Newman—'since that's how you manage it; and I'll go and see her to-morrow at the Louvre and pick out the pictures she's to copy for me.'

M. Nioche had brought a message from his daughter in acceptance of their patron's magnificent commission, the young lady declaring herself his most devoted servant, promising her most zealous endeavour and regretting that the proprieties forbade her coming to thank him in person. The morning after the conversation just narrated Newman reverted to his intention of meeting his young friend at the Louvre. M. Nioche appeared preoccupied and left his budget of anecdotes unopened; he took a great deal of snuff and sent certain oblique, appealing glances toward his stalwart pupil. At last, when taking his leave, he stood a moment, after he had polished his hat with his calico pocket-handkerchief, and fixed his small pale eyes strangely on that personage.

'Well, what's the matter?'

'Pardon the solicitude of a father's heart! You inspire me with boundless confidence, but I can't help making you an appeal. After all you're a man, and so fine a one; you're young and at liberty. Let me beseech you then to respect an innocence—!'

Newman had wondered what was coming, yet had already burst into mirth. He was on the point of pronouncing his own innocence the more exposed, but he contented himself with promising to treat the young lady with nothing less than veneration. He found her, awaiting him, seated on the great divan of the Salon Carré. She was not in the garb of labour, but wore her bonnet and gloves and carried her parasol in honour of the occasion. These articles had been selected with unerring taste, and a fresher, prettier image of youthful alertness and blooming discretion was not to be conceived. She made Newman a most respectful curtsey, she expressed her gratitude for his liberality in the neatest of little speeches. It annoyed him to have so charming a girl stand there thanking him, and it made him feel uncomfortable to think that this perfect young lady, with her excellent manners and her finished intonation, was literally in his pay. He assured her, in such French as he could muster, that the thing was not worth mentioning and that he regarded her services as a particular favour.

'Whenever you please then,' she said, 'we'll pass the review.'

They walked slowly round the room and then into the others; they strolled about with high dignity for half an hour. His companion evidently relished her situation and had no desire to bring to a close her public interview with a patron of such striking type. Newman perceived that prosperity agreed with her and that the little firm-lipped, peremptory air with which she had addressed her father on the occasion of their former meeting had given place to the prettiest, easiest prattle.

'What sort of pictures have you in mind?' she asked. 'Sacred or profane?'

'Oh, a few of each. But I want something bright and gay.'

'Something gay? There's nothing very gay in this solemn old Louvre. But we'll see what we can find. You speak French to-day like a charm. My father has done wonders.'

'Oh, I'm a thankless subject,' said Newman. 'I'm too old to learn a language.'

'Too old? *Quelle folie!*' she cried with a clear, shrill laugh. 'You're a very *beau jeune homme*. And how do you like my father?'

'He's a very nice old gentleman. He never laughs at my blunders.'

'He's very *comme il faut*, dear papa,' said Mademoiselle Noémie, 'and as honest as the day. Oh, a probity that would take a prize! You could trust him with millions.'

'Do you always mind what he says?' asked Newman.

'"Mind" it?'

'Do you do what he bids you.'

The girl stopped and looked at him; she had a spot of colour in either cheek, and in her prompt French eye, too protrusive for perfect beauty, was a sharp spark of freedom. 'Why do you ask me that?'

'Because I want to know.'

'You think me a bad little girl?' And she gave a strange smile.

Newman looked at her a moment; he saw she was pretty, but he was not in the least dazzled. He remembered poor M. Nioche's solicitude for her innocence, and he laughed out again as his eyes met this odd quantity. Her face was a rare mixture of youth and maturity, and beneath her clear, charming forehead her searching little smile seemed to contain a world of ambiguous intentions. She was pretty enough, certainly, to make her father uneasy; but as regards her innocence Newman felt ready on the spot to affirm that she had never yet sacrificed it. She had simply never had any to lose; she had been looking at the wonderful world about her since she was ten years old, and he would have been a wise man who could tell her any secret of the town. In her long mornings at the Louvre she had not only studied Madonnas and Saint Johns; she had kept an eye upon the variously-embodied human nature in which the scene no less abounded, and she had formed her conclusions. In a degree, it seemed to Newman, M. Nioche might be at rest; if his daughter should assert her liberty in some unmistakeable way she would yet never publish her imprudence. Newman, with his long-drawn, leisurely smile and his articulation that suggested confidence in nothing but its motive, was always mentally taking his time; so he asked himself now what she was looking at him in that way for. He had an impression she would like him to confess that he did think her a wretch. 'Oh no,' he said at last; 'it would be very impolite in me to judge you in any such way. I don't know you.'

'But my father has complained to you.'

'He says you're a free spirit.'

'He shouldn't go about saying such things to gentlemen! But you don't believe it?'

'Well,' said Newman conscientiously, 'I don't believe he meant any harm by it.'

She looked at him again, gave a shrug and a smile, and then pointed to a small Italian picture, a Marriage of Saint Catherine.* 'How should you like that?'

'It doesn't please me,' he presently answered. 'The young lady in the yellow dress isn't pretty enough.'

'Ah, you're a great connoisseur!' his companion sighed.

'In pictures? Oh no; I'm only picking up the rudiments of knowledge.'

'In pretty women then?'

'In that I may be coming on, but I've ground to make up.'

'What do you say to this?' the girl asked, indicating a superb Italian portrait of a lady.* 'I'll do it for you on a smaller scale.'

'On a smaller scale? Why not as large as the original?'

She glanced at the glowing splendour of the Venetian masterpiece and gave a toss of her head. 'I don't like that woman. She looks stupid.'

'Well, she makes an impression on me,' said Newman. 'Decidedly I must have her, and as large as life. And just as shiningly stupid as she stands there.'

The girl fixed her eyes on him again, and with her mocking smile: 'It certainly ought to be easy for me to make her look stupid!' And then as he but opposed his vagueness she gave another shrug. 'Seriously, you *want* that portrait—the golden hair, the purple satin, the pearl necklace, the two magnificent arms?'

'Everything—just as it is.'

'Would nothing else do instead?'

'Oh, I want some other things, but I want that too.'

She turned away a moment, walked to the other side of the hall and stood there looking vaguely about her. At last she came back. 'It must be charming to be able to order pictures at such a rate. Venetian portraits as large as life! You go at it *en prince*. And you're going to travel about Europe that way?'

'Yes, I intend to travel,' said Newman.

'Ordering, buying, spending money?'

'Of course I shall spend a certain amount of money.'

'You're very happy to have it. And you're perfectly free?'

'How do you mean, free?'

'You have nothing to *embêter* you—no father, no family, no wife, no *fiancée*?'

'Yes, I'm tolerably free.'

'You're very very happy,' said Mademoiselle Noémie gravely.

'*Je le veux bien!*' said Newman, proving that he had learned more French than he admitted.

'And how long shall you stay in Paris?' the girl went on.

'Only a few days more.'

'Why do you go away?'

'It's getting hot, and I must go to Switzerland.'

'To Switzerland? That's a fine country. I would give the clothes on my back to see it! Lakes and mountains, deep green valleys, *ranz-des-vaches*! Oh I congratulate you! Meanwhile I shall sit here through all the hot summer daubing at your pictures.'

'Ah, take your time about it,' Newman urged. 'Do them at your convenience.'

They walked further and looked at a dozen other things. He pointed out what pleased him, and Mademoiselle Noémie generally criticised it and proposed something else. Then suddenly she diverged into the intimate. 'What made you speak to me the other day in the Salon Carré?'

'I admired your picture.'

'But you hesitated a long time.'

'Oh, I do nothing foolish,' he said.

'Yes, I saw you watching me. But I never supposed you were going to speak to me. I never dreamed I should be walking about here with you to-day. It's very remarkable.'

'It's sufficiently natural,' he calmly pleaded.

'Ah, I beg your pardon: not to me. "Free spirit"—in other words horrid creature—as you think me, I have never walked about in public with a gentleman before. What was my father thinking of when he consented to our interview?'

'He was repenting of his unjust accusations.' Newman returned.

Mademoiselle Noémie remained silent; at last she dropped into a seat. 'Well then, for those five it's fixed,' she presently said. 'Five copies as brilliant and beautiful as I can make then. We've one more to choose. Shouldn't you like one of those great Rubenses—the Marriage of Marie de Médicis?* Just look at it and see how handsome it is.'

'Oh yes; I should like that,' he allowed. 'Finish off with that.'

'Finish off with that—good!' she laughed. She sat a moment looking at him, then suddenly rose and stood before him with her arms expressively folded. '*Ah ça*, I don't understand you,' she bravely broke out. 'I don't understand how a man can be so ignorant.'

'Oh, I'm ignorant certainly.' And he put his hands in his pockets.

'It's too ridiculous! I don't know how to paint *pour deux sous*.'

'You don't know how?'

'I paint like a cat; I can't draw a straight line. I never sold a picture until you bought that thing the other day.' And as she offered this surprising information she continued to smile.

Newman met it with a grimace of his own. 'Why do you make that statement?'

'Because it irritates me to see a clever man so *bête*. My copies are grotesque.'

'And the one I possess—?'

'That one's the flower of the dreadful family.'

'Well,' said Newman, 'I never outgrew a mistake but in my own time and in my own way.'

She looked at him askance. 'Your patience is very *gentille*; it's my duty to warn you before you go further. This *commande* of yours is impossible, you know. What do you take me for? It's work for ten strong men. You pick out the six most difficult pictures in the place, and you expect me to go to work as if I were sitting down to hem a dozen pocket-handkerchiefs. I wanted to see how far you'd go.'

Newman considered her in some perplexity. In spite of the blunder of which he stood convicted he was very far from being a simpleton, and he had a lively suspicion that her burst of confidence was not essentially more honest than her original pretence. She was playing a great game; she was not simply taking pity on the bloom of his barbarism. What was it she expected to gain? The stakes were high and the risk not small; the prize therefore must have been commensurate. But even granting that the prize might be great Newman could scarce resist a movement of admiration for his young friend's intrepidity. She was throwing away with one hand, whatever she might intend to do with the other, a substantial sum of money. 'Are you joking or serious?'

'Oh, *d'un sérieux*!' she cried, but with her extraordinary smile.

'I know very little about pictures or how they're really painted. If you can't do all, why then do what you conveniently can.'

'It will all be bad *à faire pleurer*,' said Mademoiselle Noémie.

'Oh,' Newman laughed, 'if you want to swindle me of course you can. But why do you go on painting badly?'

'I can do nothing else; I've neither eye nor hand nor training. Above all I haven't patience.'

'You're deceiving your father then.'

The girl just hesitated. 'He perfectly knows.'

'No,' Newman declared; 'I'm sure he believes in you.'

'He's afraid of me, poor dear. I go on painting badly, as you say, because it passes the time. I like being here; it's a place to come to every day; it's better than sitting in a little dark damp room on a court or than selling buttons and whalebones over a counter.'

'Of course it's much more amusing,' said Newman. 'But for a poor girl isn't it rather an expensive amusement?'

'Oh, I'm very wrong; there's no doubt about that,' she answered. 'But rather than earn my living as some girls do—toiling with a needle in little black holes out of the world—I'd throw myself into the Seine.'

'There's no need of that,' he presently observed.

'Your father must have mentioned to you the reason of my offer?'

'The reason—?'

'He wants you to marry, and I told him I'd give you a chance to earn your *dot*.'

'He told me all about it, and you see the account I make of it! Why should you take such an interest in my marriage?'

'My interest was in your father. I hold to my engagement. Do what you can, and I'll buy what you do.'

She stood some time in thought, her eyes on the ground. At last looking up, 'What sort of a husband can you get for twelve thousand francs?'* she asked.

'Your father tells me he knows some very good young men.'

'Grocers and butchers and little *maîtres de café's*? I won't marry at all if I can't marry more *proprement* than that.'

'I'd advise you not to be too fastidious,' said Newman. 'That's all the advice I can give you.'

'I'm vexed at what I've said!' cried his companion. 'It has done me no good. But I couldn't help it.'

'What good did you expect it to do you?'

'I couldn't help it, simply.'

He looked at her a moment. 'Well, your painting may be a fraud, but you're too honest for me all the same. I don't understand you. Good-bye!' And he put out his hand.

She made no response, she granted him no farewell. She turned away and seated herself sidewise on a bench, leaning her head on the back of her hand, which clasped the rail in front of the pictures. Newman stood near her another moment, then he turned on his heel and retreated. He had understood her better than he confessed; this singular scene was a practical commentary upon her father's description of her as a free spirit.

V

WHEN he had told Mrs Tristram the story of his fruitless visit to
Madame de Cintré she urged him not to be discouraged, but to carry
out his plan of 'seeing Europe' during the summer—after which he
might return to Paris for the autumn and then settle down comfortably for the winter. 'Claire de Cintré will be kept in a cool place for
you,' she reasoned; 'she's not a woman who'll change her condition
from one day to another.' Newman made no distinct affirmation that
he would come back to Paris; he even talked about Rome and the
Nile, and abstained from professing any especial interest in Madame
de Cintré's continued widowhood. This was a little of a false note in
his usual distinctness, and may perhaps be regarded as characteristic of the incipient stage of that passion which is more particularly
known as the romantic one. The truth is that the expression of a pair
of eyes, that were both intense and mild, had become very familiar
to his memory, and he would not easily have resigned himself to the
prospect of never looking into them again. He communicated to Mrs
Tristram a number of other facts, of greater or less importance, as
you choose; but on this particular point he kept his own counsel.
He took a kindly leave of M. Nioche, having assured him that so far
as he was concerned the blue-cloaked Madonna herself might have
been present at his interview with Mademoiselle Noémie; and left
the old man nursing his breast-pocket in an ecstasy which the
sharpest paternal discomposure might have been defied to dissipate.

He started on his travels with all his usual appearance of slow-
strolling leisure and all his essential directness and intensity of aim.
No man seemed less in a hurry and yet no man enabled brief periods
to serve him more liberally. He had practical instincts which signally
befriended him in his trade of tourist. He found his way in foreign
cities by divination, his memory was excellent when once his attention had been at all cordially given, and he emerged from dialogues
in foreign tongues, of which he had formally not understood a word,
in full possession of the particular item he had desired to elicit. His
appetite for items was large, and although many of those he noted
might have seemed woefully dry and colourless to the ordinary sentimental traveller, a careful inspection of the list would have shown

that his toughness had sensitive spots. In the charming city of Brus-
sels—his first stopping-place after leaving Paris—he asked a great
many questions about the street-cars and took extreme satisfaction
in the reappearance of this familiar symbol of American civilisation;
but he was also greatly struck with the beautiful Gothic tower of the
Hôtel de Ville and wondered if they mightn't 'get up' something
like it in San Francisco. He stood long in the crowded square before
this edifice, in imminent danger from carriage-wheels, listening to a
toothless old cicerone* mumble in broken English the touching
history of Counts Egmont and Horn;* and he wrote the names of
these gentlemen—for reasons best known to himself—on the back
of an old letter.

At the outset, on his leaving Paris, his curiosity had not been
intense; passive entertainment, in the Champs Elysées and at the
theatres, seemed about as much as he need expect of himself, and
although, as he had said to Tristram, he wanted to see the mysterious and satisfying *best*, he had not the grand tour in the least on his
conscience and was not given to worrying the thing that amused him.
He believed serenely that Europe was made for him and not he for
Europe. He had said he wanted to improve his mind, but he would
have felt a certain embarrassment, a certain shame even—a false
shame possibly—if he had caught himself looking intellectually into
the mirror. Neither in this nor in any other respect had he a high
sense of responsibility; it was his prime conviction that a man's life
should be a man's ease and that no privilege was really great enough
to take his breath away. The world, to his vision, was a great bazaar
where one might stroll about and purchase handsome things; but
he was no more conscious, individually, of social pressure than he
admitted the claim of the obligatory purchase. He had not only a
dislike but a sort of moral mistrust of thoughts too admonitory; one
shouldn't hunt about for a standard as a lost dog hunts for a master.
One's standard was the idea of one's own good-humoured prosperity, the prosperity which enabled one to give as well as take. To
expand without too much ado—without 'mean' timidity on one side
or the bravado of the big appetite on the other—to the full compass
of any such experience as was held to stir men's blood represented
his nearest approach to a high principle. He had always hated to
hurry to catch railroad-trains, and yet had always caught them; and
just so an undue solicitude for the right side seemed a sort of silly

dawdling at the station, a proceeding properly confined to women, foreigners and invalids. All this admitted, he enjoyed his journey, when once he had fairly entered the current, as intimately as if he had kept a diary of raptures. He lounged through Belgium and Holland and the Rhineland, through Switzerland and Northern Italy, planning about nothing and seeing all things. The guides and *valets de place* found him an excellent subject. He was always approachable, for he was much addicted to large lapses and long intervals, to standing about in the vestibules and porticoes of inns, and he availed himself little of the opportunities for impressive seclusion so liberally offered in Europe to gentlemen travelling with long purses. When an excursion, a church, a gallery, a ruin was proposed to him the first thing he usually did, after surveying his postulant in silence and from head to foot, was to sit down at a little table and order some light refreshment, of which he more often than not then forgot to partake. The cicerone, during this process, commonly retreated to a respectful distance; otherwise I am not sure that Newman would not have bidden him sit down and share, sit down and tell him as a decent creature if his church or his gallery were really worth one's trouble. At last he rose and stretched his long legs, beckoned to the man of monuments, looked at his watch and fixed his eye on his adversary. 'What is it and how far?' And whatever the case, though he might seem to hesitate he never declined. He stepped into an open cab, made his conductor sit beside him to answer questions, bade the driver go fast (he had a particular aversion to slow driving), and rolled, in all probability through a dusty suburb, to the goal of his pilgrimage. When the goal was a disappointment, when the church was meagre or the ruin a heap of rubbish, he never protested nor berated his adviser; he looked with an impartial eye upon great monuments and small, made the guide recite his lesson, listened to it religiously, asked if there were nothing else to be seen in the neighbourhood, and drove back again at a rattling pace. It is to be feared that his perception of the difference between the florid and the refined had not reached the stage of confidence, and that he might often have been seen—as we have already seen him—gazing with culpable serenity at inferior productions. The wrong occasion was a part of his pastime in Europe as well as the right, and his tour was altogether a pastime. But there is sometimes nothing like the imagination of those people who have none, and Newman now and then, in an unguided stroll through a foreign city, before some lonely, sad-towered church or some angular image of one who had rendered civic service in an unknown past, had felt a singular deep commotion. It was not an excitement, not a perplexity; it involved an extraordinary sense of recreation.

He encountered by chance in Holland a young American with whom he fell for a time into a tacit travellers' partnership. They were men of different enough temper, but each in his way so true to his type that each might seem to have something of value to contribute to the association. Newman's comrade, whose name was Babcock, was a young Unitarian minister;* a small, spare, neatly-attired man, with a strikingly candid countenance. He was a native of Dorchester, Massachusetts, and had spiritual charge of a small congregation in another suburb of the New England capital. His digestion was weak and he lived chiefly on Graham bread and hominy*—a regimen to which he was so much attached that his tour seemed to him destined to be blighted when, on landing on the Continent, he found these delicacies fail to flourish under the *table d'hôte* system.* In Paris he had purchased a bag of hominy at an establishment which called itself an American Agency and at which the New York illustrated papers were also to be procured, and he had carried it about with him and shown extreme serenity and fortitude in the somewhat delicate position of having his hominy prepared for him and served on odd occasions at the hotels he successively visited. Newman had once spent a morning, in the course of business, at Mr Babcock's birthplace, and, for reasons too recondite to unfold, the memory of his visit always pressed the spring of mirth. To carry out his joke, which certainly seems poor so long as it is not explained, he used often to address his companion as 'Dorchester'. Fellow-aliens cling together, on a strange soil, in spite of themselves; but it was probable that at home these unnatural intimates must have met only to part. They had indeed by habit and form as little in common as possible. Newman, who never reflected on such matters, accepted the situation with great equanimity, but Babcock used to meditate over it privately; used often indeed to retire to his room early in the evening for the express purpose of considering it conscientiously and, as he would have said, with detachment. He was not sure it was a good thing for him to have given himself up so unreservedly to our hero, whose way of taking life was so little his own.

Newman was a spirit of easy power; Mr Babcock even at times saw it clear that he was one of nature's noblemen, and certainly it was impossible not to feel strongly drawn to him. But would it not be desirable to try to produce an effect on him, to try to quicken his moral life and raise his sense of responsibility to a higher plane? He liked everything, he accepted everything, he found amusement in everything; he was not discriminating, his values were as vague and loose as if he had carried them in his trousers pocket. The young man from Dorchester accused Newman of a fault that he considered very grave and did his best himself to avoid—of what he would have called a want of moral reaction. Poor Mr Babcock was extremely fond of pictures and churches, and kept Mrs Jameson's volumes* in his trunk; he regarded works of art as questions and his relations with them as experiences, and received peculiar impressions from everything he saw. But nevertheless in his secret soul he detested Europe and felt an irritated need to protest against Newman's easy homage to so compromised a charmer, mistress of a cynicism that appeared at times to have made him cynical. Mr Babcock's moral *malaise*, I am afraid, lay deeper than where any definition of mine can reach it. He mistrusted the 'European' temperament, he suffered from the 'European' climate, he hated the 'European' dinner hour; 'European' life seemed to him unscrupulous and impure. And yet he had what he called an intimate sense of the true beautiful in life, and as this element was often inextricably associated with the above displeasing conditions, as he wished above all to be just and dispassionate and as he was furthermore extremely bent on putting his finger on the boundary-line, in the life of a School, between the sincere time and the insincere, he could not bring himself to decide that the kingdoms of the earth were utterly rotten. But he thought them in a bad way, and his quarrel with Newman was over some of the elements, insidious forms of evil, that this promiscuous feeder at the feast could swallow with no wry face. Babcock himself really knew as little about the forms of evil, in any quarter of the world, as about the forms of banking; his most vivid realisation of the most frequent form had been the discovery that one of his college classmates, a student of architecture in Paris, was carrying on a love-affair with a young woman who didn't in the least count on his marrying her. Babcock had described this situation to Newman, and our hero had applied an epithet marked by a rough but not unfriendly justice to the girl. The next day his companion asked him if he were certain he had used exactly the right word to characterise the young architect's mistress. Newman wondered and seemed amused. 'There are a great many words to express that idea,' he said; 'you can take your choice!'

'Oh, I mean,' said Babcock, 'was she possibly not to be considered in a different light? Don't you think she really *had* believed in his higher nature?'

'I'm afraid I don't know,' Newman replied. 'Very likely she had; I've no doubt she judged it by her own.' He was willing to meet his friend on any view of her.

'I didn't mean that either,' said Babcock; 'I'm not sure that she *has* a higher nature. I'm not sure—not *very* sure—every one has. I was only afraid I might have seemed yesterday not to remember—not to consider. Well, I think I'll write to Percival about it.'

And he had written to Percival (who had answered him in a manner that *was* indubitably cynical) and had reflected that Newman oughtn't to be encouraged, after all, to read a cheap idealism into flagrant cases of immorality. The levity and brevity of his comrade's judgements very often shocked and depressed him. He had a way of damning people without further appeal, or else of appearing almost in sympathy with their sinister side, which seemed unworthy of a man whose conscience could still pretend to a squirm. And yet poor Babcock yearned toward him and remembered that even if, decidedly, his sensibility would never work straight, this was not a reason for giving him up. Goethe recommended* seeing human nature in the most various forms, and Mr Babcock thought Goethe perfectly splendid. He often tried in odd half-hours of conversation to explain what he meant by some of his principal doubts, but it was like offering to read from a technical treatise. The volume might deal lucidly with Mr Babcock's subject, but what was Mr Babcock's subject without Mr Babcock's interest in it? Newman could entertain a respect for any man's subject and thought his friend fortunate to have so special a one. He accepted all the proofs of its importance that were thus anxiously offered him, and put them away in what he supposed a very safe place; but poor Babcock never afterwards recognised his gifts among the articles that Newman had in daily use.

They travelled together through Germany and into Switzerland, where for three or four weeks they trudged over rough passes and smooth and lounged by the edge and on the bosom of blue lakes. At last they crossed the Simplon* and made their way to Venice. Mr Babcock had become gloomy and even a trifle irritable; he seemed moody, absent, preoccupied; he got his plans into a tangle and talked one moment of doing one thing and the next of doing another. Newman led his own usual life, recklessly made acquaintances, took his ease in the galleries and churches, spent an unconscionable amount of time in strolling in Piazza San Marco, bought several spurious pictures and for a fortnight enjoyed Venice grossly. One evening, coming back to his inn, he found Babcock waiting for him in the little garden beside it. The young man walked up to him, looking very dismal, thrust out his hand and said with solemnity that he was afraid they must part. Newman expressed his surprise and regret; he wondered why a parting had become necessary. 'Don't be afraid I'm tired of you,' he said.

'You're not tired of me?' his companion asked, fixing him with clear but almost tragic eyes.

'Why the deuce should I be? You're a very nice man. Besides, I don't break down so easily.'

'We don't understand each other,' said poor Dorchester.

'Don't I understand you?' cried Newman. 'Why, I hoped I did. But what if I don't; where's the harm?'

'I don't understand *you*,' said Babcock. And he sat down and rested his head on his hand and looked up mournfully at his immeasurable friend.

'But why should you mind that if I don't?'

'It's very distressing to me. It keeps me in a state of unrest. It irritates me; I can't settle anything. I don't think it's good for me.'

'You worry too much; that's what's the matter with you,' said Newman.

'Of course it must seem so to you. You think I take all questions too hard, and I think you take them too superficially. We can never agree.'

'But we've agreed very well all along.'

'No, *I* haven't agreed,' said Babcock, shaking his head. 'I'm very uncomfortable. I ought to have separated from you a month ago.'

'Oh, shucks! I'll agree to anything!' cried Newman.

Mr Babcock buried his head in both hands. At last, looking up, 'I don't think you appreciate my position,' he observed. 'I try to arrive

at the truth about everything. And then you go too fast. There are
things of which you take too little account. I feel as if I ought to go
over all this ground we've traversed again by myself. I'm afraid I have
made a great many mistakes.'

'Oh, you needn't give so many reasons,' said Newman. 'You've
simply had enough of me. You've all your right to that.'

'No, no, I've *not* had enough of you!' his friend insisted. 'It would
be very wrong of me to have had enough.'

'I give it up!' laughed Newman. 'But of course it will never do to
go on making mistakes. Go your way, by all means. I shall miss you;
but you've seen I make friends very easily. You'll be lonely yourself;
but drop me a line when you feel like it, and I'll wait for you
anywhere.'

'I think I'll go back to Milan. I'm afraid I didn't do justice to
Luini.'

'Poor old Luini!'* said Newman.

'I mean I'm afraid I went too far about him. I don't think he's as
true as he at first seems.'

'Luini?' Newman exclaimed. 'There's something in the look of his
genius that's like the face of a beautiful woman. It's as if she were
coming straight *at* you, or standing very close.'

His companion frowned and winced. And it must be added that
this was, for Newman, an unusually metaphysical flight, though in
passing through Milan he had found a great attraction in the painter.
'There you are again!' said Mr Babcock. 'Yes, we had better separate.' And on the morrow he retraced his steps and proceeded to his
revisions of judgement. But presently Newman heard from him.

My dear Mr Newman,—I am afraid that my conduct at Venice a
week ago seemed to you strange and ungrateful, and I wish to explain
my position, which, as I said at the time, I do not think you appreciate. I had long had it on my mind to propose that we should part
company, and this step was not really so abrupt as it appeared. In the
first place, you know, I am travelling in Europe on funds supplied by
my congregation, who kindly offered me a vacation and an opportunity to enrich my mind with the treasures of nature and art in these
countries. I feel therefore that I ought to use my time to the very best
advantage. I've a high sense of responsibility. You appear to care only
for the pleasure of the hour, and you give yourself up to it with a

violence which I confess I'm not able to emulate. I consider that I must arrive at some conclusion and fix my convictions on certain points. Art and Life seem to me intensely serious things, and in our travels in Europe we should especially remember the rightful, indeed the solemn, message of Art. You seem to hold that if a thing amuses you for the moment this is all you need ask of it; and your relish for mere amusement is also much higher than mine. You put moreover a kind of reckless finality into your pleasures which at times, I confess, has seemed to me—shall I say it?—almost appalling. Your way, at any rate, is not my way, and it's unwise that we should attempt any longer to pull together. And yet let me add that I know there is a great deal to be said for your way; I have felt its attraction, in your society, very strongly. Save for this I should have left you long ago. But I was so deeply perplexed. I hope I have not done wrong. I feel as if I had a great deal of lost time to make up. I beg you take all this as I mean it, which heaven knows is not harshly. I have a great personal esteem for you and hope that some day when I have recovered my balance we shall meet again. But I *must* recover my balance first. I hope you will continue to enjoy your travels; only *do* remember that Life and Art *are* extremely solemn.

Believe me your sincere friend and well-wisher,

BENJAMIN BABCOCK.

P. S. I am very unhappy about Luini.

This letter produced in Newman's mind a singular mixture of exhilaration and awe. Mr Babcock's tender conscience at first seemed to him as funny as a farce, and his travelling back to Milan only to get into a deeper muddle to be, for reward of his pedantry, exquisitely and ludicrously just. Then he reflected that these are mighty mysteries; that possibly he himself *was* indeed almost unmentionably 'appalling', and that his manner of considering the treasures of art and the privileges of life lacked the last, or perhaps even the very first, refinement. Newman had a great esteem, after all, for refinement, and that evening, during the half-hour that he watched the star-sheen on the warm Adriatic, he felt rebuked and humiliated. He was unable to decide how to answer this communication. His good-nature checked his snubbing his late companion's earnestness, and his tough, inelastic sense of humour forbade his taking it seriously. He wrote no answer at all, but a day or two after he found in a curiosity-shop a grotesque little statuette in ivory, of the sixteenth century, which he sent off to Babcock without a commentary. It represented a gaunt, ascetic-looking monk, in a tattered gown and cowl, kneeling with clasped hands and pulling a portentously long face. It was a wonderfully delicate piece of carving, and in a moment, through one of the rents of his gown, you espied a fat capon hung round the monk's waist. In Newman's intention what did the figure symbolise? Did it mean that he was going to try to be as impressed with the solemnity of things as the monk looked at first, but that he feared he should succeed no better than this personage proved on a closer inspection to have done? It is not supposable he intended a satire on Babcock's own asceticism, for this would have been a truly cynical stroke. He at any rate made his late companion a valuable little present.

He went, on leaving Venice, through the Tyrol to Vienna and then returned, westward, through South Germany. The autumn found him at Baden-Baden,* where he spent several weeks. The charming place kept him from day to day; he was looking about him and deciding what to do for the winter. His summer had been very full, and as he sat under the great trees beside the miniature river that trickles past the Baden flower-beds he slowly rummaged it over. He had seen and done a great deal, enjoyed and observed a great deal; he felt older, yet felt it somehow, even at the age he had reached, as an advantage. He remembered Mr Babcock and his desire to learn the great lesson, and he remembered also that he had profited little by his friend's exhortation to cultivate the same respectable habit. Couldn't he scrape together a few great lessons? Baden-Baden was the prettiest place he had seen yet, and orchestral music in the evening, under the stars, was decidedly a great institution. This was the lesson that was clearest. But he went on to reflect that he had done very wisely to pull up stakes and come abroad; the world was apparently such an interesting thing to see. He had drawn a few morals of his own; he couldn't say just which, but he had them there under his hat-band. He had done what he wanted; he had tackled the great sights and closed with the great occasions, he had given his mind a chance to 'improve' if it would. He fondly believed it had improved a good deal. Yes, these waters of the free curiosity were very soothing, and he would splash in them till they ran dry. Forty-two years as he was on the point of numbering, he had a long course in his eye, and if the haze of the future was thick it was that of a golden afternoon. Where should he take the world next? I have said he remembered the eyes of the lady whom he had found standing in Mrs Tristram's drawing-room; four months had elapsed and he had not forgotten them yet. He had looked—he had made a point of looking—into a great many other eyes in the interval, but the only ones he thought of now were Madame de Cintré's. If he wanted to make out where the golden afternoon hung heaviest wouldn't the place perhaps be in Madame de Cintré's eyes? He would certainly find something of interest there, call it all bravely bright or call it engagingly obscure.

But there came to him sometimes too, through this vague rich forecast, the thought of his past life and the long array of years (they had begun so early) during which he had had nothing in his head but his possible 'haul'. They seemed far away now, for his present attitude was more than a holiday, it was almost a repudiation. He had told Tom Tristram the pendulum was swinging back, and the backward swing, visibly, had not yet ended. Still, the possibility of hauls, which had dropped in the other quarter, wore to his mind a different aspect at different hours. In its train a thousand forgotten episodes came trooping before him. Some of them he looked complacently enough in the face; from some he averted his head. They were old triumphs of nerve, even of bluff, mere cold memories of the heat of battle, the high competitive rage. Some of them, as they lived again, he felt decidedly proud of; he admired himself as if he had been looking at another man. And in fact many of the qualities that make a great deed were there; the decision, the resolution, the courage, the celerity, the clear eye and the firm hand. Of certain other performances it would be going too far to say he was ashamed of them, for he had doubtless never had a stomach for dirty work. He had been blessed from the first with a natural impulse to disfigure with a direct unreasoning blow the painted face of temptation. In no man, verily, could a want of the stricter scruple have been less excusable. Newman knew the crooked from the straight at a glance, and the former had received at his hands, early and late, much putting in its place. None the less, however, some of his memories wore at present a graceless and sordid mien, and it struck him that if he had never incurred any quite ineffaceable stain he had never on the other hand followed the line of beauty, as a sought direction, for a single mile of its course. He had spent his years in the unremitting effort to add thousands to thousands, and now that he stood so well outside of it the business of mere money-getting showed only, in its ugliness, as vast and vague and dark, a pirate-ship with lights turned inward. It is very well, of a truth, to think meanly of money-getting after you have filled your pockets, and our friend, it may be said, should have begun somewhat earlier to moralise with this superiority. To that it may be answered that he might have made another fortune if he chose; and we ought to add that he was not exactly moralising. It had come back to him simply that what he had been looking at all summer was a very brave and bristling world, and that it had not all been made by men 'live' in his old mean sense.

During his stay at Baden-Baden he received a letter from Mrs Tristram, scolding him for the scant tidings he had sent his friends and begging to be definitely assured that he had not even thought of not wintering within call of the Avenue d'Iéna. Newman replied as to the blast of a silver bugle.

'I supposed you knew I was a miserable letter-writer and didn't expect anything of me. I guess I've not struck off twenty letters of pure friendship in my whole life; in American I conducted my correspondence altogether by telegrams and by dictation to a shorthand reporter. This is a letter of friendship undefiled; you've got hold of a curiosity—you could really get something for it. If you want to know everything that has happened to me these three months the best way to tell you, I think, would be to send you my half-dozen guide-books with my pencil marks in the margin. Wherever you find a scratch or a cross or a "Beautiful?" or a "So true!" or a "Too thin!" you may know that I've had some one or other of the sensations I was after. That has been about my history ever since I left you. Belgium, Holland, Switzerland, Germany, Italy—I've taken the whole list as the bare-backed rider takes the paper hoops at the circus, and I'm not even yet out of breath. I carry about six volumes of Ruskin in my trunk; I've seen some grand old things and shall perhaps talk them over this winter by your fireside. You see my face isn't altogether set against Paris. I have had all kinds of plans and visions, but your letter has blown most of them away. "*L'appétit vient en mangeant*," says your proverb, and I find that the more sweet things I taste the more greedily I look over the table. Now that I'm in the shafts why shouldn't I trot to the end of the course? Sometimes I think of the far East and keep rolling the names of Eastern cities under my tongue; Damascus and Bagdad, Trebizond, Samarcand, Bokhara.* I spent a week last month in the company of a returned missionary who told me I ought to be ashamed to be loafing about Europe when there is such a treat to be had out there. I do want more treats, but I think frankly I should like best to look for them in the Rue de l'Université. Do you ever hear from that handsome tall lady? If you can get her to promise she'll be at home the next time I call I'll go back to Paris straight. So there you have a bargain. I'm more than ever in the state of mind I told you about that evening; I want a companion for life and still want her to be a star of the first magnitude. I've kept an eye on all the possible candidates for the position who have come up this summer, but none of them has filled the bill or anything like it. I should have enjoyed the whole thing a thousand times more if I had had the lady just mentioned under my arm. The nearest approach to her was a cultivated young man from Dorchester Mass., who, however, very soon demanded of me a separation for incompatibility of temper. He told me I hadn't it in me ever to raise a "tone", and he really made me half-believe him. But shortly afterwards I met an Englishman with whom I struck up an acquaintance which at first seemed to promise well—a very bright man who writes in the London papers and knows Paris nearly as well as Tristram. We knocked about for a week together, but he very soon gave me up in disgust. He pronounced me a poor creature, incapable of the joy of life*—he talked to me as if *I* had come from Dorchester. This was rather bewildering. Which of my two critics was I to believe? I didn't worry about it and very soon made up my mind they don't know everything. You come nearer that than any one I've met, and I defy any one to pretend I'm wrong when I'm more than ever your faithful friend   C.N.'

VI

HE gave up Bagdad and Bokhara and, returning to Paris before the autumn was over, established himself in rooms selected by Tom Tristram in accordance with the latter's estimate of his 'social standing'. When Newman learned that this occult attribute was to be taken into account he professed himself utterly incompetent and begged Tristram to relieve him of the care of it. 'I didn't know I "stood", socially, at all—I thought I only sat round informally, rather sprawling than anything else. Isn't a social standing to know some two or three thousand people and invite them to dinner? I know you and your wife and little old Mr Nioche, who gave me French lessons last spring. Can I invite you to dinner to meet each other? If I can you must come to-morrow.'

'That's not very grateful to me,' said Mrs Tristram, 'who introduced you last year to every creature of my acquaintance.'

'So you did; I had quite forgotten. But I thought you wanted me to forget,' said Newman in that tone of surpassing candour which frequently marked his utterance and which an observer would not have known whether to pronounce a whimsical affectation of ignorance or a modest aspiration to knowledge. 'You told me you yourself disliked them all.'

'Ah, the way you remember what I say is at least very flattering. But in future,' added Mrs Tristram, 'pray forget all the "mean" things and remember only the good. It will be easily done and won't fatigue your memory. Only I forewarn you that if you trust my husband to pick out your rooms you're in for something hideous.'

'Hideous, darling?' her husband cried.

'To-day I utter nothing base; otherwise I should use stronger language.'

'What do you think she would say, Newman?' Tristram asked. 'If she really tried now? She can polish one off for a wretch volubly—in two or three languages; that's what it is to have high culture. It gives her the start of me completely, since I can't swear, for the life of me, except in pure Anglo-Saxon. When I get mad I have to fall back on our dear old mother tongue. There's nothing like it after all.'

Newman declared that he knew nothing about tables and chairs and would accept, in the way of a lodging, with his eyes shut, anything that Tristram should offer him. This was partly pure veracity on our hero's part, but it was also partly charity. He knew that to pry about and count *casseroles* and make people open windows, to poke into beds and sofas with his cane, to gossip with landladies and ask who lived above and who below—he knew that this was of all pastimes the dearest to his friend's heart, and he felt the more disposed to put it in his way as he was conscious he had suffered the warmth of their ancient fellowship somewhat to abate. He had besides no taste for upholstery; he had even no very exquisite sense of comfort or convenience. He had a relish for luxury and splendour, but it was satisfied by rather gross contrivances. He scarcely knew a hard chair from a soft, and used an art in stretching his legs which quite dispensed with adventitious aids. His idea of material ease was to inhabit very large rooms, have a great many of them, and be conscious in them of a number of patented mechanical devices, half of which he should never have occasion to use. The apartments should be clear and high and what he called open, and he had once said that he liked rooms best in which you should want to keep on your hat. For the rest he was satisfied with the assurance of any respectable person that everything was of the latest model. Tristram accordingly secured for him an habitation over the price of which the Prince of Morocco had been haggling. It was situated on the Boulevard Haussmann,* was a first floor, and consisted of a series of rooms gilded from floor to ceiling a foot thick, draped in various light shades of satin and chiefly furnished with mirrors and clocks. Newman thought them magnificent, didn't haggle, thanked Tristram heartily, immediately took possession, and had one of his trunks standing for three months in the drawing-room.

One day Mrs Tristram told him that their tall handsome lady had returned from the country and that she had met her three days before coming out of the church of Saint Sulpice;* she herself having journeyed to that distant quarter in quest of an obscure lace-mender of whose skill she had heard high praise.

'And how were those intense mild eyes?' Newman asked.

'They were red with weeping—neither more nor less. She had been to confession.'

'It doesn't tally with your account of her,' he said, 'that she should have sins to cry about.'

'They were not sins—they were sufferings.'

'How do you know that?'

'She asked me to come and see her. I went this morning.'

'And what does she suffer from?'

'I didn't press her to tell me. With her, somehow, one is very discreet. But I guessed easily enough. She suffers from her grim old
mother and from the manner in which her elder brother, the technical head of the family, abets and hounds on the Marquise. They keep
at her hard, they keep at her all the while. But I can almost forgive
them, because, as I told you, she's simply a saint, and a persecution
is all that she needs to bring out what I call her quality.'

'That's a comfortable theory for *her*. I hope you'll never mention
it to the old folks. But why does she *let* them persecute her? Isn't she,
as a married woman, her own mistress?'

'Legally yes, I suppose; but morally no. In France you may never
say Nay to your mother, whatever she requires of you. She may be
the most abominable old woman in the world and make your life a
purgatory; but after all she's *ma mère*, and you've no right to judge
her. You've simply to obey. The thing has a fine side to it. Madame
de Cintré bows her head and folds her wings.'

'Can't she at least make her brother quit?'

'Her brother's the *chef de la famille*, the head of the clan. With
those people the family's everything; you must act not for your own
pleasure but for the advantage of your race and name.'

'But what do they want to get out of our lovely friend?' Newman
asked.

'Her submission to another marriage. They're not rich, and they
want to bring more money into the house.'

'There's where *you* come in, my boy!' Tristram interposed.

'And Madame de Cintré doesn't see it?' Newman continued.

'She has been sold for a price once; she naturally objects to being
sold a second time. It appears that the first time they greatly bungled
their bargain. M. de Cintré, before he died, managed to get through
almost everything.'

'And to whom do they want then to marry her now?'

'I thought it best not to ask; but you may be sure it is to some
horrid old nabob or to some dissipated little duke.'

'There's Mrs Tristram as large as life!' her husband cried.

'Observe the wealth of her imagination. She has not asked a single question—it's vulgar to ask questions—and yet she knows it all inside out. She has the history of Madame de Cintré's marriage at her fingers' ends. She has seen the lovely Claire on her knees with loosened tresses and streaming eyes and the rest of them standing over her with spikes and goads and red-hot irons, ready to come down if she refuses Bluebeard. The simple truth is that they've made a fuss about her milliner's bill or refused her an opera-box.'

Newman looked from Tristram to his wife with a certain reserve in each direction. 'Do you really mean,' he asked of the latter, 'that your friend is being really hustled into a marriage she really shrinks from?'

'I think it extremely probable. Those people are very capable of that sort of thing.'

'It's like something in a regular old play,' said Newman. 'That dark old house over there looks as if wicked things had been done in it and might be done again.'

'They have a still darker old house in the country, she tells me, and there, during the summer, this scheme must have been hatched.'

'*Must* have been; mind that!' Tristram echoed.

'After all,' their visitor suggested after a pause, 'she may be in trouble about something else.'

'If it's something else then it's something worse.' Mrs Tristram spoke as with high competence.

Newman, silent a while, seemed lost in meditation. 'Is it possible,' he asked at last, 'that they can do that sort of thing over here? that helpless women are thumb-screwed—sentimentally, socially, I mean—into marrying men they object to.'

'Helpless women, all over the world, have a hard time of it,' said Mrs Tristram. 'There's plenty of the thumb-screw for them every-where.'

'A great deal of that kind of thing goes on in New York,' said Tristram. 'Girls are bullied or coaxed or bribed, or all three together, into marrying, for money, horrible cads. There's no end of that always going on in Fifth Avenue, and other bad things besides. The Morals of Murray Hill!* Some one ought to show them up.'

'I don't believe it!'—Newman took it very gravely. 'I don't see how, in America, such cases can ever have occurred; for the simple reason

that the men themselves would be the first to make them impossible.
The American man sometimes takes advantage—I've known him to.
But he doesn't take advantage of women.'

'Listen to the voice of the spread eagle!' cried Tristram.

'The spread eagle should use his wings,' said his wife. 'He should
fly to the rescue of the woman of whom advantage is being taken!'

'To her rescue—?' Newman seemed to wonder.

'Pounce down, seize her in your talons and carry her off. Marry
her yourself.'

Newman, for some moments, answered nothing; but presently, 'I
guess she has heard enough of marrying,' he said. 'The kindest way
to treat her would be to care for her and yet never speak of it. But
that sort of thing's infamous,' he added. 'It's none of my business,
but it makes me feel kind of swindled to hear of it.'

He heard of it, however, more than once afterwards. Mrs Tristram
again saw Madame de Cintré and again found her looking very very
sad. But on these occasions there had been no tears; the intense
mild eyes were clear and still. 'She's cold, calm and hopeless,' Mrs
Tristram declared, and she added that on her mentioning that her
friend Mr Newman was again in Paris and was faithful in his desire
to make Madame de Cintré's acquaintance, this lovely woman had
found a smile in her despair and expressed her regret at having missed
his visit in the spring and her hope that he had not lost courage. 'I
told her something about you,' Newman's hostess wound up.

'That's a comfort,' he patiently answered. 'I seem to *want* people
to know about me.'

A few days after this, one dusky autumn afternoon, he went again
to the Rue de l'Université. The early evening had closed in as he
applied for admittance at the stoutly-guarded Hôtel de Bellegarde.
He was told that Madame la Comtesse was at home, on which he
crossed the court, entered the further door and was conducted
through a vestibule, vast, dim and cold, up a broad stone staircase
with an ancient iron balustrade, to an apartment on the first floor.
Announced and ushered in, he found himself in a large panelled
boudoir, at one end of which a lady and a gentleman were seated by
the fire. The gentleman was smoking a cigarette; there was no light
in the room save that of a couple of candles and the glow from the
hearth. Both persons rose to welcome Newman, who in the firelight
recognised Madame la Comtesse. She gave him her hand with a smile

which seemed in itself an illumination, and, pointing to her companion, murmured an allusion, 'One of my brothers.' The gentleman struck Newman as taking him, with great good-nature, for a
friend already made, and our hero then perceived him to be the young
man he had met in the court of the hotel on his former visit, the one
who had appeared of an easy commerce. 'Mrs Tristram has often
mentioned you to us.' It had an effect of prodigious benignity as
Madame de Cintré resumed her former place.

Newman, noticing in especial her 'us', began, after he had seated
himself, to consider what in truth might be his errand. He had an
unusual, unexpected sense of having wandered into a strange corner
of the world. He was not given, as a general thing, to 'borrowing
trouble' or to suspecting danger, and he had had no social tremors
on this particular occasion. He was not without presence of mind,
though he had no formed habit of prompt chatter. But his exercised
acuteness sometimes precluded detachment; with every disposition
to take things simply he couldn't but feel that some of them were
less simple than others. He felt as one feels in missing a step, in an
ascent, where one has expected to find it. This strange pretty woman
seated at fireside talk with her brother in the grey depths of her
inhospitable-looking house—what had he to say to her! She seemed
enveloped in triple defences of privacy; by what encouragement had
he presumed on his having effected a breach? It was for a moment
as if he had plunged into some medium as deep as the ocean and
must exert himself to keep from sinking. Meanwhile he was looking
at Madame la Comtesse and she was settling herself in her chair and
drawing in her long dress and vaguely, rather indirectly, turning her
face to him. Their eyes met; a moment later she looked away and
motioned to her brother to put a log on the fire. But the moment,
and the glance that lived in it, had been sufficient to relieve Newman
of the first and the last fit of sharp personal embarrassment he was
ever to know. He performed the movement frequent with him and
which was always a symbol of his taking mental possession of a
scene—he extended his long legs. The impression his hostess had
made on him at their first meeting came back in an instant; it had
been deeper than he knew. She took on a light and a grace, or, more
definitely, an interest; he had opened a book and the first lines held
his attention.

She asked him questions as if unable to do less: how lately he had seen Mrs Tristram, how long he had been in Paris, how long he expected to remain there, how he liked it. She spoke English without an accent, or rather with that absence of any one of those long familiar to him which on his arrival in Europe had struck him as constituting by itself a complete foreignness—a foreignness that in women he had come to like extremely. Here and there her utterance slightly exceeded this measure, but at the end of ten minutes he found himself waiting for these delicate discords. He enjoyed them, marvelling to hear the possible slip become the charming glide. 'You have a beautiful country of your own,' she safely enough risked.

'Oh, very fine, very fine. You ought to come over and see it.'

'I shall never go over and see it,' she answered with a smile.

'Well, why shouldn't you?'

'We don't travel; especially so far.'

'But you go away sometimes; you don't always stay right here?'

'I go away in summer—a little way, to the country.'

He wanted to ask her something more, something personal and going rather far—he hardly knew what. 'Don't you find it rather lifeless here,' he said; 'so far from the street?' Rather 'lonesome' he was going to say, but he deflected nervously, for discretion, and then felt his term an aggravation.

'Yes, it's very lifeless, if you mean very quiet; but that's exactly what we like.'

'Ah, that's exactly what you like,' he repeated. He was touched by her taking it so.

'Besides, I've lived here all my life.'

'Lived here all your life,' Newman found he could but echo.

'I was born here, and my father was born here before me, and my grandfather and my great-grandfathers. Were they not, Valentin?'—and she appealed to her brother.

'Yes, it seems a condition of our being born at all,' the young man smiled as he rose and threw the remnant of his cigarette into the fire. He remained leaning against the chimney-piece, and an observer would have guessed that he wished to take a better look at their guest, whom he covertly examined while he stroked his moustache.

'Your house is tremendously old then?' Newman pursued.

'How old is it, brother?' asked Madame de Cintré.

The young man took the two candles from the mantel, lifted one high in each hand and looked up, above the objects on the shelf, toward the cornice of the room. The chimney-piece was in white marble of the Louis-Quinze period,* but much aloft was a panelling of an earlier date, quaintly carved, painted white and here and there gilded. The white had turned to yellow and the gilding was tarnished. On the top the figures ranged themselves into a shield, on which an armorial device was cut. Above it, in relief, was a number—1627.* 'There you have a year,' said the young man. 'That's old or new, according to your point of view.'

'Well, over here,' Newman replied, 'one's point of view gets shifted round considerably.' And he threw back his head and looked about. 'Your house is of a very fine style of architecture.'

'Are you interested in questions of architecture?' asked the gentleman at the chimney-piece.

'Well, I took the trouble this summer to examine—as well as I can calculate—some four hundred and seventy churches. Do you call that interested?'

'Perhaps you're interested in religion,' said his amiable host.

Newman thought. 'Not actively.' He found himself speaking as if it were a railroad or a mine; so that the next moment, to correct this, 'Are you a Roman Catholic, madam?' he inquired of Madame de Cintré.

'I'm of the faith of my fathers,' she gravely replied.

He was struck with a sort of richness in the effect of it—he threw back his head again for contemplation. 'Had you never noticed that number up there?' he presently asked.

She hesitated a moment and then, 'In former years,' she returned.

Her brother had been watching Newman's movement. 'Perhaps you would like to examine the house.'

Our friend slowly brought down his eyes for recognition of this; he received the impression that the young man at the chimney-piece had his forms, and sought his own opportunities, of amusement. He was a handsome figure of a young man; his face wore a smile, his moustachios were curled up at the ends and there was something—more than the firelight—that played in his eyes. 'Damn his French impudence!' Newman was on the point of inwardly growling. 'What the deuce is he grinning at?' He glanced at Madame de Cintré, who was only looking at the floor. But she raised her eyes, which again met his, till she carried them to her brother. He turned again to this companion and observed that he strikingly resembled his sister. This was in his favour, and our hero's first impression of Count Valentin had moreover much engaged him. His suspicion expired and he said he should rejoice to see the house.

The young man surrendered to gaiety, laying his hand again on a light. 'It will repay your curiosity. Come then.'

But Madame de Cintré rose quickly and grasped his arm. 'Ah Valentin, what do you mean to do?'

'To show Mr Newman the house. It will be very amusing to show Mr Newman the house.'

She kept her hand on his arm and turned to their visitor with a smile. 'Don't let him take you; you won't find it remarkable. It is a musty old house like any other.'

'Ah, not like any other,' the Count still gaily protested. 'It's full of curious things. Besides a visit like Mr Newman's is just what it wants and has never had. It's a rare chance all round.'

'You're very wicked, brother,' Madame de Cintré insisted.

'Nothing venture, nothing have!' cried the young man. 'Will you come?'

She stepped toward Newman, clasping her hands and speaking, to his sense, with an exquisite grave appeal. 'Wouldn't you prefer my society here by my fire to stumbling about dark passages after—well, after nothing at all?'

'A hundred times! We'll see the house some other day.'

The young man put down his light with mock solemnity, and, shaking his head, 'Ah, you've defeated a great scheme, sir!' he sighed.

'A scheme? I don't understand,' said Newman.

'You'd have played your part in it all the better. Perhaps some day I shall have a chance to explain it.'

'Be quiet and ring for tea,' Madame de Cintré gently concluded.

Count Valentin obeyed, and presently a servant brought in a tray, which he placed on a small table. Madame de Cintré, when he had gone, busied herself, from her place, with making tea. She had but just begun when the door was thrown open and a lady rushed in with a loud rustling sound. She stared at Newman, gave a little nod and a 'Monsieur!' and then quickly approached Madame de Cintré and presented her forehead to be kissed. Madame de Cintré saluted her, but continued to watch the kettle. The rustling lady was young and pretty, it seemed to Newman; she wore her bonnet and cloak and a train of royal proportions. She began to talk rapidly in French. 'Oh, give me some tea, my beautiful one, for the love of God! I'm *anéantie*, annihilated.' Newman found himself quite unable to follow her; she spoke much less distinctly than M. Nioche.

'That's my wonderful sister-in-law,' the young man mentioned to him.

'She's very attractive,' Newman promptly responded.

'Fascinating,' the Count said; and this time again his guest suspected him of latent malice. His sister-in-law came round to the other side of the fire with her tea in her hand, holding it out at arm's length so that she mightn't spill it on her dress and uttering little cries of alarm. She placed the cup on the chimney and began to unpin her veil and pull off her gloves, looking meanwhile at Newman. 'Is there anything I can do for you, my dear lady?' the young man asked with quite extravagant solicitude.

'Present me to monsieur,' said his sister-in-law. And then when he had pronounced their visitor's name: 'I can't curtsey to you, monsieur, or I shall spill my tea. So Claire receives strangers like this?' she covertly added, in French to her brother-in-law.

'Apparently! Isn't it fun?' he returned with enthusiasm.

Newman stood a moment and then approached Madame de Cintré, who looked up at him as if she were thinking of something to say. She seemed to think of nothing, however—she simply smiled. He sat down near her and she handed him his cup. For a few moments they talked about that, and meanwhile he kept taking her in. He remembered what Mrs Tristram had told him of her 'perfection' and of her having, in combination, all the brilliant things that he dreamed of finding. This made him consider her not only without mistrust, but without uneasy conjectures; the presumption, from the first moment he looked at her, had been so in her favour. And yet if she was beautiful it was not from directly dazzling him. She was tall and moulded in long lines; she had thick fair hair and features uneven and harmonious. Her wide grey eyes were like a brace of deputed and garlanded maidens waiting with a compliment at the gate of a city, but they failed of that lamplike quality and those many-coloured fires that light up, as in a constant celebration of anniversaries, the fair front of the conquering type. Madame de Cintré was of attenuated substance and might pass for younger than she probably was. In her whole person was something still young and still passive, still uncertain and that seemed still to expect to depend, and

which yet made, in its dignity, a presence withal, and almost represented, in its serenity, an assurance. What had Tristram meant,
Newman wondered, by calling her proud? She was certainly not
proud, now, to him; or if she was it was of no use and lost on him:
she must pile it up higher if she expected him to mind it. She was a
clear, noble person—it was very easy to get on with her. And was she
then subject to that application of the idea of 'rank' which made her
a kind of historical formation? Newman had known rank but in the
old days of the army—where it had not always amounted to very
much either; and he had never seen it attributed to women, unless
perhaps to two or three rather predominant wives of generals. But
the designations representing it in France struck him as ever so
pretty and becoming, with a property in the bearer, this particular
one, that might match them and make a sense—something fair and
softly bright, that had motions of extraordinary lightness and indeed
a whole new and unfamiliar play of emphasis and pressure, a new
way, that is, of not insisting and not even, as one might think, wanting
or knowing, yet all to the effect of attracting and pleasing. She had
at last thought of something to say. 'Have you many friends in
Paris—so that you go out a great deal?'

He considered—about going out. 'Do you mean if I go to
parties—?'

'Do you go *dans le monde*, as we say?'

'I've seen a good many people. Mrs Tristram at least tells me I
have. She has taken me about. I do whatever she bids me.'

'By yourself then you're not fond of amusements?'

'Oh yes, of some sorts. I'm not fond of *very* fast rushing about,
or of sitting up half the night; I'm too old and too heavy. But I want
to be amused; I came to Europe for that.'

She appeared to think a moment, and then with a smile: 'But I
thought one can be so much amused in America.'

'I couldn't; perhaps I was too much part of the show. That's never
such fun, you know, for the animals themselves.'

At this moment young Madame de Bellegarde came back for
another cup of tea, accompanied by Count Valentin. Madame de
Cintré, when she had served her, began to talk again with Newman
and recalled what he had last said. 'In your own country you were
very much occupied?'

'I was in active business. I've been in active business since I was fifteen years old.'

'And what was your active business?' asked Madame de Belle-garde, who was decidedly not so pretty as Madame de Cintré.

'I've been in everything,' said Newman. 'At one time I sold leather; at one time I manufactured wash-tubs.'

Madame de Bellegarde made a little grimace. 'Leather? I don't like that. Wash-tubs are better. I prefer the smell of soap. I hope at least they made your fortune.' She rattled this off with the air of a woman who had the reputation of saying everything that came into her head, and with a strong French accent.

Newman had spoken with conscientious clearness, but Madame de Bellegarde's tone made him go on, after a meditative pause, with a certain light grimness of pleasantry. 'No, I lost money on wash-tubs, but I came out pretty square on leather.'

'I've made up my mind, after all,' said the Marquise, 'that the great point is—how do you call it?—to come out square. I'm on my knees to money and my worship is as public as you like. If you have it I ask no questions. For that I'm a real radical—like you, monsieur; at least as I suppose you. My *belle-sœur* is very proud; but I find that one gets much more pleasure in this sad life if one doesn't make too many difficulties.'

'Goodness gracious, chère madame, how you rush in!' Count Valentin gaily groaned.

'He's a man one can speak to, I suppose, since my sister receives him,' the lady more covertly answered. 'Besides, it's very true; those are my ideas.'

'Ah, you call them ideas?' the young man returned in a tone that Newman thought lovely.

'But Mrs Tristram told me you had been in the army—in your great war,' his beautiful sister pursued.

'Yes, but that was not business—in the paying sense. I couldn't afford it often.'

'Very true!' said Count Valentin, who looked at our hero from head to foot with his peculiar facial play, in which irony and urbanity seemed perplexingly commingled. 'Are you a brave man?'

'Well, try me.'

'Ah, then, there you are! In that case come again.'

'Dear me, what an invitation!' Madame de Cintré murmured with a smile that betrayed embarrassment.

'Oh, I want Mr Newman to come—particularly,' her brother returned. 'It will give me great pleasure. I shall feel the loss if I miss one of his visits. But I maintain he must be of high courage. A stout heart, sir, and a firm front.' And he offered Newman his hand.

'I shall not come to see you; I shall come to see Madame de Cintré,' said Newman, bent on distinctness.

'You'll need, exactly for that, all your arms.'

'Ah *de grâce*!' she appealed.

'Decidedly,' cried Madame de Bellegarde, 'I'm the only person here capable of saying something polite! Come to see me; you'll need no courage at all, monsieur.'

Newman gave a laugh which was not altogether an assent; then, shaking hands all round, marched away. Madame de Cintré failed to take up her sister's challenge to be gracious, but she looked with a certain troubled air at the retreating guest.

VII

ONE evening very late, about five days after this episode, Newman's servant brought him a card which proved to be that of young M. de Bellegarde. When a few moments later he went to receive his visitor he found him standing in the middle of the greatest of his gilded saloons and eyeing it from cornice to carpet. Count Valentin's face, it seemed to him, expressed not less than usual a sense of the inherent comedy of things. 'What the devil is he laughing at now?' our hero asked himself; but he put the question without acrimony, for he felt in Madame de Cintré's brother a free and adventurous nature, and he had a presentiment that on this basis of the natural and the bold they were destined to understand each other. Only if there was food for mirth he wished to have a glimpse of it too.

'To begin with,' said the young man as he extended his hand, 'have I come too late?'

'Too late for what?'

'To smoke a cigar with you.'

'You would have to come early to do that,' Newman said. 'I don't know how to smoke.'

'Ah, you're a strong man!'

'But I keep cigars,' he added. 'Sit down.'

His visitor looked about. 'Surely I mayn't smoke here.'

'What's the matter? Is the room too small?'

'It's too large. It's like smoking in a ball-room or a church.'

'That's what you were laughing at just now?' Newman asked; 'the size of my room?'

'It's not size only, but splendour and harmony, beauty of detail. It was the smile of sympathy and of admiration.'

Newman looked at him harder and then, 'So it *is* very ridiculous?' he enquired.

'Ridiculous, my dear sir? It's sublime.'

'That of course is the same thing,' said Newman. 'Make yourself comfortable. Your coming to see me, I take it, is an act of sympathy and a sign of confidence. You were not obliged to. Therefore if anything round here amuses you it will be all in a pleasant way. Laugh as loud as you please; I like to have my little entertainment a success.

Only I must make this request: that you explain the joke to me as soon as you can speak. I don't want to lose anything myself.'

His friend gave him a long look of unresentful perplexity. He laid his hand on his sleeve and seemed on the point of saying something, but suddenly checked himself, leaned back in his chair and puffed at his cigar. At last, however, breaking silence, 'Certainly,' he began, 'my coming to see you is the frank demonstration you recognise. I have been, nevertheless, in a measure encouraged—or urged—to the step. My sister, in a word, has asked it of me, and a request from my sister is, for me, a law. I was near you just now and I observed lights in what I supposed to be your rooms. It was not a ceremonious hour for making a call, but I was not sorry to do something that would show me as not performing a mere ceremony.'

'Well, here I am for you as large as life,' said Newman as he extended his legs.

'I don't know what you mean,' the young man went on, 'by giving me unlimited leave to laugh. Certainly I'm a great laugher; it's the only way, in general, isn't it? not to—well, not to *crever d'ennui*. But it's not in order that we may laugh together—or separately—that I have, I may say, sought your acquaintance. To speak with a confidence and a candour which I find rapidly getting the better of me, you have interested me without having done me the honour, I think, in the least to try for it—by having acted so consistently in your own interest: that, I mean, of your enlightened curiosity.' All this was uttered, to Newman's sense, with a marked proficiency, as from a habit of intercourse that was yet not 'office' intercourse, and, in spite of the speaker's excellent English, with the perfect form, as our friend supposed, of the superlative Frenchman; but there was at the same time something in it of a more personal and more pressing intention. What this might prove to have for him Newman suddenly found himself rather yearning to know. M. de Bellegarde was a foreigner to the last roll of his so frequent rotary *r*; and if he had met him out in bare Arizona he would have felt it proper to address him with a 'How-d'ye-do, Mosseer?' Yet there was that in his physiognomy which seemed to suspend a bold bridge of gilt wire over the impassable gulf produced by difference of race. He was but middling high and of robust and agile aspect. Valentin de Bellegarde, his host was afterwards to learn, had a mortal dread of not keeping the robustness down sufficiently to keep the agility up; he was afraid of growing stout; he was too short a story as he said, to afford an important digression. He rode and fenced and practised gymnastics with unremitting zeal, and you couldn't congratulate him on his appearance without making him turn pale at your imputation of its increase. He had a round head, high above the ears, a crop of hair at once dense and silky, a broad, low forehead, a short nose, of the ironical and enquiring rather than of the dogmatic or sensitive cast, and a moustache as delicate as that of a page in a romance. He resembled his sister not in feature, but in the expression of his fair open eyes, completely void, as they were in his case, of introspection, and in the fine freshness of his smile, which was like a gush of crystalline water. The charm of his face was above all in its being intensely, being frankly, ardently, gallantly alive. You might have seen it in the form of a bell with the long 'pull' dangling in the young man's conscious soul; at a touch of the silken cord the silver sound would fill the air. There was something in this quick play which assured you he was not economising his consciousness, not living in a corner of it to spare the furniture of the rest. He was squarely encamped in the centre and was keeping open house. When he flared into gaiety it was the movement of a hand that in emptying a cup turns it upside down; he gave you all the strength of the liquor. He inspired Newman with something of the kindness our hero used to feel in his earlier years for those of his companions who could perform strange and clever tricks—make their joints crack in queer places or whistle at the back of their mouths. 'My sister told me,' he said, 'that I ought to come and remove the impression I had taken such apparent pains to produce on you; the impression of my labouring under some temporary disorder. Did it strike you that what I said didn't make a sense?'

'Well, I thought I had never seen any one like you in real life,' Newman returned. 'Not in real quiet *home* life.'

'Ah then Claire's right.' And Count Valentin watched his host for a moment through his smoke-wreaths. 'And yet even if it is the case I think we had better let it stand. I had no idea of putting you off by any violence of any kind; I wanted on the contrary to produce a favourable impression. Since I did nevertheless make a fool of myself I was perhaps luckily inspired, for I mustn't seem to set up a claim for consistency which, in the sequel of our acquaintance, I may by no means justify. Set me down as a shocking trifler with intervals of high lucidity and even of extraordinary energy.'

'Oh, I guess you know what you're about,' said Newman.

'When I'm sane I'm very sane; that I admit,' his guest returned. 'But I didn't come here to talk about myself. I should like to ask you a few questions. You allow me?'

'Well, give me a specimen.'

'You live here all alone?'

'Absolutely. With whom should I live?'

'For the moment,' smiled M. de Bellegarde, 'I'm asking questions, not answering them. You've come over to Paris for your pleasure?'

Newman had a pause. 'Every one asks me that!' he said with his almost pathetic plainness. 'It sounds quite foolish—as if I were to get my pleasure somehow under a writ of extradition.'

'But at any rate you've a reason for being here.'

'Oh, call it for my pleasure!' said Newman. 'Though it represents me as trying to reclaim a hopeless absentee it describes well enough the logic of my conduct.'

'And you're enjoying what you find?'

'Well, I'm keeping my head.'

Count Valentin puffed his cigar again in silence. 'For myself,' he resumed at last, 'I'm entirely at your service. Anything I can do for you will make me very happy. Call on me at your convenience. Is there any one you wish to know—anything you wish to see? It's a pity you shouldn't fully avail yourself of Paris.'

'Well, I guess I avail myself,' said Newman serenely. 'I'm much obliged to you.'

'Honestly speaking,' his visitor went on, 'there's something absurd to me in hearing myself make you these offers. They represent a great deal of good-will, but they represent little else. You're a successful man, and I am a *raté*—by which we mean a dead failure—and it's a turning of the tables to talk as if I could lend you a hand.'

'How does it come that you haven't succeeded?' Newman ingenuously asked.

'Oh, I'm not a failure to wring your heart,' the young man returned. 'I've not fallen from a height, and my fiasco has made no noise and luckily no scandal. But you stand up, so very straight, for accomplished facts. You've made a fortune, you've raised an edifice, you're a financial, practical power, you can travel about the world till you've found a soft spot and lie down on it with the consciousness of having earned your rest. And all—so fabulously!—in the flower of your magnificent manhood. Is not that true? Well, imagine the exact reverse of all that and you have *votre serviteur*. I've done nothing, and there's not a poor pitiful thing for me to do.'

'Why what's the matter with all the things?'

'It would take me time to say. Some day I'll tell you. Meanwhile I'm right, eh? You're a horrid success? You've made more money than was ever made before by one so young and so candid? It's none of my business, but in short you're beastly rich?'

'That's another thing it sounds foolish to say,' said Newman. 'Do you think that's *all* I am?'

'No, I think you're original—that's why I'm here. We're very different, you and I, as products, I'm sure; I don't believe there's a subject on which we judge or feel alike. But I rather guess we shall get on, for there's such a thing, you know, as being—like fish and fowl—too different to quarrel.'

'Oh, I never quarrel,' said Newman rather shortly.

'You mean you just shoot? Well, I notify you that *till* I'm shot,' his visitor declared, 'I shall have had a greater sense of safety with you than I have perhaps ever known in any relation of life. And as a sense of danger is clearly a thing impossible to *you*, we shall therefore be all right.'

With the preamble embodied in these remarks he paid our hero a long visit; as the two men sat with their heels on Newman's glowing hearth they heard the small hours of the morning strike larger from a far-off belfry. Valentin de Bellegarde was by his own confession at all times a great chatterer, and on this occasion the habit of promptness of word and tone was on him almost as a fever. It was a tradition of his race that people of its blood always conferred a favour by their attentions, and, as his real confidence was as rare as his general surface was bright, he had a double reason for never fearing his friendship could be importunate. Late blossom though he might be, moreover, of an ancient stem, tradition (since I have used the word) had in his nature neither visible guards nor alarms, but was as muffled in sociability and urbanity as an old dowager in her laces and strings of pearls. Valentin was by the measure of the society about him a *gentilhomme* of purest strain, and his rule of life, so far as it was definite, had been to keep up the character. This, it seemed to him, might agreeably engage a young man of ordinary good parts. But he attained his best values by instinct rather than by theory, and

the amiability of his character was so great that certain of the aristocratic virtues lost, at his touch, their rigour without losing, as it
were, their temper. In his younger years he had been suspected of
low tastes, and his mother had greatly feared from him some such
slip in the common mire as might bespatter the family shield. He
had been treated therefore to more than his share of schooling and
drilling, but his instructors had not succeeded in mounting him upon
stilts. They had never troubled his deepest depths of serenity, and
he had remained somehow as fortunate as he was rash. He had long
been tied with so short a rope, however, that he had now a mortal
grudge against family discipline. He had been known to say within
the limits of the family that, featherhead though he might be, the
honour of the name was safer in his hands than in those of some of
its other members, and that if a day ever came to try it they would
see. He had missed no secret for making high spirits consort with
good manners, and he seemed to Newman, as afterwards young
members of the Latin races often seemed to him, now almost infan-
tile and now appallingly mature. In America, Newman reflected,
'growing' men had old heads and young hearts, or at least young
morals; here they had young heads and very aged hearts, morals the
most grizzled and wrinkled.

'What I envy you is your liberty,' Count Valentin found occasion
to observe; 'your wide range, your freedom to come and go, your not
having a lot of people, who take themselves all too seriously, expecting something of you. I live,' he added with a sigh, 'beneath the eyes
of my admirable mother.'

'Isn't it then your own fault? What's to hinder your ranging?'
Newman asked.

'There's a delightful simplicity in that question. Everything in life
is to hinder it. To begin with I haven't a penny.'

'Well, I hadn't a penny when *I* began to range.'

'Ah, but your poverty was your capital! Being of your race and
stamp, it was impossible you should remain what you were born, and
being born poor—do I understand it?—it was therefore inevitable
you should become as different from that as possible. You were in a
position that makes one's mouth water; you looked round you and
saw a world full of things you had only to step up to and take hold
of. When I was twenty I looked round me and saw a world with everything ticketed "Don't touch", and the deuce of it was that the ticket

seemed meant only for me. I couldn't go into business, I couldn't make money, because I was a Bellegarde. I couldn't go into politics because I was a Bellegarde—the Bellegardes don't recognise the Bonapartes.* I couldn't go into literature because I was a dunce. I couldn't marry a rich girl because no Bellegarde had for ages married a *roturière* and it wasn't urgent I should deviate. We shall have to face it, however—you'll see. Marriageable heiresses, *de notre bord*, are not to be had for nothing; it must be name for name and fortune for fortune. The only thing I could do was to go and fight for the Pope.* That I did, punctiliously, and received an apostolic flesh-wound at Castelfidardo.* It did neither the Holy Father nor me any good that I could make out. Rome was doubtless a very amusing place in the days of Heliogabalus,* but it has sadly fallen off since. I was immured for three years, like some of the choicest scoundrels in history, in the castle of Saint Angelo,* and then I came back to secular life.'

Newman followed very much as he had followed *ciceroni* through museums. 'So you've no active interest?—you do absolutely nothing?'

'As hard as ever I can. I'm supposed to amuse myself and to pass my time, and, to tell the truth, I've had some good moments. They come somehow, in spite of one, and the thing is then to recognise them. But you can't keep on the watch for them for ever. I'm good for three or four years more perhaps, but I foresee that after that I shall spring a leak and begin to sink. I shan't float any more, I shall go straight to the bottom. Then, at the bottom, what shall I do? I think I shall turn monk. Seriously, I think I shall tie a rope round my waist and go into a monastery. It was an old custom and the old customs were very good. People understood life quite as well as we do. They kept the pot boiling till it cracked, and then put it on the shelf altogether.'

'Do you attend church regularly?' asked Newman in a tone which gave the enquiry a quaint effect.

His friend evidently appreciated this element, yet looked at him with due decorum. 'I'm a very good Catholic. I cherish the Faith. I adore the blessed Virgin. I fear the Father of Lies.'

'Well then,' said Newman, 'you're very well fixed. You've got pleasure in the present and paradise in the future: what do you complain of?'

'It's a part of one's pleasure to complain. There's something in your own situation that rubs me up. You're the first man about whom I've ever found myself saying "Oh, if I were he—!" It's singular, but so it is. I've known many men who, besides any factitious advantages that I may possess, had money and brains into the bargain, yet they've never disturbed my inward peace. You've got something it worries me to have missed. It's not money, it's not even brains— though evidently yours have been excellent for your purpose. It's not your superfluous stature, though I should have rather liked to be a couple of inches taller. It's a sort of air you have of being imperturbably, being irremoveably and indestructibly (that's the thing!) at home in the world. When I was a boy my father assured me it was by just such an air that people recognised a Bellegarde. He called my attention to it. He didn't advise me to cultivate it; he said that as we grew up it always came of itself. I supposed it had come to me because I think I've always had the feeling it represents. My place in life had been made for me and it seemed easy to occupy. But you who, as I understand it, have made your own place, you who, as you told us the other day, have made and sold articles of vulgar household use—you strike me, in a fashion of your own, as a man who stands about at his ease and looks straight over ever so many high walls. I seem to see you move everywhere like a big stockholder on his favourite railroad. You make me feel awfully my want of shares. And yet the world used to be supposed to be ours. What is it I miss?'

'It's the proud consciousness of honest toil, of having produced something yourself that somebody has been willing to pay you for— since that's the definite measure. Since you speak of my wash-tubs— which were lovely—isn't it just they and their loveliness that make up my good conscience?'

'Oh no; I've seen men who had gone beyond wash-tubs, who had made mountains of soap—strong-smelling yellow soap, in great bars; and they've left me perfectly cold.'

'Then it's just the regular treat of being an American citizen,' said Newman. 'That sets a man right up.'

'Possibly,' his guest returned; 'but I'm forced to say I've seen a great many American citizens who didn't seem at all set up or in the least like large stockholders. I never envied them. I rather think the thing's some diabolical secret of your own.'

'Oh come,' Newman laughed, 'you'll persuade me against my humility.'

'No, I shall persuade you of nothing. You've nothing to do with humility any more than with swagger: that's just the essence of your confounded coolness. People swagger only when they've something to lose, and show their delicacy only when they've something to gain.'

'I don't know what I may have to lose,' said Newman, 'but I can quite see a situation in which I should have something to gain.'

His visitor looked at him hard. 'A situation—?'

Newman hesitated. 'Well, I'll tell you more about it when I know you better.'

'Ah, you'll soon know me by heart!' the young man sighed as he departed.

During the next three weeks they met again several times and, without formally swearing an eternal friendship, fell, for their course of life, instinctively into step together. Valentin de Bellegarde was to Newman the typical, ideal Frenchman, the Frenchman of tradition and romance, so far as our hero was acquainted with these mystic fields. Gallant, expansive, amusing, more pleased himself with the effect he produced than those (even when they were quite duly pleased) for whom he produced it; a master of all the distinctively social virtues and a votary of all the agreeable sensations; a devotee of something mysterious and sacred to which he occasionally alluded in terms more ecstatic even than those in which he spoke of the last pretty woman, and which was simply the beautiful though somewhat superannuated image of personal Honour; he was irresistibly enter-taining and enlivening, and he formed a character to which Newman was as capable of doing justice when he had once been placed in contact with it as he was unlikely, in musing upon the possible com-binations of the human mixture, mentally to have foreshadowed it. No two parties to an alliance could have come to it from a wider sepa-ration, but it was what each brought out of the queer dim distance that formed the odd attraction for the other.

Valentin lived in the basement of an old house in the Rue d'Anjou Saint Honoré,* and his small apartments lay between the court of the house and a garden of equal antiquity, which spread itself behind—one of those large, sunless, humid gardens into which you look unexpectedly in Paris from back windows, wondering how among the grudging habitations they find their space. When Newman presently called on him it was to hint that such quarters were, though in a different way, at least as funny as his own. Their oddities had another sense than those of our hero's gilded saloons on the Boulevard Haussmann: the place was low, dusky, contracted, and was crowded with curious bric-à-brac. Their proprietor, penniless patrician though he might be, was an insatiable collector, and his walls were covered with rusty arms and ancient panels and platters, his doorways draped in faded tapestries, his floors muffled in the skins of beasts. Here and there was one of those uncomfortable tributes to elegance in which the French upholsterer's art is prolific; a curtained recess with a sheet of looking-glass as dark as a haunted pool; a divan on which, for its festoons and furbelows, you could no more sit down than on a dowager's lap; a fireplace draped, flounced, frilled, by the same analogy, to the complete exclusion of fire. The young man's possessions were in picturesque disorder, and his apartment pervaded by the odour of cigars, mingled, for inhalation, with other dim ghosts of past presences. Newman thought it, as a home, damp, gloomy and perverse, and was puzzled by the romantic incoherence of the furniture.

The charming Count, like most of his countrymen, hid none of his lights under a bushel and made little of a secret of the more interesting passages of his personal history. He had inevitably a vast deal to say about women, and could frequently indulge in sentimental and ironical apostrophes to these authors of his joys and woes. 'Oh, the women, the women, and the things they've made me do!' he would exclaim with a wealth of reference. '*C'est égal*, of all the follies and stupidities I've committed for them there isn't one I would have missed!' On this subject Newman maintained an habitual reserve; to make it shine in the direct light of one's own experience had always seemed to him a proceeding vaguely analogous to the cooing of pigeons and the chattering of monkeys, and even inconsistent with a fully-developed human character. But his friend's confidences greatly amused and rarely displeased him, for the garden of the young man's past appeared to have begun from the earliest moment to bloom with rare flowers, amid which memory was as easy as a summer breeze. 'I really think', he once said, 'that I'm not more depraved than most of my contemporaries. They're *joliment* depraved, my contemporaries!' He threw off wonderfully pretty things about his female friends and, numerous and various as they had been, declared that his curiosity had survived the ordeal. 'But you're not to take that as advice,' he added, 'for as an authority I must be misleading. I'm prejudiced in their favour; I'm a *sentimental*—in other words a donkey.' Newman listened with an uncommitted smile and was glad, for his own sake, that he had fine feelings; but he mentally repudiated the idea of a Frenchman's having discovered any merit in the amiable sex he himself didn't suspect. Count Valentin, however, was not merely anecdotic and indiscreet; he welcomed every light on our hero's own life, and so far as his revelations might startle and waylay Newman could cap them as from the long habit of capping. He narrated his career, in fact, from the beginning, through all its variations, and whenever his companion's credulity or his 'standards' appeared to protest it amused him to heighten the colour of the episode. He had sat with Western humourists in circles round cast-iron stoves and seen 'tall' stories grow taller without toppling over, and his imagination had learnt the trick of building straight and high. The Count's regular attitude became at last that of lively self-defence; to mark the difference of his type from that of the occasionally witless he cultivated the wit of never being caught swallowing. The result of this was that Newman found it impossible to convince him of certain time-honoured verities.

'But the details don't matter,' Valentin said, 'since you've evidently had some such surprising adventures. You've seen some strange sides of life, you've revolved to and fro over a continent as I walk up and down the Boulevard. You're a man of the world to a livelier tune than ours. You've spent some awful, some deadly days, and you've done some extremely disagreeable things: you've shovelled sand, as a boy, for supper, and you've eaten boiled cat in a gold-digger's camp. You've stood casting up figures for ten hours at a time and you've sat through Methodist sermons for the sake of looking at a pretty girl in another pew. It can't all have been very *folichon*. But at any rate you've done something and you *are* something; you've used your faculties and you've developed your character. You've not *abruti* yourself with debauchery, and you've not mortgaged your fortune to social conveniencies. You take things as it suits you, and you've fewer prejudices even than I, who pretend to have none, but who in reality have three or four that stand in my way. Happy man, you're strong and you're free—nothing stands in yours. But what the deuce', he wound up, 'do you propose to do with such advantages? Really to use

them you need a better world than this. There's nothing worth your
while here.'

'Oh, I guess there's something,' Newman said.

'What is it?'

'Well,' he sighed, 'I'll tell you some other time!'

In this way he delayed from day to day broaching a subject he had
greatly at heart. Meanwhile, however, he was growing practically
familiar with it; in other words he had called again, three times, on
Madame de Cintré. On but two of these occasions had he found her
at home and on each of them she had other visitors. Her visitors were
numerous and, to our hero's sense, vociferous, and they exacted
much of their hostess's attention. She found time none the less to
bestow a little of it on the stranger, a quantity represented in an occasional vague smile—the very vagueness of which pleased him by
allowing him to fill it out mentally, both at the time and afterwards,
with such meanings as most fitted. He sat by without speaking,
looking at the entrances and exits, the greetings and chatterings, of
Madame de Cintré's guests. He felt as if he were at the play and as
if his own speaking would be an interruption; sometimes he wished
he had a book to follow the dialogue; he half expected to see a woman
in a white cap and pink ribbons come and offer him one for two
francs. Some of the ladies gave him a very hard or a very soft stare,
as he chose; others seemed profoundly unconscious of his presence.
The men looked only at the mistress of the scene. This was
inevitable, for whether one called her beautiful or not she entirely
occupied and filled one's vision, quite as an ample, agreeable sound
filled one's ear. Newman carried away after no more than twenty distinct words with her an impression to which solemn promises could
not have given a higher value. She was part of the play he was seeing
acted, as much a part of it as her companions, but how she filled the
stage and how she bore watching, not to say studying and throwing
bouquets to! Whether she rose or seated herself; whether she went
with her departing friends to the door and lifted up the heavy curtain
as they passed out and stood an instant looking after them and giving
them the last nod; or whether she leaned back in her chair with her
arms crossed and her eyes quiet, her face listening and smiling, she
made this particular guest desire to have her always before him,
moving through every social office open to the genius of woman, or
in other words through the whole range of exquisite hospitality. If it

might be hospitality *to* him it would be well; if it might be hospitality *for* him it would be still better. She was so high yet so slight, so active yet so still, so elegant yet so simple, so present yet so withdrawn! It was this unknown quantity that figured for him as a mystery; it was what she was off the stage, as he might feel, that interested him most of all. He could not have told you what warrant he had for talking of mysteries; if it had been his habit to express himself in poetic figures he might have said that in observing her he seemed to see the vague circle sometimes attending the partly-filled disc of the moon. It was not that she was effaced, and still less that she was 'shy'; she was, on the contrary, as distinct as the big figure on a banknote and of as straightforward a profession. But he was sure she had qualities as yet unguessed even by herself and that it was kept for Christopher Newman to bring out.

He had abstained for several reasons from saying some of these things to her brother. One reason was that before proceeding to any act he was always circumspect, conjectural, contemplative; he had little eagerness, as became a man who felt that whenever he really began to move he walked with long steps. And then it just pleased, it occupied and excited him, not to give his case, as he would have said, prematurely away. But one day Valentine—as Newman conveniently sounded the name—had been dining with him on the boulevard and their sociability was such that they had sat long over their dinner. On rising from it the young man proposed that, to help them through the rest of the evening, they should go and see Madame Dandelard.* Madame Dandelard was a little Italian lady married to a Frenchman who had proved a rake and a brute and the torment of her life. Her husband had spent all her money and then, lacking further means for alien joys, had taken, in his more intimate hours, to beating her. She had a blue spot somewhere which she showed to several persons, including the said Valentine. She had obtained a legal separation, collected the scraps of her fortune, which were meagre, and come to live in Paris, where she was staying at an *hôtel garni*. She was always looking for an apartment and visiting, with a hundred earnest questions and measurements, those of other people. She was very pretty and childlike and made very extraordinary remarks. Valentin enjoyed her acquaintance, and the source of his interest in her was, according to his declaration, an anxious curiosity as to what would become of her. 'She's poor, she's pretty and she's silly,' he said; 'it seems to me she can go only one way. It's a pity, but it can't be helped. I'll give her six months. She has nothing to fear from me, but I'm watching the process. It's merely a question of the how and the when and the where. Yes, I know what you're going to say; this horrible Paris hardens one's heart. But it quickens one's wits, and it ends by teaching one a refinement of observation. To see this little woman's little drama play itself out is now for me a pleasure of the mind.'

'If she's going to throw herself away,' Newman had said, 'you ought to stop her.'

'Stop her? How stop her?'

'Talk to her; give her some good advice.'

At which the young man laughed. ' "Some"? How much? Heaven deliver us both! Imagine the situation. Try giving her yourself exactly the right amount.'

After which it was that Newman had gone with him to see Madame Dandelard. When they came away Valentin reproached his companion. 'Where was your famous advice? I didn't hear a word of it.'

'Oh, I give it up,' Newman simply answered.

'Then you're as bad as I!'

'No, because I don't find it a pleasure of the mind to watch her prospective adventures. I don't in the least want to see her going down hill. I had rather look the other way. But why,' our friend asked in a moment, 'don't you get your sister to go and see her?'

His companion stared. 'Go and see Madame Dandelard—my sister?'

'She might talk to her to very good purpose.'

Valentin shook his head with sudden gravity. 'My sister doesn't have relations with that sort of person. Madame Dandelard's nothing at all; they'd never meet.'

'I should think,' Newman returned, 'that Madame de Cintré might see whom she pleased.' And he privately resolved that, after he should know her a little better, he would ask her to go and pick up, for such 'pressing' as might be possible, the little spotted blown leaf in the dusty Parisian alley. When they had dined, at all events, on the occasion I have mentioned, he demurred to the latter's proposal that they should go again and 'draw' the lady on the subject of her bruises. 'I've something better in mind; come home with me and finish the evening before my fire.'

Valentin always rose to any implied appeal to his expository gift, and before long the two men sat watching the blaze play over the pomp of Newman's high saloon.

VIII

'Look here—I want to know about your sister,' the elder abruptly began.

His visitor arched fine eyebrows. 'Now that I think of it you've never yet made her the subject of a question.'

'Well, I guess I know why.'

'If it's because you don't trust me, you're very right,' said Valentin. 'I can't talk of her rationally. I admire her too much.'

'Talk of her as you can,' Newman returned, 'and if I don't like it I'll stop you.'

'Well we're very good friends; such a brother and sister as haven't been known since Orestes and Electra.* You've seen her enough to have taken her in: tall, slim, imposing, gentle, half a *grande dame* and half an angel; a mixture of "type" and simplicity, of the eagle and the dove. She looks like a statue that has failed as cold stone, resigned itself to its defects and come to life as flesh and blood, to wear white capes and long soft trains. All I can say is that she really possesses every merit that the face she has, the eyes she has, the smile she has, the tone of voice she has, the whole *way* she has, lead you to expect; and isn't it saying quite enough? As a general thing when a woman seems from the first as *right* as that, she's altogether wrong—you've only to look out. But in proportion as you take Claire for right you may fold your arms and let yourself float with the current; you're safe. You'll only never imagine a person so true and so straight. She's so honest and so *gentille*. I've never seen a woman half so charming. She has every blessed thing a man wants and more; that's all I can say about her. There!' Valentin concluded: 'I told you how much I should bore you.'

Newman uttered no assurance that he was not bored; he only said after a little: 'She's remarkably *good*, eh?'

'She'd have invented goodness if it didn't exist.'

'It seems to me', Newman remarked, 'that you'd have invented *her*—! But it's all right,' he added—'I'd have invented *you*! Is she clever?' he then asked.

'Try her with something you think so yourself. Then you'll see.'

'Oh, how can I try her?' sighed Newman with a lapse. But he picked himself up. 'Is she fond of admiration?'

'*Pardieu!*' cried Valentin. 'She'd be no sister of mine if she weren't. What woman's not?'

'Well, when they're too fond of it,' Newman heard himself hypocritically temporise, 'they commit all kinds of follies to get it.'

'I didn't say she was "too" fond!' Valentin exclaimed. 'Heaven forbid I should say anything so idiotic. She's not *too* anything. If I were to say she's ugly I shouldn't mean she's "too" ugly. She's fond of pleasing, and if you're pleased she leaves it so. If you're not pleased she lets it pass, and thinks the worse neither of you nor of herself. I imagine, though, she hopes the saints in heaven are, for I'm sure she's incapable of trying to please by any means of which they'd disapprove.'

'Is she happy then?' Newman presently pursued.

'Oh, oh, oh! That's much to ask.'

'Do you mean for me—?'

'I mean for her. What should she be happy about?'

Newman wondered. 'Then she has troubles?'

'My dear man, she has what we all have—even you, strange to say. She has a history.'

'That's just what I want to hear,' said Newman.

Valentin hesitated—an embarrassment rare with him. 'Then we shall have to appoint a special séance, with music or refreshments or a turn outside between the acts. Suffice it for the present that my sister's situation has been far from *folichonne*. She made, at eighteen, a marriage that was expected to be brilliant, but that, like a lamp that goes out, turned all to smoke and bad smell. M. de Cintré was fifty-five years old and *pas du tout aimable*. He lived, however, but three or four years, and after his death his family pounced upon his money, brought a lawsuit against his widow, pushed things very hard. Their case was good, for M. de Cintré, who had been trustee for some of his relatives, appeared to have been guilty of some very irregular practices. In the course of the suit some revelations were made as to his private history which my sister found so little to her taste that she ceased to defend herself and washed her hands of all her interests. This required some strength of conviction, for she was between two fires,* her husband's family opposing her and her own family denouncing. My mother and my brother wished her to cleave to what they regarded as her rights. But she resisted firmly and at last bought her freedom—obtained my mother's assent to her compromising the suit at the price of a promise.'

'What was the promise?'

'To do anything else whatever, for the next ten years, that might be asked of her—anything, that is, but marry.'

'She had disliked her husband very much?'

'No one knows how much!'

'The marriage had been made in your vicious French way,' Newman continued—'by the two families and without her having a voice?'

'It was a first act for a melodrama. She saw M. de Cintré for the first time a month before the wedding, after everything, to the minutest detail, had been arranged. She turned white when she looked at him and white she remained—I shall never forget her face—till her wedding-day. The evening before the ceremony her nerves completely gave way and she spent the whole night in sobs. My mother sat holding her two hands and my brother walked up and down the room. I declared it was revolting and told my sister publicly that if she would really hold out I would stand by her against all comers. I was sent about my business and she became Comtesse de Cintré.'

'Your brother,' said Newman reflectively, 'must be a very nice young man.'

'He's very nice, though he's not very young. He's now upwards of fifty; fifteen years my senior. He has been a father to my sister and me. He's a type apart; he has the best manners in France. He's extremely clever; indeed he's full of accomplishment. He's writing a history of The Unmarried Princesses of the Maison de France.' This was said by Valentin with extreme gravity, in a tone that betokened no mental reservation—or that at least almost betokened none.

Our friend perhaps discovered there what little there was, for he presently said: 'You could struggle along without your brother.'

'I beg your pardon'—the young man still as gravely protested. 'A house like ours is inevitably *one*.'

'Then you want some one to come right in and break it up.'

'*Hein?*' said Valentin.

On which Newman, after an instant, put the matter another way. 'Well, I'm glad *I'm* free not to like him!'

'Wait till you know him!' Valentin returned—and this time he smiled.

'Is your mother also then a type apart?' his friend asked after a pause.

'For my mother,' the young man said, now with intense gravity, 'I have the highest admiration. She's a very extraordinary person. You can't approach her without feeling it.'

'She's the daughter, I believe, of an English nobleman?'

'Of Lord Saint Dunstans.'

'And was *he* very grand?'

'Not as grand as we. They date only from the sixteenth century. It is on my father's side that we go back—back, back, back. The family antiquaries themselves lose breath. At last they stop, panting and fanning themselves, somewhere in the ninth century, under Charlemagne. That's where we begin.'

'There is no mistake about it?' Newman demanded.

'I'm sure I hope not. We've been mistaken at least for several centuries.'

'And you've always married into—what do you call them?— "ancient houses"?'

'As a rule; though in so long a stretch of time there have been some exceptions. Three or four Bellegardes, in the seventeenth and eighteenth centuries, took wives out of the *bourgeoisie*—accepted lawyers' daughters.'

'A lawyer's daughter—that's a come-down?' Newman went on.

'A condescension. But one of us, in the Middle Ages, did better: he married a beggar-maid, like King Cophetua.* That was really more convenient; it was like pairing with a bird or a monkey; one didn't have to think about her family at all. Our women have always done well; they've never even gone into the *petite noblesse*. There is, I believe, not a case on record of a misalliance among *ces dames*.'

Newman turned this over a while and then at last: 'You offered, the first time you came to see me, to render me any service you could. I told you I'd sometime mention something you might do. Do you remember?'

'Remember? I've been counting the hours.'

'Very well; here's your chance. Do what you can to make your sister think well of me.'

The young man had a strange bright stare. 'Why, I'm sure she thinks as well of you as possible already.'

'An opinion founded on seeing me three or four times? That's putting me off with very little. I want something more. I've been thinking of it a good deal and at last I've decided to tell you. I should like very much to marry Madame de Cintré.'

Valentin had been looking at him with quickened expectancy and with the smile with which he had greeted his allusion to the promised request. At this last announcement he kept his eyes on him, but their expression went through two or three curious phases. It felt, apparently, an impulse to let itself go further; but this it immediately checked. Then it remained for some instants taking counsel with the danger of hilarity—at the end of which it decreed a retreat. It slowly effaced itself and left a sobriety modified by the desire not to be rude. Extreme surprise had in fine come into M. de Bellegarde's face; but he had reflected that it would be uncivil to leave it there. And yet what the deuce was he to do with it? He got up in his agitation and stood before the chimney-piece, still looking at his host. He was a longer time thinking what to say than one would have expected.

'If you can't render me the service I ask,' Newman pursued, 'don't be afraid to tell me, for I'll be hanged if I won't get on without you.'

'Let me hear it again distinctly, the service you ask. It's very important, you know,' Valentin went on. 'I'm to plead your cause with my sister because you want—you want to marry her? That's it, eh?'

'Oh, I don't say plead my cause exactly; I shall try and do that myself. But say a good word for me now and then—let her know at least what *you* take me for.'

This *was*, visibly, for the young man, a droll simplification. 'I shall have first, my dear fellow, to know myself!'

But Newman went on unheeding. 'What I want chiefly, after all, is just to make you aware of what I have in mind. I suppose that's what you all expect, making you formally aware, isn't it? I want always to do, over here, what's customary, what you've been used to. You seem more lost without what you've been used to than we are. If there's anything particular to be done let me know and I'll make it right. I wouldn't for the world approach Madame de Cintré save by schedule. I'd go in to her on all-fours if that's what's required. If I ought to speak to your mother first why I'll speak to her. If I ought to speak even to your brother I'll speak to *him*. I'll speak to any one you like, to the porter in his lodge or the policeman on his beat. As I don't know any one else I begin by speaking to you. But that, if it's a social obligation, is a pleasure as well.'

'Yes, I see—I see,' said Valentin, lightly stroking his chin. 'You've a very right feeling about it, but I'm glad you've begun with me.' He paused, hesitated, and then turned away and walked slowly the length of the room. Newman got up and stood leaning against the chimney with his hands in his pockets and his eyes on his friend's evolution. This personage came back and stopped in front of him. 'I give it up. I'll not pretend I'm not—well, impressed. I am—hugely! *Ouf!* It's a relief.'

'That sort of news is always a surprise,' said Newman. 'No matter what you've done, people are never prepared. But if you're impressed I hope at least you're impressed favourably.'

'Come!' the young man broke out; 'I'm going to let you have it. I don't know whether it lays me flat or makes me soar.'

'Well, if it corners you too much I'm afraid you've got to stay there, for I assure you I mean myself to fight out in the open.'

'My dear man, Samson was in the open when he pulled down the temple,* but there wasn't much left of any one else.' To which Valentin added: 'You're perfectly serious?'

'Am I a futile Frenchman that I shouldn't be?' Newman asked. 'But why is it, by the by—come to talk—that you *are* prostrated?'

The Count raised his hand to the back of his head and rubbed his hair quickly up and down, thrusting out the tip of his tongue as he did so. 'Well, for instance you're not, as we call it, if I'm not mistaken, "born."'

'The devil I'm not!' Newman exclaimed.

'Oh,' said his friend a little more seriously, 'I didn't know you had—well, your quarterings.'*

'Ah, your quarterings are your little local matter!'

Valentin just hesitated. 'But aren't we all—isn't my admirable sister in particular—our little local matter?'

Newman met his eyes with a long, hard look—exhaling at last, however, a sigh as long. 'Do you mean that I must *claim* a social standing and hang out my sign? What sort of swagger's that? If it's a question of pretensions—pretensions, that is, to effectively existing—let me make, to meet you on your own ground, the very highest. Only it isn't, it seems to me, for me vulgarly to make them; it's for you, assuming them, to invalidate them. On you, in other words, the burden of disproof.'

Valentin's fine smile suffered a further strain. 'Haven't you manufactured and placed in the market certain admirable wash-tubs?'

'With great temporary success. But it isn't a question of my achievements—it's a question of my failures. You might catch me,' said our friend, 'on two or three of those. Only then, you know,' he added, 'I should have the right to ask you about yours.'

'Oh, ours have partaken of our general brilliancy! They haven't at any rate prevented the great thing.'

'And what do you call the great thing?'

'Well,' Valentin smiled, 'our being interesting.'

Newman considered. 'To yourselves?'

'To the world. That *has* been our value—that we've had the world's attention. We've been felt to be worth it.'

'Oh,' said Newman, 'if it's but a question of what you're worth —!' He hung fire an instant, and then, 'Should you like to know what *I* am?' he demanded.

He had held his companion by his pause, and his words prolonged a little the situation. 'No, thanks,' Valentin then replied. 'It's none of my business. It's enough for me that you're worth, delightfully, my acquaintance and my wonder.'

In recognition of these last words Newman for a moment said nothing. He only coloured as with a flush of hope. Then he raised his eyes to the ceiling and stood looking at one of the rosy cherubs painted on it. 'Of course I don't expect to marry any woman for the asking,' he observed at last: 'I expect first to make myself acceptable to her. She must like me to begin with. But what I feel is how she *must*—from the moment she knows me as I want.'

'As the prince of husbands?'

'Well yes—call it the prince, as you speak of such people.'

'I believe,' said Valentin after a moment, 'that you'd be as good a prince as another.'

'I should be as good a husband.'

'And that's what you want me to tell my sister?'

'That's what I want you to tell her.'

The young man laid his hand on his companion's arm, looked at him critically, from head to foot, and then, with a loud laugh and shaking the other hand in the air, turned away. He walked again the length of the room and again he came back and stationed himself in front of Newman. 'All this is very interesting and very curious. In what I said just now I was speaking not for myself, but for my traditions and my superstitions. For myself really your idea stirs me up. It startled me at first, but the more I think of it the more I see in it. It's no use attempting to explain anything; you wouldn't, I think, follow me. After all, I don't see why you need; it's no great loss.'

'Oh, if there's anything more to explain try me with it. I guess I've had to understand some queerer things than any you're likely to tell.'

'No,' said Valentin, 'we'll do without them; we'll let them go. I took you for somebody—God knows whom or what—the first time I saw you, and I'll abide by that. It would be quite odious for me to come talking to you as if I could patronise you. I've told you before that I envy you; *vous m'imposez*, as we say—I didn't know you much till these last five minutes. So we'll let things go, and I'll say nothing to you that, with our positions reversed, you wouldn't say to me.'

I know not whether in renouncing the mysterious opportunity to which he alluded Valentin felt himself do something very generous. If so he was not rewarded; his generosity was not appreciated. Newman failed to recognise any power to disconcert or to wound him, and he had now no sense of coming off easily. He had not at his command the gratitude even of a glance; and he was in truth occupied with a particular fear, which he presently expressed. 'Do you think she may be by chance determined not to marry at all?'

'Oh, I quite think it! But that's not necessarily too much against you. Such a determination never yet spoiled a right opportunity.'

'But suppose I don't seem a right one. I'm afraid it will be hard,' Newman said with a gravity that appeared to signify at the same time a sort of lucid respect for the fact.

'I don't think it will be easy. In a general way I don't see why a widow should ever marry again. She has gained the benefits of matrimony—freedom and consideration—and she has got rid of the drawbacks. Why should she put her head back into the noose? Her usual motive is ambition—if a man can offer her a great position, make her a princess or an ambassadress.'

'And—in that way—is Madame de Cintré ambitious?'

'Who knows?' her brother asked with slightly depressing detachment. 'I don't pretend to say all she is or all she isn't. I think she might be touched by the prospect of becoming the wife of a great man. But in a certain way, I believe, whatever she does will be the *improbable*. Don't be too confident, but don't absolutely doubt. Your best chance for success will be precisely in affecting her as unusual, unexpected, original. Don't try to be any one else; be simply your-self as hard as ever you can, and harder perhaps indeed (if you under-stand) than you've ever been before. Something or other can't fail to come of *that*. I'm very curious to see what.'

'I'm much obliged to you for your curiosity,' Newman said—'if I may take it as your advice. I'm glad for your sake at least that I'm likely to prove so amusing.'

His friend, who had been staring at the fire a minute, looked up. 'It's a pity you don't fully understand me, that you don't know just what I'm doing.'

'Oh,' laughed Newman, 'don't do anything wrong! Leave me to myself rather, or defy me out and out to try it. I wouldn't lay any load on your conscience.'

Valentin sprang up again, evidently quite inflamed. 'You'll never understand—you'll never know; and if you succeed and I turn out to have helped you you'll never be grateful, not as I shall deserve you should be. You'll be an excellent fellow always, but you'll not be grateful. But it doesn't matter, for I shall get my own fun out of it.' And he broke into an extravagant laugh. 'You look worried,' he added; 'you look almost alarmed.'

'It's a pity,' said Newman, 'that I don't wholly catch on. I shall lose some very good sport.'

'I told you, you remember, that we're very strange people,' his visitor pursued. 'Well, I give you warning again. We're fit for a museum or a Balzac novel. My mother's strange, my brother's strange, and I verily believe I'm stranger than either. You'll even find my sister a little strange. Old trees have crooked branches, old houses have queer cracks, old races have odd secrets. Remember that we're eight hundred years old!'

'Very good,' said Newman; 'that's the sort of thing I came to Europe for. You're *made* for me to work right in.'

'*Touchez-là* then,' Bellegarde returned, putting out his hand. 'It's a bargain; I accept you, I espouse your cause. It's because I like you, in a great measure; but that's not the only reason.' And he stood holding Newman's hand and looking at him askance.

'What's the other one?'

'Well, I'm in the Opposition. I've a positive aversion—!'

'To your brother?' asked Newman in his unmodulated voice.

Valentin laid a finger on his lips with a whispered *hush*! 'Old races have strange secrets! Put yourself into motion. Come and see my sister and be assured of my sympathy!' With which he took leave while his host dropped into a chair before the fire. Newman stared long and late into the blaze.

IX

HE called on Madame de Cintré the very next day, and learnt from the servant that she was at home. He passed as usual up the large cold staircase and through a spacious vestibule above, where the walls seemed all composed of small door-panels touched with long-faded gilding; whence he was ushered into the sitting-room in which he had already been received. It was empty, but the footman told him that Madame la Comtesse would presently appear. He had time, while he waited, to wonder if Bellegarde had seen his sister since the evening before and if in this case he had spoken to her of their talk. In that event Madame de Cintré's receiving him was not, as he would have said, a bucket of cold water. He felt a certain trepidation as he reflected that she might come in with the knowledge of his supreme admiration and of the project he had built on it in her eyes; but the apprehension conveyed no chill. Her face could wear no look that would make it less beautiful, and he was sure beforehand that, however she might take the proposal he had in reserve, she wouldn't make him pay for it in the least to his ruin. He had a belief that if she could only look at the bottom of his heart and see it all bared to the quick for her she would be entirely kind.

She came in at last, after so long an interval that he wondered if she had been hesitating. She smiled at him, as usual, without constraint, and her great mild eyes, while she held out her hand, seemed to shine at him perhaps even straighter than before. She then remarkably observed, without a tremor in her voice, that she was glad to see him and that she hoped he was well. He found in her what he had found before—that faint perfume of a personal diffidence worn away by contact with the world, but the more perceptible the more closely she was approached. This subtle shyness gave a peculiar value to what was definite and assured in her manner, making it an acquired accomplishment, a beautiful talent, something that one might compare to an exquisite touch in a pianist. It was, in fact, her 'authority', as they say of artists, that especially impressed and fascinated him; he always came back to the feeling that, when he should have rounded out his 'success' by the right big marriage, this was the way he should like his wife to express the size of it to the world. The only trouble indeed was that when the instrument was so perfect it seemed to interpose too much between the audience and the composer. She gave him, the charming woman, the sense of an elaborate education, of her having passed through mysterious ceremonies and processes of culture in her youth, of her having been fashioned and made flexible to certain deep social needs. All this, as I have noted, made her seem rare and precious—a very expensive article, as he would have said, and one which a man with an ambition to have everything about him of the best would taste of triumph in possessing. Yet looking at the matter with an eye to private felicity he asked himself where, in so exquisite a compound, nature and art showed their dividing-line. Where did the special intention separate from the habit of good manners? Where did fine urbanity end and fine sincerity begin? He indulged in these questions even while he stood ready to accept the admired object in all its complexity; he felt indeed he could do so in profound security, examining its mechanism afterwards and at leisure. 'I'm very glad to find you alone. You know I've never had such good luck before.'

'But you've seemed before very well contented with your luck,' said Madame de Cintré. 'You've sat and watched my visitors as comfortably as from a box at the opera. What have you thought of our poor performance?'

'Oh, I've thought the ladies very bright and very graceful, wonderfully quick at repartee. But what I've chiefly thought has been that they only help me to admire *you*.' This was not the habit of the pretty speech on Newman's part, the art of the pretty speech never having attained great perfection with him. It was simply the instinct of the practical man who had made up his mind to what he wanted and was now beginning to take active steps to obtain it.

She started slightly and raised her eyebrows; she had evidently not expected so straight an advance. 'Oh, in that case,' she none the less gaily said, 'your finding me alone isn't good luck for me. I hope some one will come in quickly.'

'I hope not,' Newman returned. 'I've something particular to say to you. Have you seen your brother Valentine?'

'Yes, I saw him an hour ago.'

'Did he tell you that he had seen me last night?'

'I think he spoke of it.'

'And did he tell you what we had talked about?'

She visibly hesitated. While Newman made these enquiries she had grown a little pale, as if taking what might impend for inevitable rather than convenient. 'Did you give him a message to me?'

'It was not exactly a message. I asked him to render me a service.'

'The service was to sing your praises, was it not?' She had been clearly careful to utter this question in the tone of trifling.

'Yes, that is what it really amounts to,' said Newman. '*Did* he therefore sing my praises?'

'He spoke very well of you. But when I know that it was by special request I must of course take his eulogy with a grain of salt.'

'Ah, that makes no difference,' Newman went on. 'Your brother wouldn't have spoken well of me unless he believed what he was saying. He's too honest for that.'

'Are you a great diplomatist?' She answered. 'Are you trying to please me by praising my brother? I confess it's a good way.'

'For me any way that succeeds will be good. I'll praise your brother all day if that will help me. I just love him, you know, and I regard him as perfectly straight. He has made me feel, in promising to do what he can to help me, that I can depend upon him.'

'Don't make too much of that,' said Madame de Cintré. 'He can help you very little.'

'Of course I must work my way myself. I know that very well; I only want a chance to. In consenting to see me, after what he told you, you almost seem to be giving me a chance.'

'I'm seeing you,' she slowly and gravely pronounced, 'because I promised my brother I would.'

'Blessings on your brother's head then!' Newman cried. 'What I told him last evening was this: that I admired you more than any woman I had ever seen and that I should like extraordinarily to make you my wife.' He spoke these words with great directness and firmness and without any sense of confusion. He was full of his idea, he had completely mastered it, and he seemed to look down on the woman he addressed, and on all her gathered graces, from the height of his bracing good conscience. It is probable that this particular tone and manner were the very best he could have adopted; yet the light, just visibly forced smile with which she had listened to him died away and she sat looking at him with her lips parted and her face almost as portentous as a tragic mask. There was evidently an inconvenience amounting to pain for her in this extravagant issue; her impatience of it, however, found no angry voice. Newman wondered if he were hurting her; he couldn't imagine why the liberal devotion he meant to express should be offensive. He got up and stood before her, leaning one hand on the chimney-piece. 'I know I've seen you very little to say this, so little that it may make what I say seem disrespectful. But that's my misfortune. I could have said it at the first time I saw you. Really I had seen you before; I had seen you in imagination; you seemed almost an old friend. So what I say, you can at least believe, is not mere grand talk in the air, an exaggerated compliment. I can't talk for any effect but one I want very much to bring about, and I wouldn't to you if I could. What I say is as serious as such words can be. I feel as if I knew you and knew how fine and rare and true you are. I shall know better perhaps some day, but I have a general notion now. You're just the woman I've been looking for, except that you're far more perfect. I won't make any protestations and vows, but you can trust me. It's very soon, I know, to say all this; it may almost shock you. But why not gain time if one can? And if you want time to reflect—as of course you'd do—the sooner you begin the better for me. I don't know what you think of me; but there's no great mystery, nor anything at all difficult to tell, about me—nor difficult to understand. Your brother told me that my antecedents and occupations will be against me; that your family has a social standing so high that I can't be taken as coming up to it. Well, I don't know about coming "up"—I don't think you can very well keep me *down*, anywhere. You can't make a man feel low unless you can make him feel base; and if you may fit yourself into any class you see your way to, you can't fit *him* where he won't go. But I don't believe you care anything about that. I can assure you there's quite enough of me to last, and that if I give my mind to it I can arrange things so that in a very few years I shall not need to waste time in explaining who I am and how much I matter. You'll decide for yourself if you like me or not. I honestly believe I've no hidden vices nor nasty tricks. I'm kind, kind, kind! Everything that a man can give a woman I'll give you. I've a large fortune, a very large fortune; some day, if you'll allow me, I'll go into details. If you want grandeur, everything in the way of grandeur that money can give you, why you shall have it. And as regards anything you may give up, don't take for granted too much that its place can't be filled. Leave that to me— I've filled some places. I'll take care of you; I shall know what you need. I wouldn't talk if I didn't believe I knew how. I want you to feel I'm strong, because if you do that will be enough. There; I have said what I had on my heart. It was better to get it off. I'm very sorry if it worries you; but the air's clearer—don't you already see? If I've made a mistake we had better not have met at all; and I can't think *that*, Madame de Cintré, can *you*?' Newman asked. 'Don't answer me now, if you don't wish it. Think about it; think about it only a little at a time, if you want. Of course I haven't said, I can't say, half I mean, especially about my admiration for you. But take a favourable view of me; it will only be just.'

During this speech, the longest personal plea, of any kind, that he had ever uttered in his life, she kept her gaze fixed on him, and it expanded at the last into a sort of fascinated stare. When he ceased speaking she lowered it and sat for some moments looking down and straight before her. Then she slowly rose to her feet, and a pair of exceptionally keen eyes would have made out in her an extraordinarily fine tremor. She still looked extremely serious. 'I'm very much obliged to you for your offer. It seems to me very strange, but I'm glad you spoke without waiting any longer. It's better the subject should be dismissed between us. I appreciate immensely all you say; you do me great honour. But I've decided not to marry.'

'Oh, don't say that!' cried Newman with the very innocence of pleading desire. She had turned away, and it made her stop a moment with her back to him. 'Think better of that. You're too young, too beautiful, too much made to be happy and to make others happy. If you're afraid of losing your freedom I can assure you that this freedom here, the life you now lead, is a dreary bondage to what I'll offer you. You shall do things that I don't think you've ever thought of. I'll take you to live anywhere in the wide world you may want. Are you unhappy? You give me a feeling that you *are* unhappy. You've no right to be, or to be made so. Let me come in and put an end to it.'

The young woman waited, but looking again all away from him. If she was touched by the way he spoke the thing was conceivable. His voice, always very mild, almost flatly soft and candidly interrogative for so full an organ, had become as edgeless and as tenderly argumentative as if he had been talking to a much-loved child, He stood watching her, and she presently turned again, but with her face not really meeting his own; and she spoke with a quietness in which there was a visible trace of effort. 'There are a great many reasons why I shouldn't marry—more, I beg you to believe, than I can explain to you. As for my happiness, I'm perfectly content. If I call your proposal "strange" it's also for more reasons than I can say. Of course you've a perfect right to make it. But I can't accept it—that's impossible. Please never speak of the matter again. If you can't promise me this I must ask you not to come back.'

'Why is it impossible?' he demanded with an insistence that came easily to him now. 'You may think it is at first without its really being so. I didn't expect you to be pleased at first, but I do believe that if you'll think of it a good while you may finally be satisfied.'

'I don't know you,' she returned after a moment. 'Think how little I know you!'

'Very little of course, and therefore I don't ask for your ultimatum on the spot. I only ask you not simply to put me off. I only ask you to let me "stay round", and by so doing to let me hope. I'll wait as long as ever you want. Meanwhile you can see more of me and know me better, look at me in the light—well, of my presumption, yes, but of other things too. You can make up your mind.'

Something was going on, rapidly, in her spirit; she was weighing a question there beneath his eyes, weighing it and deciding it. 'From the moment I don't very respectfully beg you to leave the house and never return I listen to you—I seem to give you hope. I *have* listened to you—against my judgement. It's because, you see, you're eloquent. Yes,' she almost panted, 'you touch me. If I had been told this morning that I should consent to consider you as a person wishing to come so very near me I should have thought my informant a little crazy. I *am* listening to you, you see!' And she threw her arms up for a moment and let them drop with a gesture in which there was just an expression of surrendering weakness.

'Well, as far as saying goes, I've said everything,' Newman replied. 'I believe in you without restriction, and I think all the good of you it's possible to think of a human creature. I firmly believe that in marrying me you'll be *safe*. As I said just now,' he went on with his smile as of hard experience, 'I've no bad ways. I can really *do* so much for you! And if you're afraid that I'm not what you've been accustomed to, not as refined and cultivated, or even as pleasant all round, as your standard requires, you may easily carry that too far. I *am* refined—I *am* pleasant. Just you try me!'

Claire de Cintré got still further away and paused before a great plant, an azalea, which flourished in a porcelain tub before her window. She plucked off one of the flowers and, twisting it in her fingers, retraced her steps. Then she sat down in silence, and her attitude seemed a consent that he should say more. She might almost be liking it.

'Why should you say it's impossible you should marry?' he therefore continued. 'The only thing that could make it really impossible would be your being already subject to that tie!—which must be awful, I admit, when it's only a grind. Is it because you've been unhappy in marriage? That's all the more reason. Is it because your family exert a pressure on you, interfere with you or worry you? That's still another reason: you ought to be perfectly free, and marriage will make you so. I don't say anything against your family— understand that!' added Newman with an eagerness which might have made a perspicacious witness smile. 'Whatever way you feel about them is the right way, and anything you should wish me to do to make myself agreeable to them I'll do as well as I know how. They may put me through what they like—I guess I shall hold out!'

She rose again and came to the fire near which he had hovered. The expression of pain and embarrassment had passed out of her face, and it had submitted itself with a kind of grace in which there might have been indeed a kind of art. She had the air of a woman who had stepped across the frontier of friendship and looks round her a little bewildered to find the spaces larger than those marked in her customary chart. A certain checked and controlled exaltation played through the charm of her dignity. 'I won't refuse to see you again, because much of what you've said has given me pleasure. But I will see you only on this condition: that you say nothing more in the same way for a long long time.'

'What do you mean by "long long"—?'

'Well, I mean six months. It must be a solemn promise.'

'Very good; I promise.'

'Good-bye then.' And she put out her hand.

He held it a moment as if to say more. But he only looked at her— 'long, long'; then he took his departure.

That evening, on the Boulevard, he met Valentin de Bellegarde. After they had exchanged greetings he told him he had seen his sister a few hours before.

'I know it, pardieu!' said Valentin. 'I dined *là-bas*.' With which, for some moments, both men were silent. Newman wished to ask what visible impression his visit had made, but the Count had a question of his own and he ended by speaking first. 'It's none of my business, but what the deuce did you say to Claire?'

'I'm quite willing to tell you I made her an offer of marriage.'

'Already!' And the young man gave a whistle. ' "Time is money!" Is that what you say in America? And my sister—?' he discreetly added.

'She didn't close with me.'

'She couldn't, you know, in that way.'

'But I'm to see her again,' said Newman.

'Oh, the strangeness of *ces dames*!' Then he stopped and held Newman off at arm's length. 'I look at you with respect! You've achieved what we call a personal success! Immediately, now, I must present you to my brother.'

'Whenever you like!' said Newman.

X

NEWMAN continued to see his other good friends with scarce-diminished frequency, though if you had listened to Mrs Tristram's account of the matter you would have supposed they had been cynically repudiated for the sake of grander acquaintance. 'We were all very well so long as we had no rivals—we were better than nothing. But now that you've become the fashion and have your pick every day of three invitations to dinner, we're tossed into the corner. I'm sure it is very good of you to come and see us once a month; I wonder you don't send us your cards in an envelope. When you do, pray have them with black edges; it will be for the death of my last illusion.' It was in this incisive strain she moralised over Newman's so-called neglect, which was in truth a most excellent constancy. Of course she was joking, but she embroidered with a sharp needle.

'I know no better proof that I've treated you very well,' Newman had said, 'than the fact that you make so free with my character. I've let you tweak my nose, I've allowed you the run of the animal's cage. If I had a little proper pride I'd stay away a while and, when you should ask me to dinner, say I'm going to Princess Borealska's. But I haven't any pride where my pleasure's concerned, and to keep you in the humour to see me—if you must see me only to call me bad names—I'll agree to anything you choose; I'll admit I'm the biggest kind of a sneak.' Newman in fact had declined an invitation person-ally given by the Princess Borealska, an enquiring Polish lady to whom he had been presented, on the ground that on that particular day he always dined at Mrs Tristram's; and it was only a tenderly perverse theory of his hostess of the Avenue d'Iéna that he was faith-less to his early friendships. She needed the theory to explain one of her fine exasperations. Having launched our hero on the current that was bearing him so rapidly along she felt but half-pleased at its swift-ness. She had succeeded too well; she had played her game too clev-erly and wished to mix up the cards. Newman had told her, in due season, that her friend was 'quite satisfactory'. The epithet was not romantic, but Mrs Tristram had no difficulty in perceiving that in essentials the feeling which lay beneath it was. Indeed the mild expansive brevity with which it was uttered, and a certain look, at once appealing and inscrutable, that issued from her guest's half-closed eyes as he leaned his head against the back of his chair, seemed to her the most eloquent attestation of a mature sentiment that she had ever encountered. He was only abounding in her own sense,* but his temperate raptures exerted a singular effect on that enthusiasm with which she had overflowed a few months before. She now seemed inclined to take a purely critical view of Madame de Cintré, and wished to have it understood that she didn't in the least pretend to have gone into a final analysis of her life, or in other words of her honesty. 'No woman'—she played with this idea—'can be so good as that one seems. Remember what Shakespeare calls Desdemona: "a supersubtle Venetian".* Claire de Cintré's a supersubtle Parisian. She's a charming creature and has five hundred merits; but you had better keep her supersubtlety in mind.' Was Mrs Tristram simply finding herself jealous of her special favourite on the other side of the Seine, so that in undertaking to provide Newman with an ideal wife she had counted too much on the lapse of her own passions and her immunity from wild yearnings? We may be permitted to doubt it. The inconsistent little lady of the Avenue d'Iéna had an insuperable need of intellectual movement, of critical, of ironic exercise. She had a lively imagination, and was capable at times of holding views, of entertaining beliefs, directly opposed to her most cherished opinions and convictions. She got tired of thinking right, but there was no serious harm in it, as she got equally tired of thinking wrong. In the midst of her mysterious perversities she had admirable flashes of justice. One of these occurred when Newman mentioned to her that he had made their beautiful friend a formal offer of his hand. He repeated in a few words what he had said, and in a great many what she had answered, and Mrs Tristram listened with extreme interest.

'But after all,' he admitted, 'there's nothing to congratulate me upon. It is not much of a triumph.'

'I beg your pardon; it's a great triumph. It's really dazzling that she didn't silence you at the first word and request you never to come near her again.'

'Well, she wouldn't have got much by that,' he made answer.

She looked at him a moment. 'No one, I think, gets as much by anything as you. When I told you to go your own way and do what came into your head I had no idea you'd go over the ground so fast. I never dreamed you'd propose after five or six morning calls. What had you done as yet to make her like you? You had simply sat—not very straight—and stared at her. But she does like you.'

'That remains to be seen.'

'No, it only remains to be criticised. What will come of it remains to be seen. That you should make but a mouthful of her marrying you without more ado could never have come into her head. You can form very little idea of what passed through her mind as you spoke; if she ever really takes you the affair will be marked by the usual justice of all human judgements of women. You'll think you take generous views of her, but you'll never begin to know through what a strange sea of feeling she'll have passed before accepting you. As she stood there in front of you the other day she plunged into it. She said "Well, why not?" to something that a few hours earlier had been inconceivable. She turned about on a thousand gathered prejudices and traditions as on a pivot and looked where she had never looked till that instant. When I think of it, when I think of Claire de Cintré and all that she represents, there seems to me something very fine in it. When I recommended you to try your fortune with her I of course thought well of you, and in spite of your base ingratitude I think so still. But I confess I don't see quite what you are and what you've done to make such a woman go these extravagant lengths for you.'

'Oh, there's something very fine in it!'—Newman laughed as he repeated her words. He took an extreme satisfaction in hearing that there was something very fine in it. He had not the least doubt of this himself, but he had already begun to value the world's view of his possible prize as adding to the prospective glory of possession.

It was immediately after this passage that Valentin de Bellegarde came to conduct his friend to the Rue de l'Université and present him to the other members of his family. 'You're already introduced and you've begun to be talked about. My sister has mentioned your successive visits to my mother, and it was an accident that my mother was present at none of them. I've spoken of you as an American of immense wealth, and the best fellow in the world, who's looking for something quite superior in the way of a wife.'

'Do you suppose,' asked Newman, 'that Madame de Cintré has reported to your mother the last conversation I had with her?'

'I'm very certain she hasn't; she'll keep her own counsel. Meanwhile,' Valentin said, 'you must make your way with the rest of the family. Thus much is known about you—that you've made a great fortune in trade, that you're a frank outsider and an honest eccentric, and that you furiously admire our charming Claire. My sister-in-law, whom you remember seeing in Claire's sitting-room, took, it appears, a marked fancy to you; she has described you as having *beaucoup de cachet*. My mother is therefore curious to see you.'

'She expects to laugh at me, eh?' said Newman.

'She never laughs—or at least never expects to. If she doesn't like you don't hope to purchase favour by being funny. I'm funny—take warning by *me*!'

This conversation took place in the evening, and half an hour later Valentin ushered his companion into an apartment of the house of the Rue de l'Université into which he had not yet penetrated, the salon of the dowager Marquise. It was a vast high room, with elaborate and ponderous mouldings, painted a whiteish grey, along the upper portion of the walls and the ceiling; with a great deal of faded and carefully-repaired tapestry in the doorways and chair-backs; with a Turkey carpet, in light colours, still soft and rich despite great antiquity, on the floor; and with portraits of each of Madame de Bellegarde's children at the age of ten suspended against an old screen of red silk. The dimness was diminished, exactly enough for conversation, by half a dozen candles placed in odd corners and at a great distance apart. In a deep armchair near the fire sat an old lady in black; at the other end of the room another person was seated at the piano and playing a very expressive waltz. In this latter person Newman recognised the younger Marquise.

Valentin presented his friend, and Newman came sufficiently near to the old lady by the fire to take in that she would offer him no hand-shake—so that he knew he had the air of waiting, and a little like a customer in a shop, to see what she *would* offer. He received a rapid impression of a white, delicate, aged face, with a high forehead, a small mouth and a pair of cold blue eyes which had kept much of the clearness of youth. Madame de Bellegarde looked hard at him and refused what she did refuse with a sort of British positiveness which reminded him that she was the daughter of the Earl of Saint Dunstans. Her daughter-in-law stopped playing and gave him an agreeable smile. He sat down and looked about him while Valentin went and kissed the hand of the young Marquise.

'I ought to have seen you before,' said Madame de Bellegarde. 'You've paid several visits to my daughter.'

'Oh yes,' Newman liberally smiled; 'Madame de Cintré and I are old friends by this time.'

'You've gone very fast,' she went on.

'Not so fast as I should like.'

'Ah, you're very ambitious,' the old woman returned.

'Well, if I don't know what I want by this time I suppose I never shall.'

Madame de Bellegarde looked at him with her cold fine eyes, and he returned her gaze, reflecting that she was a possible adversary and trying to take her measure. Their eyes remained for some moments engaged; then she looked away and, without smiling, 'I'm very ambitious too,' she said.

Newman felt that taking her measure was not easy; she was a formidable, inscrutable little woman. She resembled her daughter as an insect might resemble a flower. The colouring in Madame de Cintré was the same, and the high delicacy of her brow and nose was hereditary. But her face was a larger and freer copy, and her mouth in especial a happy divergence from that conservative orifice, a small pair of lips at once plump and pinched, that suggested, when closed, that they could scarce open wider than to swallow a gooseberry or to emit an 'Oh dear no!' and which had probably been thought to give the finishing touch to the aristocratic prettiness of the Lady Emmeline Atheling* as represented, half a century before, in several Books of Beauty.* Madame de Cintré's face had, to Newman's eye, a range of expression as delightfully vast as the wind-streaked, cloud-flecked distance on a Western prairie; but her mother's white, intense, respectable countenance, with its formal gaze and its circumscribed smile, figured a document signed and sealed, a thing of parchment, ink and ruled lines. 'She's a woman of conventions and proprieties,' he said to himself as he considered her; 'her world's the world of things immutably decreed. But how she's at home in it and what a paradise she finds it! She walks about in it as if it were a blooming park, a Garden of Eden; and when she sees "This is genteel" or "This is improper" written on a milestone she stops as ecstatically as if she were listening to a nightingale or smelling a rose.' Madame de Bellegarde wore a little black velvet hood tied under her chin and was wrapped in an old black cashmere shawl. 'You're an American?' she went on presently. 'I've seen several Americans.'

'There are several in Paris,' Newman jocosely said.

'Oh, really? It was in England I saw these, or somewhere else; not in Paris. I think it must have been in the Pyrenees many years ago. I'm told your ladies are very pretty. One of these ladies was very pretty—with such a wonderful complexion. She presented me a note of introduction from some one—I forget whom—and she sent with it a note of her own. I kept her letter a long time afterwards, it was so strangely expressed. I used to know some of the phrases by heart. But I've forgotten them now—it's so many years ago. Since then I've seen no more Americans. I think my daugher-in-law has; she's a great gadabout; she sees every one.'

At this the younger lady came rustling forward, pinching in a very slender waist and casting idly preoccupied glances over the front of her dress, which was apparently designed for a ball. She was, in a singular way, at once ugly and pretty; she had protuberant eyes and lips that were strangely red. She reminded Newman of his friend Mademoiselle Nioche; this was what that much-hindered young lady would have liked to be. Valentin de Bellegarde walked behind her at a distance, hopping about to keep off the far-spreading train of her dress. 'You ought to show more of the small of your back,' he said very gravely. 'You might as well wear a standing ruff as such a dress as that.'

The young woman turned to the mirror over the chimney-piece the part of her person so designated, and glanced behind her to verify this judgement. The mirror descended low and yet reflected nothing but a large unclad flesh-surface. Its possessor put her hands behind her and gave a downward pull to the waist of her dress. 'Like that, you mean?'

'That's a little better,' said Valentin in the same tone, 'but it leaves a good deal to be desired.'

'Oh, I never go to extremes.' And then turning to Madame de Bellegarde, 'What were you calling me just now, madame?' her daughter-in-law enquired.

'I called you a gadabout. But I might call you something else too.'

'A gadabout? What an ugly word! What does it mean?'

'A very beautiful lady,' Newman ventured to say, seeing that it was in French.

'That's a pretty compliment but a bad translation,' the young Marquise returned. After which, looking at him a moment: 'Do you dance?'

'Not a step.'

'You lose a great deal,' she said simply. And with another look at her back in the mirror she turned away.

'Do you like Paris?' asked the old lady, who was apparently wondering what was the proper way to talk to an American.

'I think that must be the matter with me,' he smiled. And then he added with a friendly intonation: 'Don't *you* like it?'

'I can't say I know it. I know my house—I know my friends—I don't know Paris.'

'You lose a great deal, as your daughter-in-law says,' Newman replied.

Madame de Bellegarde stared; it was presumably the first time she had been condoled with on her losses. 'I'm content, I think, with what I have,' she said with dignity. Her visitor's eyes were at this moment wandering round the room, which struck him as rather sad and shabby; passing from the high casements, with their small thickly-framed panes, to the sallow tints of two or three portraits in pastel, of the last century, which hung between them. He ought obviously to have answered that the contentment of his hostess was quite natural—she had so much; but the idea didn't occur to him during the pause of some moments which followed.

'Well, my dear mother,' said Valentin while he came and leaned against the chimney-piece, 'what do you think of my good friend? Isn't he the remarkably fine man I told you of?'

'My acquaintance with Mr Newman has not gone very far,' Madame de Bellegarde replied. 'I can as yet only appreciate his great politeness.'

'My mother's a great judge of these matters,' Valentin went on to Newman. 'If you've satisfied her it's a triumph.'

'I hope I shall satisfy you some day,' said Newman to the old lady. 'I've done nothing yet.'

'You mustn't listen to my son; he'll bring you into trouble. He's a sad scatterbrain,' she declared.

Newman took it genially. 'Oh, I've got to like him so that I can't do without him.'

'He amuses you, eh?'

'I think it must be that.'

'Do you hear that, Valentin?' said his mother. 'You exist for the amusement of Mr Newman.'

'Perhaps we shall all come to that!' Valentin exclaimed.

'You must see my other son,' she pursued. 'He's much better than this one. But he'll not amuse you.'

'I don't know—I don't know!' Valentin thoughtfully objected. 'But we shall very soon see. Here comes *monsieur mon frère*.' The door had just opened to give ingress to a gentleman who stepped forward and whose face Newman remembered as that of the author of his discomfiture the first time of his calling. Valentin went to meet his brother, looked at him a moment and then, taking him by the arm, led him up to their guest. 'This is my excellent friend Mr Newman,' he said very blandly. 'You must know him if you can.'

'I'm delighted to know Mr Newman,' said the Marquis with an unaccompanied salutation.

'He's the old woman at second-hand,' Newman reflected with the sense of having his health drunk from an empty glass. And this was the starting-point of a speculative theory, in his mind, that the late head of this noble family had been a very amiable foreigner with an inclination to take life easily and a sense that it was difficult for the husband of the stilted little lady by the fire to do so. But if he had found small comfort in his wife he had found much in his two younger children, who were after his own heart, while Madame de Bellegarde had paired with her eldest-born.

'My brother has spoken to me of you,' said M. de Bellegarde, 'and as you are also acquainted with my sister it was time we should meet.' He turned to his mother and gallantly bent over her hand, touching it with his lips; after which he assumed a position before the chimney-piece. With his long lean face, his high-bridged nose and small opaque eyes he favoured, in the old phrase, the English strain in his blood. His whiskers were fair and glossy and he had a large dimple, of unmistakeable British origin, in the middle of his handsome chin. He was 'distinguished' to the tips of his polished nails, and there was not a movement of his fine perpendicular person that was not noble and majestic. Newman had never yet been confronted with such an incarnation of the maintained attitude; he felt himself in presence of something high and unusual.

'Urbain,' said young Madame de Bellegarde, who had apparently been waiting for her husband to take her to her ball, 'I call your attention to the fact that I'm dressed.'

'That's a good idea—to show what you claim for it,' Valentin commented.

'I'm at your orders, dear friend,' said M. de Bellegarde. 'Only you must allow me first the pleasure of a little conversation with Mr Newman.'

'Oh, if you're going to a party don't let me keep you; I'm so sure we shall meet again. Indeed if you'd like to meet me I'll gladly name an hour.' He was eager to make it known that he would readily answer all questions and satisfy all exactions.

M. de Bellegarde stood in a well-balanced position before the fire, caressing one of his fair whiskers with one of his white hands and looking at our friend, half-askance, with eyes from which a particular ray of observation made its way through a general meaningless smile. 'It's very kind of you to make such an offer. If I'm not mistaken your occupations are such as to make your time precious. You're in—a—as we say—a—*dans les affaires?*'

'In business, you mean? Oh no, I've thrown business overboard for the present. I'm regularly "loafing", as *we* say. My time's quite my own.'

'Ah, you're taking a holiday,' rejoined M. de Bellegarde. '"Loafing." Yes, I've heard that expression.'

'Mr Newman's a distinguished American,' Madame de Bellegarde observed.

'My brother's a great ethnologist,' said Valentin.

'An ethnologist?'—and Newman groped for gaiety. 'You collect negroes' skulls and that sort of thing?'

The Marquis looked hard at his brother and began to caress his other whisker. Then turning to their new acquaintance with sustained urbanity: 'You're travelling for pure recreation?'

'Well, I'm visiting your country, sir,' Newman replied with a certain conscious patience—a patience he felt he on his side too could push, should need be, to stiffness; 'and I confess I'm having a good time in it. Of course I get a good deal of pleasure out of it.'

'What more especially interests you?' the Marquis benevolently pursued.

'Well,' our friend continued, 'the life of the people, for one thing, interests me. Your people are very taking. But economically, technically, as it were, manufactures are what I care most about.'

'Those—a—products have been your speciality?'

'I can't say I have had any speciality. My speciality has been to accumulate the largest convenient competency in the shortest possible time.' Newman made this last remark very designedly and deliberately; he wished to open the way, should it be necessary, to an authoritative statement of his means.

'M. de Bellegarde laughed agreeably. 'I hope you enjoy the sense of that success.'

'Oh, one has still, at my age, the sense also of what's left to do. I'm not so very old,' our hero candidly explained.

'Well, Paris is a very good place to spend a fortune. I wish you all the advantages of yours.' And M. de Bellegarde drew forth his gloves and began to put them on.

Newman for a few moments watched him sliding his fair, fat hands into the pearly kid, and as he did so his feelings took a singular turn. M. de Bellegarde's good wishes seemed to flutter down on him from the cold upper air with the soft, scattered movement of a shower of snowflakes. Yet he was not irritated; he didn't feel that he was being patronised; he was conscious of no especial impulse to introduce a discord into so noble a harmony. Only he felt himself suddenly in personal contact with the forces with which his so valued backer had told him that he would have to contend, and he became sensible of their intensity. He wished to make some answering manifestation, to stretch himself out at his own length, to sound a note at the uttermost end of *his* scale. It must be added that if this impulse was neither vicious nor malicious, it was yet by no means unattended by the play in him of his occasional disposition to ironic adventure. He hated the idea of shocking people, he respected the liability to be shocked. But there were impressions that threw him back, after all, on his own measures of proportion. 'Paris', he presently remarked, 'is a very good place for people who take a great deal of stock, as we say, *in* their location, and want to be very much aware of it all the time; or it's a very good place if your family has been settled here for a long time and you've made acquaintances and got your relations round you; or if you've got a big house like this and a wife and children and mother and sister—everything right there. I don't like that way that prevails in many of your districts of people's living all in rooms door to door with each other. But I'm not, as I may put it, a *natural*, a real inspired loafer. I'm a poor imitation and it goes against the grain. My business habits are too deep-seated. Then I haven't any house to call my own or anything in the way of a family. My sisters are five thousand miles away, my mother died when I was pretty small, and I haven't what a man has when he has taken the regular way to get it—if I express myself clearly; and I often miss *that* pleasantness very much. So you see I'm sometimes rather conscious of a void. I'm not proficient in literature, as you are, sir, and I get tired of dining out and going to the opera. I miss my business activity. You see I began to earn my living when I was almost a baby, and until a few months ago I've never had my hand off the plough. I miss the regular call on my attention.'

This speech was followed by a profound silence of some moments on the part of Newman's entertainers. Valentin stood looking at him fixedly, hands in pockets, and then slowly, with a half-sidling motion, went out of the room. The Marquis continued to draw on his gloves and to smile benignantly. 'You began to earn your living in the cradle?' said the old Marquise, who appeared to wish to encourage, a little grimly, yet not wholly without an effect of pleasantry, her guest's autobiographic strain.

'Well, madam, I'm not absolutely convinced I *had* a cradle!'

'You say you're not proficient in literature,' M. de Bellegarde resumed; 'but you must do yourself the justice to remember that your studies were interrupted early.'

'That's very true; on my tenth birthday my schooling stopped short. I thought that a grand way to keep it. Still, I *have* picked up knowledge,' Newman smiled.

'You have some sisters?' Madame de Bellegarde enquired.

'Yes, two splendid sisters. I wish you knew *them*!'

'I hope that for *ces dames* the hardships of life commenced less early.'

'They married very early indeed, if you call that a hardship—as girls do in our Western country. The husband of one of them is the owner of the largest india-rubber house in the West.'

'Ah, you make houses also of india-rubber?' the Marquise asked.

'You can stretch them as your family increases,' said her daughter-in-law, now enveloped in a soft shining cape. Newman indulged at this in a burst of hilarity and explained that the house in which his relatives lived was a large wooden structure, but that they manufactured and sold india-rubber on a colossal scale. 'My children have some little india-rubber shoes which they put on when they go to play in the Tuileries* in damp weather,' the young Marquise accordingly pursued. 'I wonder if your brother-in-law made them.'

'I guess he did,—and *if* he did you may be very sure you've got a good article.'

'Well, you mustn't be too much discouraged,' said M. de Bellegarde with vague benevolence.

'Oh, I don't mean to be. I've a project—really a grand one—which gives me plenty to think about, and that's an occupation.' And then Newman waited, hesitating yet debating rapidly; he wished again to get near his point, though to do so forced him to depart still further from the form of not asking favours. He *had* to ask that of their attention. 'Nevertheless,' he continued, addressing himself to old Madame de Bellegarde, 'I'll tell you my great idea; perhaps you can help me. I want not only to marry, but to marry remarkably well.'

'It's a very good project, but I never made a match in all my life,' said his hostess with her odd mincing plainness.

Newman looked at her an instant and then all sincerely, 'I should have thought you a great hand,' he declared.

Madame de Bellegarde might well have thought him too sincere. She murmured something sharply in French and fixed her eyes on her son. At this moment the door of the room was thrown open, and with a rapid step Valentin reappeared. 'I've a message for you,' he said to his sister-in-law. 'Claire bids me ask you not to start for your ball. If you'll wait a minute she'll go with you.'

'Claire will go with us?' cried the young Marquise. '*En voilà du nouveau!*'

'She has changed her mind; she decided half an hour ago and is sticking the last diamond into her hair!' said Valentin.

'What on earth has taken possession of my daughter?' Madame de Bellegarde asked with a coldness of amazement. 'She has not been this age where any candle was lighted. Does she take such a step at half an hour's notice and without consulting me?'

'She consulted me, dear mother, five minutes since,' said Valentin, 'and I told her that such a beautiful woman—she's more beautiful than ever, you'll see—has no right to bury herself alive.'

'You should have referred Claire to her mother, my brother,' said M. de Bellegarde in French. 'This is not the way—!'

'I refer her to the whole company!' Valentin broke in. 'Here she comes!'—and he went to the open door, met Madame de Cintré on the threshold, took her by the hand and led her into the room. She was dressed in white, but a cloak of dark blue, which hung almost to her feet, was fastened across her shoulders by a silver clasp. She had tossed it back, however, and her long white arms were uncovered. In her dense fair hair there glittered a dozen diamonds. She looked serious and, Newman thought, rather pale; but she glanced round her and, when she saw him, smiled and put out her hand. He thought her at this moment far and away the handsomest woman he had ever seen. He had a chance to look her full in the face, for she stood a little in the centre of the room, where she seemed to consider what she should do, without meeting his eyes. Then she went up to her mother, who sat in the deep chair by the fire with an air of immeasurable detachment. Her back turned to the others, Madame de Cintré held her cloak apart to show her dress.

'What do you think of me?'

'I think you seem to have lost your head. It was but three days ago, when I asked you as a particular favour to myself to go to the Duchesse de Lusignan's, that you told me you were going nowhere and that one must be consistent. Is this your consistency? Why should you distinguish Madame Robineau? Who is it you wish to please to-night?'

'I wish to please myself, dear mother,' said Madame de Cintré. And she bent over and kissed the old lady.

'I don't like violent surprises, my sister,' said Urbain de Bellegarde; 'especially when one's on the point of entering a drawing-room.'

Newman at this juncture felt inspired to speak. 'Oh, if you're going anywhere with this lady you needn't be afraid of being noticed yourself!'

M. de Bellegarde turned to his sister with an intense little glare. 'I hope you appreciate a compliment that's paid at your brother's expense. *Venez donc*, madame.' And offering Madame de Cintré his arm he led her rapidly out of the room. Valentin rendered the same service to young Madame de Bellegarde, who had apparently been reflecting on the fact that the ball-dress of her sister-in-law was much less brilliant than her own, and yet had failed to derive absolute comfort from the reflexion. With a leave-taking smile she sought the complement of her consolation in the eyes of the American visitor, and, perceiving in them an almost unnatural glitter, not improbably may have flattered herself she had found it.

Newman, left alone with his hostess, if she might so be called, stood before her a few moments in silence. 'Your daughter's very beautiful,' he said at last.

'She's very perverse,' the old woman returned.

'I'm glad to hear it,' he smiled. 'It makes me hope.'

'Hope what?'

'That she'll consent some day to marry me.'

She slowly got up. 'That really is your "great idea"?'

'Yes. Will you give it any countenance?'

Madame de Bellegarde looked at him hard and shook her head. Then her so peculiarly little mouth rounded itself to a 'No!' which she seemed to blow at him as for a mortal chill.

'Will you then just let me alone with my chance?'

'You don't know what you ask. I'm a very proud and meddlesome old person.'

'Well, I'm very rich,' he returned with a world of desperate intention.

She fixed her eyes on the floor, and he thought it probable she was weighing the reasons in favour of resenting his so calculated directness. But at last looking up, 'How rich?' she simply articulated.

He gave her, at this, the figure of his income—gave it in a round number which had the magnificent sound that large aggregations of dollars put on when translated into francs. He added to the enunciation of mere brute quantity certain financial particulars which completed a sufficiently striking presentment of his resources.

Madame de Bellegarde had let him enjoy her undisguised attention. 'You're very frank,' she finally said, 'and I'll be the same. I would rather, on the whole, get all the good of you there is—rather, I mean, than, as you call it, let you alone. I would rather,' she coldly smiled, 'take you in our way than in your way. I think it will be easier.'

'I'm thankful for any terms,' Newman quite radiantly answered. 'It's enough for me to feel I'm taken. But it needn't be, for you,' he at the same time rather grimly laughed, 'in too big doses to begin with. Good-night!'—and he rapidly quitted her.

XI

HE had not, on his return to Paris, resumed the study of French conversation with M. Nioche; he had been conscious of too many other uses for his time. That amiable man, however, came to see him very promptly, having ascertained his whereabouts by some art of curiosity too subtle to be challenged. He repeated his visit more than once; he seemed oppressed by an humiliating sense of having been overpaid, and wished apparently to redeem his debt by the offer of grammatical and statistical information in small instalments. He exhaled the same decent melancholy as a few months before; a few months more or less of brushing could make little difference in the antique lustre of his coat and hat. But his spirit itself was a trifle more threadbare; it had clearly received some hard rubs during the summer. Newman asked with interest about Mademoiselle Noémie, and M. Nioche at first, for answer, simply looked at him in lachrymose silence.

'Don't press me on that subject, sir. I sit and watch her, but I can do nothing.'

'Do you mean she gives you serious cause—?'

'I don't know, sir, *what* I mean! I can't follow her. I don't understand her. She has something in her head; who can say what's in the head of a little person so independent, so dreadful—and so pleasing? She's too deep for her poor papa.'

'Does she continue to go to the Musée? Has she made any of those copies for me?' Newman continued.

'She goes to the Musée, but I see nothing of the copies. She has something on her easel; I suppose it's one of the pictures you ordered. Such a splendid commission ought to give her fairy fingers. But she's not in earnest. I can't say anything to her; I'm afraid of her, if you must know. One evening last summer when I took her to walk in the Champs Elysées she said to me things that made me turn cold.'

'And what things?'

'Excuse an unhappy father from telling you,' said M. Nioche while he unfolded his calico pocket-handkerchief.

Newman promised himself to pay Mademoiselle Noémie another visit at the Louvre. He was curious of the progress of his copies, but it must be added that he was still more curious of the personal progress of the copyist. He went one afternoon to the great museum, but wandered through several of the rooms without finding her; after which, on his way to the long hall of the Italian masters,* he stopped face to face with Valentin de Bellegarde. The young Frenchman eagerly greeted him, assuring him he was a godsend. He himself was in the worst of humours and wanted some one to contradict. 'In a bad humour among all these beautiful things? I thought you were so fond of pictures, especially the grand old black ones,' Newman said. 'There are two or three here that ought to keep you in spirits.'

'Oh, to-day,' Valentin returned, 'I'm not in a mood for gimcracks, and the more remarkable they are the less I like them. The great staring eyes and fixed positions of all these dolls and mannikins irritate me. I feel as if I were at some big dull party, a roomful of people I shouldn't wish to speak to. What should I care for their beauty? It's a bore and, worse still, it's a reproach. I've a *tas d'ennuis*. I feel damnably vicious.'

'If this grand sight works you up so why do you expose yourself?' Newman asked with his quiet play of reason.

'That's one of my worries. I came to meet my cousin—a dreadful English cousin, a member of my mother's family—who's in Paris for a week with her husband and who wishes me to point out the "principal beauties". Imagine a woman who wears a green crape bonnet in December and has straps sticking out of the ankles of her interminable boots! My mother begged I would do something to oblige them. I've undertaken to play *valet de place* this afternoon. They were to have met me here at two o'clock, and I've been waiting for them twenty minutes. Why doesn't she arrive? She has at least a pair of feet to carry her. I don't know whether to be furious at their playing me false or to toss up my hat for the joy of escaping them.'

'I think in your place I'd be furious,' said Newman, 'because they may arrive yet, and then your fury will still be of use to you. Whereas if you were delighted and they were afterwards to turn up, you mightn't know what to do—well, with your hat.'

'You give me excellent advice, and I already feel better. I'll be furious; I'll let them go to the deuce and I myself will go with *you*— unless by chance you too have a rendezvous.'

'It's not exactly a rendezvous,' Newman returned. 'But I've in fact come to see a person, not a picture.'

'A woman, presumably?'

'A young lady.'

'Well,' said Valentin, 'I hope for you, with all my heart, that she's not clothed in green tulle* and that her feet are not too much out of focus.'

'I don't know much about her feet, but she has very pretty hands.'

The young man breathed all his sadness. 'And on that assurance I must part with you?'

'I'm not certain of finding my young lady,' said Newman, 'and I'm not quite prepared to lose your company on the chance. It doesn't strike me quite as good business to introduce you to her, and yet I should rather like to have your opinion of her.'

'Is she formed to please?'

'Well, I guess you'll think so.'

Valentin passed his arm into that of his companion. 'Conduct me to her on the instant! I should be ashamed to make a pretty woman wait for my verdict.'

Newman suffered himself to be gently propelled in the direction in which he had been walking, but his step was not rapid. He was turning something over in his mind. The two men passed into the long gallery of the Italian masters, and our friend, after having scanned for a moment its brilliant vista, turned aside into the smaller apartment devoted to the same school on the left.* It contained very few persons, but at the further end of it Mademoiselle Nioche sat before her easel. She was not at work; her palette and brushes had been laid down beside her, her hands were folded in her lap and she had relapsed into her seat to look intently at two ladies on the other side of the hall, who, with their backs turned to her, had stopped before one of the pictures. These ladies were apparently persons of high fashion, they were dressed with great splendour and their long silken trains and furbelows were spread over the polished floor. It was on their dresses the young woman had fixed her eyes, though what she was thinking of I am unable to say. I hazard the hypothesis of her mutely remarking that to carry about such a mass of ponderable pleasure would surely be one of the highest uses of freedom. Her reflections, at any rate, were disturbed by the advent of her unannounced visitors, whom, as she rose and stood before her easel, she greeted with a precipitation of eye and lip that was like the glad clap of a pair of hands.

'I came here on purpose to see you—*seulement vous*, expray, expray,'* Newman said in his fairest, squarest, distinctest French. And then, like a good American, he introduced Valentin formally: 'Allow me to make you acquainted with Comte Valentin de Bellegarde.'

Valentin made a bow which must have seemed to her quite in harmony with the impressiveness of his title, but the graceful brevity of her response was a negation of underbred surprise. She turned to her generous patron, putting up her hands to her hair and smoothing its delicately-felt roughness. Then, rapidly, she turned the canvas that graced her easel over on its face. 'You've not forgotten me?'

'I shall never forget you. You may be sure of that.'

'Oh,' she protested, 'there are a great many different ways of remembering a person.' And she looked straight at the Comte de Bellegarde, who was looking at her as a gentleman may when a verdict is expected of him.

'Have you painted me a pretty picture?' Newman went on. 'Have you shown *beaucoup d'industrie*?'

'No, I've done nothing.' And, taking up her palette, she began to mix her colours at random.

'But your father tells me your attendance has been regular.'

'I've nowhere else to go! Where do you suppose, cher monsieur —? Here, all summer, one could breathe at least.'

'Being here then,' said Newman, 'don't you think you might have tried something?'

'I told you before,' she sweetly answered, 'that I haven't the advantage of knowing how to paint.'

'But you've something of interest on your easel now,' Valentin gaily objected, 'if you'd only let me see it.'

She spread out her two hands, with the fingers expanded, over the back of the canvas—those hands which Newman had called pretty and which, in spite of several little smudges of colour, Valentin could now admire. 'My painting isn't of interest.'

'It's the only thing about you that is not, then, mademoiselle,' the young man gallantly returned.

She took up her shamefaced study and silently passed it to him. He looked at it, and in a moment she said: 'I'm sure you're a great judge.'

'Yes,' he admitted; 'I recognise merit.'

'Only when it's there, I hope! I've given up,' she bravely declared, 'trying to have it.'

He faced her, with a smile, over her demoralised little daub. 'If one hasn't one sort one can always have another.'

She considered with downcast eyes—which, however, she presently raised. 'We're talking of the sort of which you're a judge.' Then, as to anticipate too obvious a rejoinder, she turned, for more urgent good manners, to Newman. 'Where have you been all these months? You took those great journeys, you amused yourself well?'

'Oh yes,' our hero returned—'always beaucoup, beaucoup!'

'Ah, so much the better.' She spoke with charming unction and, having taken back her canvas from Valentin, who meanwhile had looked at his friend with eyes of rich meaning, began again to dabble in her colours. She was singularly pretty, with the look of serious sympathy she threw into her face. 'Tell me,' she continued, 'a little of all you've done.'

'Oh, I went to Switzerland—to Geneva and Zermatt and Zürich and all those places, you know; and down to Venice, and all through Germany, and down the Rhine, and into Holland and Belgium—the regular round. How do you say that in French—the regular round?' Newman asked of Valentin.

Mademoiselle Nioche fixed her eyes an instant on their companion, and then with all the candour of her appeal: 'I don't understand monsieur when he says so much at once. Would you be so good as to translate?'

'I'd rather talk to you out of my own head,' Valentin boldly declared.

'No,' said Newman gravely, still in his formal French, 'you mustn't talk to Mademoiselle Nioche, because you say discouraging things. You ought to tell her to work, to persevere.'

'And we Parisians, mademoiselle,' the young man exclaimed, 'are accused of paying hollow compliments and of being false flatterers!'

'Ah, I don't want any compliments,' the girl protested, 'I want only the cruel truth. But if I didn't know it by this time—!'

'I utter no truth more cruel,' Valentin returned, 'than that there are probably many things you *can* do very well.'

'Oh, I can at least do *this*!' And dipping a brush into a clot of red paint she drew a great horizontal daub across her unfinished picture.

'What are you making that mark for?' Newman asked with his impartial interest.

Without answering, she drew another long crimson daub, in a vertical direction, down the middle of her canvas and so in a moment completed the rough indication of a cross. 'It's the sign of the cruel truth.'

The two men looked at each other, Valentin as with vivid intelligence. 'You've spoiled my picture,' said his friend.

'I know that very well. It was the only thing to do with it. I had sat looking at it all day without touching it. I had begun to hate it. It seemed to me something was going to happen.'

'I like it better that way than as it was before,' said Valentin. 'Now it's more interesting. It tells a little story now. Is it for sale, mademoiselle?'

'Everything I have is for sale,' she promptly replied.

'How much then is this object?'

'Ten thousand francs—and very cheap!'

'Everything mademoiselle may do at present is mine in advance,' Newman interposed. 'It makes part of an order I gave her some months ago. So you can't have that!'

'Monsieur will lose nothing by it,' said mademoiselle with her charming eyes on Valentin. And she began to put up her utensils.

'I shall have gained an ineffaceable memory,' Valentin smiled. 'You're going away? your day's over?'

'My father comes to fetch me,' the young lady replied.

She had hardly spoken when, through the door behind her, which opens on one of the great white stone staircases of the Louvre, M. Nioche made his appearance. He came in with his usual patient shuffle, indulging in a low salute to the gentlemen who had done him the honour to gather about his daughter. Newman shook his hand with muscular friendliness and Valentin returned his greeting with high consideration. While the old man stood waiting for Noémie to make a parcel of her implements he let his mild oblique gaze play over this new acquaintance, who was watching her put on her bonnet and mantle. Valentin was at no pains to disguise the benevolence of his own interest. He looked at a pretty person as he would have listened to a good piece of music. Intelligent participation was in such a case simple good manners. M. Nioche at last took his daughter's paintbox in one hand and the bedaubed canvas, after giving it a solemn puzzled stare, in the other, and led the way to the door. Noémie followed him after making her late interlocutors the formal obeisance of the perfectly-educated female young.

'Well,' said Newman, 'what do you think of her?'

'She's very remarkable. *Diable, diable, diable!*' his friend reflectively repeated; 'she's the perfection of the type.'

'I'm afraid she's a sad little trifler,' Newman conscientiously remarked.

'Not a little one—rather an immense one. She has all the material.' And Valentin began to walk slowly off, looking vaguely, though with eyes now so opened, at the pictures on the walls. Nothing could have appealed to his imagination more than the possible futility of a young lady so equipped for futility. 'She's very interesting,' he went on. 'Yes, the type shines out in her.'

' "The type"? The type of what?'

'Well, of soaring, of almost sublime ambition! She's a very bad little copyist, but, endowed with the artistic sense in another line, I suspect her none the less of a strong feeling for her great originals.'

Newman wondered, but presently followed. 'Surely her great originals will have had more beauty.'

'Not always. She has enough to look as if she had more, and that's always plenty. It's a face and figure in which everything tells. If she were prettier she would be less intelligent, and her intelligence is half her charm.'

'In what way does her intelligence strike you as so remarkable?' asked Newman, at once puzzled, impressed and vaguely scandalised by his friend's investment of such a subject with so much of the dignity of demonstration.

'She has taken the measure of life, and she has determined to *be* something—to succeed at any cost. Her smearing of colours is of course a mere trick to gain time. She's waiting for her chance; she wishes to launch herself, and to do it *right*. Nobody, my dear man, can ever have *had* such a love of the right. She knows her Paris. She's one of fifty thousand, so far as her impatiences and appetites go, but I'm sure she has an exceptional number of ideas.'

Newman raised his strong eyebrows. 'Are you also sure they're really good ones?'

'Ah, "good, good"!' cried Valentin: 'you people are too wonderful with your goodness. Good for what, please—? They'll be excellent,

I warrant, for some things! They'll be much better than the hopeless game she has just given up. They'll be good enough to make her, I dare say, one of the celebrities of the future.'

'Lord o' mercy, you *have* sized her up! But don't—I must really ask it of you—let her quite run away with you,' Newman went on. 'I shall owe it to her good old father not to have upset her balance. For he's a real nice man.'

'Oh, oh, oh, her good old father!' Valentin incorrigibly mocked. And then as his companion looked grave: 'He expects her to assure his future.'

'I thought he rather expected *me!* And don't you judge him, as a friend of mine,' Newman asked, 'too cruelly? He's as poor as a rat, but very high-toned.'

'Why, mon cher, I should adore his tone, and you're right to do the same: it's much better than mine, and he'll do you more good as a companion, he'll protect your innocence better, than ever I shall. I don't mean,' Valentin explained, 'that he wouldn't much rather his daughter were a good girl, that she remained as "nice"—as worthy, that is, say, of your particular use—as he may himself remain. But all the same he won't, if the worst comes to the worst—well, he won't do what Virginius* did. He doesn't want her to be a failure—as why should he?—and if she isn't a failure it's plain she'll be a success. On the whole he has confidence.'

'He has touching fears, sir—I admit he has betrayed *them* to me.' Newman felt himself loyally concerned to defend a character that had struck him as pleasingly complete—though completeness was, after all, what Valentin also claimed for it. The difference was in their view of that picturesque grace, and Newman would, to an appreciable degree, have sentimentally suffered from not being able to keep Monsieur Nioche before him as he had first seen him. He was, to an extent he never fully revealed, a collector of impressions as romantically concrete, even when profane, as the blest images and sanctified relics of one of the systematically devout, and he at bottom liked as little to hear anything he had picked up with the hand of the spirit pronounced unauthentic. 'I don't quite remember what Virginius did,' he presently pursued, 'and I don't say for certain that my old friend would shoot. He doesn't affect me—no—as a shooting man. But I guess he wouldn't want to *make* very much out of anything.'

'Then he'll be very different,' Valentin laughed, 'from any of the rest of his species! Why, my dear fellow, we all here in Paris want to make as much as possible out of everything. That's how we differ, I conceive, from the people of *your* country: the objects of your exploitation appear to be fewer, and above all of fewer kinds. I don't mind telling you,' he declared in the same tone, 'that I don't see the end of what I might be capable of making out of *this*.'

'Of "this"—?'

'Of the relation of Monsieur Nioche to his daughter, and of the relation of his daughter to—well, to as many other persons as you like!'

'I shan't at all like *you* to be one of them,' Newman still gravely returned. 'I didn't ask you to come round with me just to set you after her.'

The young man appeared for an instant embarrassed. 'Do you object then to her having engaged my enlightened curiosity?'

Newman considered. 'Well, no—since, from the moment I recognise she'll never deliver my goods I don't quite see where I stand or how I can improve her.'

'Oh, you certainly can't improve her!' Valentin gaily cried.

Newman looked at him a moment. 'I should like then to improve *you*. I guess at any rate you had better leave her alone.'

'Oh, oh, oh!' his companion exclaimed, at this, with an accent that made him pull up. 'Do you mean, my dear fellow, that you warn me off?'

They had stopped a minute before, and he stood there staring. 'Hanged if I don't believe you suppose I'm afraid of you!'

Valentin had given a cock to his moustache, and he stroked it an instant, meeting this exclamation with a glance of some ambiguity and a smile just slightly strained. 'Oh, I shouldn't put it that way: you don't even yet know me enough to fear me! Which gives you the advantage—for you've yourself attitudes that, I confess, make me tremble. I think you're afraid, at most,' he continued, 'of my bad example.'

Newman had again—for he had had it before—a strange fine sense of something he would have called, in relation to this brilliant friend, the waste of animadversion. It was somehow one with the accepted economic need of keeping him pleasantly in view. Even to argue with him was somehow to misuse a luxury, and to think of him as perverse was somehow to miss an occasion. No one had ever given him that impression, which he might have compared to the absolute plea-sure, for the palate, of wine of the highest savour. One didn't put anything 'into' such a vintage and there was a way of handling the very bottle. The grace of him, of Valentin, was all precious, the growth of him all fortunate, the quantity of him elsewhere all doubt-less limited. 'I *might* perhaps have been a factor in that young lady's moral future,' Newman presently said—'but I don't come in now. And evidently,' he added 'you've no room for me in yours.'

The young man gave a laugh, and the next moment, arm in arm, they had resumed their walk. 'Oh, on the contrary,' Valentin then replied; 'since what I want, precisely, is to keep it spacious and capa-cious—at least on the scale, if you please, of my moral past; which indeed seems to me, when I look back on it, as boundless as the desert. It's a prospect that, at all events, such figures as you and your wonderful friends help to people. And I may say about *them*,' he went on, 'that I should like really—in the interest of the impression that I confess the young lady makes on me—to propose to you a fair agreement.'

On which, amusedly enough, Newman debated as they went. 'That I shall shut my eyes to what you want to do?'

'Well, yes—say I may expect you'll shut them to me as soon as I shall find you've opened them to the grand manner in which your old gentleman *is* a man of the world. You'll be obliged, I'm con-vinced, to recognise it, and I only ask you to let me know, in all honesty, when you've done so.'

'So that *you*, in all honesty—?'

'Well, call it in all delicacy!' Valentin suggested.

Newman continued to wonder. 'May have a free hand—?'

'Without your being shocked,' the young man gracefully said.

But it only made our friend rather quaintly groan. 'I think it's your delicacies, all round, that shock me most!'

'Ah, don't say,' Valentin pleaded, 'that I'm not at the worst a man of duty! See for yourself!' His English cousins had come into view, and he advanced gallantly to meet the lady in the green crape bonnet.

XII

COMING in toward evening, three days after his introduction to the family of Madame de Cintré, Newman found on his table the card of the Marquis de Bellegarde. On the following day he received a note informing him that this gentleman's mother requested the pleasure of his company at dinner. He went of course, though he had first to disengage himself from appeals that struck him as in comparison the babble of vain things. He was ushered into the room in which Madame de Bellegarde had received him before, and here he found his venerable hostess surrounded by her entire family. The room was lighted only by the crackling fire, which illumined the very small pink shoes of a lady who, from a low chair, stretched out her toes to it. This lady was the younger Madame de Bellegarde, always less effectively present, somehow, than perceptibly posted. Madame de Cintré, not posted at all, but oh so present, was seated at the other end of the room, holding a little girl against her knee, the child of her brother Urbain, to whom she was apparently relating a wonderful story. Valentin had perched on a puff* close to his sister-in-law, into whose ear he was certainly distilling the finest nonsense. The Marquis was stationed before the chimney, his head erect and his hands behind him in an attitude of formal expectancy.

The old Marquise stood up to give Newman her greeting, and there was that in the way she did so which seemed to measure narrowly the quantity of importance such a demonstration might appear to attach to him. 'We're all alone, you see; we've asked no one else,' she said austerely.

'I'm very glad you didn't; this is much more sociable. I wish you good-evening, sir'—and Newman offered his hand to the Marquis.

M. de Bellegarde was affable, yet in spite of his dignity was restless. He changed his place, fidgeted about, looked out of the long windows, took up books and laid them down again. Young Madame de Bellegarde gave their guest her hand without moving and without looking at him.

'You may think that's coldness,' Valentin freely explained; 'but it's not, it's the last confidence, and you'll grow up to it. It shows she's treating you as an intimate. Now she detests me, and yet she's always looking at me.'

'No wonder I detest you if I'm always looking at you!' cried the lady. 'If Mr Newman doesn't like my way of shaking hands I'll do it for him again.'

But this charming privilege was lost on our hero who was already making his way over to Madame de Cintré. She raised her eyes to him as she accepted from him the customary form, but she went on with the story she was telling her little niece. She had only two or three phrases to add, but they were apparently of great moment. She deepened her voice, smiling as she did so, and the little girl immensely gazed at her. 'But in the end the young prince married the beautiful Florabella, and carried her off to live with him in the Land of the Pink Sky. There she was so happy that she forgot all her troubles and went out to drive every day of her life in an ivory coach drawn by five hundred white mice. Poor Florabella,' she mentioned to Newman, 'had suffered terribly.'

'She had had nothing to eat for six months,' said little Blanche.

'Yes, but when the six months were over she had a plum-cake as big as that ottoman,' Madame de Cintré insisted. 'That quite set her up again.'

'What a strong constitution and what a chequered career!' said Newman. 'Are you very fond of children?' He was certain she must be, but wished to make her say it.

'I like to talk with them; we can talk with them so much more seriously than with grown persons. That's great nonsense I've been telling Blanche, but it has much more value than most of what we say in society.'

'I wish you would talk to me then as if I were Blanche's age,' Newman laughed. 'Were you happy at your ball the other night?'

'Extravagantly!'

'Now you're talking the nonsense that we talk in society,' said Newman. 'I don't believe that.'

'It was my own fault if I wasn't happy. The ball was very pretty and every one very amiable.'

'It was on your conscience,' he presently risked, 'that you had annoyed your mother and your brother.'

She looked at him a moment in silence. 'That's possible—I had undertaken more than I could carry out. I've very little courage; I'm not a heroine.' She said this, he could feel, to be very true with him; and it touched him as if she had pressed into his hand, for reminder, some note she had scrawled or some ribbon or ring she had worn. Then changing her tone, 'I could never have gone through the sufferings of the beautiful Florabella,' she added, 'not even for her prospective rewards.'

Dinner was announced and he betook himself to the side of old Madame de Bellegarde. The dining-room, at the end of a cold corridor, was vast and sombre; the dinner was simple and delicately excellent. Newman wondered if the daughter of the house had had to do with ordering the repast, and, with a fine applied power of remote projection, hoped this might have been. Once seated at table, with the various members of so rigidly closed a circle round him, he asked himself the meaning of his position. Was the old lady responding to his advances? Did the fact that he was a solitary guest augment his credit or diminish it? Were they ashamed to show him to other people or did they wish to give him a sign of sudden adoption into their last reserve of favour? He was on his guard; he was watchful and conjectural, yet at the same time he was vaguely indifferent. Whether they gave him a long rope or a short he was there now, and Madame de Cintré was opposite him. She had a tall candlestick on each side of her; she would sit there for the next hour, and that was enough. The dinner was extremely solemn and measured; he wondered if this was always the state of things in old families. Madame de Bellegarde held her head very high and fixed her eyes, which looked peculiarly sharp in her little finely-wrinkled white face, very intently on the table-service. The Marquis appeared to have decided that the fine arts offered a safe subject of conversation, as not leading to uncouth personal revelations. Every now and then, having learned from Newman that he had been through the museums of Europe, he uttered some polished aphorism on the flesh-tints of Rubens or the good taste of Sansovino.* He struck his guest as precautionary, as apprehensive; his manner seemed to indicate a fine nervous dread that something disagreeable might happen if the atmosphere were not kept clear of stray currents from windows opened at hazard. 'What under the sun is he afraid of?' Newman asked himself. 'Does he think I'm going to offer to swap jack-knives with him?' It was useless to shut his eyes to the fact that the Marquis was as disagreeable to him as some queer, rare, possibly dangerous biped, perturbingly akin to humanity, in one of the cages of a 'show'. He had never been a man of strong personal aversions; his nerves had not been at the mercy of the mystical qualities of his neighbours. But here was a figure in respect to which he was irresistibly in opposition; a figure of forms and phrases and postures; a figure of possible impertinences and treacheries. M. de Bellegarde made him feel as if he were standing barefooted on a marble floor; and yet to gain his desire, he felt perfectly able to stand. He asked himself what Madame de Cintré thought of his being accepted—if it was acceptance that was conveyed to him. There was no judging from her face, which expressed simply the desire to show kindness in a manner requiring as little explicit recognition as possible. Young Madame de Belle-garde had always the same manner; preoccupied, distracted, listen-ing to everything and hearing nothing, looking at her dress, her rings, her finger-nails and seeming ineffably bored, she yet defied you to pronounce on her ideal of social diversion. Newman was enlightened on this point later. Even Valentin failed quite to seem master of his wits; his vivacity was fitful and forced, but his friend felt his firm eyes shine through the lapses of the talk very much as to the effect of one's being pinched by him very hard in the dark. Newman himself, for the first time in his life, was *not* himself; he measured his motions and counted his words; he had the sense of sitting in a boat that required inordinate trimming and that a wrong movement might cause to overturn.

After dinner M. de Bellegarde proposed the smoking-room and led the way to a small and somewhat musty apartment, the walls of which were ornamented with old hangings of stamped leather and trophies of rusty arms. Newman refused a cigar, but established himself on one of the divans while the Marquis puffed his own weed before the fireplace and Valentin sat looking through the light fumes of a cigarette from one to the other. 'I can't keep quiet any longer,' this member of the family broke out at last. 'I must tell you the news and congratulate you. My brother seems unable to come to the point; he revolves round his announcement even as the priest round the altar. You're accepted as a candidate for the hand of our sister.'

'Valentin, be a little proper!' murmured the Marquis, the bridge of whose high nose yielded to a fold of fine irritation.

'There has been a family council,' his brother nevertheless con-tinued; 'my mother and he have put their heads together, and even my testimony has not been altogether excluded. My mother and Urbain sat at a table covered with green cloth; my sister-in-law and I were on a bench against the wall. It was like a committee at the Corps Législatif.* We were called up one after the other to testify. We spoke of you very handsomely. Madame de Bellegarde said that if she had not been told who you were she'd have taken you for a duke—an American duke, the Duke of California. I said I could warrant you grateful for the smallest favours—modest, humble, unassuming. I was sure you'd know your own place always and never give us occasion to remind you of certain differences. You couldn't help it, after all, if you had not come in for a dukedom. There were none in your country; but if there had been it was certain that with your energy and ability you'd have got the pick of the honours. At this point I was ordered to sit down, but I think I made an impression in your favour.'

M. de Bellegarde looked at his brother as Newman had seen those unfortunates looked at who have told, before waiting auditors, stories of no effect. Then he removed a spark of cigar-ashes from the sleeve of his coat; he fixed his eyes for a while on the cornice of the room, and at last he inserted one of his white hands into the breast of his waistcoat. 'I must apologise to you for Valentin's inveterate bad taste, as well as notify you that this is probably not the last time that his want of tact will cause you serious embarrassment.'

'No, I confess, I've no tact,' said Valentin. 'Is your embarrassment really serious, Newman? Urbain will put you right again; he'll know just how you feel.'

'My brother, I'm sorry to say,' the Marquis pursued, 'has never had the real sense of his duties or his opportunities—of what one must after all call his position. It has been a great pain to his mother, who's very fond of the old traditions. But you must remember that he speaks for no one but himself.'

'Oh, I don't mind him, sir'—Newman was all good-humour. 'I know what the Valentines of this world amount to.'

'In the good old times,' the young man said, 'marquises and counts used to have their appointed buffoons and jesters to crack jokes for them. Nowadays we see a great strapping democrat keeping one of "us", as Urbain would say, about him to play the fool. It's a good situation, but I certainly am very degenerate.'

The Marquis fixed his eyes for some time on the floor. 'My mother has let me know,' he presently resumed, 'of the announcement that you made her the other evening.'

'That I want so much to marry your sister?'

'That you desire to approach the Comtesse de Cintré with that idea, and ask of us therefore your facility for so doing. The proposal gave my mother—you can perhaps even yourself imagine—a great deal to think about. She naturally took me into her counsels, and the subject has had my most careful attention. There was a great deal to be considered; more than you perhaps appear to conceive. We have viewed the question on all its faces, we have weighed one thing against another. Our conclusion has been that we see no reason to oppose your pretension—though of course the matter, the question of your success, rests mainly with yourself. My mother has wished me to inform you then of our favourable attitude. She'll have the honour of saying a few words to you on the subject herself. Meanwhile you have our sanction, as heads of the family.'

Newman got up and came nearer. 'You personally will do all you can to back me up, eh?'

'I engage to you to throw my weight into the scale of your success.'

Newman passed his hand over his face and pressed it for a moment upon his eyes. This promise had a great sound, and yet the pleasure he took in it was embittered by his having to stand there so and receive, as he might say, this prodigious person's damned permission. The idea of having the elder M. de Bellegarde mixed up with his wooing and wedding was more and more unpleasant to him. But he had resolved to go through the mill, as he had imaged it, and he wouldn't cry out at the first turn of the wheel. He was silent a while and then said with a certain dryness which Valentin told him afterwards had a very grand air: 'I'm much obliged to you.'

'I take note of the promise,' said Valentin; 'I register the vow.'

M. de Bellegarde began to gaze at the cornice again; he apparently had more to say. 'I must do my mother the justice, I must do myself the justice, to make the point that our decision was not easy. Such an arrangement was not what we had expected. The idea that my sister should marry a gentleman so intimately involved in—a—business, was something of a novelty.'

'So I told you, you know!' Valentin recalled to Newman with a fine admonitory finger.

'The incongruity has not quite worn off, I confess,' the Marquis

went on; 'perhaps it never will entirely. But possibly that's not altogether to be regretted'; and he went through that odd dim form of
a smile that affected his guest as the scraping of a match that doesn't
light. 'It may be that the time has come when we should make some
concession to the spirit of the day. There had been no such positive
sacrifice in our house for a great many years. I made the remark to
my mother, and she did me the honour to admit that it was worthy
of attention.'

'My dear brother,' interrupted Valentin, 'is not your memory just
here leading you the least bit astray? Our mother is, I may say, distinguished by her small respect for abstract reasoning. Are you very
sure she replied to your striking proposition in the gracious manner
you describe? You know how, when it suits her, she goes straight to
the point—*au pas de charge*! Didn't she rather do you the honour to
say: "A fiddlestick for your fine phrases! There are better reasons than
that"?'

'Other reasons were discussed,' said the Marquis without looking
at Valentin, but with a slightly more nasal pitch; 'some of them possibly were better. We're highly conservative, Mr Newman, but we
have never, I trust, been stupidly narrow. We're judging this so interesting question on its merits only. We've no doubt we shall be fully
justified. We've no doubt everything will be comfortable.'

Newman had stood listening to these remarks with his arms folded
and his eyes fastened on the speaker. 'Justified?' he echoed with his
way of putting rather less than more sense into words he repeated.
'Why shouldn't we be? I assure you I've no fear for myself. Why
shouldn't we be comfortable? If you're not it will be your own fault.
I've everything to make *me* so.'

'My brother means that with the lapse of time you may get used
to the difference.' And Valentin paused to light another cigarette.

'What difference?' Newman unimaginatively asked.

'Urbain,' said Valentin very gravely, 'I'm afraid that Mr Newman
doesn't quite realise the difference. We ought to insist on that.'

'My brother goes too far,' M. de Bellegarde observed to Newman.
'He has no nice sense of what shouldn't be said. It's my mother's
wish and mine that no comparisons should be made. Pray never make
them yourself. We prefer to assume that the person accepted as the
possible husband of my sister is one of ourselves, and that he should
feel no explanations necessary. With a little tact on both sides every-

thing ought to be easy. That's exactly what I wished to say—that we quite understand what we've undertaken and that you may depend on our not breaking down.'

Valentin shook his hands in the air and then buried his face in them. 'I don't quite steer clear myself, no doubt, but oh, my brother, if you knew what *you* are saying!' And he went off into a sound that combined a long laugh with a long wail.

M. de Bellegarde's face flushed a little, but he held his head higher, as if to repudiate this concession to vulgar perturbability. 'I'm sure you quite know what I mean,' he said to Newman.

'Oh no, not quite—or perhaps not at all,' Newman answered. 'But you needn't mind that. I don't care whether I know—or even, really, care, I think, what you say; for if I did there might be things I shouldn't like, should in fact, quite *dis*like, and that wouldn't suit me at all, you know. I want, very originally, no doubt, but very obstinately, to marry your sister and nobody other whomsoever—that's all; to do it as quickly as possible and to do as little else among you besides. I don't care therefore *how* I do it—as regards the rest of you! And that's all I have to say.'

'You had better, nevertheless, receive the last word from my mother,' said the Marquis, who hadn't blanched.

'Very good; I'll go and get it.' And Newman prepared to return to the drawing-room.

M. de Bellegarde made a motion for him to pass first, and on his doing so shut himself into the room with Valentin. Newman had been a trifle bewildered by the free play of his friend's wit and had not needed its aid to feel the limits of the elder brother's. That was what he had heard of as patronage—a great historic and traditionary force that he now personally encountered for the first time in his life. Didn't it consist in calling your attention to the impertinences it spared you? But he had recognised all the bravery of Valentin's backing that underlay Valentin's comedy, and he was unwilling so fine a comedian should pay a tax on it. He paused a moment in the corridor, after he had gone a few steps, expecting to hear the resonance of M. de Bellegarde's displeasure; but he detected only a perfect stillness. The stillness itself seemed a trifle portentous; he reflected, however, that he had no right to stand listening and made his way back to the salon. In his absence several persons had come in. They were scattered about the room in groups, two or three of them having passed into a small boudoir, next to the drawing-room, which had now been lighted and opened. Madame de Bellegarde was in her place by the fire, talking to an antique gentleman in a wig and a profuse white neckcloth of the fashion of 1820. Madame de Cintré had bent a listening head to the historic confidences of an old lady who was presumably the wife of this personage, an old lady in a red satin dress and an ermine cape, whose forehead was adorned with a topaz set in a velvet band. The young Marquise, when he came in, left some people among whom she was sitting and took the place she had occupied before dinner. Then she gave a little push to the puff that stood near her and seemed to indicate by a glance that she had placed it in position for him. He went and took possession of it; the young Marquise amused and puzzled him.

'I know your secret,' she said in her bad but charming English; 'you need make no mystery of it. You wish to marry my sister-in-law. *C'est un beau choix.* A man like you ought in effect to marry a very tall and very thin woman. You must know that I've spoken in your favour, I'm really on your side and in your interest. You owe me a famous taper!'

'You've spoken well of me to Madame de Cintré?' Newman asked.

'Oh no, not that. You may think it strange, but my sister-in-law and I are not so intimate as that. Taking my courage in my hands, I put in my word for you to my husband and to my mother-in-law. I said I was sure we could do what we choose with you.'

'I'm much obliged to you,' laughed Newman, 'but I guess you'll find you can't.'

'I know that very well; I didn't believe a word of it. But I wanted you to come into the house; I thought we should be friends.'

'I'm very sure of it,' said Newman.

'Don't be too sure. If you like the Comtesse so much perhaps you won't like me. We're as different—well, as this fan and that poker. But you and I have something in common. I've come into this family by marriage; you want to come into it in the same way.'

'Oh no, I don't want to come into it at all,' he interrupted—'not a wee mite! I only want to take Madame de Cintré out of it.'

'Well, to cast your nets you have to go into the water. Our positions are alike; we shall be able to compare notes. What do you think of my husband? It's a strange question, isn't it? But I shall ask you some stranger ones yet.'

'Perhaps a stranger one will be easier to answer,' Newman said. 'You might try me.'

'Oh, you get off very well; the old Comte de la Rochefidèle,* yonder, couldn't do it better. I told them that if we only gave you a chance you'd be one of our *plus fins causeurs*. I know something about men. Besides, you and I belong to the same camp. I'm a ferocious modern. I'm more modern than you, you know—because I've been *through* this and come out, very far out; which you haven't. Oh, you don't know what this is! *Vous allez bien voir*. By birth I'm *vieille roche*; a good little bit of the history of France is the history of my family. Oh, you never heard of us, of course! *Ce que c'est que la gloire de race*. We're much better than the Bellegardes, at any rate. But I don't care a pin for my pedigree—I only want to belong to my time. So, being a reactionary—from the reaction—I'm sure I go beyond you. That's what you look, you know—that you're not reactionary enough. But I like clever people, wherever they come from, and I take my amusement wherever I find it. I don't pout at the Empire;* here all the world pouts at the Empire. Of course I've to mind what I say, but I expect to take my revenge with *you*.' The little lady discoursed for some time longer in this sympathetic strain, with an eager abundance indicating that her opportunities for revealing her esoteric philosophy were indeed rare. She hoped Newman would never be afraid of her, however he might be with the others, for really she went very far indeed. 'Strong people'—*les gens forts*—were in her opinion equal all the world over. Newman listened to her with an attention at once beguiled and irritated. He wondered what the deuce she too was driving at, with her hope he wouldn't be afraid of her and her protestations of equality. In so far as he could understand her she was wrong—he didn't admit her equality; a silly rattling woman was never on a level with a sensible man, a man preoccupied with an ambitious passion. The young Marquise stopped suddenly and looked at him sharply, shaking her fan. 'I see you don't believe me, you're too much on your guard. You won't form an alliance, offensive or defensive? You're very wrong; I could really help you.'

Newman answered that he was very grateful and that he would certainly ask for help; she should see. 'But first of all,' he said, 'I must help myself.' And he went to join Madame de Cintré.

'I've been telling Madame de la Rochefidèle that you're an American,' she said as he came up. 'It interests her greatly. Her favourite uncle went over with the French troops to help you in your battles in the last century,* and she has always, in consequence, wanted greatly to see one of your people. But she has never succeeded till to-night. You're the first—to her knowledge—that she has ever looked at.'

Madame de la Rochefidèle had an aged cadaverous face, with a falling of the lower jaw which prevented her bringing her lips together and reduced her conversation to a series of impressive but inarticulate gutturals. She raised an antique eye-glass, elaborately mounted in chased silver, and looked at Newman from head to foot. Then she said something to which he listened deferentially but which conveyed to him no idea whatever.

'Madame de la Rochefidèle says she's convinced she must have seen Americans without knowing it,' Madame de Cintré explained. Newman thought it probable she had seen a great many things without knowing it; and the old lady, again addressing herself to utterance, declared—as interpreted by Madame de Cintré—that she wished she *had* known it.

At this moment the old gentleman who had been talking to their hostess drew near, leading that lady on his arm. His wife pointed out Newman to him apparently explaining his remarkable origin. M. de la Rochefidèle, whose old age was as rosy and round and polished as an imitation apple, spoke very neatly and cheerily; almost as prettily, Newman thought, as M. Nioche, and much more hopefully. When he had been enlightened he turned to Newman with an inimitable elderly grace. 'Monsieur is by no means the first American I have seen. Almost the first person I *ever* saw—to notice him—was an American.'

'Ah!' said Newman sympathetically.

'The great Dr Franklin.* Of course I was very very young. I believe I had but just come into the world. He was received very well *dans le nôtre.*'

'Not better than Mr Newman,' said Madame de Bellegarde. 'I beg he'll offer me his arm into the other room. I could have offered no higher privilege to Dr Franklin.' Newman, complying with her request, perceived that her two sons had returned to the drawing-room. He scanned their faces an instant for traces of the scene that had followed his separation from them, but if the Marquis had been ruffled he stepped all the more like some high-crested though distinctly domestic fowl who had always the alternative of the perch. Valentin, on his side, was kissing ladies' hands as much as ever as if there were nothing else in the world but these and sundry other invitations to the moustachioed lip. Madame de Bellegarde gave a glance at her elder son, and by the time she had crossed the threshold of her boudoir he was at her side. The room was now empty and offered a sufficient privacy. She disengaged herself from Newman's arm and rested her hand on that of their companion; and in this position she stood a moment, bridling, almost quivering, causing her ornaments, her earrings and brooches and buckles, somehow doubly to twinkle, and pursing, as from simple force of character, her portentous little mouth. I am afraid the picture was lost on Newman, but she was in fact at this moment a striking image of the dignity which—even in the case of a small time-shrunken old lady—may reside in the habit of unquestioned authority and the absoluteness of a social theory favourable to the person holding it. 'My son has spoken to you as I desired, and you'll understand that you've nothing to fear from our opposition. The rest will lie with yourself.'

'M. de Bellegarde told me several things I didn't understand,' said Newman, 'but I made out that. You'll let me stand on my merits. I'm much obliged.'

'I wish nevertheless to add a word that my son probably didn't feel at liberty to say,' the Marquise pursued. 'I must say it for my own peace of mind. We've stretched a point; we've gone very far to meet you.'

'Oh, your son said it very well; didn't you, Marquis?' Newman asked.

'Not so well as my mother,' the Marquis declared.

'Well,' Newman returned, 'I don't know what I can do but make a note of it and try to profit by it.'

'It's proper I should tell you,' Madame de Bellegarde went on as if to relieve an insistent inward need, 'that I'm a very stiff old person and that I don't pretend not to be. I may be wrong to feel certain things as I do, but it's too late for me to change. At least I know it—as I know also why. Don't flatter yourself that my daughter also isn't proud. She's proud in her own way—a somewhat different way from mine. You'll have to make your terms with that. Even Valentin's proud, if you touch the right spot—or the wrong one. Urbain's proud—that you see for yourself. Sometimes I think he's a little too proud; but I wouldn't change him. He's the best of my children; he cleaves to his old mother. I've said, in any case, enough to show you that we are all very much aware of ourselves and very absurd and rather impossible together. It's well you should know the sort of people you have come among.'

'Well,' said Newman, 'I can only say that I hope I'm as little like you then as may be. But though I don't think I'm easy to scare, you speak as if you quite intended to be as disagreeable as you know how.'

His hostess fixed him a moment. 'I shall not enjoy it if my daughter decides to marry you, and I shall not pretend to enjoy it. If you don't mind that, so much the better.'

'If you stick to your own side of the contract we shall not quarrel; that's all I ask of you,' Newman replied. 'Keep your hands off—I shall mind my own business. I'm very much in earnest and there's not the slightest danger of my getting discouraged or backing out. You'll have me constantly before your eyes, so that if you don't like it I'm sorry for you. I'll do for your daughter, if she'll accept me, everything that a man can do for a woman. I'm happy to tell you that, as a promise—a pledge. I consider that on your side you take an equally definite engagement. You'll not back out, eh?'

'I don't know what you mean by "backing out",' said the Marquise with no small majesty. 'It suggests a movement of which I think no Bellegarde has ever been guilty.'

'Our word's our word,' Urbain pronounced. 'We recognise that we've given it.'

'Well then,' said Newman. 'I'm very glad of your pride and your pretensions. You'll have to keep your word to keep *them* up.'

The Marquise was silent a little; after which suddenly, 'I shall always be polite to you, Mr Newman,' she declared, 'but decidedly I shall never like you.'

'Don't be too sure, madam!' her visitor laughed.

'I'm so sure that I shall ask you to take me back to my armchair without the least fear of having my sentiments modified by the service you render me.' And Madame de Bellegarde took his arm and returned to the salon and to her customary place.

M. de la Rochefidèle and his wife were preparing to take their leave, and Madame de Cintré's interview with the mumbling old lady was at an end. She stood looking about her, asking herself apparently to whom she should next speak, when Newman approached.

'Your mother has given me leave—very solemnly—to come here often. I intend to come often.'

'I shall be glad to see you,' she answered simply. And then in a moment: 'You probably think it very strange that there should be such a solemnity—as you say—about your coming.'

'Well yes; I do, rather.'

'Do you remember what my brother Valentin said the first day you came to see me?—that we're a strange, strange family.'

'It wasn't the first day I came, but the second,' Newman amended.

'Very true. Valentin annoyed me at the time, but now I know you better I may tell you he was right. If you come often you'll see!' And Madame de Cintré turned away.

He watched her a while as she talked with other people and then took his leave. It was practically indeed to Valentin alone that he so addressed himself, and his friend followed him to the top of the staircase. 'Well, you've taken out your passport,' said that young man. 'I hope you liked the process and that you admire our red tape.'

'I like your sister better than ever. But don't worry your poor brother any more for my sweet sake,' Newman added. 'There must be something the matter with him.'

'There's a good deal!'

'Well, I don't seem to mind him—I don't seem to mind anything!' Newman just a bit musingly acknowledged. 'I was only afraid he came down on you in the smoking-room after I went out.'

'When my brother comes down on me,' said Valentin, 'he drops hard. I've a particular way of receiving him. I must say,' he continued, 'that they've fallen into line—for it has been a muster of all our forefathers too!—sooner than I expected. I don't understand it; they must really have put forward their clock! It's a tribute to your solidity.'

'Well, if my solidity's all they want—!' Newman again rather pensively breathed.

'You can cut them a daily slice of it and let them have it with their morning coffee?' But he was turning away when Valentin more effectually stopped him. 'I should like to know whether, within a few days, you've seen your venerable friend M. Nioche.'

'He was yesterday at my rooms.'

'What had he to tell you?'

'Nothing particular.'

'You didn't see the weapon of Virginius sticking out of his pocket?'

'What are you driving at?' Newman demanded. 'I thought he seemed rather cheerful, for him.'

Valentin broke into a laugh. 'I'm delighted to hear of his high spirits—they make me so beautifully right and so innocently happy. For what they mean, you see, must be that his charming child is favourably placed, at last, for the real exercise of her talents, and that the pair are relieved, almost equally, from the awkwardness of a false position. And M. Nioche is rather cheerful—*for him!* Don't brandish your tomahawk at that rate,' the young man went on; 'I've not seen her nor communicated with her since that day at the Louvre. Andromeda has found another Perseus* than I. My information's exact; on such matters it always is. I suppose,' he wound up, 'that I may now cease so elaborately to neglect her?'

Newman, struggling up out of intenser inward visions, listened as he could, and then, having listened, remained with his eyes on his friend's face. 'It would do you good to fall in love. You want it badly,' he at last remarked.

'Well, that's perhaps exactly what, according to my perpetual happy instinct, I'm now trying to do!'

'Oh hell!' said our hero impatiently as he broke away again.

XIII

HE kept his promise, or his menace, of presenting himself often in the Rue de l'Université, and during the next six weeks saw Madame de Cintré more times than he could have numbered. He flattered himself *he* had not fallen, and hadn't needed to fall, after the fashion enjoined by him on Valentin, in love, but his biographer may be supposed to know better what, as he would have said, was the matter with him. He claimed certainly none of the exemptions and emoluments of the merely infatuated state. That state, he considered, was too consistent with asininity, and he had never had a firmer control of his reason or a higher opinion of his judgement. What he was conscious of, none the less, was an intense all-consuming tenderness, which had for its object an extraordinarily graceful and harmonious, yet at the same time insidiously agitating woman who lived in a grand grey house on the left bank of the Seine. His theory of his relation to her was that he had become conscious of how beautifully she might, for the question of his future, come to his aid; but this left unexplained the fact that his confidence had somehow turned to a strange, muffled heartache. He was in truth infinitely anxious, and, when he questioned his anxiety, knew it was not all for himself. If she might come to his aid he might come to hers; and he had the imagination—more than he had ever had in his life about anything— of fantastic straits or splendid miseries in the midst of which, standing before her with wide arms out, he would have seen her let herself, even if still just desperately and blindly, make for his close embrace as for a refuge.

He really wouldn't have minded if some harsh need for mere money had most driven her; the creak of that hinge would have been sweet to him had it meant the giving way of the door of separation. What he wanted was to *take* her, and that her feeling herself taken should come back to him for their common relief. The full surrender, so long as she didn't make it, left the full assurance and unrest and a yearning—from which all his own refuge was in the fine ingenuity, the almost grim extravagance, of the prospective provision he was allowing to accumulate. She gave him the sense of 'suiting' him so, exactly as she was, that his desire to interpose for her and close about her had something of the quality of that solicitude with which a fond mother might watch from the window even the restricted garden-play of a child recovering from an accident. But he was above all simply charmed, and the more for feeling wonder-struck, as the days went on, at the proved rightness both of the instinct and of the calculation that had originally moved him. It was as if there took place for him, each day, such a revelation of the possible number of forms of the 'personal' appeal as he could otherwise never have enjoyed, and as made him yet ask himself how, *how*, all unaided (save as Mrs Tristram, subtle woman, had aided him!) he could have known. For he *had*, amazingly, known. And the impression must now thereby have been for him, he thought, very much that of the wistful critic or artist who studies 'style' in some exquisite work or some quiet genius, and who sees it come and come and come, and still never fail, like the truth of a perfect voice or the safety of a perfect temper. Just as such a student might say to himself, 'How could I have got on without this particular research?' so Christopher Newman could only say, 'Fancy this being to be had and—with my general need—my not having it!'

He made no violent love and, as he would have said, no obvious statements; he just attended regularly, as he would also have said, in the manner of the 'interested party' present at some great liquidation where he must keep his eye on what concerns him. He never trespassed on ground she had made him regard, ruefully enough, as forbidden; but he had none the less a sustaining sense that she knew better from day to day all the good he thought of her. Though in general no great talker, and almost incapable, on any occasion, of pitching his voice for the gallery, he now had his advances as well as his retreats, and felt that he often succeeded in bringing her, as he might again have called it, into the open. He determined early not to care if he should bore her, whether by speech or by silence—since he certainly meant she should so suffer, at need, before he had done; and he seemed at least to know that even if she actually suffered she liked him better, on the whole, with too few fears than with too many. Her visitors, coming in often while he sat there, found a tall, lean, slightly flushed and considerably silent man, with a lounging, permanent-looking seat, who laughed out sometimes when no one had meant to be droll, and yet remained grave in presence of those calculated witticisms and those initiated gaieties for the appreciation of which he apparently lacked the proper culture and the right acquaintances. It had to be confessed that the number of the subjects upon which he was without ideas was only equalled by the number of the families to which he was not allied; and it might have been added more gravely still that as regards those subjects upon which he was without ideas he was also quite without professions. He had little of the small change of conversation and rarely rose to reach down one of those ready-made forms and phrases that drape, whether fresh or frayed, the hooks and pegs of the general wardrobe of talk—that repository in which alone so many persons qualify for the discipline of society, as supernumerary actors prepare, amid a like provision, for the ordeal of the footlights. He was able on the other hand, at need, to make from where he sat one of the long arms that stretch quite out of the place—to the effect, as might mostly be felt, of coming back with some proposition as odd as a single shoe.

Bent, at any rate, on possession, he had at his command treasures of attention and never measured the possibilities of interest in a topic by his own power of contribution to it: he liked topics to grow at least big enough for him to walk round them and see. This made, for his advantage, to his being little acquainted with satiety either of sound or of sense; he was not himself more often bored than he was often alarmed, and there was no man with whom it would have been a greater mistake than to take his intermissions always for absences or his absences always for holidays. What it was that entertained or that occupied him during some of his speechless sessions I shall not, however, undertake fully to say. The Marquise Urbain had once found occasion to declare to him that he reminded her, in company, of a swimming-master she had once had who would never himself go into the water and who yet, at the baths, *en costume de ville*, managed to control and direct the floundering scene without so much as getting splashed. He had so made her angry, she professed, when he turned her awkwardness to ridicule. Newman affected her in like manner as keeping much too dry: it was urgent for her that *he* should be splashed—otherwise what was he doing at the baths?—and she even hoped to get him into the water. We know in a general way that many things which were old stories to those about him had for him the sharp high note, but we should probably find a complete list of his new impressions surprising enough. He told Madame de Cintré stories, sometimes not brief, from his own repertory; he was full of

reference to his own great country, over the greatness of which it
seldom occurred to him that every one mightn't, on occasion offered,
more or less insatiably yearn; and he explained to her, in so dis-
coursing, the play of a hundred of its institutions and the ingenuity
of almost all its arrangements. Judging by the sequel, judging even
by the manner in which she suffered his good faith to lay an
apparent spell upon her attitude, she was mildly—oh mildly and
inscrutably!—beguiled; but one wouldn't have been sure beforehand
of the shade of her submission. As regards any communication she
herself meanwhile made him he couldn't nevertheless but guess that
on the whole she 'wanted' to make it. This was in so far an amend-
ment to the portrait Mrs Tristram had drawn of her.

He had been right at first in feeling her a little—or more than a
little—proudly shy; her shyness, in a woman whose circumstances
and tranquil beauty afforded every facility for sublime self-
possession, was only a charm the more. For Newman it had lasted
some time and had, even when it went, left something behind it that
for a while performed the same office. Was this the uneasy secret of
which Mrs Tristram had had a glimpse, and of which, as of her
friend's reserve, her high breeding and her profundity, she had given
a sketch marked by outlines perhaps rather too emphatic? He supposed so, yet to find himself, as a result, wondering rather less what
Madame de Cintré's secrets might consist of, and convinced rather
more that secrets would be in themselves hateful and inconvenient
things, things as depressing and detestable as inferior securities, for
such a woman to have to lug, as he inwardly put it, round with her.
She was a creature for the sun and the air, for no sort of hereditary
shade or equivocal gloom; and her natural line was neither imposed
reserve nor mysterious melancholy, but positive life, the life of the
great world—*his* great world, not the *grand monde* as there understood if he wasn't mistaken, which seemed squeezeable into a couple
of rooms of that inconvenient and ill-warmed house: all with nothing
worse to brood about, when necessary, than the mystery perhaps of
the happiness that would so queerly have come to her. To some perception of his view and his judgement, and of the patience with
which he was prepared to insist on them, he fondly believed himself
to be day by day bringing her round. She mightn't, she couldn't yet,
no doubt, wholly fall in with them, but she saw, he made out, that

he had built a bridge which would bear the very greatest weight she should throw on it, and it was for him often, all charmingly, as if she were admiring from this side and that the bold span of arch and the high line of the parapet—as if indeed on occasion she stood straight there at the spring, just watching him at *his* extremity and with nothing, when the hour should strike, to prevent her crossing with a rush.

He often spent an evening's end, when she had so appointed—her motives and her method and her logic being meanwhile something of her own, though something thus beautifully *between them*, even if never named, and which he wouldn't for the world have asked her to name—he often passed a stiff succession of minutes at the somewhat chill fireside of Madame de Bellegarde; contenting himself there for the most part with looking across the room, through narrowed eyelids, at his mistress, who always made a point, before her family, of talking to some one else. Her mother, on that scene, would sit by the fire conversing neatly and coldly with whomsoever approached her and yet detaching for his own especial benefit a glance that seemed to say: 'See how completely I'm interested, how agreeably I'm occupied, how deeply I'm absorbed.' He often wondered what those supposedly honoured by this intensity of participation thought of her at such moments, and he sometimes answered her look by looking at *them*; but no one, for all the fine community of taste, that air in the place as of bitter convictions dissolved in iced indifference and partaken of for refreshment with small rare old 'family' spoons, appeared to meet him on any such particular question any more intimately than on any other—and all by direct default of ability; which would have made him again ask himself, but for his constant anxious ache, what he was doing in so deadly a hole at all. To ache very hard at one point, he found, was practically to be unconscious of punctures at any other. When he at all events made his bow to the old lady by the fire he always asked her with a laugh whether she could 'stand him' another evening, and she replied without a laugh, that, thank God, she had always been able to do her duty. Talking of her once to Mrs Tristram he had remarked that, after all, it was very easy to get on with her; it always was easy to get on with out-and-out rascals.

'And is it by that elegant term that you designate the Marquise?'

'Well, she's a bad, bold woman. She's a wicked old sinner.'

'What then has been her sin?'

He thought a little. 'I shouldn't wonder if she had done some one to death—all of course from a high sense of duty.'

'How can you be so dreadful?' Mrs Tristram had luxuriously sighed.

'I'm not dreadful. I am speaking of her favourably.'

'Pray what will you say then when you want to be severe?'

'I shall keep my severity for some one else—say for that prize donkey of a Marquis. There's a man I can't swallow, mix the drink as I will.'

'And what has *he* done?'

'I can't quite make out, but it's something very nice of its kind—I mean of a kind elegantly sneaking and fastidiously base; not redeemed as in his mother's case by a fine little rage of passion at some part of the business. If he has never committed murder he has at least turned his back and looked the other way while some one else was committing it.'

In spite of this free fancy, which indeed struck his friend as, for a specimen of American humour, exceptionally sardonic, Newman did his best to maintain an easy and friendly style of communication with M. de Bellegarde. So long as he was in personal contact with people he disliked extremely to have anything to forgive them, and was capable of a good deal of unsuspected imaginative effort (for the working of the relation) to assume them to be of a human substance and a social elasticity not alien to his own. He did his best to treat the Marquis as practically akin to him; he believed honestly, moreover, that he couldn't in reason be such a confounded fool as he seemed. Newman's assumptions, none the less, were never importunate; his habit of sinking differences and supposing equalities was not an aggressive taste nor an æsthetic theory, but something as natural and organic as a physical appetite which had never been put on a scant allowance and had consequently never turned rabid. His air as of not having to account for his own place in the social scale was probably irritating to Urbain, for whom it could but represent a failure to conceive of other places either, and who thus saw himself reflected in the mind of his potential brother-in-law in a crude and colourless form, unpleasantly dissimilar to the impressive image thrown upon his own intellectual mirror. He never forgot himself an instant, and replied with mechanical politeness to the large bright vaguenesses that he was apparently justified in regarding as this visitor's wanton advances. Newman, who was constantly forgetting himself and indulging in an unlimited amount of irresponsible enquiry and conjecture, now and then found himself confronted by these obscure abysses of criticism. What in the world M. de Bellegarde was falling back either from or on he was at a loss to divine. M. de Bellegarde's general orderly retreat may meanwhile be supposed to have been, for himself, a compromise between a great many emotions. So long as he ambiguously smiled—and what could make more for order?—he was polite, and it was proper he should be polite. A smile moreover committed him to nothing more than politeness; it left the degree of politeness agreeably vague. Civil ambiguity too—and it was perfectly civil—was neither dissent, which was too serious, nor agreement, which might have brought on terrible complications. And then it covered his own personal dignity, which at such a crisis he was resolved to keep immaculate: it was quite enough that the glory of his house should pass into eclipse. Between him and Newman, his whole manner seemed to declare, there could be no interchange of opinion; he could but hold his breath so as not to inhale the strong smell—since who liked such *very* strong smells?—of a democracy so gregarious as to be unable *not* to engender heat and perspiration.

Newman was far from being versed in 'European' issues, as he liked to call them; but he was now on the very basis of aspiring to light, and it had more than once occurred to him that he might here both arrive at it and give this acquaintance the pleasure of his treating him as an oracle. Interrogated, however, as to what he thought of public affairs, M. de Bellegarde answered on each occasion, and quite indeed as if thanking him for the opportunity, that he thought as ill of them as possible, that they were going from bad to worse, though there was always at least the comfort of their being too dreadful to touch. This gave our friend, momentarily, almost an indulgence for a spirit so depressed; he pitied the man who had to look at him in such a fashion when he ventured to insist, particularly about their great shining France, 'Why, don't you see anything anywhere?'—and he was brought by it to an attempt, possibly indiscreet, to call attention to some of the great features of the world's progress. This had presently led the Marquis to observe, once for all, that he entertained but a single political conviction—dearer to him, however, than all the others, put together, that other people might entertain: he believed, namely, in the divine right of Henry of Bourbon, Fifth of his name,* to the throne of France. This had in truth, upon Newman, as many successive distinct effects as the speaker could conceivably have desired. It made him in the first place look at the latter very hard, harder than he had ever done before; which had the appearance somehow of affording M. de Bellegarde another of the occasions he personally appreciated. It was as if he had never yet shown how he could return such a look; whereby, producing that weapon of his armoury, he made the demonstration brilliant. Then he reduced his guest, further, just to staring with a conscious, foolish failure of every resource, at one of the old portraits on the wall, out of which some dim light for him might in fact have presently glimmered. Lastly it determined on Newman's part a wise silence as to matters he didn't understand. He relapsed, to his own sense, into silence very much as he would have laid down, on consulting it by mistake, some flat-looking back-number or some superseded time-table. It might do for the 'collection' craze but wouldn't do for use.

One afternoon, on his presenting himself, he was requested by the servant to be so good as to wait, a very few minutes, till Madame la Comtesse should be at liberty. He moved about the room a little, taking up a book here and there as with a vibration of tact in his long and strong fingers; he hovered, with a bent head, before flowers that he recognised as of a 'lot' he himself must have sent; he raised his eyes to old framed prints and grouped miniatures and disposed photographs, ten times as many of which she should some day possess; and at last he heard the opening of a door to which his back was turned. On the threshold stood an old woman whom he remembered to have met more than once in entering and leaving the house. She was tall and straight and dressed in black, and she wore a cap which, if Newman had been initiated into such mysteries, would have sufficiently assured him she was not a Frenchwoman; a cap of pure British composition. She had a pale, decent, depressed-looking face and a clear, dull English eye. She looked at Newman a moment, both intently and timidly, and then she dropped a short, straight English curtsey. 'The Countess begs you'll kindly wait, sir. She has just come in; she'll soon have finished dressing.'

'Oh, I'll wait as long as she wants,' said Newman. 'Pray tell her not to hurry.'

'Thank you, sir,' said the woman softly, and then instead of retiring with the message advanced into the room. She looked about her a moment and presently went to a table and began to dispose again several small articles. Newman was struck with the high respectability of her appearance; he was afraid to address her as a servant. She busied herself with ordering various trifles, with patting out cushions and pulling curtains straight, while our hero rather attentively hovered. He perceived at last, from her reflexion in the mirror as he was passing, that her hands were idle and her eyes fixed on him. She evidently wished to say something, and, now aware of it, he helped her to begin.

'I guess you're English, ain't you?'

'Oh dear, yes,' she answered, quickly and softly. 'I was born in Wiltshire, sir.'

'And what do you think of Paris?'

'Oh, I don't think of Paris, sir,' she said in the same tone. 'It's so long that I've been here.'

'Ah, you have been here very long?'

'More than forty years, sir. I came over with Lady Emmeline.'

'You mean with old Madame de Bellegarde?'

'Yes, sir. I came with her when she married. I was my lady's own woman.'

'And you've been with her ever since?'

'I've been in the house ever since. My lady has taken a younger person. You see I'm very old. I do nothing regular now. But I keep about.'

'You keep about remarkably well,' said Newman, observing the erectness of her figure and a certain venerable pink in her cheek. 'I like,' he genially added, 'to *see* you about.'

'Very good of you, sir. Thank God I'm not ill. I hope I know my duty too well to go panting and coughing over the house. But I'm an old woman, sir, and it's as an old woman that I venture to speak to you.'

'Oh, speak, if you like, as you never spoke!' said Newman curiously. 'You needn't be afraid of me.'

'Yes, sir, I think you're kind. I've seen you before.'

'On the stairs, you mean?'

'Yes, sir. When you've been coming to see the Countess. I've taken the liberty of noticing that you come often.'

'Oh yes; I come very often,' he laughed. 'You needn't have been very much emancipated to notice that.'

'I've noticed it with pleasure, sir,' said this interesting member of the family. And she stood looking at him with a strange expression of face. The old instinct of deference and humility was there; the habit of decent self-effacement and the knowledge of her appointed orbit. But there mingled with it an impulse born of the occasion and of a sense, probably, of this free stranger's unprecedented affability; and, beyond this, a vague indifference to the old proprieties, as if my lady's own woman had at last begun to reflect that, since my lady had taken another person, she had a slight reversionary property in herself.

'You take a great interest in our friends?' he asked.

She looked at him as if she admired that expression and had never heard anything quite like it. 'A deep interest, sir. Especially in the Countess.'

'I'm glad of that,' said Newman. And he smilingly followed it up. 'You can't take more than I do!'

'So I supposed, sir. We can't help noticing these things and having our ideas; can we, sir?'

'You mean as an old employee?'

'Ah, there it is, sir. I'm afraid that when I let my thoughts meddle with such matters I rather step out of my place. But I'm so devoted to the Countess; if she were my own child I couldn't love her more. That's how I come to be so bold, sir.' Her boldness failed her a moment, but she brought it round with a turn. 'They say in the house, sir, that you want to marry her.'

Newman eyed his interlocutress, and, as if something had suddenly begun to depend on it, made up his mind about her. Something at least passed between them with his exchange of distinct truths, and at the end of a minute he felt almost like a lost child kindly taken by the hand. He gave the hand a responsive grasp. He looked quite up into the deep mild face. 'I want to marry Madame de Cintré more than I ever wanted anything in my life.'

'And to take her away to America?'

'I'll take her wherever she wants to go.'

'The further away the better, sir!' exclaimed the old woman with sudden intensity. But she checked herself and, taking up a paperweight in mosaic, began to polish it with her black apron. 'I don't mean anything about the house or the family, sir. But I think a great change would do the poor Countess good. There's no very grand life here.'

'Oh, grand life—!' he quite sarcastically sighed. 'But Madame de Cintré,' he added, 'has great courage in her heart.'

'She has everything in her heart that's good. You'll not be vexed to hear that she has been more her natural self these two months past than she had been for many a day before.'

Newman was delighted to gather this testimony to the progress of his suit, but he kept his expression within bounds. 'Had she been *very* long as you didn't want to see her?'

'Well, sir, she had good reason not to be gay. The Count was no natural husband for a young lady like that. And it isn't as if, in this house, there were other great pleasures—to make up, I mean, for anything so sad. It's better, in my humble opinion, that she should leave it altogether. So if you'll pardon my saying such a thing, I hope very much she'll see her blessed way—!'

'You can't hope it as much as I do!' Newman returned.

'But you mustn't lose courage, sir, if she doesn't make up her mind at once. That's what I wanted to beg of you,' his friend proceeded. 'Don't give it up, sir. You'll not take it ill if I say it's a great risk for any lady at any time; all the more when she has got rid of one bad bargain. But if she can take advantage of a good, kind, respectable gentleman I think she had better make up her mind. They speak very well of you, sir, in the house—I mean in my part of it; and, if you'll allow me to say so, there's everything in your appearance—! You've a very different one to the late Count; he wasn't, really sir, much more than five feet high. And they say your fortune's beyond everything. There's no harm in that. So I entreat you to be patient, sir, and to bide your time. If I don't say it to you perhaps no one will. Of course it's not for me to make any promises. I can answer for nothing. But I believe in your chance because I believe in your spirit. I'm nothing but a weary old woman in my quiet corner, but one of us poor things here may understand another, and I don't think I could ever mistake the Countess. I received her in my arms when she came into the world, and her first wedding-day was the saddest of my life. She owes it to me to show me another and a brighter. If you'll but hold on fast, sir—and you look as if you would—I think we may see it.'

Newman had listened to this slow, plain, deliberate speech, the first evidently of much waiting and wishing, with as hushed and grateful a pleasure as he had ever had for some grand passage at the opera. 'Why, my dear madam, I just love you for your encouragement. One can't have too much, and I mean to hold on fast—you may bet your life on that. And if Madame de Cintré does see her way you must just come and live with her.'

The old woman looked at him with grave lifeless eyes. 'It may seem a heartless thing to say, sir, when one has been forty years in a house, but I promise you I should like to leave this place.'

'Why, it's just the *time* to promise,' said Newman with ingenuity. 'After forty years one wants a big change. That's what *I'm* going in for,' he smiled.

'You're very kind indeed, sir,'—and this faithful servant dropped another curtsey and seemed disposed to retire. She moved slowly, however, and gave while she lingered a dim joyless smile. Newman was disappointed, and his fingers stole so impatiently to his waistcoat-pocket that his informant noticed the gesture. 'Ah, thank God I'm not a mercenary French person! If I were I would tell you with a brazen simper, old as I am, that if you please, monsieur, my information is worth something. Yet let me tell you so after all in my own decent English way. It *is* worth something.'

'How much, please?'

'Simply this, sir: your solemn promise not to hint by a single word to the Countess that I've gone so far.'

'Oh, I promise all right,' said Newman. 'And when I promise—!'

'I do believe you keep, sir! That's all, sir. Thank you, sir. Goodday, sir.' And having once more slid down telescope-wise into her scant petticoats, his visitor departed. At the same moment Madame de Cintré came in by an opposite door. She noticed the movement of the other *portière* and asked Newman who had been entertaining him.

'The British female—in her most venerable form. An old lady in a black dress and a cap, who bobs up and down and expresses herself ever so well.'

'An old lady who bobs and expresses herself? Ah, you mean poor Mrs Bread. I happen to know you've made a conquest of her.'

'Mrs Cake, she ought to be called,' Newman declared. 'She's very sweet. She's a delicious old woman.'

His friend looked at him a moment. 'What can she have said to you? She's an excellent creature, but we think her rather dismal.'

'I suppose,' he presently answered, 'that I like her so much because she has lived near you so long. Since your birth, she told me.'

'Yes—such an age as that makes! She's very faithful,' Madame de Cintré went on simply. 'I can absolutely trust her.'

Newman, however that might be, had never made a reflexion to this lady on her mother and her brother Urbain—he had given no hint of the impression they made on him. But, as if she could perfectly guess his feeling and subtly spare his nerves, she had markedly avoided any occasion for making him speak of them. She never alluded to her mother's domestic decrees; she never quoted the opinions of the Marquis. They had talked, it was true, of Valentin, and she had made no secret of her extreme affection for her younger brother. Newman listened sometimes with a vague, irrepressible pang; if he could only have caught in his own cup a few drops of that overflow! She once spoke to him with candid elation of something Valentin had done which she thought very much to his honour. It was a service he had rendered to an old friend of the family—something more 'serious' and useful than he was usually supposed capable of achieving. Newman said he was glad to hear of it, and then began to talk of a matter more personal to himself. His companion listened, but after a while she said: 'I don't like the way you speak of poor Valentin.' At which, rather surprised, he protested he had never spoken of him save in kindness.

'Well, it's just the sort of kindness,' she smiled, 'the kindness that costs nothing, the kindness you show to a child. It's as if you rather looked down on him. It's as if you didn't respect him.'

'Respect him? Why, respect's a big feeling. But I guess I do.'

'You guess? If you're not sure, it's no respect.'

'Do *you* respect him?' Newman asked. 'If you do then I do.'

'If one loves a person, that's a question one's not bound to answer,' said Madame de Cintré.

'You shouldn't have asked it of me then. I'm very fond of your brother.'

'He amuses you. But you wouldn't like to resemble him.'

'I shouldn't like to resemble any one. It's hard enough work resembling one's self.'

'What do you mean,' she demanded, 'by resembling one's self?'

'Why, doing what's expected of one. Doing one's duty.'

'But that's hard—or at any rate it's urgent—only when one's very good.'

'Well, a great many people are good enough—so long as they insist on being so!' he optimistically laughed. 'Valentine, at all events, is good enough for *me*.'

She was silent a little, and then, with inconsequence, 'Ah, I could wish him rather better!' she declared. 'I could wish he would do something.'

Her companion considered: after which, candidly: 'What in the world can Valentine "do"?'

'Well, he's very clever.'

'But I guess it's a proof of power,' Newman reasoned, 'to be so happy without doing anything.'

'Ah, but I don't think Valentin's really so happy. He's intelligent, generous, brave—but what is there to show for it? To me there's something sad in his life, and sometimes I have a sort of foreboding about him. I don't know why, but it seems to come to me that he may have some great trouble—perhaps a really unhappy end.'

'Oh, leave him to me,' Newman cheerfully returned. 'I guess I can keep him all right.'

One evening, however, in spite of such passages as these, the conversation in Madame de Bellegarde's own apartment had flagged most sensibly. The Marquis walked up and down in silence, like a sentinel at the door of some menaced citadel of the proprieties; his mother sat staring at the fire; his wife worked at an enormous band of tapestry. Usually there were three or four visitors, but on this occasion a violent storm sufficiently accounted for the absence even of the most assiduous. In the long silences the howling of the wind and the beating of the rain were distinctly audible. Newman sat perfectly still, watching the clock, determined to stay till the stroke of eleven and not a moment longer. Madame de Cintré had turned her back to the circle and had been standing for some time within the uplifted curtain of a window, her forehead against the pane and her eyes reaching out to the deluged darkness. Suddenly she turned round to her sister-in-law. 'For heaven's sake,' she said with peculiar eagerness, 'go to the piano and play something.'

The young Marquise held up her tapestry and pointed to a little white flower. 'Don't ask me to leave this. I'm in the midst of a masterpiece. My little flower's going to smell very sweet; I'm putting in the smell with this gold-coloured silk. I'm holding my breath; I can't leave off. Play something yourself.'

'It's absurd for me to play when you're present,' Claire returned; yet the next moment she had plunged, as it were, into the source of music, had begun to strike the keys with vehemence. She sounded them for some time, to a great, and almost startling effect; when she stopped Newman went over and asked her to begin again. She shook her head and, on his insisting, said: 'I've not been playing for you, I've been playing for myself.' She went back to the window again and looked out, and shortly afterwards she left the room.

When he took leave Urbain de Bellegarde accompanied him, as always, just three steps down the staircase. At the bottom stood a servant with his overcoat. He had just put it on when he saw Madame de Cintré come to him across the vestibule. 'Shall you be at home on Friday?' he asked.

She looked at him a moment before answering, and the servant moved away to the great house-door. 'You don't like my mother and my brother. Ah, but not the least little bit!'

He hesitated a moment and then said ever so mildly: 'Well, since you mention it—!'

She laid her hand on the balustrade and prepared to ascend the stairs, fixing her eyes on the first step. 'I shall be at home on Friday,' she brought out; and she passed up while he watched her. But on the Friday, as soon as he came in, she asked him to be so good as to tell her why he had such an aversion to her family.

'Such an aversion? Did I call it that? Don't think I make too much of it. See how easily I work it.'

'I wish you would tell me what you think of them,' she simply said.

'I don't think of any of them but you.'

'That's because you dislike them too much. Speak the truth; you can't offend me.'

'Well, I could live at a pinch without the Marquis,' Newman confessed. 'It comes to me now, if you mention it. But what's the use of our bringing it up? I don't think of him.'

'You're too good-natured,' Madame de Cintré gravely said. Then, as if to avoid the appearance of inviting him to speak ill of her brother, she turned away, motioning him to sit down.

But he remained there before her. 'What's of much more importance is that they can scarcely stand me.'

'Scarcely,' she said with the gentlest, oddest distinctness.

'And don't you think they're wrong? I don't strike myself as a man
to hate.'

'I suppose a man who may inspire strong feelings,' she thoughtfully opined, 'must take his chance of what they are. But have my
brother and my mother made you hate *them*?'

'Oh, I don't sling my passions about—I've put all my capital into
one good thing,' he smiled. 'Yet I may have spent about ten cents on
the luxury of rage.'

'You've never then let me see you doing it.'

'Ah, I don't do it here,' he still sturdily smiled.

She dropped her eyes, and it somehow held him a minute in suspense. But 'They think they've treated you rather handsomely' was,
however, all she said at last.

'Well, I've no doubt they could have been much worse. They must
have let me off pretty easily,' he went on; 'for see how little I feel
damaged. And I think I show you everything. Honestly.'

She faced him again, at this, as if really to take the measure, more
than she had done yet, of what he showed her. 'You're very generous. It's a painful position.'

'For them, you mean. Not for me.'

'For me,' said Madame de Cintré.

'Not when their sins are forgiven!' Newman laughed. 'They don't
think I'm as good as themselves. I do, you see. What should I be—
well, even for you—if I didn't? But we shan't quarrel about it.'

'I can't even agree with you without saying something that has a
sound I dislike. The presumption, if I may put it so, was against you.
That you probably don't understand.'

He sat down before her, all carefully and considerately, as he might
have placed himself at the feet of a teacher. 'I don't think I really
understand it. But when you say it I believe it.'

She gave, still with her charming eyes on him, the slowest,
gentlest headshake. 'That's a poor reason.'

'No, it's a very good one. I believe everything you say, and I know
why—if you'll let me tell you. You've a high spirit, a high standard;
but with you it's all natural and unaffected: you don't seem to have
stuck your head into a vise, as if you were sitting for the photograph

of propriety. Yet you do also think of me, I guess, as a sort of animal that has had no idea in life but to make money and drive sharp bargains. Well, that's a fair description,' he pursued, 'but it's not the whole. A man ought to care for something else—I'm alive to that and always was, even if I don't know exactly for what. I cared for money-making, but I never cared so very terribly for the money. There was nothing else to do, and I take it you don't see me *always* on the loaf. I've been very easy to others, and I've tried always to know where I was myself. I've done most of the things that people have asked me— I don't mean scoundrels. I guess no one has suffered by me very badly. As regards your mother and your brother,' he added, 'there's only one point on which I feel that I might quarrel with them. I don't ask them to sing my praises to you, but I ask them to let you alone. If I thought they talked against me to you at all badly'—and he just paused—'why I'd have to come in somewhere on *that*.'

She reassured him. 'They've let me alone, as you say. They haven't talked against you to me at all badly.'

It gave him, and for the first time, the exquisite pleasure of her apparently liking to use and adopt his words. 'Well then I'm ready to declare them only too good for this world!'

This brought something into her face that—as it seemingly wasn't relief—he didn't quite understand, and she might have spoken in a sense to explain it if the door at the moment had not been thrown open and Urbain de Bellegarde had not stepped across the threshold. He appeared surprised at finding Newman; but his surprise was but a momentary shadow across the surface of an unwonted cheer. His guest had never seen him so exhilarated; he produced the effect of an old faded portrait that had suddenly undergone restoration. He held open the door for some one else to enter, and was presently followed by the old Marquise, supported on the arm of a gentleman whom Newman saw for the first time. He was already on his feet, and Madame de Cintré rose, as she always did before her mother. The Marquis, who had greeted him almost genially, stood apart and slowly rubbed his hands; his mother came forward with her companion. She gave Newman a majestic little nod and then released the other visitor, that he might make his bow to her daughter. 'I've brought you an unknown relative, Lord Deepmere, Lord Deepmere who's our cousin, but who has done only to-day what he ought to have done long ago, come to make our acquaintance.'

Madame de Cintré dropped her soft but steady light on this personage, who had advanced to take her hand. 'It's very extraordinary,' he ingenuously remarked, 'but this is the first time in my life I've been in Paris for more than three or four weeks.'

'And how long have you been here now?' she enquired with a certain detachment.

'Oh, for the last two months.' The young man—he was still a young man—showed no hesitation. His artless observations might have constituted an impertinence; but a glance at his face would have satisfied you, as it apparently satisfied Madame de Cintré, that nothing about him could well be explained save in the light of his simplicity. When their group was seated Newman, who was out of the conversation, reflected, observing him, that unless he had the benefit of that he hadn't the benefit of very much. His other advantages—beyond his three or four and thirty years—were a scant stature and an odd figure, a bald head, a short nose, round clear blue eyes and a frank and natural smile, which made the loss of a couple of front teeth by some rude misadventure constantly conspicuous. Perceptibly embarrassed, by more than one sign, he laughed as if he were bold and free, catching his breath with a loud startling sound. He admitted that Paris was charming, but pleaded that he was a wild, bog-trotting Paddy who preferred his Dublin even to his London and who would never be caught where they had caught him save for his taste for light music. He came over for the new Offenbach things, since, though they always brought them out in Dublin, it was perhaps with a whiff too much of the brogue. He had been nine times to hear 'La Pomme de Paris'.* Had Madame de Cintré ever been to Dublin? They must all come over some day and he'd show them some grand old Irish sport. His younger kinswoman, leaning back with her arms folded and her eyes set in a certain dimness of wonder, might have been drifting away from him, conveniently and resignedly, on some deep slow current. Her mother's face, on the other hand, was lighted as if in honour of the hour, and Newman felt himself make out in it a queer prehistoric prettiness. The Marquis noted that among light operas his favourite was 'La Gazza Ladra'.* The Marquise, however, began a series of enquiries about the duke and the cardinal, the old duchess and Lady Barbara, after listening to which and to Lord Deepmere's somewhat irreverent responses for a quarter of an hour,

our friend rose to take his leave. The Marquis went with him their three usual steps into the hall.

'He *is* a real Paddy!'—and Newman nodded in the direction of the visitor.

His companion took it coldly. 'His mother was the daughter of Lord Finucane; he has great Irish estates. Lady Bridget, in the complete absence of male heirs, either direct or collateral—a most extraordinary circumstance—came in for no end of things. Lord Deepmere takes his principal title, however, from his English property, which is immense. He's a charming young man.'

Newman answered nothing, but he detained the Marquis as the latter was beginning gracefully to recede. 'It's a good time for me to thank you for sticking so punctiliously to our bargain—for doing so much to help me with your sister.'

The Marquis stared. 'Really, I've done nothing that I can boast of.'

'Oh, don't be modest,' Newman genially urged. 'I can't flatter myself I'm doing so well—so well, that is, as I hope and pray—simply by my own merit. Please tell your mother too, won't you? how thoroughly I feel it.' And, turning away with a sense of the fair thing done now, after all, all round, he left M. de Bellegarde looking after him more ambiguously than he knew.

XIV

THE next time Newman came to the Rue de l'Université he had the good fortune to find Madame de Cintré alone. He arrived with a definite intention and lost no time in applying it, for she wore even to his impatience an expectant, waiting look. 'I've been coming to see you for six months now and have never spoken to you a second time of marriage. That was what you asked me—I obeyed. Could any man have done better?'

'You've acted with great delicacy,' she said.

'Well, I'm going to change now. I don't mean I'm going to risk offending, but I'm going to go back to where I began. I *am* back there. I've been all round the circle. Or rather I've never been away from there. I've never ceased to want what I wanted then. Only now I'm more sure of it, if possible; I'm more sure of myself and more sure of you. I know you better, though I don't know anything I didn't believe three months ago. You're everything, you're beyond everything, I can imagine or desire. You know me now—you *must* know me. I won't say you've seen the best, but you've seen the worst. I hope you've been thinking all this while. You must have seen I was only waiting; you can't suppose I was changing. What will you say to me now? Say that everything is clear and reasonable and that I've been very patient and considerate and deserve my reward. And then give me your hand. Madame de Cintré, do that. Do it.'

'I knew you were only waiting,' she answered, 'and I was sure this day would come. I've thought about it a great deal. At first I was half afraid of it. But I'm not afraid of it now.' She paused a moment and then added: 'It's a relief.'

She sat on a low chair and Newman on an ottoman near her; he leaned a little and took her hand, which for an instant she let him keep. 'That means that I've not waited for nothing.' She looked at him a moment, and he saw her eyes fill with tears. 'With me,' he went on, 'you'll be as safe—as safe'—and even in his ardour he hesitated for a comparison—'as safe', he said with a kind of simple solemnity, 'as in your father's arms.'

Still she looked at him and her tears flowed; then she buried her face on the cushioned arm of the sofa beside her chair and broke into noiseless sobs. 'I'm weak—I'm weak,' it made him fairly tremble to hear her say.

'All the more reason why you should give yourself up to me,' he pleaded. 'Why are you troubled? There's nothing here that should trouble you. I offer you nothing but happiness. Is that so hard to believe?'

'To you everything seems so simple,' she said as she raised her head. 'But things are not so. I like you—oh, I like you. I liked you six months ago, and now I'm sure of it, as you say *you're* sure. But it's not easy, simply for that, to decide for what you ask. There are so many things to think about.'

'There ought to be only one thing—that we love each other.' And as she remained silent he quickly added: 'Very good; if you can't accept that, don't tell me.'

'I should be very glad to think of nothing,' she returned at last; 'not to think at all—only to shut both my eyes and give myself up. But I can't. I'm cold, I'm old, I'm a coward. I never supposed I should ever marry again,' she continued, 'and it seems to me too strange I should ever have listened to you. When I used to think, as a girl, of what I should do if I were to marry freely, by my own choice, I thought of a very different man from you.'

'That's nothing against me,' said Newman with an immense smile. 'Your taste wasn't formed.'

His smile lighted her own face. 'Have you formed it?' And then she said in a different tone: 'Where do you wish to live?'

'Anywhere in the wide world you like. We can easily settle that.'

'I don't know why I ask you,' she presently went on—'I care so very little. I think that if I were to marry you I could live almost anywhere. You've some false ideas about me, you think I need a great many things—that I must have a brilliant worldly life. I'm sure you're prepared to take a great deal of trouble to give me such things. But that's very arbitrary; I've done nothing to show that.' She paused again, looking at him, and her mingled sound and silence were so sweet to him that he had no more wish to hurry her than he would have had to hurry the slow flushing of the east at dawn. 'Your being so different, which at first seemed a difficulty, a danger, began one day to seem to me a pleasure, a great pleasure. I was glad you were different. And yet if I had said so no one would have understood me. And I don't mean simply my family.'

'*They* at least would have said I was a queer monster, eh?' he asked.

'They would have said I could never be happy with you—you were too different; and I would have said it was just *because* you were so different that I might be happy. But they would have given better reasons than I. My only reason—!' And she paused again.

But this time, before his golden sunrise, he felt the impulse to grasp at a rosy cloud. 'Your only reason is that you love me!' he almost groaned for deep insistence; and he laid his two hands on her with a persuasion that she rose to meet. He let her feel as he drew her close, bending his face to her, the fullest force of his imposition; and she took it from him with a silent, fragrant, flexible surrender which—since she seemed to keep back nothing—affected him as sufficiently prolonged to pledge her to everything.

He came back the next day and in the vestibule, as he entered the house, encountered his friend Mrs Bread. She was wandering about in honourable idleness and when his eyes fell upon her delivered to him straight one of her Wiltshire curtsies; then turning to the servant who had admitted him she said with a cognate respectability to which evidently a proper pronunciation of French had never had anything to add: 'You may retire; I'll have the honour of conducting monsieur.' In spite of this clean consciousness, however, it appeared to Newman that her voice had a queer quaver, as if the tone of uncontested authority were not habitual to it. The man gave her an impertinent stare, but he walked slowly away, and she led Newman upstairs. At half its course the staircase put forth two arms with an ample rest between. In a niche of this landing stood an indifferent statue of an eighteenth-century nymph, simpering with studied elegance. Here Mrs Bread stopped and looked with shy kindness at her companion. 'I know the good news, sir.'

'You've a good right to be first to know it; you've taken such a friendly interest.' And then as she turned away and began to blow the dust off the image as if this might but be free pleasantry, 'I suppose you want to congratulate me,' Newman went on, 'and I'm greatly obliged.' To which he added: 'You gave me much pleasure the other day.'

She turned round, apparently reassured. 'You're not to think I've been told anything—I've only guessed. But when I looked at you as you came in I was sure I had guessed right.'

'You're really a grand judge,' said Newman. 'I'm sure that what you don't see isn't worth seeing.'

'I'm not a fool, sir, thank God. I've guessed something else beside,' said Mrs Bread.

'What's that?'

'I needn't tell you, sir; I don't think you'd believe it. At any rate it wouldn't please you.'

'Oh, tell me nothing but what *will* please me,' he laughed. 'That's the way you began.'

'Well, sir,' she went on, 'I suppose you won't be vexed to hear that the sooner everything's over the better.'

'The sooner we're married, you mean? The better for me, certainly.'

'The better for every one.'

'The better for you perhaps. You know you're coming to live with us,' said Newman.

'I'm extremely obliged to you, sir, but it's not of my poor self I was thinking. I only wanted, if I might take the liberty, to recommend you to lose no time.'

'Who are you afraid of?'

Mrs Bread looked up the staircase and then down, and then looked at the undusted nymph as if she possibly had sentient ears. 'I'm afraid of every one.'

'What an uncomfortable state of mind!' said Newman. 'Does "every one" wish to prevent my marriage?'

'I'm afraid of already having said too much,' Mrs Bread replied. 'I won't take it back, but I won't say any more.' And she kept her course up the staircase again and led him into her mistress's salon.

Newman indulged in a brief and silent imprecation when he found this lady not alone. With her sat her mother, and toward the middle of the room stood young Madame de Bellegarde in bonnet and mantle. The old Marquise, who leant back in her chair clasping the knob of each arm, looked at him hard and without moving. She seemed barely conscious of his greeting; she might have had too much else to think of. Newman said to himself that her daughter had been announcing their engagement and that she found the morsel hard to swallow. But Madame de Cintré, as she gave him her hand, gave him also a look by which she appeared to mean that he should understand something. Was it a warning or a request? Did she wish to enjoin speech or silence? He was puzzled, and young Madame de Bellegarde's pretty grin gave him no information.

'I've not told my mother,' said Madame de Cintré abruptly and with her eyes on him.

'Told me what?' the Marquise demanded. 'You tell me too little. You should tell me everything.'

'That's what I do,' laughed Madame Urbain with all her bravery.

'Let *me* tell your mother,' said Newman.

The old woman stared at him again and then turned to her daughter. 'You're going to marry him?' she brought out.

'Oui, ma mère,' said Madame de Cintré.

'Your daughter has consented, to my very great happiness,' Newman announced.

'And when was this arrangement made?' asked Madame de Bellegarde. 'I seem to be picking up the news by chance!'

'My suspense came to an end yesterday,' said Newman.

'And how long was mine to have lasted?' the Marquise further enquired of her daughter. She spoke without irritation, with cold, noble displeasure.

Madame de Cintré stood silent and with her eyes on the ground. 'It's over at all events now.'

'Where's my son—where's Urbain?' asked the Marquise. 'Send for your brother and let him know.'

Young Madame de Bellegarde laid her hand on the bell-rope. 'He was to make some visits with me, and I was to go and knock—very softly, very softly—at the door of his study. But he can come to *me*!' She pulled the bell and in a few moments Mrs Bread appeared with a face of calm enquiry.

'Send for your brother,' the old lady went on to Claire.

But Newman felt an irresistible impulse to speak—and to speak in a certain way. 'Please tell the Marquis we want him immediately,' he said to Mrs Bread, who quietly retired.

Young Madame de Bellegarde approached her sister-in-law and embraced her, and then she turned, intensely smiling, to Newman. 'She's as charming as you like. I congratulate you.'

'I do the same, Mr Newman,' said Madame de Bellegarde with extreme solemnity. 'My daughter's an extraordinarily good woman. She may have faults, but I don't know them.'

'My mother doesn't often make jokes,' Madame de Cintré observed; 'but when she does they're terrible.'

'She's a pearl, she's adorable,' the Marquise Urbain resumed, looking at her sister-in-law with her head on one side. 'Yes, I congratulate you.'

Madame de Cintré turned away and, taking up a piece of tapestry, began to ply the needle. Some minutes of silence elapsed, which were interrupted by the arrival of M. de Bellegarde. He came in with hat in hand and irreproachably gloved, and was followed by his brother Valentin, who appeared to have just entered the house. The Marquis looked round the circle and administered to Newman his due little measure of recognition. Valentin saluted his mother and sisters and, as he shook hands with his friend, appeared to put him a sharp mute question.

'*Arrivez donc, messieurs!*' cried the young Marquise. 'We've great news for you.'

'Speak to your brother, my daughter,' said the old woman to Claire.

Madame de Cintré had been looking at her tapestry, but on this she raised her eyes. 'I've accepted Mr Newman, Urbain.'

'Yes, sir, your sister has nobly consented,' said Newman. 'You see after all I knew what I was about.'

'I beg you to believe I'm charmed!' M. de Bellegarde replied with superior benignity.

'So am I, my dear man,' said Valentin to Newman. 'The Marquis and I are charmed. I can't marry myself, but I can understand it in others when the inducements to it are overwhelming. I can't stand on my head, but I can applaud a clever acrobat when he brings down the house. My dear sister, I bless your union with this delightful gentleman.'

The Marquis stood looking for a while into the crown of his hat. 'We've been prepared,' he said at last, 'but it's inevitable that in the face of the event we should *éprouver* a certain emotion.' And he gave the oddest smile his visitor had ever beheld.

'I feel no emotion that I was not perfectly prepared for,' his mother, upon this, remarked.

'I can't say that for myself,' said Newman, who felt in his face a different light from that of the Marquis. 'I'm distinctly happier than I expected to be. I suppose it's the sight of all your happiness!'

'Don't exaggerate that,' said Madame de Bellegarde as she got up and laid her hand on her daughter's arm. 'You can't expect an honest old woman to thank you for taking away her beautiful only daughter.'

'You forget *me*, dear madame,' the young Marquise demurely interposed.

'Yes, she's very, very beautiful,' Newman agreed while he covered Claire with his bright still protection.

'And when is the wedding, pray?' asked young Madame de Bellegarde. 'I must have a month to think over the question of my falbalas.'*

'Ah, the time must be particularly discussed,' said the Marquise.

'Oh, we'll discuss it thoroughly, and we'll promptly let you know!' Newman gaily declared.

'I make very little doubt we shall agree,' said Urbain.

'If you don't agree with Madame de Cintré you'll be very unreasonable,' his visitor went on.

'Come, come, Urbain,' said young Madame de Bellegarde, 'I must go straight to my tailor's.'

The old lady had been standing with her hand on her daughter's arm and her eyes on her face. Madame de Cintré had got up; she seemed inscrutably to wait. Her mother exhaled a long heavy breath. 'No, I can't say I had been sure of you. You're a very lucky gentleman,' she added with a rather grand turn to their guest.

'Oh, I know that!' he answered. 'I feel tremendously proud. I feel like crying it on the house-tops—like stopping people in the street to tell them.'

Madame de Bellegarde narrowed her lips. 'Pray do nothing of the sort.'

'Oh, the more people who know it the better,' Newman roundly returned. 'I haven't yet announced it here, but I cabled it this morning to America.'

'"Cabled" it?' She spoke as if—what indeed well might be—she had never heard the expression.

'To New York, to Saint Louis and to San Francisco; those are the principal cities you know. To-morrow I shall tell my friends here.'

'Have you so many?' asked Madame de Bellegarde in a tone of which he perhaps but partly measured the impertinence.

'Enough to bring me a great many hand-shakes and congratulations. To say nothing,' he added in a moment, 'of those I shall receive from your own friends.'

'Our own won't use the telegraph,' said the Marquise as she took her departure.

M. de Bellegarde, whose wife, her imagination having apparently taken flight to the tailor's, was fluttering her silken wings in emulation, shook hands with Newman very pertinently and said with a more persuasive accent than the latter had ever heard him use: 'I beg you to count on me for everything.' Then his wife led him away.

Valentin, on this, stood looking from his sister to his friend. 'I hope you've both reflected very seriously.'

Madame de Cintré smiled. 'We've neither your powers of reflexion nor your depth of seriousness, but we've done our best.'

'Well, I've a great regard for each of you,' the young man continued. 'You're charming, innocent, beautiful creatures. But I'm not satisfied, on the whole, that you belong to that small and superior class—that exquisite group—composed of persons who are worthy to remain unmarried. These are rare souls, they're the salt of the earth. But I don't mean to be invidious; the marrying people are often very *gentils*.'

'Valentin holds that women should marry and that men shouldn't,' said Madame de Cintré. 'I don't know how he arranges it.'

'I arrange it by adoring you, my sister,' he ardently answered.

'You had better adore some one you can marry, by my example,' Newman laughed. 'I'll arrange *that* for you some day. I foresee I'm going to turn apostle.'

Valentin was on the threshold; he looked back a moment with a face that had grown grave. 'I adore some one I *can't* marry!' And he dropped the portière and departed.

'They don't really like it, you know,' Newman said as he stood there before his mistress.

'No,' she returned after a moment, 'they don't really like it.'

'Well now, do you mind that?' he asked.

'Yes!' she said after another interval.

'But isn't that a mistake?'

'It may be, but I can't help it. I should prefer that my mother were pleased.'

'Why the dickens then,' he yearningly enquired, '*isn't* she pleased? She gave you leave to accept me.'

'Very true; I don't understand it. And yet I do "mind" it, as you say. You'll call that superstitious.'

'That will depend on how much you let it worry you. Then I shall call it an awful bore.'

'I'll keep it to myself,' said Madame de Cintré. 'It shall not, I promise, worry *you*.' And they then talked of their marriage-day, and she assented unreservedly to his desire to have it fixed for an early date.

His messages by cable were answered promptly and with interest. Having despatched in reality but three of these, he received, for fruit of his investment, as he called it, no less than eight electrical out-pourings, all concisely humorous, which he put into his pocket-book and, the next time he encountered Madame de Bellegarde, drew forth and displayed to her. This, it must be confessed, was a slightly malicious stroke; the reader will judge in what degree the offence was venial. He knew she would dislike his barbaric trophies, but he was himself possessed by a certain hardness of triumph. Madame de Cintré, on the other hand, quite artlessly, quite touch-ingly admired them, and, most of them being of a wit quainter than any she had ever encountered, laughed at them immoderately and enquired into the character of their authors. Newman, now that his prize was gained, felt a peculiar desire that his triumph should be manifest. He more than suspected the Bellegardes of keeping quiet about it and allowing it, in their select circle, but a limited resonance; and it pleased him to think that if he were to take the trouble he might, as he phrased it, break all their windows. No honest man ever enjoys any sign of his not being acknowledged in his totality, and yet our friend, with his lucid vision, was not conscious of humiliation. He had not this good excuse for his somewhat aggressive impulse to promulgate his felicity; his sentiment was of another degree. He wanted for once to make the heads of the house of Bellegarde simply feel the weight of his hand; for when should he have another chance? He had had for the past six months a sense of the old woman's and her elder son's looking straight over *his* head, and he was now resolved that they should toe a mark which he would give himself the satisfaction of drawing.

'It's like seeing a bottle emptied when the wine's poured too slowly,' he said to Mrs Tristram. 'They make me want to joggle their elbows and force them to spill their wine.'

To this Mrs Tristram answered that he had better leave them alone and let them do things in their own way. 'You must make allowances for them—it's natural enough they should hang fire a little. They thought they accepted you when you made your application; but they're not people of imagination, they couldn't project themselves into the future, and now they'll have to begin again. But they *are* people of honour and they'll do whatever's necessary.'

Newman spent a few moments in narrow-eyed meditation. 'I'm not hard on them,' he presently said, 'and to prove it I'll invite them all to a festival.'

'A festival—?'

'You've been laughing at my great gilded rooms all winter; I'll show you they're good for something. I'll give a party. What's the grandest thing one can do here? I'll hire all the great singers from the opera and all the first people from the Théâtre Français, and I'll hold an entertainment—the biggest kind of show'.

'And who will you invite?'

'You two, first of all. And the old woman, damn her, and her son and her son's wife. And Valentin of course—for the fun of him. And then every one of their friends whom I have met at their house or elsewhere, every one who has shown me the minimum of politeness, every duke of them, such as they are, every doddering old duchess, every "great name" in the place. And then all my friends, without exception—Miss Kitty Upjohn, Miss Dora Finch, General Packard, C. P. Hatch, every pet horror even of yours. And every one shall know what it's about—to celebrate my engagement to the Countess de Cintré, who shall sit, through it all, on a golden chair above their heads and look as beautiful—and perhaps, poor dear, as bored—as a saint in paradise. What do you think of the idea?'

'I think it odious!' said Mrs Tristram. And then in a moment: 'I think it delicious!'

The very next evening Newman repaired to Madame de Bellegarde's own drawing-room, where he found her surrounded by her children and invited her to honour his poor dwelling by her presence on a certain evening a fortnight distant.

The Marquise stared a moment. 'My dear sir,' she cried, 'what on earth do you want to do to me?'

'To make you acquainted with a few people and then to place you in a very easy chair and ask you to listen to Madame Frezzolini's* singing.'

'You mean to give a concert?'

'Something of that sort.'

'And to have a crowd of people?'

'All my friends, and I hope some of yours and your daughter's. I want to celebrate my engagement.'

It seemed to him she had turned perceptibly pale. She opened her fan, a fine old painted fan of the last century, and looked at the picture, which represented a *fête champêtre*—a lady singing to a guitar and a group of dancers round a garlanded Hermes. 'We go out so little,' her elder son murmured, 'since my poor father's death.'

'But *my* poor father's still alive, my friend,' said his wife. 'I'm only waiting for my invitation to accept it;' and she glanced with amiable confidence at Newman. 'It will be magnificent, I'm sure of that.'

I am sorry to say, to the discredit of Newman's gallantry, that this lady's invitation was not then and there bestowed; he was giving all his attention to her mother-in-law. Madame de Bellegarde looked up at last with a prodigious extemporised grace. 'I can't think of letting you offer me a fête until I've offered you one. We want to present you to our friends; we'll invite them all. We have it very much at heart. We must do things in order. Come to me about the twenty-fifth; I'll let you know the exact day immediately. We shall not have any one so fine as Madame Frezzolini, but we shall have some very good people. After that you may talk of your own party.' She spoke with a certain quick eagerness, smiling more agreeably as she went on.

It seemed to Newman a handsome proposal, and such proposals always touched the sources of his good-nature. He replied after a little discussion that he would be glad to come on the twenty-fifth or any other day, and that it mattered very little whether he met his friends at her house or his own. We have noted him for observant, yet on this occasion he failed to catch a thin sharp eyebeam, as cold as a flash of steel, which passed between Madame de Bellegarde and the Marquis and which we may presume to have been a commentary on the innocence displayed in that latter clause of his speech.

Count Valentin walked away with him that evening and, when they had left the scene of so many anxieties well behind them, said reflectively: 'My mother's very strong—ah, but uncommonly strong.' Then in answer to an interrogative movement of Newman's: 'She was driven to the wall, but you'd never have thought it. Her party on the twenty-fifth was an invention of the moment. She had no idea

whatever of giving one, but, finding it the only issue from your proposal, she looked straight at the dose—pardon the expression—and
bolted it, as you saw, without winking. She's really rather grand, you
know.'

'Well, I wonder!' said Newman, divided, this time, rather whim-
sically, quite appreciatively, between the sense of his own force and
the sense of hers. 'I don't care a straw for her fiddles and ices; I'm
willing to take the will for the deed.'

'No, no!'—and Valentin showed an inconsequent touch of family
pride. 'The thing will be done now, and I dare say it will be quite
folichon!'

XV

VALENTIN's ironic forecast of the secession of Mademoiselle
Nioche from her father's domicile and his irreverent reflexion on the
attitude of this anxious parent in so grave a catastrophe received a
practical commentary in the fact that M. Nioche was slow to seek
another interview with his late pupil. It had cost Newman some
disgust to be forced to assent to his friend's expert analysis of the old
man's philosophy, and, though circumstances seemed to indicate that
he had not given himself up to a noble despair, our hero thought it
possible he might be suffering more keenly than he allowed to
become flagrant. M. Nioche had been in the habit of paying him a
respectful little visit every two or three weeks, and his absence might
be a proof quite as much of extreme depression as of a desire to
conceal the success with which he had patched up his sorrow.
Newman presently gathered in the bright garden of Valentin's talk
several of the flowers of the young woman's recent history.

'I told you she was remarkable,' this consistent reasoner declared,
'and it's proved by the way she has managed this most important of
all her steps. She has had other chances, but she was resolved to take
none but the best. She did you the honour to think for a while that
you might be such a chance. You were not; so she gathered up her
patience and waited a little longer. At last her occasion arrived, and
she made her move with her eyes open. I'm very sure she had no
innocence to lose, but she had all her respectability. Dubious little
damsel as you thought her she had kept a firm hold of that; nothing
could be proved against her, and she was determined not to let her
reputation go till she had got her equivalent. About her equivalent
she had high ideas. Apparently her requirements have been met.
Well, they've been met in a superior form. The form's fifty years old,
baldheaded and deaf, but he's very easy about money.'

'And where in the world,' asked Newman, 'did you pick up this
valuable information?'

'In animated conversation. Remember my frivolous habits. Conversation—and this time not criminal!—with a young woman
engaged in the humble trade of glove-cleaner who keeps a small shop
in the Rue Saint-Roch.* M. Nioche lives in the same house, up six

pairs of stairs, across the court in and out of whose ill-swept doorway Miss Noémie has been flitting for the last five years. The little glove-cleaner was an old acquaintance; she used to be the friend of a friend of mine—the foolish friend of a foolish friend—who has married and given up friendship. I often saw her in his society. As soon as I made her out behind her clear little window-pane I recollected her. I had on a spotlessly fresh pair of gloves, but I went in and held up my hands and said to her: "Dear mademoiselle, what will you ask me for cleaning these?" "Dear Count," she answered immediately, "I'll clean them for *you* for nothing." She had instantly recognised me and I had to hear her history from ever so far back. But after that I put her on that of her neighbours. She knows and admires Noémie, and she told me what I've just repeated.'

A month elapsed without any reappearance of M. Nioche, and Newman, who every morning read, for practice, about the suicides of the day in a newspaper, began to suspect that, mortification proving stubborn, he had sought a balm for his wounded pride in the waters of the Seine. He had a note of the poor gentleman's address in his pocket-book, and, finding himself one day in the *quartier*, determined, so far as he might, to clear up his doubts. He repaired to the house in the Rue Saint-Roch which bore the recorded number, and observed in a neighbouring basement, behind a dangling row of neatly inflated gloves, the unmistakeable face of Valentin's informant—a sallow person in a dressing-gown—peering into the street as if in expectation that this amiable nobleman would pass again. But it was not to her that Newman applied; he simply enquired of the portress if M. Nioche were at home. The portress replied, as the portress invariably replies, that her lodger had gone out barely three minutes before, but then, through the little square hole of her lodge-window, taking the measure of Newman's resources and seeing them, by an unspecified process, refresh the dry places of servitude to occupants of fifth floors on courts, she added that M. Nioche would have had just time to reach the Café de la Patrie, round the second turning to the left, at which establishment he regularly spent his afternoons. Newman thanked her for the information, took the second turning to the left and arrived at the Café de la Patrie. He felt a momentary hesitation to go in; was it not rather mean to press so hard on humiliated dignity? There passed across his vision an image of a haggard little septuagenarian taking measured sips of a glass of sugar and water and finding them quite impotent to sweeten his desolation. But he opened the door and entered, perceiving nothing at first but a dense cloud of tobacco-smoke. Across this, however, in a corner, he presently descried the figure of M. Nioche, stirring the contents of a deep glass and with a lady seated in front of him. The lady's back was presented, but her companion promptly perceived and recognised his visitor. Newman had gone forward, and the old man rose slowly, gazing at him with a more blighted expression even than usual.

'If you're drinking hot punch,' Newman said, 'I suppose you're not dead. That's all right. You needn't move to show it.'

M. Nioche stood staring with a fallen jaw, not risking any confidence. The lady who faced him turned round in her place and glanced up with a spirited toss of her head, displaying the agreeable features of his daughter. She looked at Newman hard, to see how he was looking at her, then—I don't know what she discovered—she said graciously: 'How d'ye do, monsieur? won't you come into our little corner?'

'Did you come—did you come after *me*, monsieur?' asked M. Nioche very softly.

'I went to your house to see what had become of you. I thought you might be sick,' monsieur said mildly enough.

'It's very good of you, as always,' the old man returned. 'No, I'm not well. Yes, I'm *seek*.'

'Ask monsieur to sit down,' said Mademoiselle Nioche. 'Garçon, bring a chair for monsieur.'

'Will you do us the honour to *seat*?' M. Nioche enquired timorously and with a double foreignness of accent.

Newman said to himself that he had better see the thing out, and he took a place at the end of the table with the brilliant girl on his left and the dingy old man on the other side. 'You'll take something of course,' said Miss Noémie, who was sipping a brown *màdère*. Newman said he guessed not, and then she turned to her parent with a smile. 'What an honour, eh?—he has only come for us.' M. Nioche drained his pungent glass at a long draught and looked out from eyes more lachrymose in consequence. 'But you didn't come for *me*, eh?' Noémie went on. 'You didn't expect to find me here?'

He observed the change in her appearance and that she was very elegant, really prettier than before; she looked a year or two older, and it was noticeable that, to the eye, she had only added a sharp accent to her appearance of 'propriety', only taken a longer step toward distinction. She was dressed in quiet colours and wore her expensively unobtrusive gear with a grace that might have come from years of practice. Her presence of mind, her perfect equilibrium, struck Newman as portentous, and he inclined to agree with Valentin that the young lady was very remarkable. 'No, to tell the truth, I didn't come for you,' he said, 'and I didn't expect to find you. I was told,' he added in a moment, 'that you had left your good father.'

'*Quelle horreur!*' she cried with the brightest of all her smiles. 'Does one *ever* leave one's good father? You've the happy proof of the contrary.'

'Yes, convincing proof,' said Newman with his almost embarrassed eyes on M. Nioche. The old man caught his glance obliquely, with his faded deprecation, and then, lifting his empty glass, pretended to drink again.

'Who told you that?' Noémie demanded. 'But I know very well. It was M. de Bellegarde. Why don't you say yes? You're not polite.'

'I'm so shy and simple and stupid,' Newman said with a certain fond good faith.

'I set you a better example. I know M. de Bellegarde told you. He knows a great deal about me—or he thinks he does. He has taken a great deal of trouble to find out, but half of it isn't true. In the first place I haven't left my father, any more than he has left me. I'm much too fond of him, and never so fond as now, when he has been *gentil, mais gentil*—! Isn't it so, little father? Haven't you been *gentil, mais gentil*? M. de Bellegarde's a charming young man; it's impossible to *mieux causer*. I know a good deal about *him* too; you can tell him that when you next see him.'

'No,' said Newman with a sturdy grin; 'I won't carry any messages from you.'

'Just as you please,' his young friend placidly returned. 'I don't depend on you, nor does M. de Bellegarde either. He's very much interested in me, he can be left to his own devices. He's a contrast to *you*, monsieur,' Noémie went on with a fine little flight of dignity.

'Oh, he's a great contrast to me, I've no doubt,' said Newman. 'But I don't exactly know how you mean it.'

'I mean it in this way. First of all he never offered to help me to a *dot* and a husband.' And Mademoiselle Nioche expressively paused.

'I won't say that's in his favour, for I do you justice. What led you, by the way, to make me such a monstrous offer? You didn't care for me.'

'Oh yes—I did,' said Newman.

'Well, how much?'

'It would have given me real pleasure to see you married to a respectable young fellow.'

'With six thousand francs of income!' Noémie cried. 'Do you call that caring for me? I'm afraid you know little about women. You were not *galant*; you were not what you might have been.'

Newman flushed a trifle fiercely. 'I say!' he exclaimed, 'that's rather strong. I had no idea I had been so shabby.'

She laughed out as she took up her muff—it was almost her only hint of vulgarity. 'It's something at any rate to have made you angry.'

Her father had leaned both his elbows on the table, and his head, bent forward, was supported on his hands, the thin white fingers of which were pressed over his ears. In this position he stared fixedly at the bottom of his empty glass, and Newman supposed he was not hearing. Noémie buttoned her furred jacket and pushed back her chair, casting a glance charged with the consciousness of an expensive appearance first down over her flounces and then up at Newman.

'You had better have remained an honest girl,' his obstinate sense of his old friend's painful situation prompted him at last to remark.

M. Nioche continued to stare at the bottom of his glass, and his daughter got up, still bravely smiling. 'You mean that I look so much like one? That's more than most women do nowadays. Don't judge me yet a while,' she added. 'I mean to succeed; that's what I mean to do. I leave you; I don't mean to be seen in such places as this, for one thing. I can't think what you want of my poor father; he's very comfortable now. It isn't his fault either. *Au revoir*, little father.' And she tapped the old man on the head with her muff. Then she stopped a minute, looking again at their visitor. 'Tell M. de Bellegarde, when he wants news of me, to come and get it from *me*!' And she turned and departed, the white-aproned waiter, with a bow, holding the door wide open for her.

M. Nioche sat motionless, and Newman hardly knew what to say to him. The old man looked dismally foolish. 'So you determined not to shoot her, after all,' Newman said presently.

M. Nioche, without moving, raised his eyes and let all their confession quite dismally and abjectly come. They didn't somehow presume to ask for pity, yet they doubtless pretended even less to a rugged ability to do without it. They might have expressed the state of mind of an innocuous insect, flat in shape, conscious of the impending pressure of a boot-sole and reflecting that he was perhaps too flat to be crushed. M. Nioche's gaze was a profession of moral flatness. 'You despise me terribly', he said in the weakest possible voice.

'Oh no; it's not your own affair. And hanged if I understand your institutions anyway!'

'I made you too many fine speeches,' M. Nioche added. 'I meant them at the time.'

'I'm sure I'm very glad you didn't shoot her,' Newman went on. 'I was afraid you might have shot yourself. That's why I came to look you up.' And he began to button his coat.

'Neither, *hélas*! You despise me and I can't explain to you. I hoped I shouldn't see you again.'

'Why, that's pretty mean,' said Newman. 'You shouldn't drop your friends that way. Besides, the last time you came to see me I thought you felt rather fine.'

'Yes, I remember'—M. Nioche musingly recalled it. 'I must have been, I *was*, in a fever. I didn't know what I said, what I did. I spoke, no doubt, wild words.'

'Ah well, you're quieter now.'

M. Nioche bethought himself. 'As quiet as the grave,' he then struck off.

'Are you very unhappy?' Newman more ingenuously asked.

M. Nioche rubbed his forehead slowly and even pushed back his wig a little, looking askance at his empty glass. 'Yes—yes. But that's an old story. I've always been unhappy. My daughter does what she will with me. I take what she gives me—I make a face, but I take it. I've no pluck, and when you've no pluck you must keep quiet: you can't go about telling people. I shan't trouble you any more.'

'Well,' said Newman, rather disgusted at the smooth operation of the old man's philosophy, 'that's as you please.'

M. Nioche seemed to have been prepared to be despised, but he nevertheless appealed feebly from his patron's faint praise. 'After all she's my daughter and I can still look after her. If she has her bad idea, why she has it and she won't let go of it. And then *now*,' he pointed out—'it's fine talking! But there are many different paths, there are degrees. I can place at her disposal the benefit, the benefit'—and he paused, staring vaguely at his friend, who began to suspect his mind of really giving way—'the benefit of my experience.'

'Your experience?' Newman inquired, both amused and amazed.

'My experience of business,' said M. Nioche gravely.

'Ah yes,' Newman laughed, 'that will be a great advantage to her!' And then he said good-bye and offered the poor foolish old man his hand.

M. Nioche took it and leaned back against the wall, holding it a moment and looking up at him. 'I suppose you think my wits are going. Very likely; I've always a pain in my head. That's why I can't explain, I can't present the case. And she's so strong, she makes me walk as she will—anywhere! But there's this—there's this.' And he stopped, still staring up at his visitor. His little white eyes expanded and glittered for a moment like those of a cat in the dark. 'It's not as it seems. I haven't forgiven her. Oh, *par exemple*, no!'

'That's right, don't let up on it. If you should, you don't know what she still *might* do!'

'It's horrible, it's terrible,' said M. Nioche; 'but do you want to know the truth? I hate her! I take what she gives me, and I hate her more. To-day she brought me three hundred francs; they're here in my waistcoat-pocket. Now I hate her almost cruelly. No, I haven't forgiven her.'

Newman had a return of his candour. 'Why then did you accept the money?'

'If I hadn't I should have hated her still more. That, you see, is the nature of misery. No, I haven't forgiven her.'

'Well, take care you don't hurt her!' Newman laughed again. And with this he took his leave. As he passed along the glazed side of the café, on reaching the street, he saw the old man motion the waiter, with a melancholy gesture, to replenish his glass.

A week after his visit to the Café de la Patrie he called one morning on Valentin de Bellegarde and by good fortune found him at home. He spoke of his interview with M. Nioche and his daughter, and said he was afraid Valentin had judged the old man correctly. He had found the couple hobnobbing together in amity; the old gentleman's rigour was purely theoretic. Newman confessed he was disappointed; he should have expected to see his venerable friend take high ground.

'High ground, my dear fellow!' Valentin returned; 'there's no high ground for him to take. The only perceptible eminence in M. Nioche's horizon is Montmartre,* which isn't an edifying quarter. You can't go mountaineering in a flat country.'

'He remarked indeed,' said Newman, 'that he had not forgiven her. But she'll never find it out.'

'We must do him the justice to suppose he intensely disapproves. His gifted child,' Valentin added, 'is like one of the great artists whose biographies we read, those who at the beginning of their career suffered opposition in the domestic circle. Their vocation was not recognised by their families, but the world has done it justice. Noémie has a vocation.'

'Damn her vocation! Oh,' added Newman impatiently, 'you're a cold-blooded crew!'

Valentin sounded him a moment with curious eyes. 'You must be very fond of boiled beef and cabbage to have such a suspicion of ripe peaches and plums.'

But Newman sturdily met his look. 'I shouldn't think I'd have to tell *you* what fruit I gather!'

The young man, at this, closed his eyes an instant and then, with a motion of his hand, shook his head. After which he gravely said: 'I back you more than ever!'

'Let me then,' his companion returned, 'do what I suppose you'd call the fair thing by you. Miss Noémie desired me to tell you—but hanged if I know what!'

'Bless your quiet imagination,' said Valentin, 'do you suppose I've been waiting for you? I've been to see her for myself—no less than three times these five days. She's a charming hostess; we attack the noblest subjects of discussion. She's really very clever and a rare and remarkable type; not at all low nor wanting to be low—determined not to be. She means to take very good care of herself. She's as perfect as you please, and as hard and clear-cut as some little figure of a sea-nymph on an antique intaglio;* and I warrant she hasn't a grain more true sensibility than if she was scooped out of a big amethyst. You can't scratch her even with a diamond. Extremely pretty—really, when you know her, she's wonderfully pretty—intelligent, determined, ambitious, unscrupulous, capable of seeing a man strangled

without changing colour, she's, upon my honour, remarkably
agreeable.'

'Well,' said Newman after reflexion, 'I once saw in a needle-factory
a gentleman from the city, who had stopped too near a machine that
struck him as curious, picked up as clean as if he had been removed
by a silver fork from a china plate, and swallowed down and ground
to small pieces!'

Re-entering his rooms late in the evening, three days after
Madame de Bellegarde had struck her bargain with him, as he might
feel, over the entertainment at which she was to present him to the
world, he found on his table a goodly card of announcement to the
effect that she would be at home on the twenty-seventh of the month
and at ten o'clock in the evening. He stuck it into the frame of his
mirror and eyed it with some complacency; it seemed to him a document of importance and an emblem of triumph. Stretched out in a
chair he looked at it lovingly, and while he so revelled Valentin was
shown into the place. The young man's glance presently followed the
direction of Newman's and he perceived his mother's invitation.

'And what have they put into the corner? Not the customary
"music", "dancing", or "*tableaux vivants*"?* They ought at least to
put "An American of Americans".'

'Oh, there are to be several of us,' Newman said. 'Mrs Tristram
told me to-day she had received a card and sent an acceptance.'

'Ah then, with Mrs Tristram and her husband you'll have support.
My mother might have put on her card "Three Americans in a
Row"—which you can pronounce in either way you like, though I
know the way I should suppose most American. I dare say at least
you'll not lack amusement. You'll see a great many of the best people
in France—I mean of the long pedigrees, and the *beaux noms*, and
the great fidelities, and the rare stupidities, and the faces and figures
that, after all, sometimes, I suppose God did make. We've already
shown you specimens in numbers—you know by which end to take
them.'

'Oh, they haven't hurt me yet,' said Newman, 'and I guess they
would, by this time, if they were going to. I seem to want to like
people, these days—seem regularly to *like* liking them, and almost
any one will do. I feel so good that if I wasn't sure I'm going to be
married I might think I'm going to die.'

'Do you make,' the young man enquired, 'so much of a distinction?' But he dropped rather wearily into a chair and went on before his host could answer. 'Happy man, only remember that there are poor devils whom the flaunted happiness of others sometimes irritates.'

'Do you call a person a poor devil,' demanded Newman, 'who's as good as my brother-in-law?'

'Your brother-in-law?' his friend a trifle musingly echoed.

'Say then my brother,' Newman kindly returned—'and leave the other description for yours.'

It made Valentin after an instant rise to him. 'You're really very charming. You have your own way for it—which must have been your way of making love. Well,' he sighed with a dimmer smile than usual, 'I don't wonder and I don't question! Only you *are*, I understand'— he immediately took himself up—'"really and truly" in love?'

'Yes, sir!' said Newman after a pause.

'And do you hold that *she* is?'

'You had better ask her,' Newman answered. 'Not for me, but for yourself.'

'I never ask anything for myself. Haven't you noticed that? Besides, she wouldn't tell me, and it's after all none of my business.'

Newman hesitated, but 'She doesn't know!' he the next thing brought out. 'However, she *will* know.'

'Ah then, *you* will—which I see you don't yet. But what you'll know will be what you want, for that's the way things turn out for you.' And Valentin's grave fine eyes, as if under some impression oddly quickened, measured him again a moment up and down. 'The way you cover the ground! However, being as you are a giant, you move naturally in seven-league boots.' With which again he turned restlessly off.

Newman's attention, from before the fire, followed him a little. 'There's something the matter with you to-night: you're kind of perverse—you're almost kind of vicious. But wait till I'm through with my business—to which I wish to give just now my undivided attention—and then we'll talk. By which I mean I'll fix you somehow.'

'Ah, there will be plenty of me for you, such as I am—for you always. Only when, then,' Valentin asked, '*is* the event?'

'About five weeks hence—on a day not quite yet settled.'

He accepted this answer with interest, in spite of which, however, 'You feel very confident of the future?' he next attentively
demanded.

'Confident,' said Newman with the large accent from which semi-
tones were more than ever absent. 'I knew what I wanted exactly, and
now I know what I've got.'

'You're sure then you're going to be happy?'

'Sure?'—Newman competently weighed it. 'So foolish a question
deserves a foolish answer. Yes—I'll be hanged if I ain't sure!'

Well, if Valentin was to pass for perverse it would not be, he
seemed to wish to show, for nothing. 'You're not afraid of anything?'

'What should I be afraid of? You can't hurt me unless you kill me
by some violent means. That I should indeed regard as a tremendous
sell. I want to live and I mean to live: I mean to have a good time. I
can't die of sickness, because I'm naturally healthy, and the time for
dying of old age won't come round yet a while. I can't lose my wife,
I shall take too good care of her. I can't lose my money, or much of
it—I've fixed it so on purpose. So what have I to be afraid of?'

'You're not afraid it may be rather a mistake for such an infuriated
modern to marry—well, such an old-fashioned rococo product; a
daughter, as one may say, of the Crusaders, almost of the Patriarchs?'

Newman, who had been moving about as they talked, stopped
before his visitor. 'Does that mean you're worried for her?'

Valentin met his eyes. 'I'm worried for everything.'

'Ah, if that's all—!' And then: 'Trust me—*because* I'm modern
and can compare all round—to know where I stand!' With which, as
from the impulse to celebrate his happy certitude by a bonfire, he
turned to throw a couple of logs on the already blazing hearth.
Valentin watched a few moments the quickened flame; after which,
with his elbow supported on the chimney and his head on his hand,
he gave an expressive sigh. 'Got a headache?' Newman asked.

'*Je suis triste*,' he answered with Gallic simplicity.

Newman stared at the remark as if it had been scrawled on a slate
by a school-boy—a weakling whom he wouldn't wish, however, too
harshly to snub. 'You've got a sentimental stomach-ache, eh? Have
you caught it from the lady you told me the other night you adored
and couldn't marry?'

'Did I really speak of her?' Valentin asked as if a little struck. 'I
was afraid afterwards I had made some low allusion—for I don't as

a general thing (and it's a rare scruple I have!) drag in *ces dames* before Claire. But I was feeling the bitterness of life, as who should say, when I spoke; and—yes, if you want to know—I've my mouth full of it still. Why did you ever introduce me to that girl?'

'Oh, it's Noémie, is it? Lord deliver us! You don't mean to say you're lovesick about *her*?'

'Lovesick, no; it's not a grand passion. But the cold-blooded little demon sticks in my thoughts; she has bitten me with those even little teeth of hers; I feel as if I might turn rabid and do something crazy in consequence. It's very low, it's disgustingly low. She's the most mercenary little jade in Europe. Yet she really affects my peace of mind; she's always running in my head. It's a striking and a vile contrast to your noble and virtuous attachment. It's rather pitiful that it should be the best I'm able to do for myself at my present respectable age. I'm a nice young man, eh, *en somme*? You can't warrant my future as you do your own.'

'Drop the creature right here,' said Newman; 'don't go near her again, and your future will be all right. Come over to America and I'll get you a place in a bank.'

'It's easy to say drop her'—Valentin spoke with a certain gravity in his lucidity. 'You might as well drop a pretty panther who has every one of her claws in your flesh and who's in the act of biting your heart out. One *has* to keep up the acquaintance, if only to show one isn't afraid.'

'You've better things to keep up, it seems to me, than such acquaintances. Remember too,' Newman went on, 'that I didn't want to introduce you to her; you insisted. I had a sort of creepy feeling about it even at the time.'

'Oh, I no more reproach you with misleading my innocence than I reproach myself with practising on hers. She's really extraordinary. The way she has already spread her wings is amazing. I don't know when a woman has amused me more. But pardon me,' he added in an instant; 'she doesn't amuse *you*, at second-hand; your interest appears to flag just where that of many men would wake up. Let us talk of something else.' Valentin introduced another topic, but he had within five minutes reverted by a bold transition to Mademoiselle Nioche and was throwing off pictures of her 'home' and quoting specimens of her *mots*. These latter were very droll and, for a young woman who six months before had been dabbling in sacred subjects, remarkably profane. But at last, abruptly, he stopped, became thoughtful and for some time afterwards said nothing. When he rose to go it was evident that his thoughts were still running on his rare young friend. 'Yes,' he wound up, 'she's a beautiful little monster!'

XVI

THE next ten days were to be the happiest Newman had ever known. He saw Madame de Cintré every day, and never saw either her mother or the elder of his prospective brothers-in-law. The woman of his choice at last seemed to think it becoming to apologise for their never being present. 'They're much taken up,' she said, 'with doing the honours of Paris to Lord Deepmere.' Her gravity as she made this declaration was almost prodigious, and it even deepened as she added: 'He's our seventh cousin, you know, and blood's thicker than water. And then he's so interesting!' And with this she strangely smiled.

He met young Madame de Bellegarde two or three times, always roaming about with graceful vagueness and as if in search of an un-attainable ideal of diversion. She reminded him of some elegant painted phial, cracked and fragrantly exhaling; but he felt he owed indulgence to a lady who on her side owed submission to Urbain de Bellegarde. He pitied that nobleman's wife the more, also, that she was a silly, thirstily-smiling little brunette with a suggestion of the unregulated heart. The small Marquise sometimes looked at him with an intensity too marked not to be innocent, since vicious advances, he conceived, were usually much less direct. She appar-ently wanted to ask him something; he wondered what it might be. But he was shy of giving her an opportunity, because, if her com-munication bore upon the aridity of her matrimonial lot, he was at a loss to see how he could help her. He had a fancy, however, of her coming up to him some day and saying (after looking round behind her) with a little passionate hiss: 'I know you detest my husband; let me have the pleasure of promising you that you're right. Pity a poor woman who's married to a clock-image in *papier-mâché*!' Possessing, at any rate, in default of a competent knowledge of the principles of etiquette, a very downright sense of the 'meanness' of certain actions, it seemed to him to belong to his proper position to keep on his guard; he was not going to put it into the power of these people to say he had done in their house anything not absolutely straight. As it was, Madame de Bellegarde used to give him news of the dress she meant to wear at his wedding, and which had not yet, in her creative imagination, in spite of many interviews with the tailor, resolved itself into its composite totality. 'I told you pale blue bows on the sleeves, at the elbow,' she would say. 'But to-day I don't see my blue bows at all. I don't know what has become of them. To-day I see pink—a tender sort of *cuisse de nymphe* pink. And then I pass through strange desolate phases in which neither blue nor pink says anything to me. And yet I must have the bows.'

'Have them green or yellow,'* Newman sometimes suggested.

'*Malheureux!*' the little Marquise would then piercingly cry. 'I hope you're not going to pretend to dress your wife. Claire's an angel, yes, but her bows, already, are—well, quite of another world!'

Madame de Cintré was calmly content before society, but her lover had the felicity of feeling that before him, when society was absent, her sense of security overflowed. She said charming and tender things. 'I take no pleasure in you. You never give me a chance to scold you, to correct you. I bargained for that; I expected to enjoy it. But you won't do anything wrong or queer or dreadful, and yet you won't even look as if you were trying to do right. You're easier than we are, you're easier than I am, and I quite see that you've reasons, of some sort, that are as good as ours. It's dull for me therefore,' she smiled, 'and it's rather disappointing, not to have anything to show you or to tell you or to teach you, anything that you don't seem already quite capable of knowing and doing and feeling. What's left of all the good one was going to do you? It's very stupid, there's no excitement for me; I might as well be marrying some one—well, some one *not* impossible.'

'I'm afraid I'm as impossible as I know how to be, and that it's all the worst I can do in the time,' Newman would say in answer to this. 'Kindly make the best of *any* inconvenience.' He assured her that he would never visit on her any sense of her own deficiencies; he would treat her at least as if she were perfectly satisfactory. 'Oh,' he then broke out, 'if you only knew how exactly you're what I coveted! I'm beginning to understand why I wanted it; the having it makes all the difference that I expected. Never was a man so pleased with his good fortune. You've been holding your head for a week past just as I wanted my wife to hold hers. You say just the things I want her to say. You walk about the room just as I want her to walk. You've just the taste in dress I want her to have. In short you come up to the mark, and, I can tell you, my mark was high.'

These assurances tended to make his friend more grave. At last she said: 'Depend on it I don't come up to the mark at all; your mark's much too high. I'm not all you suppose; I'm a much smaller affair. She's a magnificent person, the person you imagine. Pray how did she come to such perfection?'

'She was never anything *but* perfection,' Newman replied.

'I really believe,' his companion went on, 'that she's better than any fond flight of my own ambition. Do you know that's a very handsome compliment? Well, sir, I'll *make* her my ambition!'

Mrs Tristram came to see her dear Claire after Newman had announced his engagement, and she observed to our hero the next day that his fortune was simply absurd. 'For the ridiculous part of it is that you're evidently going to be as happy as if you were marrying Miss Smith or Miss Brown. I call it a brilliant match for you, but you get brilliancy without paying any tax on it. Those things are usually a compromise, but here you've everything, and nothing crowds anything else out. You'll be brilliantly happy—with the rest of the brilliancy. I consider really that I've done it for you, but it's almost more than I can myself bear.' Newman thanked her for her pleasant encouraging way of saying things; no woman could encourage or discourage better. Tristram's way was different; he had been taken by his wife to call on Madame de Cintré and he gave an account of the expedition.

'You don't catch me risking a personal estimate this time, I guess, do you? I put my foot in it for you once. That's a jolly underhand thing to do, by the way—coming round to sound a fellow on the woman you're going to marry. You deserve anything you get. Then of course you rush and tell her, and she takes care to make it pleasant for the spiteful wretch the first time he calls. I'll do you the justice to say, however, that you don't seem to have told your present friend—or if you did she let me down easy. She was very nice; she was tremendously polite. She and Lizzie sat on the sofa pressing each other's hands and calling each other *chère belle*, and Madame de Cintré sent me every third word a magnificent smile, as if to give me to understand that I too was a beauty and a darling. She made up for past neglect, I assure you; she was very pleasant and sociable. Only in an evil hour it came into her head to say that she must present us to her mother—her mother wished to know any good friends of yours. I didn't want to know her mother, and I was on the point of telling Lizzie to go in alone and let me wait for her outside. But Lizzie, with her usual infernal ingenuity, guessed my purpose and looked me into obedience. So they marched off arm-in-arm and I followed as I could. We found the old lady in her armchair twiddling her aristocratic thumbs. She eyed Lizzie hard, from head to foot; but at that game Lizzie, to do her justice, was a match for her. My wife told her we were great friends of Mr Newman. The Marquise stared a moment and then said: "Oh, Mr Newman? My daughter has made up her mind to marry a Mr Newman." Then Madame de Cintré began to fondle Lizzie again and said it was this dear lady who had had the idea and brought them together. "Oh, it's you I have to thank for my American son-in-law?" Madame de Bellegarde said to Mrs Tristram. "It was a very clever thought of yours. Be sure of my high appreciation." With which she began to look at me too, and presently said: "Pray, are you engaged in some species of manufacture?" I wanted to say that I manufactured broomsticks for old witches to ride on, but Lizzie got in ahead of me. "My husband, madame la Marquise, belongs to that unfortunate class of persons who have no profession and no occupation, and who thereby do very little good in the world." To get her poke at the old woman she didn't care where she shoved *me*. "Dear me," said the Marquise, "we all have our duties." "I'm sorry mine compel me to take leave of you," said Lizzie. And we bundled out again. But you have a mother-in-law in all the force of the time-honoured term.'

'Oh,' Newman made answer, 'my mother-in-law desires nothing better than to let me alone!'

Betimes, on the evening of the twenty-seventh, he went to Madame de Bellegarde's ball. The old house in the Rue de l'Université shone strangely in his eyes. In the circle of light projected from the outer gate a detachment of the populace stood watching the carriages roll in; the court was illumined with flaring torches and the portico draped and carpeted. When Newman arrived there were but few persons present. The Marquise and her two daughters were on the top landing of the staircase, where the ancient marble nymph peeped out from a bower of plants. Madame de Bellegarde, in purple and pearls and fine laces, resembled some historic figure painted by Vandyke;* she made her daughter, in comparative vaguenesses of white, splendid and pale, seem, for his joy of possession, infinitely modern and near. His hostess greeted him with a fine hard urbanity and, looking round, called to several of the persons standing at hand. They were elderly gentlemen with faces as marked and featured and filled-in, for some science of social topography, as, to Newman's whimsical sense, any of the little towered and battered old towns, on high eminences, that his tour of several countries during the previous summer had shown him; they were adorned with strange insignia, cordons and ribbons and orders, as if the old cities were flying flags and streamers and hanging out shields for a celebration, and they approached with measured alertness while the Marquise presented them the good friend of the family who was to marry her daughter. The good friend heard a confused enumeration of titles and names that matched, to his fancy, the rest of the paraphernalia; the gentlemen bowed and smiled and murmured without reserve, and he indulged in a series of impartial hand-shakes, accompanied in each case by a 'Very happy to meet you, sir.' He looked at Madame de Cintré, but her attention was absent. If his personal self-consciousness had been of a nature to make him constantly refer to her as to the critic before whom in company he played his part, he might have found it a flattering proof of her confidence that he never caught her eyes resting on him. It is a reflexion he didn't make, but we may nevertheless risk it, that in spite of this circumstance she probably saw every movement of his little finger. The Marquise Urbain was wondrously dressed in crimson crape bestrewn with huge silver moons—full discs and fine crescents, half the features of the firmament.

'You don't say anything about my *toilette*,' she impatiently observed to him.

'Well, I feel as if I were looking at you through a telescope. You put me in mind of some lurid comet, something grand and wild.'

'Ah, if I'm grand and wild I match the occasion! But I'm not a heavenly body.'

'I never saw the sky at midnight that particular shade of crimson,' Newman said.

'That's just my originality: any fool could have chosen blue. My sister-in-law would have chosen a lovely shade of that colour, with a dozen little delicate moons. But I think crimson much more amusing. And I give my idea, which is moonshine.'

'Moonshine and bloodshed,' said Newman.

'A murder by moonlight,' the young woman laughed. 'What a

delicious idea for a toilet! To make it complete there's a dagger of diamonds, you see, stuck into my hair. But here comes Lord Deepmere,' she added in a moment; 'I must find out what he thinks of it.' Lord Deepmere came up very red in the face and very light, apparently, at heart; at once very much amused and very little committed. 'My Lord Deepmere can't decide which he prefers, my sister-in-law or me,' Madame Urbain went on. 'He likes Claire because she's his cousin, and me because I'm not. But he has no right to make love to Claire, whereas I'm perfectly *disponible*. It's very wrong to make love to a woman who's engaged, but it's very wrong *not* to make love to a woman who's married.'

'Oh, it's very jolly making love to married women,' the young man said, 'because they can't ask you to marry them.'

'Is that what the others do—the spinsters?' Newman enquired.

'Oh dear, yes—in England all the girls ask a fellow to marry them.'

'And a fellow brutally refuses,' Madame Urbain commented.

'Why, really, you know, a fellow can't marry any girl that asks him,' said his lordship.

'Your cousin won't ask you. She's going to marry Mr Newman.'

'Oh, that's a very different thing!' Lord Deepmere readily agreed.

'You'd have accepted *her*, I suppose. That makes me hope that, after all, you prefer me.'

'Oh, when things are nice I never prefer one to the other,' said the young man. 'I take them all.'

'Ah, what a horror! I won't be taken in that way, especially as a "thing",' cried his interlocutress. 'Mr Newman's much better; he knows how to choose. Oh, he chooses as if he were threading a needle. He prefers the Comtesse to any rival attraction, however brilliant.'

'Well, you can't help my being her cousin,' said Lord Deepmere to Newman with candid hilarity.

'Oh no, I can't help that,' Newman laughed back. 'Neither can she!'

'And you can't help my dancing with her,' said Lord Deepmere with sturdy simplicity.

'I could prevent that only by dancing with her myself,' Newman returned. 'But unfortunately I don't know how to dance.'

'Oh, you may dance without knowing how; may you not, milord?' Madame Urbain asked. But to this Lord Deepmere replied that a fellow ought to know how to dance if he didn't want to make an ass of himself; and at this same moment the Marquis joined the group, slow-stepping and with his hands behind him.

'This is a very splendid entertainment,' Newman cheerfully observed. 'The old house looks very pleasant and bright.'

'If you're pleased we're content.' And the Marquis lifted his shoulders and bent them forward.

'Oh, I suspect every one's pleased,' said Newman. 'How can they help being pleased when the first thing they see as they come in is your sister standing there as beautiful as an angel of light and of charity?'

'Yes, she's very beautiful,' the Marquis a little distantly admitted. 'But that's not so great a source of satisfaction to other people, naturally, as to you.'

'Well, I *am* satisfied and suited, Marquis—there's no doubt but what I *am*,' said Newman with his protracted enunciation. 'And now tell me,' he added, taking in more of the scene, 'who some of these pleasant folks are.'

M. de Bellegarde looked about him in silence, with his head bent and his hand raised to his lower lip, which he slowly rubbed. A stream of people had been pouring into the salon in which Newman stood with his host, the rooms were filling up and the place, all light and colour and fine resonance, looked rich and congressional. It borrowed its splendour largely from the shining shoulders and profuse jewels of the woman, and from the rest of their festal array. There were uniforms, but not many, as Madame de Bellegarde's door was inexorably closed against the mere myrmidons of the upstart power which then flourished on the soil of France, and the great company of smiling and chattering faces was not, as to line and feature, a collection of gold or silver medals. It was a pity for our friend, nevertheless, that he had not been a physiognomist, for these mobile masks, much more a matter of wax than of bronze, were the picture of a world and the vivid translation, as might have seemed to him, of a text that had had otherwise its obscurities. If the occasion had been different they would hardly have pleased him; he would have found in the women too little beauty and in the men too many smirks; but he was now in a humour to receive none but fair impressions, and it sufficed him to note that every one was charged with some vivacity or some solemnity and to feel that the whole great sum of character and confidence was part of his credit. 'I'll present you to some people,' said M. de Bellegarde after a while. 'I'll make a point of it in fact. You'll allow me?—if I may exercise my judgement.'

'Oh, I'll shake hands with any one you want,' Newman returned. 'Your mother just introduced me to half a dozen old gentlemen. Take care you don't pick out the same parties again.'

'Who are the gentlemen to whom my mother presented you?'

'Upon my word I forget them,' Newman had to confess. 'I'm afraid I've got them rather mixed; and don't all Chinamen—even great mandarins!—look very much the same to Occidentals?'

'I suspect they've not forgotten you,' said the Marquis; and he began to walk through the rooms. Newman, to keep near him in the crowd, took his arm; after which, for some time, the Marquis walked straight on in silence. At last, reaching the further end of the apartments, Newman found himself in the presence of a lady of monstrous proportions* seated in a very capacious armchair and with several persons standing in a semicircle round her. This little group had divided as the Marquis came up, and he stepped forward and stood for an instant silent and obsequious, his flattened hat raised to his lips as Newman had seen gentlemen stand in churches as soon as they entered their pews. The lady indeed bore a very fair likeness to a revered effigy in some idolatrous shrine. She was monumentally stout and imperturbably serene. Her aspect was to Newman almost formidable; he had a troubled consciousness of a triple chin, a pair of eyes that twinkled in her face like a pair of polished pin-heads in a cushion, a vast expanse of uncovered bosom, a nodding and twinkling tiara of plumes and gems, an immense circumference of satin petticoat. With her little circle of beholders this remarkable woman reminded him of the Fat Lady at a fair. She fixed her small unwinking gaze at the newcomers.

'Dear Duchess,' said the Marquis, 'let me present you our good friend Mr Newman, of whom you've heard us speak. Wishing to make Mr Newman known to those who are dear to us, I couldn't possibly fail to begin with you.'

'Charmed, dear friend; charmed, monsieur,' said the Duchess in a voice which, though small and shrill, was not disagreeable, while Newman performed with all his length his liberal obeisance. He always made his bow, as he wrote his name, very distinctly. 'I came on purpose to see monsieur. I hope he appreciates the compliment.

You've only to look at me to do so, sir,' she continued, sweeping her person with a much-encompassing glance. Newman hardly knew what to say, though it seemed that to a duchess who joked about her corpulence one might say almost anything. On hearing she had come on purpose to see this object of interest the gentlemen who surrounded her turned a little and looked at him with grave, with almost overdone consideration. The Marquis, with supernatural gravity, mentioned to him the name of each, while the gentleman who bore it bowed; and these pronouncements again affected Newman as some enumeration of the titles of books, of the performers on playbills, of the items of indexes. 'I wanted extremely to see you,' the Duchess went on. '*C'est positif.* In the first place I'm very fond of the person you're going to marry; she's the most charming creature in France. Mind you treat her well or you'll have news of me. But *vous avez l'air bien honnête*, and I'm told you're very remarkable. I've heard all sorts of extraordinary things about you. *Voyons*, are they true?'

'I don't know what you can have heard,' Newman promptly pleaded.

'Oh, you've had your *légende*. You've had a career the most chequered, the most *bizarre*. What's that about your having founded a city some ten years ago in the great West, a city which contains to-day half a million of inhabitants? Isn't it half a million, messieurs? You're exclusive proprietor of the wonderful place and are consequently fabulously rich, and you'd be richer still if you didn't grant lands and houses free of rent to all newcomers who'll pledge themselves never to smoke cigars. At this game, in three years, we're told, you're going to become President of all the Americas.'

The Duchess recited this quaint fable with a smooth self-possession which gave it to Newman's ear the sound of an amusing passage in a play interpreted by a veteran comic actress. Before she had ceased speaking he had relieved himself, applausively, by laughter as frank as clapping or stamping. 'Dear Duchess, dear Duchess!' the Marquis began to murmur soothingly. Two or three persons came to the door of the room to see who was laughing at the Duchess. But the lady continued with the soft, serene assurance of a person who, as a great lady, was certain of being listened to, and, as a garrulous woman, was independent of the pulse of her auditors. 'But I know you're very remarkable. You must be, to have endeared yourself to our good Urbain and to his admirable mother. They don't scatter their approval about. They're very exacting. I myself am not very sure at this hour of really enjoying their esteem—eh, Marquis? But your real triumph, cher monsieur, is in pleasing the Comtesse; she's as difficult as a princess in a fairy-tale. Your success is a miracle. What's your secret? I don't ask you to reveal it before all these gentlemen, but you must come and see me some day and show me how you proceed.'

'The secret is with Madame de Cintré,' Newman found a face to answer. 'You must ask her for it. It consists in her having a great deal of charity.'

'Very pretty!' the Duchess pronounced. 'That, to begin with, is a nice specimen of your system. What, Marquis, are you already taking monsieur away?'

'I've a duty to perform, dear friend,' said Urbain, pointing to the other groups.

'Ah, for you I know what that means! Well, I've seen monsieur; that's what I wanted. He can't persuade me he hasn't something wonder-working. Au revoir, monsieur.'

As Newman passed on with his host he asked who the Duchess might be. 'The greatest lady in France!' the Marquis hereupon reservedly replied. He then presented his prospective brother-in-law to some twenty other persons of both sexes, selected apparently for some recognised value of name or fame or attitude. In some cases their honours were written in a good round hand on the countenance of the wearer; in others Newman was thankful for such help as his companion's impressively brief intimation, measured as to his scant capacity, contributed to the discovery of them. There were large, heavy imperturbable gentlemen and small insinuating extravagant ones; there were ugly ladies in yellow lace and quaint jewels, and pretty ladies with reaches of white denudation that even their wealth of precious stones scarce availed to overtake. Every one gave Newman extreme attention, every one lighted up for him regardless, as he would have said, of expense, every one was enchanted to make his acquaintance, every one looked at him with that fraudulent intensity of good society which puts out its bountiful hand but keeps the fingers closed over the coin. If the Marquis was going about as a bear-leader, if the fiction of Beauty and the Beast was supposed to show thus its companion-piece, the general impression appeared that the bear was a very fair imitation of humanity. Newman found his reception in the charmed circle very handsome—he liked, handsomely, himself, not to say less than that for it. It was handsome to be treated with so much explicit politeness; it was handsome to meet civilities as pointed as witticisms, and to hear them so syllabled and articulated that they suggested handfuls of crisp counted notes pushed over by a banker's clerk; it was handsome of clever Frenchwomen— they all seemed clever—to turn their backs to their partners for a good look at the slightly gaunt outsider whom Claire de Cintré was to marry, and then shine on the subject as if they quite understood. At last as he turned away from a battery of vivid grimaces and other amenities, Newman caught the eye of the Marquis fixed on him inscrutably, and thereupon, for a single instant, he checked himself. 'Am I behaving like a blamed fool?' he wondered. 'Am I stepping about like a terrier on his hind legs?' At this moment he perceived Mrs Tristram at the other side of the room and waved his hand in farewell to M. de Bellegarde in order to make his way toward her.

'Am I holding my head too high and opening my mouth too wide?' he demanded. 'Do I look as if they were saying "Catch" and I were snapping down what they throw me and licking my lips?'

'You look like all very successful men—fatuous without knowing it. Women triumph with more tact, just as they suffer with more grace. Therefore it's the usual thing for such situations—neither better nor worse. I've been watching you for the last ten minutes, and I've been watching M. de Bellegarde. He doesn't like what he has to do.'

'The more credit to him for putting it through,' Newman returned. 'But I shall be generous. I shan't trouble him any more. Only I'm very happy. I can't stand still here. Please take my arm and we'll go for a walk.'

He led Mrs Tristram from one room to another, where, scattering wide glances and soft, sharp comments, she reminded him of the pausing wayfarer who studies the contents of the confectioner's window, with platonic discriminations, through a firm plate of glass. But he made vague answers; he scarcely heard her; his thoughts were elsewhere. They were lost in the vastness of this attested truth of his having come out where he wanted. His momentary consciousness of perhaps too broad a grin passed away, and he felt, the next thing, almost solemnly quiet. Yes, he had 'got there', and now it was, all-powerfully, to stay. These prodigies of gain were in a general way familiar to him, but the sense of what he had 'made' by an anxious operation had never been so deep and sweet. The lights, the flowers, the music, the 'associations', vague and confused to him, yet hovering like some odour of dried spices, something far-away and, as he had hinted to the Marquis, Mongolian; the splendid women, the splendid jewels, the strangeness even of the universal sense of a tongue that seemed the language of society as Italian was the language of opera: these things were all a gage of his having worked, from the old first years, under some better star than he knew. Yet if he showed again and again so many of his fine strong teeth, it was not tickled vanity that pulled the exhibition-string: he had no wish to be pointed at with the finger or to be considered by these people for himself. If he could have looked down at the scene invisibly, as from a hole in the roof, he would have enjoyed it quite as much. It would have spoken to him of his energy and prosperity and deepened that view of his effective 'handling' of life to which, sooner or later, he made all experience contribute. Just now the cup seemed full.

'It's all very fine and very funny, I mean very special and quite thrilling and almost interesting,' said Mrs Tristram while they circulated. 'I've seen nothing objectionable except my husband leaning against that adorably faded strawberry damask of the other room and talking to an individual whom I suppose he takes for a prince, but whom I more than suspect to be the functionary taking care of the lamps. Do you think you could separate them? Do knock over a lamp!'

I doubt whether Newman, who saw no harm in Tristram's conversing with an ingenious mechanic, would have complied with this request; but at this moment Valentin de Bellegarde drew near. Newman, some weeks previously, had presented Madame de Cintré's youngest brother to Mrs Tristram, for whose rather shy and subtle merit the young man promptly professed an intelligent relish and to whom he had paid several visits.

'Did you ever read', she asked, 'Keats's "Belle Dame sans Merci"?* You remind me of the hero of the ballad:

> ' "Oh, what can ail thee, knight-at-arms,
>   Alone and palely loitering?" '

'If I'm alone it's because I've been deprived of your society,' Valentin returned. 'Besides, it's good manners for no man except

Newman to look happy. This is all to his address. It's not for you and me to go before the curtain.'

'You prophesied to me last spring,' said Newman to Mrs Tristram, 'that six months from that time I should get into a tearing rage. It seems to me the time's up, and yet the nearest I can now come to doing anything rough is to offer you a café glacé.'

'I promised you we should do things grandly,' Valentin observed. 'I don't allude to the cafés glacés. But every one's here, and my sister told me just now that Urbain has been adorable.'

'He's a real nice man—all the way through. If I don't look out,' Newman went on—'or if *he* doesn't—I shall begin to love him as a brother. That reminds me that I ought to go and say something enthusiastic to your mother.'

'Let it be something very enthusiastic indeed,' said Valentin. 'It may be the last time you'll feel so much in the vein.'

Newman walked away almost disposed to clasp Madame de Bellegarde round the waist. He passed through several rooms and at last found her in the first saloon, seated on a sofa with her young kinsman Lord Deepmere beside her. The young man unmistakeably felt the strain; his hands were thrust into his pockets and his eyes fixed on the toes of his shoes, his feet being thrust out in front of him. His hostess appeared to have been addressing him with some intensity and to be now waiting for an answer to what she had said or for some other sign of the effect of her words. Her hands were folded in her lap and she considered his lordship's simple physiognomy as she might have studied some brief but baffling sentence in an obscure text. He looked up as Newman approached, met his eyes and changed colour. On which the latter said: 'I'm afraid I disturb an interesting interview.'

Madame de Bellegarde rose, and, her companion rising at the same time, she put her hand into his arm. She answered nothing for an instant, and then as he remained silent brought out with a smile: 'It would be amiable for Lord Deepmere to say it was very interesting.'

'Oh, I'm not amiable!' cried his lordship. 'But it was all right.'

'Madame de Bellegarde was giving you some good advice, eh?' Newman asked: 'preaching you, with her high authority, the way you should go? In your place I'd go it then—blind!'

'I was giving him some excellent advice,' said the Marquise, fixing her fresh cold eyes on our hero. 'It's for him to take it.'

'Take it, sir, take it!' Newman exclaimed. 'Any advice she gives you to-night must be good; for to-night, Marquise, you must speak from a cheerful, comfortable spirit, and that makes for good ideas. You see everything going on so brightly and successfully round you. Your party's magnificent; it was a very happy thought. It's a much better show than that feeble effort of mine would have been.'

'If you're pleased I'm satisfied,' she answered with rare accommodation. 'My desire was to please you.'

'Do you want to please me a little more then?' Newman went on. 'Just let Lord Deepmere digest your wisdom and take care of himself a little; and then take my arm and walk through the rooms.'

'My desire was to please you,' the Marquise rather stiffly repeated; and as she liberated her companion our friend wondered at her docility. 'If this young man is wise,' she added, 'he'll go and find my daughter and ask her to dance.'

'I've been endorsing your advice,' said Newman, bending over her and laughing; 'I suppose therefore I must let him cut in where I can neither lead nor follow.'

Lord Deepmere wiped his forehead and departed, and Madame de Bellegarde took Newman's arm. 'Yes, it has been a real friendly, hearty, jolly idea,' he declared as they proceeded on their circuit. 'Every one seems to know every one and to be glad to see every one. The Marquis has made me acquainted with ever so many people, and I feel quite like one of the family. It's an occasion,' Newman continued, wanting still more to express appreciation without an afterthought, 'that I shall always remember, and remember very pleasantly.'

'I think it's an occasion that we shall none of us ever forget,' said the Marquise with her pure, neat enunciation.

People made way for her as she passed, others turned round and looked at her, and she received a great many greetings and pressings of the hand, all of which she accepted with a smooth good grace. But though she smiled on every one she said nothing till she reached the last of the rooms, where she found her elder son. Then 'This is enough, sir,' she observed with her dignity of distinctness, turning at the same time from Newman to Urbain. He put out both his hands and took both hers, drawing her to a seat with an air of the tenderest veneration. It appeared to attest between them the need of more intimate communion, and Newman discreetly retired. He moved through the rooms for some time longer, circulating freely, overtopping most people by his great height, renewing acquaintance with some of the groups to which the Marquis had presented him, and expending generally the surplus of his equanimity. He continued to find it all a regular celebration, but even the Fourth of July of his childhood used to have an end, and the revelry on this occasion began to deepen to a close. The music was sounding its last strains and people about to take their leave were looking for their hostess. There seemed to be some difficulty in finding her, and he caught a report that she had left the ball in an access of fatigue or of faintness. 'She has succumbed to the emotions of the evening,' he heard a voluble lady say. 'Poor dear Marquise; I can imagine all they may have been for her!'

But he learned immediately afterwards that she had recovered herself and was seated in an armchair near the doorway, receiving final honours from members of her own sex who insisted upon her not rising. He himself had set out in quest of Madame de Cintré, whom he had seen move past him many times in the rapid circles of a waltz, but with whom, also, conforming to her explicit instructions, he had exchanged no word since the beginning of the evening. The whole house having been thrown open the apartments of the rez-de-chaussée were also accessible, though a smaller number of persons had gathered there. Newman wandered through them, observing a few scattered couples to whom this comparative seclusion appeared grateful, and reached a small conservatory which opened into the garden. The end of the conservatory was formed by a clear sheet of glass, unmasked by plants and admitting the winter starlight so directly that a person standing there would seem to have passed into the open air. Two persons stood there now, a lady and a gentleman; the lady Newman, from within the room and although she had turned her back to it, immediately recognised as his friend. He hesitated as to whether he should advance, but as he did so she looked round, feeling apparently that he was there. She rested her eyes on him a moment and then turned again to her companion.

'It's almost a pity not to tell Mr Newman,' she said with restraint, but in a tone Newman could hear.

'Tell him if you like!' the gentleman answered in the voice of Lord Deepmere.

'Oh, tell me by all means!'—and our hero came straight forward.

Lord Deepmere, he observed, was very red in the face and had twisted his gloves into as tight a cord as if squeezing them dry. These, presumably, were tokens of violent emotion, and it struck him that the traces of a corresponding agitation were visible in Madame de Cintré. The two had been talking with extreme animation. 'What I should tell you is only to milord's credit,' said Madame de Cintré, however, with a clear enough smile.

'It wouldn't please him any better for that!' cried milord with his awkward laugh.

'Come; what's the mystery?' Newman demanded. 'Clear it up. I don't like what I don't understand.'

'We must have some things we don't like, and go without some we do,' said the ruddy young nobleman, still almost unnaturally exhilarated.

'It's to Lord Deepmere's credit, but it's not to every one's,' Madame de Cintré imperfectly explained. 'So I shall say nothing about it. You may be sure,' she added; and she put out her hand to the Englishman, who took it with more force than grace. 'And now go and dance hard!' she said.

'Oh yes, I feel awfully like dancing hard! I shall go and drink champagne—as hard as I can!' And he walked away with a gloomy guffaw.

'What has happened between you?' Newman asked.

'I can't tell you—now,' she said. 'Nothing that need make you unhappy.'

'Has that weak brother been trying to make love to you?'

She hesitated, then uttered a grave 'No!—He's a perfectly honest young man.'

'But you've been somehow upset and are still worried. Something's the matter.'

'Nothing, I repeat, that need make you unhappy. I've completely recovered my balance—if I had lost it: which I hadn't! Some day I'll tell you what it was; not now. I can't now,' she insisted.

'Well, I confess,' Newman returned, 'I don't want to hear anything out of key. I'm satisfied with everything—most of all with you, I've seen all the ladies and talked with a great many of them; but I'm really satisfied with you.' The charming woman covered him for a moment with her bright mildness, and then turned her eyes away into the starry night. So they stood silent a moment, side by side. 'Say you're really satisfied with *me*,' Newman said.

He had to wait a moment for the answer; but it came at last, low yet distinct. 'I'm very very happy.'

It was presently followed by a few words from another source which made them both turn round. 'I'm sadly afraid Madame la Comtesse will take a chill. I've ventured to bring a shawl.' Mrs Bread stood there softly solicitous, holding a white drapery in her hand.

'Thank you, *ma bonne*,' said Madame de Cintré; 'the sight of those cold stars gives one a sense of frost. I won't take your shawl, but we'll go back into the house.'

She passed back and Newman followed her, Mrs Bread standing respectfully aside to make way for them. Newman paused an instant before the old woman and she glanced up at him with a silent greeting. 'Oh yes,' he said, 'you must come and live with us.'

'Well then, sir, if you will,' she answered, 'you've not seen the last of me!'

XVII

NEWMAN was fond of music, and went often to the opera, where, a couple of evenings after Madame de Bellegarde's ball, he sat listening to 'Don Giovanni';* having in honour of this work, which he had never yet seen represented, come to occupy his orchestra-chair before the rising of the curtain. Frequently he took a large box and invited a group of his compatriots; this was a mode of recreation to which he was much addicted. He liked making up parties of his friends and conducting them to the theatre or taking them to drive on mail-coaches and dine at restaurants renowned, by what he could a trifle artlessly ascertain, for special and incomparable dishes. He liked doing things that involved his paying for people; the vulgar truth is he enjoyed 'treating' them. This was not because he was what is called purse-proud; handling money in public was, on the contrary, positively disagreeable to him; he had a sort of personal modesty about it akin to what he would have felt about making a toilet before spectators. But just as it was a gratification to him to be nobly dressed, just so it was a private satisfaction (for he kept the full flavour of it quite delicately to himself) to see people occupied and amused at his pecuniary expense and by his profuse interposition. To set a large body of them in motion and transport them to a distance, to have special conveyances, to charter railway-carriages and steamboats, harmonised with his relish for bold processes and made hospitality the potent thing it should ideally be. A few evenings before the occasion of which I speak he had invited several ladies and gentlemen to the opera to listen to the young and wondrous Adelina Patti*—a party which included Miss Dora Finch. It befell, however, that Miss Dora Finch, sitting near him in the box, discoursed brilliantly, not only during the entr'actes but during many of the finest portions of the performance, so that he had really come away with an irritated sense that the new rare diva had a thin, shrill voice and that her roulades* resembled giggles. After this he promised himself to go for a while to the opera alone.

When the curtain had fallen on the first act of 'Don Giovanni' he turned round in his place to observe the audience. Presently, in one of the boxes, he perceived Urbain de Bellegarde and his wife. The little Marquise swept the house very busily with a glass, and Newman, supposing she saw him, determined to go and bid her good-evening. M. de Bellegarde leaned against a column, motionless, looking straight in front of him, one hand in the breast of his white waistcoat and the other resting his hat on his thigh. Newman was about to leave his place when he noticed in that obscure region devoted to the small boxes which in French are called, not inaptly, bathtubs, from their promoting at least immersion through the action of the pores, a face which even the dim light and the distance could not make wholly indistinct. It was the face of a young and pretty woman, crowned with an arrangement of pink roses and diamonds. This person looked round the house while her fan moved with practised grace; when she lowered it Newman perceived a pair of plump white shoulders and the edge of a rose-coloured dress. Beside her, very close to the shoulders and talking, apparently with an earnestness which it suited her scantly to heed, sat a young man with a red face and a very low shirt-collar. A moment's consideration left Newman no doubts; the pretty young woman was Noémie Nioche. He looked hard into the depths of the box, thinking her father might perhaps be in attendance, but from what he could see the young man's eloquence had no other auditor. Newman at last made his way out, and in doing so passed beneath the *baignoire* of his former client. She saw him as he approached, giving him a nod and smile which seemed meant as a hint that her enviable rise in the world had not made her inhuman. He passed into the *foyer* and walked through it, but suddenly to pause before a gentleman seated on one of the divans. The gentleman's elbows were on his knees; he leaned forward and stared at the pavement, lost apparently in meditations of a gloomy cast. But in spite of his bent head Newman recognised him and in a moment had sat down beside him. Then the gentleman looked up and displayed the expressive countenance of Valentin de Bellegarde. 'What in the world are you thinking of so hard?'

'A subject that requires hard thinking to do it justice,' Valentin promptly replied. 'My immeasurable idiocy.'

'What's the matter now?'

'The matter now is that, as I'm a madman with lucid intervals, I'm having one of them now. But I came within an ace of entertaining a sentiment—!'

'For the young lady below stairs, in a *baignoire*, in a pink dress?'

'Did you notice what a rare kind of pink it was?' Valentin enquired by way of answer. 'It makes her look as white as new milk.'

Newman had a stare of some wonderment, and then: 'Is *she* what you call *crème de la crème*?' But as Valentin's face pronounced this a witticism below the Parisian standard he went on: 'You've stopped then, at any rate, going to see her?'

'Oh bless you, no. Why should I stop? I've changed, but she hasn't,' said Valentin. 'The more I see her the more sure I am—well, that I see her right. She has awfully pretty arms, and several other things, but she's not really a bit *gentille*. The other day she had the bad taste to begin to abuse her father, to his face, in my presence. I shouldn't have expected it of her; it was a disappointment. Heigho!'

'Why, she cares no more for her father than for her door-mat,' Newman declared. 'I discovered that the first time I saw her.'

'Oh, that's another affair; she may think of the poor old beggar what she pleases. But it was base in her to call him bad names; it spoiled my reckoning and quite threw me off. It was about a frilled petticoat that he was to have fetched from the washerwoman's; he appeared to have forgotten the frilled petticoat. She almost boxed his ears. He stood there staring at her with his little blank eyes and smoothing his old hat with his coat-tail. At last he turned round and went out without a word. Then I told her it was in very bad taste to speak so even to an unnatural father. She said she should be so thankful to me if I would mention it to her whenever her taste was at fault; she had immense confidence in mine. I told her I couldn't have the inconvenience of forming her manners; I had had an idea they were already formed, after the best models. She had quite put me out. But I shall get over it,' said Valentin gaily.

'Oh, time's a great consoler!' Newman answered with humorous sobriety. He was silent a moment and then added in another tone: 'I wish you'd think of what I said to you the other day. Come over to America with us and I'll put you in the way of doing some business. You've got a very fine mind if you'd only give it a chance.'

Valentin made a genial grimace. 'My mind's much obliged to you: you make it feel finer than ever. Would the "chance" be that place in a bank?'

'There are several places, but I suppose you'd consider the bank the most aristocratic.'

Valentin burst into a laugh. 'My dear fellow, at night all cats are grey?* When one falls from such a height there are no degrees!'

Newman answered nothing for a minute. Then, 'I think you'll find there are degrees in success,' he said with his most exemplary mild distinctness.

Valentin had leaned forward again with his elbows on his knees and was scratching the pavement with his stick. At last, looking up, 'Do you really think I ought to do something?' he asked.

Newman laid his hand on his companion's arm and eyed him a moment through measuring lids. 'Try it and see. I'm not sure you're not too bright to live; but why not find out how bright a man can *afford* to be?'

'Do you really think I can make some money? Once when I was a small boy I found a silver piece under a door-mat. I should like awfully to see how it feels to find a gold one.'

'Well, do what I tell you and you shall find salvation,' said Newman, 'Think of it well,' And he looked at his watch and prepared to resume his way to Madame de Bellegarde's box.

'Upon my honour I *will* think of it,' Valentin returned. 'I'll go and listen to Mozart another half-hour—I can always think better to music—and profoundly meditate on it.'

The Marquis was with his wife when Newman entered their box; he was as remotely bland as usual, but the great demonstration in which he had lately played his part appeared to have been a draw-bridge lowered and lifted again. Newman was once more outside the castle and its master perched on the battlements. 'What do you think of the opera?' our hero none the less artlessly demanded. 'What do you think of the cool old Don?'

'He doesn't remain so very cool,' the Marquis amusedly replied. 'But we all know what Mozart is; our impressions don't date from this evening. Mozart is youth, freshness, brilliancy, facility—facility perhaps a little too unbroken. But the execution is here and there deplorably rough.'

'I'm very curious to see how it ends,' Newman less critically continued.

'You speak as if it were a feuilleton in the *Figaro*,'* observed the Marquis. 'You've surely seen the opera before?'

'Never—I'm sure I should have remembered it. Donna Elvira*

reminds me of Madame de Cintré; I don't mean in her situation, but in her lovely tone.'

'It's a very nice distinction,' the Marquis neatly conceded. 'There's no possibility, I imagine, of my sister's being forsaken.'

'That's right, sir,' Newman said. 'But what becomes of the Don?'

'The Devil comes down—or comes up—and carries him off,' Madame Urbain replied. 'I suppose Zerlina* reminds you of me.'

'I'll go to the *foyer* for a few moments,' said her husband, 'and give you a chance to say that I'm like the Commander—the man of stone.'* With which he passed out of the box.

The little Marquise stared an instant at the velvet ledge of the balcony and then murmured: 'Not a man of stone, a man of wood!' Newman had taken her husband's empty chair; she made no protest, but turned suddenly and laid her closed fan on his arm. 'I'm very glad you came in; I want to ask you a favour. I wanted to do so on Thursday, at my mother-in-law's ball, but you would give me no chance. You were in such very good spirits that I thought you might grant my little prayer then; not that you look particularly doleful now. It's something you must promise me; now's the time to take you; after you're married you'll be good for nothing. *Allons*, promise!'

'I never sign a paper without reading it first,' said Newman. 'Show me your document.'

'No, you must sign with your eyes shut; I'll hold your hand. *Voyons*, before you put your head into the noose you ought to be thankful for me giving you a chance to do something amusing.'

'If it's so amusing,' said Newman, 'it will be in even better season after I'm married.'

'In other words,' she cried, 'you'll not do it at all, for then you'll be afraid of your wife.'

'Oh, if the thing violates the moral law—pardon my strong language!—I won't go into it. If it doesn't I shall be quite as ready for it after my marriage.'

'Oh, you people, with your moral law—I wonder that with such big words in your mouth you don't all die of choking!' Madame Urbain declared. 'You talk like a treatise on logic, and English logic into the bargain. Promise then after you're married,' she went on. 'After all, I shall enjoy keeping you to it.'

'Well, then after I'm married,' said Newman serenely.

She hesitated a moment, looking at him, and he wondered what was coming. 'I suppose you know what my life is,' she presently said. 'I've no pleasure, I see nothing, I do nothing. I live in Paris as I might live at Poitiers.* My mother-in-law calls me—what is the pretty word?—a gadabout; accuses me of going to unheard-of places and thinks it ought to be joy enough for me to sit at home and count over my ancestors on my fingers. But why should I bother about my ancestors? I'm sure they never bothered about me. I don't propose to live with a green shade over my eyes; I hold that the only thing you can do with things arranged in a row before you is see them. My husband, you know, has principles, and the first on the list is that the Tuileries are dreadfully vulgar.* If the Tuileries are vulgar his principles are imbecile. If I chose I might have principles quite as well as he. If they grew on one's family tree I should only have to give mine a shake to bring down a shower of the finest. At any rate I prefer clever Bonapartes to stupid Bourbons.'

'Oh, I see; you want to go to court,' said Newman, fantastically wondering if she mightn't wish him to smooth her way to the imperial halls through some ingenious use of the American Legation.

The Marquise gave a little sharp laugh. 'You're a thousand miles away. I'll take care of the Tuileries myself; the day I decide to go they'll be glad enough to have me. Sooner or later I shall dance in an imperial quadrille. I know what you're going to say: "How will you dare?" But I *shall* dare. I'm afraid of my husband; he's soft, smooth, irreproachable, everything you know; but I'm afraid of him—horribly afraid of him. And yet I shall arrive at the Tuileries. But that will not be this winter, nor perhaps next, and meantime I must live. For the moment I want to go somewhere else; it's my dream. I want to go to the Bal Bullier.'

'To the Bal Bullier?' repeated Newman, for whom the words at first meant nothing.

'The ball in the Latin Quarter,* where the students dance with their mistresses. Don't tell me you've not heard of it.'

'Oh yes,' said Newman; 'I've heard of it; I remember now. I've even been there. And you want to go there?'

'It's *bête*, it's low, it's anything you please. But I want to go. Some of my friends have been, and they say it's very curious. My friends go everywhere; it's only I who sit moping at home.'

'It seems to me you're not at home now,' said Newman, 'and I shouldn't exactly say you were moping.'

'I'm bored to death. I've been to the opera twice a week for the last eight years. Whenever I ask for anything my mouth is stopped with that: Pray, madame, haven't you your *loge aux Italiens*? Could a woman of taste want more? In the first place my box was down in my *contrat*; they have to give it to me. To-night, for instance, I should have preferred a thousand times to go to the Palais Royal. But my husband won't go to the Palais Royal because the ladies of the court go there so much. You may imagine then whether he would take me to Bullier's; he says it is a mere imitation—and a bad one—of what they do in the imperial *intimité*. But as I'm not yet for a little in the imperial *intimité*—which must be charming—why shouldn't I look in where you can get the nearest notion of it? It's my dream at any rate; it's a fixed idea. All I ask of you is to give me your arm; you're less compromising than any one else. I don't know why, but you are. I can arrange it. I shall risk something, but that's my own affair. Besides, fortune favours the bold. Don't refuse me; it is my dream!'

Newman gave a loud laugh. It seemed to him hardly worth while to be the wife of the Marquis de Bellegarde, a daughter of the crusaders, heiress of six centuries of glories and traditions, only to have centred one's aspirations upon the sight of fifty young ladies kicking off the hats of a hundred young men. It struck him as a theme for the moralist, but he had no time to moralise. The curtain rose again; M. de Bellegarde returned and he went back to his seat.

He observed that Valentin had taken his place in the *baignoire* of Mademoiselle Nioche, behind this young lady and her companion, where he was visible only if one carefully looked for him. In the next act Newman met him in the lobby and asked him if he had reflected upon possible emigration. 'If you really meant to meditate,' he said, 'you might have chosen a better place for it.'

'Oh, the place wasn't bad,' Valentin replied. 'I wasn't thinking of that girl. I listened to the music and, heedless of the play and without looking at the stage, turned over your handsome proposal. At first it seemed quite fantastic. And then a certain fiddle in the orchestra—I could distinguish it—began to say as it scraped away: "Why not, why not, why not?" And then in that rapid movement all the fiddles took it up and the conductor's stick seemed to beat it in the air: "Why not, why not, why not?" I'm sure I can't say! I don't see why not. I don't see why I shouldn't do something. It appears to me a really very bright idea. This sort of thing is certainly very stale. And then

I should come back with a trunk full of dollars. Besides, I might possibly find it amusing. They call me an extravagant *raffiné*; who knows but that I might discover an unsuspected charm in shopkeeping? It would really have a certain rare and romantic side; it would look well in my biography. It would look as if I were a strong man, an *homme de premier ordre*, a man who dominated circumstances.'

'I guess you had better not mind how it would look,' said Newman. 'It always looks well to have half a million of dollars. There's no reason why you shouldn't have them if you'll mind what I tell you— I alone—and not fool round with other parties.' He passed his arm into that of his friend, and the two walked for some time up and down one of the less frequented corridors. Newman's imagination began to glow with the idea of converting this irresistible idler into a first-class man of business. He felt for the moment a spiritual zeal, the zeal of the propagandist. Its ardour was in part the result of that general discomfort which the sight of all uninvested capital produced in him; so charming an intelligence ought to be dedicated to fine uses. The finest uses known to Newman's experience were transcendent operations in ferocious markets. And then his zeal was quickened by personal kindness; he entertained a form of pity which he was well aware he never could have made the Comte de Bellegarde understand. He never lost a sense of its being pitiable that so bright a figure should think it a large life to revolve in varnished boots between the Rue d'Anjou and the Rue de l'Université, taking the Boulevard des Italiens on the way, when over there in America one's promenade was a continent and one's boulevard stretched from one world-sea to another. It mortified him moreover to have to understand that Valentin wanted for money; it wasn't business, that was what was the matter with it, he would have said; it was unpractical, unsuitable, unsightly—very much as if he hadn't known how to spell or to ride. There was something almost ridiculously anomalous to Newman in the sight of lively pretensions unaccompanied by a considerable control of Western railroads; though I may add that he would not have maintained that such advantages were in themselves a proper ground for pretensions. 'I'll put you into something,' he said at any rate; 'I'll see you through. I know half a dozen things in which we can make a place for you. You'll find it a big rush and you'll see some high jumps; it will take you a little while to get used to the scale. But you'll work in before long and at the end of six months—after you've tasted blood, after you've done a thing or two on your own account—you'll have some good times. And then it will be very pleasant for you having your sister over there. It will be pleasant for her to have you too. Yes, Valentine,' he continued, pressing his comrade's arm genially, 'I think I see just the opening for you. Keep quiet, and I'll find something nice—I'll fix you all right.'

Newman pursued this favouring strain over a wide stretch of prospect; the two men strolled about for a quarter of an hour. Valentin listened and questioned, making his friend laugh at his ignorance of the very alphabet of affairs, smiling himself too, half ironical and half curious. And yet he was serious and nearly convinced, fascinated as by the biggest, plainest map of the great land of El Dorado ever spread before him. It is true, withal, that if it might be bold, original and even amusing to surrender his faded escutcheon to the process, the smart patent transatlantic process, of heavy regilding, he didn't quite relish the freedom with which it might be handled, and yet suddenly felt eager to know the worst that might await him. So that when the bell rang to indicate the close of the entr'acte there was a certain mock-heroism in his saying all gaily: 'Well then, put me through; locate me and fix me! I make myself over to you. Dip me into the pot and turn me into gold.'

They had passed into the corridor which encircled the row of *baignoires*, and Valentin stopped in front of the dusky little box in which Mademoiselle Nioche had bestowed herself, laying his hand on the door-knob. 'Oh come, are you going back there?' Newman hereupon asked.

'*Mon Dieu, oui*,' said Valentin.

'Haven't you another place?'

'Yes, I've my usual place in the stalls.'

'You had better go then and occupy it.'

'I see her very well from there too,' Valentin went on serenely; 'and to-night she's worth seeing. But,' he added in a moment, 'I've a particular reason for going back just now.'

'Oh, I give you up,' said Newman. 'You're sunk in depravity and don't know the light when you see it.'

'No, it's only this. There's a young man in the box whom I shall worry by going in, and I really want to worry him.'

'Why, you cold-blooded calculating wretch!' Newman cried. 'Can't you give the poor devil a chance?'

'No, he has trod with all his weight on my toes. The box is not his; Noémie came alone and installed herself. I went and spoke to her, and in a few moments she asked me to go and get her fan from the pocket of her cloak, which the greedy *ouvreuse* had carried off, with her eye to a fee, instead of hanging it up on a peg. In my absence a gentleman came in and took the chair beside her in which I had been sitting. My reappearance put him out, and he had the grossness to show it. He came within an ace of being impertinent. I don't know who he is—a big hard-breathing red-faced animal. I can't think where she picks up such acquaintances. He has been drinking too, but he knows what he's about. Just now, in the second act, the brute did unmistakeably betray an intention. I shall put in another appearance for ten minutes—time enough to give him an opportunity to commit himself if he feels inclined. I really can't let him suppose he's keeping me out of the box.'

'My poor dear boy,' said Newman remonstrantly, 'why shouldn't he have his good time? You're not going to pick a quarrel about such an article as that, I hope.'

'The nature of the article—if you mean of the young lady—has nothing to do with it, and I've no intention of picking a quarrel. I'm not a bully nor a fire-eater, I simply wish to make a point that a gentleman must.'

'Oh, damn your point!' Newman impatiently returned. 'That's the trouble with you Frenchmen; you must be always making points. Well,' he added, 'be lively, or I shall pack you off first to a country where you'll find half your points already made and the other half quite unnoticed.'

'Very good,' Valentin answered, 'whenever you like. But if I go to America I mustn't let the fellow suppose it's to run away from him.'

And they separated. At the end of the act Newman observed that Valentin was still in the *baignoire*. He strolled into the corridor again, expecting to meet him, and when he was within a few yards of Noémie's retreat saw his friend pass out accompanied by the young man who had been seated beside its more interesting occupant. The two walked with some quickness of step to a distant part of the lobby, where Newman perceived them stop and stand talking. The manner of each was quiet enough, but the stranger, who was strikingly flushed, had begun to wipe his face very emphatically with his pocket-handkerchief. By this time Newman was abreast of the *baignoire*; the door had been left ajar and he could see a pink dress inside. He immediately went in. Noémie turned on him a glitter of interest.

'Ah, if you've at last decided to come and see me you but just save your politeness. You find me in a fine moment. Sit down.' She looked, it had to be owned, exceedingly pretty and perverse and animated and elegant, and quite as if she had had some very good news.

'Something has happened here!' Newman said while he kept his feet.

'You find me in a very fine moment,' she repeated. 'Two gentlemen—one of them's M. de Bellegarde, the pleasure of whose acquaintance I owe to you—have just had words about your humble servant. Very sharp words too. They can't come off without its going further. A meeting and a big noise—that will give me a push!' said Noémie, clapping with a soft thud her little pearl-coloured hands. '*C'est ça qui pose une femme!*'

'You don't mean to say Bellegarde's going to fight about *you*!' Newman disgustedly cried.

'Nothing less!'—and she looked at him with a hard little smile. 'No, no, you're not *galant*! And if you prevent this affair I shall owe you a grudge—and pay my debt!'

Newman uttered one of the least attenuated imprecations that had ever passed his lips, and then, turning his back without more ceremony on the pink dress, went out of the box. In the corridor he found Valentin and his companion walking toward him. The latter had apparently just thrust a card into his waistcoat pocket. Noémie's jealous votary was an immense, robust young man with a candid, excited glare, a thick nose and a thick mouth, the certainty of a thick articulation; also with a pair of very large white gloves and a very massive, voluminous watch-chain. When they reached the box Valentin, over whom he towered, made with an emphasised bow way for him to pass in first. Newman touched his friend's arm as a sign he wished to speak with him, and Valentin answered that he would be with him in an instant. Valentin entered the box after the robust young man, but a couple of minutes later reappeared in a state of aggravated gaiety. 'She's immensely set up—she says we'll make her fortune. I don't want to be fatuous, but I think it very possible.'

'So you're going to fight?' Newman asked.

'My dear fellow, don't look at me as if I had told you I'm *not*! It was not my own choice. The thing's perfectly settled.'

'I told you so!' groaned Newman.

'I told *him* so,' smiled Valentin.

'What the hell did he ever do to you?'

'My good friend, it doesn't matter what. It seems to me you don't understand these things. He used an expression—I took it up.'

'But I insist on knowing; I can't, as your elder brother, let you give way to public tantrums—!'

'I'm, as your younger brother, very much obliged to you,' said Valentin. 'I've nothing to conceal, but I can't go into particulars now and here.'

'We'll leave this place then. You can tell me outside.'

'Oh no, I can't leave this place; why should I hurry away? I'll go to my stall and sit out the opera.'

'You'll not enjoy it.'

Valentin looked at him a moment, coloured a little, smiled and patted his arm. 'You'd have been an ornament to the Golden Age. Before an affair a man's quiet. The quietest thing I can do is to go straight to my place.'

'Ah,' said Newman, 'you want her to see you there—you and your quietness. Your quietness will drown the orchestra. I'm not so undeveloped. It's the damnedest foolery.'

Valentin remained, and the two men, in their respective places, sat out the rest of the performance, which was also enjoyed by Mademoiselle Nioche and her truculent admirer. At the end Newman joined his friend again, and they went out into the street together. The young man shook his head at the proposal that he should get into Newman's own vehicle and stopped on the edge of the pavement. 'I must go off alone; must look up a couple of friends who'll be so good as to act for me.'

'I'll be so good as to act for you,' Newman declared. 'Put the case into my hands.'

'You're very kind, but that's hardly possible. In the first place you're, as you said just now, almost my brother; you're going to marry my sister. That alone disqualifies you; it casts doubts on your impartiality. And if it didn't it would be enough for me that you haven't, as I say, God forgive you, the sentiment of certain shades. You'd only try to prevent a meeting.'

'Of course I should,' said Newman. 'Whoever your friends are they'll be ruffians if they don't do that.'

'Unquestionably then they'll do it. They'll urge that excuses be made, the most proper excuses. But you'd be much too *coulant*. You won't do.'

Newman was silent a moment. He was in presence, it seemed to him, of a vain and grotesque parade, poor, restricted, indirect as a salve to an insult or a righting of a wrong, and yet pretentious and pompous as an accommodation. But he saw it useless to attempt interference. 'When is this precious performance to come off?' he could only ask.

'The sooner the better. The day after to-morrow I hope.'

'Well,' Newman went on, 'I've certainly a claim to know the facts. I can't consent to shut my eyes to a single one of them.'

'I shall be most happy to tell you them all then. They're very simple and it will be quickly done. But now everything depends on my putting my hands on my friends without delay. I'll jump into a cab; you had better drive to my rooms and wait for me there. I'll turn up at the end of an hour.'

Newman assented protestingly, let him go, and then betook himself to the encumbered little apartment in the Rue d'Anjou. It was more than an hour before Valentin returned, but when he did so he was able to announce that he had found one of his accessories and that this gentleman had taken upon himself the care of securing the other. Newman had been sitting without lights by the faded fire, on which he had thrown a log; the blaze played over the rich multifarious properties of the place and produced fantastic gleams and shadows. He listened in silence to Valentin's account of what had passed between him and the gentleman whose card he had in his pocket— M. Stanislas Kapp of Strasbourg—after his return to the society of their common hostess. This acute young woman had espied an acquaintance on the other side of the house and had expressed her displeasure at his not having the civility to come and pay her a visit. 'Oh, let him alone,' M. Stanislas Kapp had hereupon exclaimed; 'there are too many people in the box already!' And he had fixed his eyes on his fellow-guest with the utmost ferocity. Valentin had promptly retorted that if there were too many people in the box it was easy for M. Kapp to diminish the number. 'I shall be most happy to open the door for *you*!' M. Kapp had exclaimed: 'And I shall be delighted to fling you into the pit!' Valentin had as promptly retorted. 'Oh do make a rumpus and get into the papers!' Miss Noémie had gleefully ejaculated. 'M. Kapp, turn him out; or, M. de

Bellegarde, pitch him into the pit, into the orchestra—anywhere! I don't care who does which, so long as you make a scene.' Valentin had answered that they would make no scene, but that the gentleman would be so good as to step into the corridor with him. In the corridor, after a brief further exchange of words, there had been an exchange of cards. M. Stanislas Kapp had pressed on his intention, the flat-faced imbecile, with all his weight; and there were fifty tons, at the least, of that.

'Well, say there *are*! If you hadn't gone back into the box the thing wouldn't have happened.'

'Why, don't you see,' Valentin replied, 'that the event proves the extreme propriety of my going back into the box? M. Kapp wished to provoke me; he was awaiting his chance. In such a case—that is, when he has been, so to speak, notified—a man must be on hand to receive the provocation. My not returning would simply have been tantamount to my saying to M. Stanislas Kapp: "Oh, if you're going to be offensive—!"'

'"You must manage it by yourself; damned if I'll help you!" That would have been a thoroughly sensible thing to say. The only attraction for you seems to have been the idea that you *could* help him,' Newman went on. 'You told me you were not going back for that minx herself.'

'Oh, don't mention her ever, ever any more!' Valentin almost plaintively sighed. 'She's really quite a bad bore.'

'With all my heart. But if that's the way you feel about her, why couldn't you let her alone?'

Valentin shook his head with a fine smile. 'I don't think you quite understand, and I don't believe I can make you. She understood the situation; she knew what was in the air; she was watching us.'

'Then you *are* doing it for *her*?' Newman railed.

'I'm doing it for myself, and you must leave me judge of what concerns my honour.'

'Well, I'll leave you judge if you'll leave me to, quite impartially, kick somebody!'

'It's vain talking,' Valentin replied to this. 'Words have passed and the thing's settled.'

Newman turned away, taking his hat. Then pausing as if with interest, his hand on the door: 'You're going to use knives?'

'That's for M. Stanislas Kapp, as the challenged party, to decide.

My own choice would be a short, light sword. I handle it well. I'm an indifferent shot.'

Newman had put on his hat; he pushed it back, gently scratching his forehead high up. 'I wish it were guns,' he said. 'I could show you how to hold one.'

Valentin gave him a hard look and then broke into a laugh. 'Murderer!' he cried with some intensity, but agreeing to see him again on the morrow, after the details of the meeting with M. Stanislas Kapp should have been arranged.

In the course of the day Newman received three lines from him to the effect that it had been decided he should cross the frontier with his adversary, and that he was accordingly to take the night express to Geneva. They should have time, however, to dine together. In the afternoon Newman called on Madame de Cintré for the single daily hour of reinvoked and reasserted confidence—a solemnity but the more exquisite with repetition—to which she had, a little strangely, given him to understand it was convenient, important, in fact vital to her, that their communion, for their strained interval, should be restricted, even though this reduced him for so many other recurrent hours, the hours of evening in particular, the worst of the probation, to the state of a restless, prowling, time-keeping ghost, a taker of long night-walks through streets that affected him at moments as the alleys of a great darkened bankrupt bazaar. But his visit to-day had a worry to reckon with—all the more that it had as well so much of one to conceal. She shone upon him, as always, with that light of her gentleness which might have been figured, in the heat-thickened air, by a sultry harvest moon; but she was visibly bedimmed, and she confessed, on his charging her with her red eyes, that she had been, for a vague vain reason, crying them half out. Valentin had been with her a couple of hours before and had somehow troubled her without in the least intending it. He had laughed and gossiped, had brought her no bad news, had only been, in taking leave of her, rather 'dearer', poor boy, than usual. A certain extravagance of tenderness in him had in fact touched her to positive pain, so that on his departure she had burst into miserable tears. She had felt as if something strange and wrong were hanging about them—ah, she had had that feeling in other connexions too; nervous, always nervous, she had tried to reason away the fear, but the effort had only given her a headache. Newman was of course tongue-tied on what he himself knew, and, his power of simulation and his general art of optimism breaking down on this occasion as if some long needle-point had suddenly passed, to make him wince, through the sole crevice of his armour, he could, to his high chagrin, but cut his call short. Before he retreated, however, he asked if Valentin had seen his mother.

'Yes; but he didn't make *her* cry!'

It was in Newman's own apartments that the young man dined, having sent his servant and his effects to await him at the railway. M. Stanislas Kapp had positively declined to make excuses, and he on his side had obviously none to offer. Valentin had found out with whom he was dealing, and that his adversary was the son and heir of a rich brewer of Strasbourg, a youth sanguineous, brawny, bull-headed, and lately much occupied in making ducks and drakes of the paternal brewery. Though passing in a general way for a good companion, he had already been noted as apt to quarrel after dinner and to be disposed then to charge with his head down. 'Que voulez-vous?' said Valentin: 'brought up on beer how could he stand such champagne as Noémie, cup-bearer to the infernal gods, had poured out for him?' He had chosen the weapon known to Newman as the gun. Valentin had an excellent appetite: he made a point, in view of his long journey, of eating more than usual: one of the points, no doubt, that his friend had accused him of always needing to make. He took the liberty of suggesting to the latter the difference of the suspicion of a shade in the composition of a fish-sauce; he thought it worth hinting, with precautions, to the cook. But Newman had no mind for sauces; there was more in the dish itself, the mixture now presented to him, than he could swallow; he was in short 'nervous' to a tune of which he felt almost ashamed as he watched his inimitable friend go through their superior meal without skipping a step or missing a savour; the exposure, the possible sacrifice, of so charming a life on the altar of a stupid tradition struck him as intolerably wrong. He exaggerated the perversity of Noémie, the ferocity of M. Kapp, the grimness of M. Kapp's friends, and only knew that he did yearn now as a brother.

'This sort of thing may be all very well,' he broke out at last, 'but I'll be blamed if I see it. I can't stop you perhaps, but at least I can swear at you handsomely. Take me as doing so in the most awful terms.'

'My dear fellow, don't make a scene'—Valentin was almost sententious. 'Scenes in these cases are in very bad taste.'

'Your duel itself is a scene,' Newman said; 'a scene of the most flagrant description. It's a wretched theatrical affair. Why don't you take a band of music with you outright? It's G— d— barbarous, and yet it's G— d— effete.'

'Oh, I can't begin at this time of day to defend the theory of duelling,' the young man blandly reasoned. 'It's our only resource at given moments, and I hold it a good thing. Quite apart from the merit of the cause in which a meeting may take place, it strikes a romantic note that seems to me in this age of vile prose greatly to recommend it. It's a remnant of a higher-tempered time; one ought to cling to it. It's a way of more decently testifying. Testify when you can!'

'I don't know what you mean by a higher-tempered time,' Newman retorted. 'Because your great-grandfather liked to prance, is that any reason for you, who have got beyond it? For my part I think we had better let our temper take care of itself; it generally seems to me quite high enough; I'm not more of a fire-eater than most, but I'm not afraid of being too mild. If your great-grandfather were to make himself unpleasant to me I think I could tackle him yet.'

'My dear friend'—Valentin was perfectly patient with him—'you can't invent anything that will take the place of satisfaction for an insult. To demand it and to give it are equally excellent arrangements.'

'Do you call this sort of thing satisfaction?' Newman groaned. 'Does it satisfy you to put yourself at the disposal of a bigger fool even than yourself? I'd see him somewhere first! Does it satisfy you that he should set up this ridiculous relation with *you*? I'd like to see him try anything of the sort with *me*! If a man has a bad intention on you it's his own affair till it takes effect; but when it does, give him one in the eye. If you don't know *how* to do that—straight— you're not fit to go round alone. But I'm talking of those who claim they *are*, and that they don't require some one to take care of them.'

'Well,' Valentin smiled, 'it would be interesting truly to go round with *you*. But to get the full good of that, alas, I should have begun earlier!'

Newman could scarcely bear even the possible pertinence of

his 'alas'. 'See here,' he said at the last: 'if any one ever hurts you again—!'

'Well, *mon bon?*'—and Valentin, with his eyes on his friend's, might now have been much moved.

'Come straight to me about it. *I'll* go for him.'

'*Matamore!*' the young man laughed as they parted.

XVIII

IT was the next morning that, by exception, Newman went to see Madame de Cintré, timing his visit so as to arrive after the noonday breakfast. In the court of the hôtel, before the portico, stood Madame de Bellegarde's old square heavy carriage. The servant who opened the door answered his enquiry with a slightly embarrassed and hesitating murmur, and at the same moment Mrs Bread appeared in the background, dim-visaged as usual and wearing a large black bonnet and shawl.

'What's the matter?' he asked. 'Is Madame la Comtesse at home or not?'

Mrs Bread advanced, fixing her eyes on him; he observed that she held a sealed letter, very delicately, in her fingers. 'The Countess has left a message for you, sir; she has left this.' And the good woman held out the missive, which he took.

'Left it? Is she out? Is she gone away?'

'She's going away, sir; she's leaving town,' said Mrs Bread.

'Leaving town!' he exclaimed. 'What in the world has happened?'

'It is not for me to say, sir.' And Mrs Bread cast her eyes to the ground. 'But I thought it would come.'

'What would come, pray?' Newman demanded. He had broken the seal of the letter, but he still questioned. 'She's in the house? She's visible?'

'I don't think she expected you this morning,' his venerable friend replied. 'She was to leave immediately.'

'Where is she going?'

'To Fleurières.'

'Away off there? But surely I can see her?'

Mrs Bread hesitated, but then, clasping together her black-gloved hands, 'I'll take you!' she rather desperately said. And she led the way upstairs. At the top of the staircase, however, she paused and fixed her dry sad eyes on him. 'Be very easy with her. Nobody else is.' Then she went on to Madame de Cintré's apartment. Newman, perplexed and alarmed, followed her fast. She threw open the door and he pushed back the curtain at the further side of its deep embrasure. In the middle of the room stood Madame de Cintré; her face was flushed and marked and she was dressed for travelling. Behind her, before the fireplace, stood Urbain de Bellegarde and looked at his finger-nails; near the Marquis sat his mother, buried in an arm-chair and with her eyes immediately fixing themselves on the invader, as he felt them pronounce him. He knew himself, as he entered, in the presence of something evil; he was as startled and pained as he would have been by a threatening cry in the stillness of the night. He walked straight to Madame de Cintré and seized her by the hand.

'What's the matter?' he asked commandingly; 'what's happening?'

Urbain de Bellegarde stared, then left his place and came and leaned on the back of his mother's chair. Newman's sudden irrup-tion had evidently discomposed them both. Madame de Cintré stood silent and with her eyes resting on her friend's. She had often looked at him with all her soul, as it seemed to him; but in this present gaze there was a bottomless depth. She was in distress, and—mon-strously—was somehow to her own sense helpless. It would have been the most touching thing he had ever seen if it hadn't been the most absurd. His heart rose into his throat and he was on the point of turning to her companions with an angry challenge; but she checked him, pressing the hand of which she had possessed herself.

'Something very grave has happened,' she brought out. 'I can't marry you.'

Newman dropped her hand—as if, suddenly and unnaturally acting with the others, she had planted a knife in his side: he stood staring, first at her and then at them. 'Why not?' he asked as quietly as his quick gasp permitted.

Madame de Cintré almost smiled, but the attempt was strange. 'You must ask my mother. You must ask my brother.'

'Why can't she marry me?'—and he looked all at them.

Madame de Bellegarde never moved in her seat, but her con-sciousness had paled her face. The Marquis hovered protectingly. She said nothing for some moments, but she kept her keen clear eyes on their visitor. The Marquis drew himself up and considered the ceiling. 'It's impossible!' he finely articulated.

'It's improper,' said Madame de Bellegarde.

Newman began to laugh. 'Oh, you're fooling!' he exclaimed.

'My sister, you've no time; you're losing your train,' the Marquis went on.

'Come, is he mad?' Newman asked.

'No; don't think that,' said Madame de Cintré. 'But I'm going away.'

'Where are you going?'

'To the country; to Fleurières; to be alone.'

'To leave *me* alone?' Newman put it.

'I can't see you now,' she simply answered.

' "Now"—why not?'

'I'm ashamed,' she still more simply confessed.

Newman turned to the Marquis. 'What have you done to her—what does it mean?' he asked with the same effort at calmness, the fruit of his constant practice in taking things easily. He was excited, but excitement with him was only an intenser deliberateness; it was the plunger stripped.

'It means that I've given you up,' said Madame de Cintré. 'It means that.'

Her appearance was too charged with tragic expression not fully to confirm her words. Newman was profoundly shocked, but he felt as yet no resentment against her. He was amazed, bewildered, and the presence of the Marquise and her son seemed to smite his eyes like the glare of a watchman's lantern. 'Can't I see you alone?' he asked.

'It would be only more painful. I hoped I shouldn't see you—that I should escape. I wrote to you, but only three words. Good-bye.' And she put out her hand again.

Newman put both his own into his pockets. 'I'll simply go with you.'

She laid her two hands on his arm. 'Will you grant me a last request?'—and as she looked at him, urging this, her eyes filled with tears. 'Let me go alone—let me go in peace. Peace I say—though it's really death. But let me bury myself. So—good-bye.'

Newman passed his hand into his hair and stood slowly rubbing his head and looking through his keenly-narrowed eyes from one to the other of the three persons before him. His lips were compressed, and the two strong lines formed beside his mouth and riding hard, as it were, his restive moustache, might have at first suggested a wide grimace. I have said that his excitement was an intenser deliberateness, and now his deliberation was grim. 'It seems very much as if you had interfered, Marquis,' he said slowly. 'I thought you said you wouldn't interfere. I know you didn't like me; but that doesn't make any difference. I thought you promised me you wouldn't interfere. I thought you swore on your honour that you wouldn't interfere. Don't you remember, Marquis?'

The Marquis lifted his eyebrows, but he was apparently determined to be even more urbane than usual. He rested his two hands upon the back of his mother's chair and bent forward as if he were leaning over the edge of a pulpit or a lecture-desk. He didn't smile, but he looked softly grave. 'Pardon me, sir—what I assured you was that I wouldn't influence my sister's decision. I adhered to the letter to my engagement. Did I not, my sister?'

'Don't appeal, my son,' said the Marquise. 'Your word's all sufficient.'

'Yes—she accepted me,' said Newman. 'That's very true; I can't deny that. At least,' he added in a different tone while he turned to Madame de Cintré, 'you *did* accept me?' The effect of deep irony in it—even if there had been nothing else—appeared to move her strongly, and she turned away, burying her face in her hands. 'But you've interfered now, haven't you?' he went on to the Marquis.

'Neither then nor now have I attempted to influence my sister. I used no persuasion then—I've used no persuasion to-day.'

'And what have you used?'

'We've used authority,' said Madame de Bellegarde in a rich, bell-like voice.

'Ah, you've used authority!' Newman wonderfully echoed. 'They've used authority—' He turned to Madame de Cintré. 'What in the world is their authority and how do they apply it?'

'My mother addressed me her command,' Madame de Cintré said with a sound that was the strangest yet.

'Her command that you should give me up—I see. And you obey—I see. But *why* do you obey?' Newman pursued.

Madame de Cintré looked across at the old Marquise, measuring her from head to foot. Then she spoke again with simplicity. 'I'm afraid of my mother.'

Madame de Bellegarde rose with a certain quickness. 'This is a most indecent scene!'

'I've no wish to prolong it,' said Madame de Cintré; and, turning to the door, she put out her hand again. 'If you can pity me a little, let me go alone.'

Newman held her quietly and firmly. 'I'll come right down there.'

The portière dropped behind her, and he sank with a long breath into the nearest chair. He leaned back in it, resting his hands on the knobs of the arms and looking at Madame de Bellegarde and Urbain. There was a long silence. They stood side by side, their heads high and their handsome eyebrows arched. 'So you make a distinction?' he went on at last. 'You make a distinction between persuading and commanding? It's very neat. But the distinction's in favour of commanding. That rather spoils it.'

'We've not the least objection to defining our position,' said M. de Bellegarde. 'We quite understand that it shouldn't at first appear to you altogether clear. We rather expect indeed that you'll not do us justice.'

'Oh, I'll do you justice,' said Newman. 'Don't be afraid. Only give me a chance!'

The Marquise laid her hand on her son's arm as if to deprecate the attempt to marshal reasons or to meet their friend again, on any ground, too intimately. 'It's quite useless,' she opined, 'to try and arrange this matter so as to make it agreeable to you. It's a disappointment, and disappointments are—I grant it—sometimes odious things. I thought our necessity over—that of letting you know that we don't after all see our way! I considered carefully and tried to arrange it better; but I only gave myself bad headaches and lost my sleep. Say what we will you'll think yourself ill-treated and will publish your wrong among your friends. But we're not afraid of that. Besides, your friends are not our friends, and it will matter by so much the less. Think of us as you like—you don't really know us. I only beg you not to be violent. I've never in my life been present at any sort of roughness, and I think my age should now protect me.'

'Is *that* all you have to say?' asked Newman, slowly rising from his chair. 'That's a poor show for a clever lady like you, Marquise. Come, try again.'

'My mother goes to the point with her usual honesty and intrepidity,' said the Marquis, toying with his watchguard. 'But it's perhaps right I should add another word. We of course quite repudiate the charge of having broken faith with you. We left you entirely at liberty to make yourself agreeable to my sister. We left her quite at liberty to entertain your proposal. When she accepted you we said nothing. We therefore wholly observed our promise. It was only at a later stage of the affair, and on quite a different basis, as it were, that we determined to speak. It would have been better perhaps if we had spoken before. But really, you see, nothing has yet been done.'

'Nothing has yet been done?'—Newman repeated the words as if unconscious of their comical effect. He had lost the sense of what the Marquis was saying; M. de Bellegarde's superior style was a mere humming in his ears. All he understood, in his deep and simple wrath, was that the matter was not a violent joke and that the people before him were perfectly serious. 'Do you suppose I can take this from you?' he wonderingly asked. 'Do you suppose it can matter to me what you say? Do you suppose I'm an idiot that you can so put off?'

Madame de Bellegarde gave a rattle of her fan in the hollow of her hand. 'If you don't take it you can leave it, sir. It matters very little what you do. The simple fact is that my daughter has given you up.'

'She doesn't mean it,' Newman declared after a moment.

'I think I can assure you that she does,' the Marquis fluted.

'Poor stricken woman, poor bleeding heart, what damnable thing have you done to her?' Newman demanded.

'Gently, gently!' murmured M. de Bellegarde as he rocked on his neat foundations.

'She told you,' his mother said. 'I expressed my final wish.'

Newman shook his head heavily. 'This sort of thing can't be, you know. A man can't be used in this fashion. You not only have no right that isn't a preposterous pretence, but you haven't a pennyworth of power.'

'My power,' Madame de Bellegarde observed, 'is in my children's obedience.'

'In their fear, your daughter said. There's something very strange in it. Why should any one be afraid of you?' added Newman after looking at her a moment. 'There has been something at play I don't know and can't guess.'

She met his gaze without flinching and as if neither hearing nor heeding. 'I did my best,' she said quietly. 'I could bear it no longer.'

'It was a bold experiment!' the Marquis pursued.

Newman felt disposed to walk to him and clutch his neck with irresistible firm fingers and a prolongation of thumb-pressure on the windpipe. 'I needn't tell you how you strike me,' he said, however, instead of this; 'of course you know that. But I should think you'd be afraid of your friends—all those people you introduced me to the other night. There were some decent people apparently among them; you may depend upon it there were some good, honest men and women.'

'Our friends approve us,' said M. de Bellegarde; 'there's not a responsible *chef de famille* among them who would have acted otherwise. And however that may be we take the cue from no one. We've been much more used—since one really has to tell you—to setting the example than to waiting for it.'

'You'd have waited long before any one would have set you such an example as this, I guess!' Newman cried. 'Have I done anything wrong or mean or base?' he rang out. 'Have I given you any reason to change your opinion? Have you found out anything against me? Hanged if I can imagine!'

'Our opinion,' said Madame de Bellegarde, 'is quite the same as at first—exactly. We've no ill-will towards yourself; we're very far from accusing you of misconduct. Since your relations with us began you've been, I frankly confess, less eccentric than I expected. It's not your personal character that we object to, it's your professional—it's your antecedents. We really can't reconcile ourselves to a commercial person. We tried to believe in an evil hour it was possible, and that effort was our great misfortune. We determined to persevere to the end and to give you every advantage. I was resolved you should have no reason to accuse me of a want of loyalty. We let the thing certainly go very far—we introduced you to our friends. To tell the truth it was that, I think, that broke me down. I succumbed to the scene that took place the other night in these rooms. You must pardon me if what I say is disagreeable to you, but you've insisted, with violence, on an explanation.'

'There's no better proof of our good faith,' the Marquis superadded, 'than our committing ourselves to you in the eyes of the world three evenings since. We endeavoured to bind ourselves—to tie our hands and cut off our retreat. Could we have done more?'

'But it was that,' his mother subjoined, 'that opened our eyes and broke our bonds. We should have been deeply uncomfortable with any such continuance. You know,' she wound up in a moment, 'that you were forewarned as to our high, stiff way of carrying ourselves. Oh, I grant you that we're as proud and odious as you please! But we didn't seek your acquaintance. You sought ours.'

Newman took up his hat and began mechanically to smooth it; the very fierceness of his scorn kept him from speaking. 'You're certainly odious enough,' he cried at last, 'but it strikes me your pride falls short altogether.'

'In the whole matter,' said the Marquis, still as with a fine note of cool reason, 'I really see nothing but our humility.'

'Let us have no more painful discussion than is necessary,' his mother resumed. 'My daughter told you everything when she said she gives you up.'

'I'm not in the least satisfied about your daughter,' Newman insisted: 'I want to know what you did to her. It's all very easy talking about authority and saying she likes your orders. She didn't accept me blindly and she wouldn't give me up blindly. Not that I believe yet she has really done it after what has passed between us; she'll talk it over with me. But you've frightened her, you've bullied her, you've *hurt* her. What was it you did to her?'

'I had very little to do,' said Madame de Bellegarde in a tone which gave him a chill when he afterwards remembered it.

'Let me remind you that we offered you this amount of consideration,' the Marquis observed, 'with the express understanding that you should abstain from intemperance.'

'I'm not intemperate,' Newman answered; 'it's you who are intemperate. You stab me in the back and I turn on you; is it *I* who am offensive? But I don't know that I've much more to say to you. What you expect of me, apparently, is to go on my way—in the manner most convenient to you—thanking you for favours received and promising never to trouble you again.'

'We expect of you to act like an *homme d'esprit*,' said Madame de Bellegarde. 'You've shown yourself remarkably that, already, and what we've done is altogether based upon your being so. When one must recognise a situation—well, one must. That's all that we've done. Since my daughter absolutely withdraws, what do you gain by making a noise under our windows? You proclaim, at the best, your discomfiture.'

'It remains to be seen if your daughter absolutely withdraws. Your daughter and I are still very good friends; nothing's changed in that. As I say, there has been that between us that must make her recognise at least my claim to some light of mercy from her.'

'I recommend you in your own interest not to expect more than you'll get,' the Marquis returned with firmness. 'I know her well

enough to know that a meaning signified as she just now signified
hers to you is final. Besides, she has given me her word.'

'I've no doubt her word's worth a great deal more than your own,'
said Newman. 'Nevertheless I don't give her up.'

'There's nothing of course to prevent your saying so! But if she
won't even see you—and she won't—your constancy must remain
very much on your hands.'

Newman feigned in truth a greater confidence than he felt.
Madame de Cintré's strange intensity had really struck a chill to his
heart; her face, still impressed on his vision, had been a terrible image
of deep renunciation. He felt sick and suddenly helpless. He turned
away and stood a moment with his hand on the door; then he faced
about and, after the briefest hesitation, broke out with another
accent. 'Come, think of what this must be to me, and leave her to
herself and to the man whom, before God I believe, she loves! Why
should you object to me—what's the matter with me? I can't hurt
you, I wouldn't if I could. I'm the most unobjectionable man in the
world. What if I *am* a commercial person? What under the sun do
you mean? A commercial person? I'll be any sort of person you want.
I never talked to you about business—where on earth does it come
in? Let her go and I'll ask no questions. I'll take her away and you
shall never see me or hear of me again. I'll stay in America if you
like. I'll sign a paper promising never to come back to Europe. All I
want is not to lose her!'

His companions exchanged a glance of mutual re-enforcement,
and Urbain said: 'My dear sir, what you propose is hardly an
improvement. We've not the slightest objection to seeing you, as an
amiable foreigner, and we've every reason for not wishing to be eternally separated from my sister. We object to her marriage; and in that
way'—M. de Bellegarde gave a small, thin laugh—'she'd be more
married than ever.'

'Well then,' Newman presently broke out again, 'where's this
interesting place of yours—Fleurières? I know it's near some old city
on a hill.'

'Precisely. Poitiers is on a hill,' the Marquise admitted. 'I don't
know exactly how old it is. We're not afraid to tell you.'

'It's Poitiers, is it? Very good,' said Newman. 'I shall immediately
follow Madame de Cintré.'

'The trains after this hour won't serve you,' Urbain appeared to judge it his duty to mention.

'I shall then hire a special train.'

'That will be a very foolish waste of money,' said Madame de Bellegarde.

'It will be time enough to talk about waste three days hence,' Newman answered; with which, clapping his hat on his head, he departed.

He didn't immediately start for Fleurières; he was too stunned and wounded for consecutive action. He simply walked; he walked straight before him, following the river till he got out of the stony circle of Paris.* He had a burning, tingling sense of personal outrage. He had never in his life received so absolute a check; he had never been pulled up, or, as he would have said, 'let down', so short, and he found the sensation intolerable as he strode along tapping the trees and lamp-posts fiercely with his stick and inwardly raging. To lose such a woman after taking such jubilant and triumphant possession of her was as great an affront to his pride as it was an injury to his happiness. And to lose her by the interference and the dictation of others, by an impudent old hag's and a pretentious coxcomb's stepping in with their 'authority'! It was too preposterous, it was too pitiful. Upon what he deemed the unblushing treachery of the Bellegardes he wasted little thought; he consigned it once for all to eternal perdition. But the treachery of Madame de Cintré herself amazed and confounded him; there was a key to the mystery, of course, but he groped for it in vain. Only three days had elapsed since she stood beside him in the starlight, beautiful and tranquil as the trust with which he had inspired her, and told him she was happy in the prospect of their marriage. What was the meaning of the change? of what infernal potion had she tasted? He had, however, a terrible apprehension that she had really changed. His very admiration for her attached the idea of force and weight to her rupture. But he didn't rail at her as false, for he was sure she was unhappy. In his walk he had crossed one of the bridges of the Seine, and he still followed unheedingly the long and unbroken quay. He had left Paris behind and was almost in the country; he was in the pleasant suburb of Auteuil.* He stopped at last, looked about at it without seeing or caring for its pleasantness, and then slowly turned round and at a

slower pace retraced his steps. When he came abreast of the fantastic embankment known as the Trocadéro* he reflected, through his
throbbing pain, that he was near Mrs Tristram's dwelling and that
Mrs Tristram, on particular occasions, had much of a woman's kindness in her chords. He felt he needed to pour out his ire, and he took
the road to her house. She was at home and alone, and as soon as she
had looked at him, on his entering the room, she told him she knew
what he had come for. He sat down heavily, in silence, with his eyes
on her.

'They've backed out!' she said without his even needing to tell her.
'Well, you may think it strange, but I felt something the other night
in the air.' Presently he gave her his account; she listened while her
whole face took it in. When he had finished she said quietly: 'They
want her to marry Lord Deepmere.' Newman stared—he didn't
know she knew anything about Lord Deepmere. 'But I don't think
she will,' Mrs Tristram added.

'*She* marry that poor little cub!' cried Newman. 'Oh Lord save us!
And yet why else can she have so horribly treated me?'

'But that isn't the only thing,' said Mrs Tristram. 'They really
couldn't *live* with you any longer. They had overrated their courage.
I must say, to give the devil his due, that there's something rather
fine in that. It was your commercial quality in the abstract, and the
mere historic facts of your wash-tubs and other lucrative wares, that
they couldn't swallow. That's really consistent—the inconsistency
had been the other way. They wanted your money, but they've given
you up for an idea.'

Newman frowned most ruefully and took up his hat again. 'I
thought you'd encourage me!' he brought out with almost juvenile
sadness.

'Pardon my trying to understand—of course it doesn't concern
you to understand,' she answered very gently. 'I feel none the less
sorry for you, especially as I'm at the bottom of your troubles. I've
not forgotten that I suggested the marriage to you. I don't believe
Claire has any intention of consenting to marry Lord Deepmere. It's
true he's not younger than she, as he might pass for being. He's
thirty-three years old; I looked in the Peerage. But no—I can't
believe her so hideously, cruelly false.'

'Please say nothing against her!' Newman strangely cried.

'Poor woman,' she none the less continued, 'she *is* cruel. But of course you'll go after her and you'll plead powerfully. Do you know that as you are now,' Mrs Tristram added with characteristic audacity of comment, 'you're extremely eloquent, even without speaking? To resist you a woman must have a very fixed idea or a very bad conscience. I wish I had done you a wrong—that you might come to me and make me so feel it; and feel *you*, dear man, just you.' She looked at him an instant, then had one of her odd little outbreaks. 'You're lamentable—you're splendid! Go to Madame de Cintré, at any rate, and tell her that she's a puzzle even to one of the intelligent, like me, who so greatly admires her. I'm very curious to see how far family discipline in a fine case like this does go.'

Newman sat a while longer, leaning his elbows on his knees and his head in his hands, and Mrs Tristram continued to temper charity with reason and compassion with criticism. At last she inquired: 'And what does Count Valentin say to it?' Newman started; he had not thought of Valentin and his errand on the Swiss frontier since the morning. The reflexion made him restless again, and he broke away on a promise that his hostess should have without delay his next news. He went straight to his apartment, where, on the table in the vestibule, he found a waiting telegram. 'I'm seriously ill and should be glad to see you as soon as possible.—VALENTIN.' He had a savage groan for this miserable news and for the interruption of his journey to Fleurières. But he addressed to Madame de Cintré a brief, the briefest, statement of these things; it formed a response as well to the ten words of the note that had come to him by Mrs Bread, and was now all the time allowed him.

'I don't give you up and don't really believe you speak your own intention. I don't understand it, but am sure we shall clear it up together. I can't follow you to-day, as I'm called to see a friend at a distance who's very ill, perhaps dying. Why shouldn't I tell you he's your brother?—C.N.'

XIX

HE had a rare gift for sitting still when nothing else would serve, and rare was his opportunity to use it on his journey to Switzerland. The successive hours of the night brought him no sleep; but he kept motionless in his corner of the railway-carriage, his eyes closed, and the most observant of his fellow-travellers might have envied him his apparent rest. Toward morning rest really came, as an effect of mental rather than of physical fatigue. He slept for a couple of hours, and at last, waking, found his eyes attach themselves to one of the snow-powdered peaks of the Jura,* behind which the sky was just reddening with the dawn. But he took in neither the cold mountain nor the warm light: his consciousness began to throb again, on the very instant, with a sense of his wrong. He got out of the train half an hour before it reached Geneva—alighted in the pale early glow and at the station indicated in Valentin's telegram. A drowsy station-master was on the platform with a lantern and the hood of his over-coat over his head, and near him stood a gentleman who advanced to meet Newman. This personage, a man of about forty, showed a tall lean figure, a long brown face, marked eyebrows, high moustaches and fresh light gloves. He took off his hat, looking very grave, and articulated, 'Monsieur!' To which our hero replied: 'You've been acting, in this tragedy, for the Count?'

'I unite with you in having been chosen for that sad honour,' said the gentleman. 'I had placed myself at M. de Bellegarde's service in this melancholy affair, together with M. de Grosjoyaux, who is now at his bedside. M. de Grosjoyaux, I believe, has had the honour of meeting you in Paris, but as he is a better nurse than I, he remained with our poor friend. Bellegarde has been eagerly expecting you.'

'And how *is* the rascal?' said Newman. 'He was badly hit?'

'The doctor has condemned him; we brought a surgeon with us. But he will die in the best sentiments. I sent last evening for the curé of the nearest French village, who spent an hour with him. The curé was quite satisfied.'

'Heaven forgive us!' groaned Newman. 'I'd rather the surgeon were so! And can he see me—shall he know me?'

'When I left him, half an hour ago, he had fallen asleep—after a

feverish, wakeful night. But we shall see.' And this companion proceeded to lead the way out of the station to the village, explaining as
he went that the little party was lodged in the humblest of Swiss inns,
where, however, they had succeeded in making M. de Bellegarde
much more comfortable than could at first have been expected.
'We're old companions-in-arms,' the personage said; 'it's not the first
time one of us has helped the other to lie easy. It's a very nasty
wound, and the nastiest thing about it is that Valentin's adversary
was no shot. He put his beastly bullet where he could. It entered,
accursedly, our poor friend's left side, just below the heart.'

As they picked their way, in the grey, deceptive dawn, between the
manure-heaps of the village street, Newman's new acquaintance narrated the particulars of the meeting. The conditions had been that
if the first exchange of shots should fail to satisfy one of the parties
a second should take place. Valentin's first bullet had done exactly
what Newman's companion was convinced he had intended it to do;
it had grazed the arm of M. Stanislas Kapp, just scratching the flesh.
M. Kapp's own projectile, meanwhile, had passed at ten good inches
from the person of Valentin. The representatives of M. Stanislas
had demanded another shot, which was then, on Valentin's absolute
insistence, granted. But Valentin had fired into space, and the young
Alsatian had done effective execution. 'I saw, when we met him on
the ground,' said Newman's informant, 'that he was not going to be
commode. A mixture of the donkey and the buffalo—with no sense
whatever of proportion.' Valentin had immediately been installed at
the inn, while M. Stanislas and his friends had withdrawn to regions
unknown. The police authorities of the canton* had waited upon the
others, had placed them under technical arrest and had drawn up a
long *procès-verbal*; but as the wine had been drawn—alas!—the
powers would have to drink it. Newman asked if a message had not
been sent to the family, and learned that up to a late hour of the previous night Valentin had opposed it. He had refused to believe his
wound dangerous. After his interview with the curé, however, he had
consented, and a telegram had been despatched to his mother. 'But
the Marquise will scarcely have time—!' So judged Newman's
conductor.

'Well, it's a wicked, wanton, infernal affair!' So judged Newman
himself.

'Ah, you don't approve?' his friend gravely questioned, while he himself remained passionately careless of the involved reflexion on this gentleman's control of the encounter.

'Approve?' cried Newman. 'I wish that when I had him there night before last I had locked him up in my *cabinet de toilette*!'

Valentin's supporter opened his eyes and shook his head up and down two or three times, portentously, with a little flute-like whistle. But he had evidently been prepared, in respect to this outer barbarian, for some oddity of emotion and expression. They had in any case reached the inn, where a stout maid-servant in a nightcap was on the threshold, with a lantern, to take the traveller's bag from the porter who trudged behind him. Valentin was lodged on the ground floor at the back of the house, and Newman's companion went along a stone-faced passage and softly opened a door. Then he beckoned to the visitor, who advanced and looked into the room, lighted by a single shaded candle. Beside the fire sat M. de Grosjoyaux asleep in his dressing-gown—a short stout fair man, with an air of gay surprise, whom Newman had seen several times in Valentin's company. On the bed lay Valentin, pale and still, his eyes closed—a figure very shocking to Newman, who had known it hitherto awake to its finger-tips. M. de Grosjoyaux's colleague pointed to an open door beyond and whispered that the doctor was within, where he kept guard. So long as Valentin slept, or seemed to sleep, of course he was not to be approached; so our hero withdrew for the present, committing himself to the care of the half-waked *bonne*. She took him to a room above-stairs and introduced him to a bed on which a magnified bolster, in yellow calico, figured as a counterpane. He lay down and, in spite of his counterpane and most other things, slept for three or four hours. When he awoke the morning was advanced and the sun filling his window, outside of which he heard the clucking of hens.

While he was dressing there came to his door a message from M. de Grosjoyaux and his companion, who amiably proposed he should breakfast with them. Presently he went downstairs to the little stone-paved dining-room, where the maid-servant, who had taken off her nightcap, was serving the repast. M. de Grosjoyaux was there, surprisingly fresh for a gentleman who had been playing sick-nurse half the night; he now rubbed his hands very constantly and very hard and watched the breakfast-table attentively. Newman renewed acquaintance with him and learned that Valentin was still in a doze; the doctor, who had had a fairly tranquil night, was at present sitting

with him. Before M. de Grosjoyaux's associate reappeared Newman
learned that his name was M. Ledoux and that Bellegarde's acquaintance with him dated from the days when they served together in the
Pontifical Zouaves. M. Ledoux was the nephew of a distinguished
Ultramontane bishop. At last he came in with an effect of dress in
which an ingenious attempt at adjustment at once to a confirmed
style and to the peculiar situation was visible, and with a gravity
tempered by a decent deference to the best breakfast the Croix
Helvétique had ever set forth. Valentin's servant, who was allowed
but with restrictions the honour of attending his master, had been
lending a light Parisian hand in the kitchen. The two Frenchmen did
their best to prove that if circumstances might overshadow they
couldn't really obscure the national gift for good talk, and M. Ledoux
delivered a neat little eulogy on poor Bellegarde, whom he pronounced the most charming Englishman he had ever known.

'Do you call him an Englishman?' Newman asked.

M. Ledoux smiled a moment and then just fell short of an
epigram: '*C'est plus qu'un Anglais, le cher homme—c'est un Anglomane!*' Newman returned, sturdily and handsomely, that any country
might have been proud to claim him, and M. de Grosjoyaux
remarked that it was really too soon to deliver a funeral oration on
poor Bellegarde. 'Evidently,' said M. Ledoux. 'But I couldn't help
observing this morning to Mr Newman that when a man has taken
such excellent measures for his salvation as our dear friend did last
evening, it seems almost a pity he should put it in peril again by
coming back to the world.' M. Ledoux was a great Catholic, and
Newman thought him a queer mixture. His countenance, by day-
light, had an amiably saturnine cast; he had a large lean nose and
looked like an old Spanish picture. He appeared to think the use of
pistols at thirty paces a very perfect arrangement, provided, should
one get hit, one might promptly see the priest. He took, clearly, a
great satisfaction in Valentin's interview with that functionary, and
yet his general tone was far from indicating a sanctimonious habit of
mind. M. Ledoux had evidently a high sense of propriety and was
furnished, in respect to everything, with an explanation and a grave
grin that combined together to push his moustache up under his
nose. *Savoir-vivre*—knowing how to live—was his strong point, in
which he included knowing how to die; but, as Newman reflected
with a good deal of dumb irritation, he seemed disposed to delegate

to others the application of his mastery of this latter resource. M. de Grosjoyaux was quite of another complexion and could but have regarded his friend's theological unction as the sign of an inaccessibly superior spirit. His surprise was so bright that it made him look amused; as if, under the impression of M. Kapp's mere mass, he couldn't recover from the oddity of these hazards, that of the translation of so much large looseness into a thing so fine as a direction— even, as it were, a dreadfully wrong one. He could have understood the *coup* if it had been his own indeed, and he kept looking through the window, over the shoulder of M. Ledoux, at a slender tree by the end of a lane opposite the inn, as if measuring its distance from his extended arm and secretly wishing that, since the association of ideas was so close, he might indulge in a little speculative practice.

Newman found his company depressing, almost irritating. He himself could neither eat nor talk; his soul was sore with grief and anger and the weight of his double sorrow intolerable. He sat with his eyes on his plate, counting the minutes, wishing at one moment that Valentin would see him and leave him free to go in quest of Madame de Cintré and his lost happiness, and mentally calling himself a vile brute the next, for the egotism of his impatience. He at least was poor enough company, and even his acute preoccupation and his general lack of the habit, determined by all his need, of pondering the impression he produced, didn't prevent his guessing the others to be puzzled at poor Bellegarde's taking such a fancy to a dull barbarian as to desire him at his deathbed. After breakfast he strolled forth alone into the village and looked at the fountain, the geese, the open barn-doors, the brown, bent old women who showed their hugely-darned stocking-heels at the end of their slowly-clicking sabots,* as well as at the beautiful view of snowy Alp and purple Jura hanging across either end of the rude street. The day was brilliant; early spring was in the air and the sunshine, and the winter's damp trickled out of the cottage eaves. It was birth and brightness for all nature, even for chirping chickens and other feathered waddling particles, and it was to be death and burial for poor foolish, generous, precious Valentin. Newman walked as far as the village church and went into the small graveyard beside it, where he sat down and looked at the awkward tablets planted about. They were all sordid and hideous, and he could feel only the hardness and coldness of death. He got up and came back to the inn, where he found M. Ledoux having coffee and a cigarette at a little green table which he had caused to be carried into the small garden. Newman, learning that the doctor was still sitting with Valentin, asked if he mightn't be allowed to relieve him; he had a great desire to be useful to their patient. This was, through M. Ledoux, easily arranged; the doctor was very glad to go to bed. He was a youthful and rather jaunty practitioner, but he had a clever face and the ribbon of the Legion of Honour in his buttonhole; Newman listened attentively to his instructions and took mechanically from his hand an old book that had lain on the windowseat of the inn, recommended by him as a help to wakefulness and which proved an odd volume of 'Les Liaisons Dangereuses'.*

Valentin still lay with his eyes closed and without visible change of condition. Newman sat down near him and for a long time narrowly watched him. Then he let his vision stray with his consciousness of his own situation—range away and rest on the chain of the Alps disclosed by the drawing of the scant white cotton curtain of the window, through which the sunshine passed and lay in squares on the red-tiled floor. He tried to interweave his gloom with strains of hope, but only half succeeded. What had happened to him was violent and insolent, like all great strokes of evil; unnatural and monstrous, it showed the hard hand of the Fate that rejoices in the groans and the blood of men, in the tears and the terrors of women, and he had no arms against it. At last a sound struck on the stillness and he heard Valentin's voice.

'It can't be about *me* you're pulling that long face!' He found when he turned that his patient lay in the same position, but with eyes now open and showing the glimmer of a smile. It was with a very slender strength that he felt the pressure of his hand answered. 'I've been watching you for a quarter of an hour,' Valentin went on; 'you've been looking as if you too had had to swallow some vile drug. You're greatly disgusted with me, I see. Well, of course! So am I!'

'Oh, I shan't abuse you,' said Newman. 'I feel too badly. And how are you getting on?'

'Oh, I'm getting *off*! They've quite settled that. Aren't you here to *see* me off?'

'That's for you to settle; you can get well if you try.' Newman declared with a queer strained quaver.

'My dear fellow, how can I try? Trying's violent exercise, and that sort of thing isn't in order for a man with a hole in his side as big as your hat, which begins to bleed if he moves a hair's breadth. I knew you'd come,' he continued; 'I knew I should wake up and find you here; so I'm not surprised. But last night I was very impatient. I didn't see how I could keep still without you. It was a matter of keeping still, just like this; as still as a mummy in his case. You talk about trying; I tried that! Well, here I am yet—these twenty hours. It's more like twenty days.' Valentin's speech was slowly taken, with strange precautions and punctuations, but it had, however faint, the flicker of his gaiety, and he seemed almost to say what he wanted. It was visible, however, that he was in extreme pain, and at last he again closed his eyes. Newman begged him to make no effort—just, as he called it, to take his ease; the doctor had left urgent orders against worry. 'Oh,' returned Valentin, 'let us eat and drink, for to-morrow—to-morrow—!' And he paused again. 'No, not to-morrow, perhaps, but to-day. I can't eat and drink, but I can talk. What's to be gained, at this pass, by renun—renunciation? I mustn't use such big words. I was always a chatterer; Lord, how I've *bavardé* in my day!'

'That's a reason for keeping quiet now,' said Newman. 'We know how beautifully you talk—it's all right about that.'

But Valentin, without heeding him, went on with the same effect of trouble and of pluck. 'I wanted to see you because you've seen my sister. Does she know—will she come?'

Newman felt himself the poorest of deceivers. 'Yes, by this time she must know.'

'Didn't you tell her?' Valentin asked. And then, in a moment: 'Didn't you bring me any message from her?' His eyes now covered his friend like lifted lamps.

'I didn't see her after I got your telegram. I wrote to her.'

'And she sent you no answer?'

Newman managed to reply that Madame de Cintré had left Paris. 'She went yesterday to Fleurières.'

'Yesterday—to Fleurières? Why did she go to Fleurières? What day is this? What day was yesterday? Ah then, I shan't see her,' Valentin moaned. 'Fleurières is too far!' And he became dark and dumb again, only breathing a little harder. Newman sat silent, invoking duplicity, but was relieved at being able soon to believe him really too weak to be curious. He did, however, at last break out again. 'And my mother—and my brother—will they come? Are they at Fleurières?'

'They were in Paris, but I didn't see them either,' Newman answered. 'If they received your telegram in time they'll have started this morning. Otherwise they'll be obliged to wait for the night express and change, and will arrive at the same hour I did.'

'They won't thank me—they won't thank me,' Valentin murmured. 'They'll pass an atrocious night, and Urbain doesn't like the early morning air. I don't remember ever in my life to have seen him before noon—before breakfast. No one ever saw him. We don't know how he is then. Perhaps he's different. Who knows? Posterity perhaps will know. That's the time he works in his *cabinet*, at the history of the Princesses. But I had to send for them—hadn't I? And then I want to see my mother sit there where you sit and say good-bye to her—hear her above all say hers to me. Perhaps, after all, I don't know her—she may have some surprise for me. Don't think you know her yet, yourself; perhaps she may surprise *you*. But if I can't see Claire I don't care—what do you call it?—a red cent. Have you then green *sous* or blue ones or any other colour? *Ah vous, mon cher, vous en avez, vous, de toutes les couleurs!* But what's the matter—while I've been dreaming of her? Why did she go to Fleurières to-day? She never told me. What has happened? Ah, she ought to have guessed I'm here—in this bad way. It's the first time in her life she ever disappointed me. Poor, poor Claire!'

'You know we're not man and wife quite yet—your sister and I,' said Newman. 'She doesn't yet account to me for all her actions.' He tried to throw off this statement with grace, but felt how little the muscles of his face served him.

Valentin looked at him harder. 'Have you two unimaginably quarrelled?'

'Never, never, never!' Newman exclaimed.

'How happily you say that!' said Valentin. 'You're going to be happy—la-la!' In answer to this stroke of irony, none the less powerful for being so unconscious, all poor Newman could do was to give a helpless and ridiculous grin, for the conscious failure of which he then more ridiculously blushed. Valentin, still playing over him the fitful light of fever, presently said: 'But something *is* the matter with you. I watched you just now; you haven't a bridegroom's face.'

'My dear fellow,' Newman desperately pleaded, 'how can I show *you* a bridegroom's face? If you think I enjoy seeing you lie here and not being able to help you—!'

'Why, you're just the man to be jolly and—what do you call it?—to crow; don't forfeit your right to it! I'm a proof of your wisdom. When was a man ever down when he could say "I told you so!" You told me so, you know. You did what you could about it. You said some very good things; I've thought them carefully over. But, my dear friend, I was right, all the same. This is the regular way.'

'I didn't do what I ought,' said Newman. 'I ought to have done something better.'

'For instance?'

'Oh, something or other. I ought to have treated you as a vicious small boy and have locked you up.'

'Well, I'm a very small boy now,' Valentin softly sighed, 'and God knows I've been vicious enough! I'm even rather less than an infant. An infant's helpless, but it's generally voted promising. I'm not promising, eh? Society can't lose a less valuable member.' Newman was strongly moved. He got up and turned his back on his friend and walked away to the window, where he stood looking out but only vaguely seeing. 'No, I don't like the look of your back,' Valentin continued. 'I've always been an observer of backs; yours is quite out of sorts.'

Newman returned to his bedside and begged him to be quiet. 'Only rest and get well, give yourself the very best chance. That's what you want and what you must do. Get well and help me.'

'I told you you were in trouble! But how can I "help" you?' Valentin wailed.

'I'll let you know when you're better. You were always awfully enquiring; there's something to get well *for*!' Newman answered with resolute animation.

Valentin relapsed once more and lay a long time without speaking. He seemed even to have fallen asleep. But at the end of half an hour he was again conversing. 'I'm rather sorry about that place in the bank. Who knows but I might have become another Rothschild?* But I wasn't meant for a banker; bankers are not so easy to kill. Don't you think I've been very easy to kill? It's not like a serious man. It's really very mortifying. It's like telling your hostess you must go, when you count upon her begging you to stay, and then finding she does no such thing. "Really—so soon? You've only just come!" This beastly underbred life of ours doesn't make me any such polite little speech.'

Newman for some time said nothing, but at last he broke out. 'It's a bad case—it's a bad case—it's the worst case I ever met. I don't want to say anything unpleasant, but I can't help it. I've seen men dying before—and I've seen men shot. I've seen men in the worst kind of holes—worse even than yours. But it always seemed more natural; they were of no account compared to you—and at any rate *I* didn't care. But *now*—damnation, damnation! You might have done something more to the purpose. It's about the meanest wind-up of a man's legitimate business I can imagine!'

Valentin feebly waved his hand to and fro. 'Don't insist—don't insist! It's taking a mean advantage. For you see at the bottom—down at the bottom in a little place as small as the end of a wine-funnel— I agree with you!' A few moments after this the doctor put his head through the half-opened door and, perceiving his charge was awake, came in to feel his pulse. He shook his head and declared he had talked too much—ten times too much. 'Nonsense!' his patient protested; 'a man sentenced to death is allowed to get in first all he can. He can't talk *after*, and if he was ever a talker—! Have you never read an account of an execution in a newspaper?' he went on. 'Don't they always set a lot of people at the prisoner—lawyers, reporters, priests—to *make* him talk? But it's not Newman's fault; he sits there as mum as a death's-head.'

The doctor observed that it was time the wound should be dressed again; MM. de Grosjoyaux and Ledoux, who had already witnessed this delicate operation, taking Newman's place as assistants. Newman withdrew, learning from his fellow-watchers in the other room that they had received a telegram from the Marquis to the effect that their message had been delivered in the Rue de l'Université too late to allow him to take the morning train, but that he would start with his mother in the evening. Our friend wandered away into the village again and walked about restlessly for two or three hours. The day had, in its regulated gloom, the length of some interminable classic tragedy. At dusk he came back and dined with the doctor and M. Ledoux. The dressing of Valentin's wound had been a very critical business; the question was definitely whether he could bear a repetition of it. He then declared that he must beg of Mr Newman to deny himself for the present the satisfaction of sitting with M. de

Bellegarde; more than any one else, apparently, he had the flattering but fatal gift of interesting him more than he could bear. M. Ledoux, at this, swallowed a glass of wine in silence; he must have been wondering what the deuce Bellegarde found so exciting in the American.

Newman, after dinner, went up to his room, where, flinging himself too on his bed at his grim length, he lay staring, for blank weariness, at the lighted candle and thinking that Valentin was dying downstairs. Late, when the candle had burnt low, came a soft tap at his door. The doctor stood there with another light and a motion of despair.

'He must *faire la fête toujours*! He insists on seeing you, and I'm afraid you must come. I think that at this rate he'll hardly outlast the night.'

Newman went back to Valentin's room, which he found lighted by a taper on the hearth, but with its occupant begging for something brighter. 'I want to see your face. They say you work me up,' he went on as Newman complied with this request, 'and I confess I've felt worked up; but it isn't you—it's my own great intelligence, that sacred spark, of which you've such an opinion. Sit down there and let me look at you again.' Newman seated himself, folded his arms and bent a heavy gaze on his friend. He felt as if he were now playing a part, mechanically, in the most lugubrious of comedies. Valentin faced him thus for some time. 'Yes, this morning I was right; you've something on your mind heavier than ever I've had. Come, I'm a dying man, and it's indecent to deceive me. Something happened after I left Paris. It wasn't for nothing that my sister started off at this season of the year for Fleurières. Why was it? It sticks in my crop. I've been thinking it over, and if you don't tell me I shall guess.'

'I had better not tell you,' Newman mildly reasoned. 'It won't do you any good.'

'If you think it will do me any good not to tell me you're very much mistaken. There's trouble about your marriage.'

'Yes. There's trouble about my marriage.'

'Good!' With which Valentin again waited a little. 'They've stopped it off.'

'They've stopped it off,' Newman admitted. Now that he had spoken out he found in it a relief that deepened as he went on. 'Your mother and brother have broken faith. They've decided that it can't take place. They've decided I'm not good enough—when they come to think of it. They've taken back their word. Since you want to know, there it is!' Valentin uttered a strange sound, thrice lifting his hands and letting them drop. 'I'm sorry not to have anything better to tell you of them,' Newman pursued. 'But it's not my fault. I was indeed bewildered enough when your telegram reached me; I was quite upside down. You may imagine whether I feel any better now.'

Valentin gasped and moaned as if his wound were throbbing. 'Broken faith, broken faith! And my sister—my sister?'

'Your sister's very unhappy; she has consented to give me up. I don't know why—I don't know what they've done to her; it must be something pretty bad. In justice to her you ought to know. They've made her suffer—what it is they must have put her through! I haven't seen her alone, but only before them. We had an interview yesterday morning. They let me have it full in the face. They told me to go about my business. It seems to me a very bad case. I'm sorry to have such a report to make of them. I'm angry, I'm sore, I'm sick.'

Valentin lay there staring, his eyes more brilliantly lighted, his lips soundlessly parted, a flush of colour in his pale face. Newman had never before uttered so many words in the plaintive key, but now, in speaking to his friend in that friend's extremity, he had a sense of making his lament somewhere within the presence of the power that men pray to in trouble; he felt his outgush of resentment as a spiritual act, an appeal to higher protection. 'And Claire,' the young man breathed; 'Claire? She has given you up?'

'I don't really believe it.'

'No, don't believe it, don't believe it. She's gaining time. Believe that.'

'I immensely pity her!' said Newman.

'Poor, poor Claire!' Valentin sighed. 'But they—but they—?' And he paused again. 'You saw them; they dismissed you, face to face?'

'Face to face—rather!'

'What did they say?'

'They said they couldn't stand a commercial person.'

Valentin put out his hand and laid it on Newman's arm. 'And about their promise—their engagement with you?'

'They made a distinction. They said it was to hold good only until Madame de Cintré accepted me.'

'But since she did—!'

'Well, since she did—*after* she did—they found, as I understand, that they couldn't.'

Valentin lay staring—his flush died away. 'Don't tell me any more. I'm ashamed.'

'You? You're the soul of honour,' said Newman very simply.

Valentin groaned and averted his head. For some time nothing more was said. Then he turned back again and found a certain force to press Newman's arm. 'It's very bad—very bad. When my people—when my "race"—come to that, it is time for me to pass away. I believe in my sister; she'll explain. Pardon her, allow for her, be patient with her; wait for that. If she can't—if she can't make her conduct clear: well, forgive her somehow; at any rate don't curse her. She'll pay—she *has* paid; with her one chance of happiness. But for the others it's very bad—very bad. You take it very hard? No, it's a shame to make you say so.' He closed his eyes and again there was a silence. Newman felt almost awed; he had stirred his companion to depths down into which he now shrank from looking. Presently Valentin fixed him again, releasing his arm. 'I apologise. Do you understand? Here on my deathbed. I apologise for my family. For my mother. For my brother. For the name I *was* proud of. Voilà!' he added softly.

Newman for all answer took his hand and kept it in his own. He remained quiet, and at the end of half an hour the doctor noiselessly returned. Behind him, through the half-open door, Newman saw the two questioning faces of MM. de Grosjoyaux and Ledoux. The doctor laid a hand on the patient's wrist and sat looking at him. He gave no sign, and the two gentlemen came in, M. Ledoux having first beckoned to some one outside. This was M. le curé, who carried in his hand an object unknown to Newman and covered with a white napkin. M. le curé was short, round and red: he advanced, pulling off his little black cap to Newman, and deposited his burden on the table; and then he sat down in the best armchair, folding his hands across his person. The other gentlemen had exchanged glances which expressed unanimity as to the timeliness of their presence. But for a long time Valentin neither spoke nor moved. It was Newman's belief afterwards that M. le curé had gone to sleep. At last, abruptly, their friend pronounced Newman's name. This visitor went to him and he said in French: 'You're not alone. I want to speak to you alone.'

Newman looked at the doctor and the doctor looked at the curé, who looked back at him; and then the doctor and the curé together gave a shrug. 'Alone—for five minutes,' Valentin repeated. 'Please leave us.' The curé took up his burden again and led the way out, followed by his companions. Newman closed the door behind them and came back to Valentin, who had watched all this intently.

'It's very bad, it's very bad,' he said after Newman had seated himself close. 'The more I think of it the worse it is.'

'Oh, don't think of it!' Newman groaned.

But his friend went on without heeding him. 'Even if they should come round again the shame—the baseness—is there.'

'Oh, they won't come round!' said Newman.

'Well, you can make them.'

'Make them?'

'I can tell you something—a great secret—an immense secret. You can use it against them—frighten them, coerce them.'

'A secret!' Newman repeated. The idea of letting Valentin, on his deathbed, confide to him any matter sacredly intimate, shocked him, for the moment, and made him draw back. It seemed an illicit way of arriving at information and even had a vague analogy with listening at a keyhole. Then suddenly the thought of reducing Madame de Bellegarde and her son to the forms of submission became attractive, and, as to lose in any case no last breath of the spirit for which he had felt such a kindness, he brought his head nearer. For some time, however, nothing more came. Valentin but covered him with kindled, expanded, troubled eyes, and he began to believe he had spoken in delirium. But at last he spoke again.

'There was something done—something done at Fleurières. It was some wrong, some violence, I believe some cruelty. It may have been—God forgive me *now*—some crime. My father—something happened to him: I don't know what; I've been ashamed, afraid, to know. But a bad business—a worse even than yours—there was *that*. My mother knows—Urbain knows.'

'Something happened to your father?' Newman permitted himself to ask.

Valentin looked at him still more wide-eyed. 'He didn't get well. They didn't let him.'

'"Let" him?'—Newman stared back. 'Get well of what?'

But the immense effort he had made, first to decide to utter these words and then to bring them out, appeared to have taken his last strength. He lapsed again into silence and Newman sat watching him. 'Do you understand?' he began again presently. 'At Fleurières. You can find out. Mrs Bread knows. Tell her I made this point—at this hour—of your asking her. She'll give you the truth itself—and then you'll show them you know it. It may do something for you. It may make the difference. If it doesn't, tell every one. It will—it will'—here Valentin's voice sank to the feeblest murmur—'it will pay them.'

'Pay them?'—Newman wondered.

'What you owe them!'

The words died away in a long vague wail. Newman stood up, deeply impressed, not knowing what to say; his heart was beating as never. 'Thank you,' he said at last. 'I'm much obliged.' But Valentin seemed not to hear him; he remained silent and his silence continued. At last Newman went and opened the door. M. de curé re-entered, bearing his sacred vessel* and followed by a young ministrant at his altar in a white stole, by the three gentlemen and by Valentin's servant. It was quite processional.

XX

VALENTIN DE BELLEGARDE died tranquilly, just as the cold faint March dawn began to clear the grave faces of the little knot of friends gathered about his bedside. An hour later Newman left the inn and drove to Geneva. He was naturally unwilling to be present at the arrival of Madame de Bellegarde and her first-born. At Geneva, for the moment, he remained. He was like a man who has had a fall and wants to sit still and count his bruises. He instantly wrote to Madame de Cintré, detailing to her the circumstances of her brother's death—with certain exceptions—and asking her what was the earliest moment at which he might hope she would consent to see him. M. Ledoux had told him he had reason to know that Valentin's will—he had had a great deal of light but pleasant personal property to dispose of—contained a request that he should be buried near his father in the churchyard of Fleurières, and Newman intended that the state of his own relations with the family should not deprive him of the satisfaction of helping to pay the last earthly honours to the best fellow in the world. He reflected that Valentin's friendship was older than Urbain's enmity, and that at a funeral it was easy to escape notice. Madame de Cintré's answer to his letter enabled him to time his arrival at Fleurières. This answer was very brief; it ran as follows;

'I thank you for your letter and for your being with Valentin. It is the most inexpressible sorrow to me that I was not. To see you will be only anguish; there's no need therefore to wait for what you call brighter days. It is all one now, and I shall have no brighter days. Come when you please; only notify me first. My brother is to be buried here on Friday, and my family is to remain.—C. DE C.'

On receipt of this Newman had gone straight to Paris and to Poitiers. The journey had taken him far southward, through green Touraine and across the far-shining Loire, into a country where the early spring deepened divinely about him, but he had never made one during which he had heeded less the lay of the land. He alighted at an hotel in respect to which he scarce knew whether the wealth of its provincial note more graced or compromised it, and the next morning drove in couple of hours to the village of Fleurières. But here, for all his melancholy, he couldn't resist the intensity of an impression. The *petit bourg* lay at the base of a huge mound, on the summit of which stood the crumbling ruins of a feudal castle, much of whose sturdy material, as well as that of the wall that dropped along the hill to enclose the clustered houses defensively, had been absorbed into the very substance of the village. The church was simply the former chapel of the castle, fronting upon its grass-grown court, which, however, was of generous enough width to have given up its quaintest corner to a small place of interment. Here the very headstones themselves seemed to sleep as they slanted into the grass; the patient elbow of the rampart held them together on one side, and in front, far beneath their mossy lids, the green plains and blue distances stretched away. The approach to the church, up the hill, defied all wheels. It was lined with peasants two or three rows deep, who stood watching old Madame de Bellegarde slowly ascend on the arm of her elder son and behind the pall-bearers of the other. Newman chose to lurk among the common mourners who murmured 'Madame la Comtesse' as a particular tall slimness almost bowed beneath its ensigns of woe passed before them. He stood in the dusky little church while the service was going forward, but at the dismal tombside he turned away and walked down the hill. He went back to Poitiers and spent two days in which patience and revolt were confounded in a single ache. On the third day he sent Madame de Cintré a note to the effect that he would call on her in the afternoon, and in accordance with this he again took his way to Fleurières. He left his vehicle at the tavern in the village street and obeyed the simple instructions given him for finding the château.

'It's just beyond there,' said the landlord, and pointed to the tree-tops of the *parc* above the opposite houses. Newman followed the first cross-road to the right—it was bordered with mouldy cottages—and in a few moments saw before him the peaked roofs of the towers. Advancing further he found himself before a vast iron gate, rusty and closed; here he paused a moment, looking through the bars. The residence was near the road, as if the very highway belonged to it; this gave it a fine old masterly air. Newman learned afterwards, from a guide-book of the province, that it dated from the reign of Henry III.* It presented to the wide-paved area which preceded it, and which was edged with shabby farm-buildings, an immense façade of dark time-stained brick, flanked by two low wings, each of which terminated in a little Dutch-looking pavilion* capped with a fantastic roof. Two towers rose behind, and behind the towers was a grand group of elms and beeches, now just faintly green. The great feature, however, was a wide green river, which washed the foundations of the pile. The whole mass rose from an island in the circling stream, so that this formed a perfect moat, spanned by a two-arched bridge without a parapet. The dull brick walls, which here and there made a grand straight sweep, the ugly little cupolas of the wings, the deep-set windows, the long steep pinnacles of mossy slate, all mirrored themselves in the quiet water.

Newman rang at the gate, and was almost frightened at the tone with which a big rusty bell above his head replied to him. An old woman came out from the gatehouse and opened the creaking portal just wide enough for him to pass, on which he went in and across the dry bare court and the little cracked white slabs of the causeway on the moat. At the door of the house he waited for some moments, and this gave him a chance to observe that Fleurières was not 'kept up' and to reflect that it was a melancholy place of residence. 'It looks,' he said to himself—and I give the comparison for what it is worth— 'like a Chinese penitentiary.' At last the door was opened by a servant whom he remembered to have seen in the Rue de l'Université. The man's dull face brightened as he perceived our hero, the case always being that Newman, for indefinable reasons, enjoyed the confidence of the liveried gentry. The footman led the way across a great main vestibule, with a pyramid of plants at its centre and glass doors all around, to what appeared to be the principal saloon. The visitor crossed the threshold of a room of superb proportions, which made him feel at first like a tourist with a guide-book and a cicerone awaiting a fee. But when his guide had left him alone after observing that he would call Madame la Comtesse, he saw the place contained little that was remarkable beyond a dusky ceiling with curiously carved beams, a set of curtains of elaborate antiquated tapestry and a dark oaken floor polished like a mirror. He waited some minutes, walking up and down; then at last, as he turned at the end of the room, saw Madame de Cintré had come in by a distant door. She wore a black dress—she stood looking at him. As the length of the immense room lay between them he had time to take her well in before they met in the middle of it.

He was dismayed at the change in her appearance. Pale, heavy-browed, almost haggard with a monastic rigidity in her dress, she had little but her pure features in common with the woman whose radiant good grace he had hitherto admired. She let her eyes rest on his own and surrendered to him her hand; but the eyes were like two rainy autumn moons and the touch portentously lifeless. 'I was at your brother's funeral,' he said. 'Then I waited three days. But I could wait no longer.'

'Nothing can be lost or gained by waiting,' she answered. 'But it was very considerate of you to wait, horribly wronged as you've been.'

'I'm glad you think I've been horribly wronged,' said Newman with that vague effect of whimsicality with which he often uttered words of the gravest meaning.

'Do I need to say so?' she asked. 'I don't think I've wronged, seriously, many persons; certainly not consciously. To you, to whom I have done this hard and cruel thing, the only reparation I can make is to say that I know it, that I feel it. But such words are pitifully poor.'

'Oh, they're a great step forward!' said Newman with a fixed and ah—as he even himself felt—such an anxious smile of encouragement. He pushed a chair toward her and held it, looking at her urgently. She sat down mechanically and he seated himself near her; but in a moment he got up and stood restlessly before her. She remained there like a troubled creature who had passed through the stage of restlessness.

'I say nothing's to be gained by my seeing you,' she went on, 'and yet I'm very glad you came. Now I can tell you what I feel. It's a selfish pleasure, but it's one of the last I shall have.' And she paused with her great misty eyes on him. 'I know how I've deceived and injured you; I know how cruel and cowardly I've been. I see it as vividly as you do—I feel it to the ends of my fingers.' And she unclasped her hands, which were locked together in her lap, lifted them and dropped them at her side. 'Anything that you may have said of me in your angriest passion is nothing to what I have said to myself.'

'In my angriest passion,' said Newman, 'I've said nothing hard of you. The very worst thing I've said of you yet is that you're the most perfect of women.' And he seated himself before her again abruptly.

She flushed a little, but even her flush was dim. 'That's because you think I'll come back. But I shall not come back. It's in that hope you have come here, I know; I'm very sorry for you. I'd do almost anything for you. To say that, after what I have done, seems simply impudent; but what can I say that will not seem impudent? To wrong you and apologise—that's easy enough. I should not, heaven forgive me, have wronged you.' She stopped a moment, always with her tragic eyes on him, but motioned him to let her talk. 'I ought never to have listened to you at first; that was the wrong. No good could come of it. I felt it, and yet I listened; that was your fault. I liked you too much; I believed in you.'

'And don't you believe in me now?'

'More than ever. But now it doesn't matter. I've given you up.'

Newman gave a great thump with his clenched fist upon his knee. 'Why, why, why?' he cried. 'Give me a reason—a decent reason. You're not a child—you're not a minor nor an idiot. You're not obliged to drop me because your mother told you to. Such a reason isn't worthy of you.'

'I know that; it's not worthy of me. But it's the only one I have to give. After all,' said Madame de Cintré, throwing out vain hands, 'think me an idiot and forget me! That will be the simplest way.'

He got up and walked away with a crushing sense that his cause was lost and yet with an equal inability to give up fighting. He went to one of the great windows and looked out at the stiffly-embanked river and the formal gardens beyond it. When he turned round she had risen; she stood there silent and passive, so passive that it told terribly of her detachment. 'You're not frank,' he began again; 'you're not really honest any more than you're merciful. Instead of saying you're imbecile you should say that other people are wicked. Your mother and your brother have been false and cruel; they have been so to me, and I'm sure they have been so to you. Why do you try to shield them? Why do you sacrifice me to *them*? I'm not false; I'm not cruel. You don't know what you give up; I can tell you that— you *don't*. They bully you and plot about you; and I—I—' And he paused, lifting the strong arms to which she wouldn't come. She but turned away and began to leave him. 'You told me the other day that you were afraid of your mother,' he followed her to say. 'It must have meant something. What therefore *did* it mean?'

She shook her head. 'I remember. I was sorry afterwards.'

'You were sorry when she came down on you and used some atrocious advantage. In God's name, what *is* it she does to you?'

'Nothing. Nothing that you can understand. And now that I've given you up I mustn't complain of her to you.'

'That's no reasoning!' cried Newman. 'Complain of her, on the contrary, for all you're worth. To whom on God's earth *but* to me? Tell me all about it, frankly and trustfully, as you ought, and we'll talk it over so satisfactorily that you'll keep your plighted faith.'

Madame de Cintré looked down some moments fixedly; at last she raised her eyes. 'One good at least has come of this: I've made you judge me more fairly. You thought of me in a way that did me great honour; I don't know why you had taken it into your head. But it left me no loophole for escape—no chance to be the common weak creature I am. It was not my fault; I warned you from the first. But I ought to have warned you more. I ought to have convinced you that I was doomed to disappoint you. But I *was*, in a way, too proud. You see what my superiority amounts to, I hope!' she went on, raising her voice with a tremor that even then and there he found all so inconsequently sweet. 'I'm too proud to be honest, I'm not too proud to be faithless. I'm timid and cold and selfish. I'm afraid of being uncomfortable.'

'And you call marrying me uncomfortable?' he stared.

She flushed as with the sense of being only shut up in her pain, and seemed to say that if begging his pardon in words had that effect of an easy condition for her she might at least thus mutely express her perfect comprehension of his finding her conduct odious. 'It's not marrying you; it's doing all that would go with it. It's the rupture, the defiance, the insisting upon being happy in my own way. What right have I to be happy when—when—?' Again she broke down.

'When what?' he pressed.

'When others have so suffered.'

'What others?' he demanded. 'What have you to do with any others but me? Besides, you said just now that you wanted happiness and that you should find it by obeying your mother. You strangely contradict yourself.'

'Yes, I strangely contradict myself; that shows you—strangely enough too—that I'm not even intelligent.'

'You're laughing at me!' he cried. 'It's as if you were horribly mocking!'

She looked at him intently, and an observer might have believed her to be asking herself if she shouldn't most quickly end their common pain by confessing to some such monstrosity. Yet 'No; I'm not,' was what she presently said.

'Granting that you're not intelligent,' he went on, 'that you're weak, that you're common, that you're nothing I've believed you to be—what I ask of you is not an heroic effort, it's a very easy and possible effort. There's a great deal on my side to make it so. The simple truth is that you don't care enough for me to make it.'

'I'm cold,' said Madame de Cintré. 'I'm as cold as that flowing river.'

Newman gave a great rap on the floor with his stick and a long grim laugh. 'Ah, not you! You go altogether too far—you overshoot the mark. There isn't a woman in the world as bad as you would make yourself out. I see your game; it's what I said. You're blackening yourself to whiten others. You don't want to give me up at all; you like me—you like me, God help you! I know you do; you've shown it, and I've felt it and adored you for it! After that you may be as cold as you please! They've bullied you, I say; they've tortured you. It's an outrage, and I insist on saving you from the extravagance of your generosity. Would you chop off your hand if your mother required it?'

She gave at this the long sigh of a creature too hard pressed. 'I spoke of my mother too blindly the other day. I'm my own mistress, by law and by her approval. She can do nothing to me; she has done nothing. She has never alluded to those hard words I used about her.'

'She has made you feel them, I'll promise you!' said Newman.

'It's my conscience that makes me feel them.'

'Your conscience then seems to me rather extraordinarily mixed!' he passionately returned.

'It has been in great trouble, but now it's very clear. I don't give you up for any worldly advantage or for any worldly happiness.'

'Oh, you don't give me up for Lord Deepmere, I know,' he agreed. 'I won't pretend, even to provoke you, that I think that. But that's what your mother and your brother wanted, and your mother, at that villainous ball of hers—I liked it at the time, but the very thought of it now is a bath of fire!—tried to push him on to make up to you.'

'Who told you this?' she asked with her strange, stricken mildness.

'Not Valentin, I observed it. I guessed it. I didn't know at the time that I was observing it, but it stuck in my memory. And afterwards, you recollect, I saw Lord Deepmere with you in the conservatory. You said then that you would tell me at another time what he had said to you.'

'That was before—before *this*,' she immediately pleaded.

'It doesn't matter,' said Newman; 'and, besides, I think I know. He's an honest little Englishman. He came and told you what your mother was up to—that she wanted him to supplant me; not being a commercial person. If he would make you an offer she would undertake to bring you over and give me the slip—getting rid of me easily, or at least decently, somehow. Lord Deepmere isn't remarkably bright, so she had to spell it out to him. He said he admired you "no end", and that he wanted you to know it; but he didn't like being mixed up with that sort of treachery, and he came to you and told tales. That was about the size of it, wasn't it? And then you said you were perfectly happy.'

'I don't see why we should talk of Lord Deepmere,' she returned. 'It wasn't for that you came here; and about my mother it doesn't matter what you suspect and what you know. When once my mind has been made up, as it is now, I shouldn't discuss these things. Discussing anything now is very vain and only a fresh torment. We must try and live each as we can. I believe you'll be happy again; even, sometimes, when you think of *me*. When you do so, think this—that it was not easy and that I did the best I could. I've things to reckon with that you don't know. I mean I've feelings. I must do as they force me—I must, I must. They'd haunt me otherwise,' she cried, with vehemence; 'they'd give me no rest and would kill me!'

'I know what your feelings are: they're perversities and superstitions! They're the feeling that after all, though I *am* a good fellow, I've been in business; the feeling that your mother's looks are law and your brother's words are gospel; that you all hang together and that it's a part of the everlasting great order, *your* order, that they should have a hand in everything you do. It makes my blood boil. That *is* cold; you're right. And what I feel here,' and Newman struck his heart and became more eloquent than he knew, 'is a glowing fire!'

A spectator less preoccupied than Madame de Cintré's distracted wooer would have felt sure from the first that her appealing calm of manner was the result of violent effort, in spite of which the tide of agitation was rapidly rising. On these last words of Newman's it overflowed, though at first she spoke low, for fear her voice might betray her. 'No, I was not right—I'm not cold! I believe that if I'm doing what seems so bad it's not mere weakness and falsity. My dear friend, my best of friends, it's like a religion. I can't tell you—I can't! It's cruel of you to insist, I don't see why I shouldn't ask you to believe me—and pity me. It's like a religion. There's a curse upon the house; I don't know what—I don't know why—don't ask me. We must all bear it. I've been too selfish; I wanted to escape from it. You offered me a great chance—besides my liking you. I liked you more than I ever liked any one,' she insisted to him with a beauty and purity of clearness, and yet with the sad fallacy of thinking, apparently, that she made the case less tragic for him by making it more tragic for herself. 'It seemed good to change completely, to break, to go away. And then I admired you, I admired you,' she so nobly and decently repeated. 'But I can't—it has overtaken and come back to me.' Her self-control had now completely abandoned her, and her words were broken with long sobs. 'Why do such dreadful things happen to us— why is my brother Valentin killed, like a beast, in the beauty of his youth and his gaiety and his brightness and all that we loved him for? Why are there things I can't ask about—that I'm afraid, for my life, to know? Why are there places I can't look at, sounds I can't hear? Why is it given to me to choose, to decide, in a case so hard and so terrible as this? I'm not meant for that—I'm not made for boldness and defiance. I was made to be happy in a quiet natural way.' At this Newman gave a most expressive groan, but she quavered heartbreakingly on: 'I was made to do gladly and gratefully what's expected of me. My mother has always been very good to me; that's all I can say. I mustn't judge her; I mustn't criticise her. If I did it would come dreadfully back to me. I can't change!'

'No,' said Newman bitterly; '*I* must change—if I break in two in the effort!'

'You're different. You're a man; you'll get over it. You'll live, you'll do things, you can't not do good, therefore you can't not be happy: you'll find all kinds of consolation. You were born—you were trained—to changes. Besides, besides, I shall always think of you.'

'I don't care for that!' he almost shouted. 'You're cruel—you're terribly cruel, God forgive you! You may have the best reasons and the finest feelings in the world; that makes no difference. You're a mystery to me; I don't see how such hardness can go with anything so divine!'

Madame de Cintré fixed him a moment with her swimming eyes. 'You believe I'm hard then?'

He glared as if at her drowning beyond help; then he broke out: 'You're a perfect, faultless, priceless creature! For God's sake, stay by me!'

'Of course I'm hard *in effect*,' she pitifully reasoned; 'though if ever a creature was innocent, in intention—! Whenever we give pain we're hard. And we *must* give pain; that's the world—the hateful miserable world! Ah!' and she gave a sigh as sharp as the shudder of an ague, 'I can't even say I'm glad to have known you—though I am. That too is to wrong you. I can say nothing that's not cruel. Therefore let us part without more of this. Good-bye!' And she put out her hand.

Newman stood and looked at it without taking it, and then raised his eyes to her face. He felt in them the rising tears of rage. 'What do you mean to do? Where are you going?'

'Where I shall give no more pain and suspect no more evil. I'm going out of the world.'

'Out of the world?'

'I'm going into a convent.'

'Into a convent!' He repeated the words with the deepest dismay; it was as if she had said she was going into an hospital for incurables. 'Into a convent—*you*!'

'I told you that it was not for my worldly advantage or pleasure I was leaving you.'

But still he hardly understood. 'You're going to be a nun,' he went on; 'in a cell—for life—with a gown and a black veil?'

'A nun—a blest Carmelite nun,'* said Madame de Cintré. 'For life, with God's leave and mercy.'

The image rose there, at her words, too dark and horrible for belief, and affected him as if she had told him she was going to mutilate her beautiful face or drink some potion that would make her mad. He clasped his hands and began to tremble visibly. 'Madame de Cintré, don't, don't, I beseech you! On my knees, if you like, I'll beseech you.'

She laid her hand on his arm with a tender, pitying, almost reassuring gesture, 'You don't understand, you've wrong ideas. It's nothing horrible. It's only peace and safety. It's to be out of the world, where such troubles as this come to the innocent, to the best. And for life—that's the blessing of it! They can't begin again.'

He dropped into a chair and sat looking at her with a long inarticulate wail. That this superb woman, in whom he had seen all human grace, the rarest personal resource, should turn from him and all the brightness he offered her—him and his future and his fortune and his fidelity—to muffle herself in ascetic rags and entomb herself in a cell, was a confounding combination of the merciless and the impossible. As the vision spread before him the impossibility turned to the monstrous; it was a reduction to the absurd of the trial to which he was subjected. 'You—you a nun; you with your beauty defaced and your nature wasted—you behind locks and bars! Never, never, if I can prevent it!' And he sprang to his feet in loud derision.

'You can't prevent it,' she returned, 'and it ought—a little—to satisfy you. Do you suppose I'll go on living in the world, still beside you, and yet not *with* you? It's all arranged. Good-bye, good-bye.'

This time he took her hand, took it in both his own. 'For ever?' he said. Her lips made an inaudible movement and his own sounded a deep imprecation. She closed her eyes as if with the pain of hearing it; then he drew her toward him and clasped her to his breast. He kissed her white face again and again, as to leave less of it for his loss; for an instant she resisted and for a minute she submitted; then, with a force that threw him back panting, she disengaged herself and hurried away over the long shining floor. The next moment the door closed behind her, and after another he had made his way out as he could.

XXI

THERE is a pretty public walk at Poitiers, laid out upon the crest of the high hill around which the little city clusters, planted with thick trees and looking down on the fertile fields in which the old English princes fought for their right and held it. Newman paced up and down this retreat for the greater part of the next day, letting his eyes wander over the historic prospect; but he would have been sadly at a loss to tell you afterwards if the latter was made up of coal-fields or of vineyards. He was wholly possessed by his pang, of which reflection by no means diminished the ache. He feared the creature he had thus learned to adore was irretrievably lost; and yet in what case of straight violation of his right or property had he ever merely sat down and groaned? In what case had he not made some attempt at recovery? Wholly unused to giving up in difficulties, he found it impossible to turn his back upon Fleurières and its inhabitants; it seemed to him some germ of hope or reparation must lurk there somewhere if he could only stretch his arm out far enough to pluck it. It was as if he had his hand on a door-knob and were closing his clenched fist on it: he had thumped, he had called, he had pressed the door with his powerful knee and shaken it with all his strength, and dead, damning silence had answered him. And yet something held him there—something hardened the grasp of his fingers. His satisfaction had been too intense, his whole plan too deliberate and mature, his prospect of happiness too rich and comprehensive, for this fine moral fabric to crumble at a stroke. The very foundation seemed fatally injured and yet he felt a stubborn desire still to try to save the edifice. He was filled with a sorer sense of wrong than he had ever known, or than he had supposed it possible he should know. To accept his injury and walk away without looking behind him was a stretch of accommodation of which he found himself incapable. He looked behind him intently and continually, and what he saw there didn't assuage his resentment. He saw himself trustful, generous, liberal, patient, easy, pocketing frequent irritation and furnishing unlimited modesty. To have eaten humble pie, to have been snubbed and patronised and satirised, and have consented to take it as one of the conditions of the bargain—

to have done this, and done it all for nothing, surely gave one a right to protest.

And to be turned off because one was a commercial person! As if he had ever talked or dreamt of the commercial since his connexion with the Bellegardes began—as if he had made the least circumstance of the commercial—as if he wouldn't have consented to confound the commercial fifty times a day if it might have increased by a hair's breadth the chance of his not suffering this so much more than commercial treachery! Granted one's being commercial was fair ground for one's being cleverly 'sold', how little they knew about the class so designated and its enterprising way of not standing on trifles! It was in the light of his injury that the weight of his past endurance seemed so heavy; his current irritation had not been so great, merged as it was in his vision of the cloudless blue that overarched his more intimate relation. But now his sense of outrage was deep, rancorous and ever-present; he felt himself as swindled as he had been confiding. As for his friend's spiritual position, it moved him but to dismal mystification; it struck him with a kind of awe, and the fact that he was powerless to understand it or feel the reality of its motives only made it a deadlier oppression. He had never let the fact of her religious faith trouble him; Catholicism was only a name to him, and to express a mistrust of her forms of worship would have implied that he had other and finer ones to offer: which was as little possible as might be. If such flawless white flowers as that could bloom in Catholic soil they but attested its richness. But it was one thing to be a Catholic and another to turn nun—on your hands! There was something lugubriously comical in the way Newman's thoroughly contemporaneous optimism was confronted with this dusky old-world expedient. To see a woman made for him and for motherhood to his children juggled away in this tragic travesty—it was a thing to rub one's eyes over, a nightmare, an extravagance, a hoax. But the hours passed without disproving anything, passed leaving him only the aftertaste of the vehemence with which he had held her to his heart. He remembered her words and her looks—he lived through again the sense of her short submission; he turned them over and tried to make them square with the saving of something from his wreck. How had she meant that the force driving her was, as a thing apart from the conventual question, a 'religion'? It was the religion simply of the family laws, the religion of which her implacable mother was priestess. Twist the thing about as her generosity would, the one certain fact was that they had been able to determine her act. Her generosity had tried to screen them, but Newman's heart rose into his throat at the thought that they should go scot-free.

The twenty-four hours spent themselves, and the next morning he sprang to his feet with the resolution to return to Fleurières and demand another interview with Madame de Bellegarde and her son. He lost no time in putting it into practice. As he rolled swiftly over the excellent road in the little calèche furnished him at the inn at Poitiers, he drew forth, as it were, from the very safe place in his mind to which he had consigned it, the last information given him by poor Valentin. Valentin had told him he could do something with it, and Newman thought it would be well to have it at hand. This was of course not the first time, lately, that he had given it his attention. It was information in the rough—it was formless and obscure; but he was neither helpless nor afraid. Valentin had clearly meant to put him in possession of a weapon he could use, though he couldn't be said to have placed the handle very securely in his grasp. But if he had told him nothing definite he had at least given him a clue— a clue of which the decidedly remarkable Mrs Bread held the other end. Mrs Bread had always looked to Newman as if she held clues; and as he apparently enjoyed her esteem he suspected she might be induced to share with him her knowledge. So long as there was only Mrs Bread to deal with he felt easy. As to what there was to find out, he had only one fear—that it might not be bad enough. Then, when the image of the Marquise and her son rose before him again, standing side by side, the old woman's hand in Urbain's arm and the same cold guarded glare in the eyes of each, he cried out to himself that the fear was groundless. There was crime in the air at the very least! He arrived at Fleurières almost in a state of elation; he had satisfied himself, logically, that in the presence of his threat of penetration they would, as he mentally phrased it, rattle down like loosened buckets. He remembered indeed that he must first catch his hare— first ascertain what there was to penetrate; but after that why shouldn't his happiness be as good as new? Mother and son, dropping in terror the tender victim they had mauled, would take to hiding, and Madame de Cintré, left to herself, would surely come back to him. Give her a chance and she would rise to the surface and return to the light. How could she fail to perceive that his house would have all the security of a convent and none of the dampness?

Newman, as he had done before, left his conveyance at the inn and walked the short remaining distance to the château. When he reached the gate, however, a singular feeling took possession of him—a feeling which, strange as it may seem, had its source in his unfathomable good-nature. He stood there a while, looking through the bars at the large time-stained face beyond and wondering to what special misdeed it was that the dark old dwelling with the flowery name had given convenient occasion. It had given occasion, first and last, to tyrannies and sufferings enough, Newman said to himself; it was an evil-looking place to live in. Then suddenly came the reflexion: what a horrible rubbish-heap of iniquity to fumble through! The attitude of inquisitor turned its ignoble face, and with the same movement he declared that the Bellegardes should have another chance. He would appeal once more directly to their sense of fairness and not to their fear; and if they should be accessible to reason he need know nothing worse about them than what he already knew. That was bad enough.

The gate-keeper let him in through the same 'mean' crevice of aperture—for so he qualified it—as before, and he passed through the court and over the rustic bridge of the moat. The door was opened before he had reached it, and, as if to put his clemency to rout with the suggestion of a richer opportunity, Mrs Bread stood there awaiting him. Her face, as usual, looked hopelessly blank, like the tide-smoothed sea-sand, and her black garments hung as heavy as if soaked in salt tears. Newman had already learned how interesting she could make the expression of nothing at all, and he scarce knew whether she now struck him as almost dumb or as almost effusive. 'I thought you would try again, sir. I was looking out for you.'

'I'm glad to see you,' he answered; 'I think you're my friend.'

Mrs Bread looked at him opaquely. 'I wish you well, sir; but it's vain wishing now.'

'You know then how they've treated me?'

'Oh, sir,' she dryly returned, 'I know everything.'

He frankly enough wondered. 'Everything?'

Her eyes just visibly lighted. 'I know at least too much.'

'One can never know too much. I congratulate you on every scrap of it. I've come to see Madame de Bellegarde and her son,' Newman added. 'Are they at home? If they're not I'll wait.'

'My lady's always at home,' Mrs Bread replied, 'and the Marquis is mostly with her.'

'Please then tell them—one or the other, or both—that I'm here and that I should like to see them.'

Mrs Bread hesitated. 'May I take a great liberty, sir?'

'You've never taken a liberty but you've justified it,' said Newman with diplomatic urbanity.

She dropped her wrinkled eyelids as if she were curtseying; but the curtsey stopped there: the occasion was too grave. 'You've come to plead with them again, sir? Perhaps you don't know this—that the poor Countess returned this morning to Paris.'

'Ah, she's gone!' And Newman, groaning, smote the pavement with his stick.

'She's gone straight to the convent—the Carmelites, you know, is the miserable name. I see you do know, sir. My lady and the Marquis take it very ill. It was only last night she told them.'

'Ah, she had kept it back then?' he cried. 'Well, that's all right. And they're highly worked up?'

'They're certainly not pleased. But they may well dislike it. They tell me it's most dreadful, sir; of all the nuns in Christendom the Carmelites are the worst. They're so unnatural that you may say they're really not human; they make you give up everything in the world you have—for ever and for ever. And to think of *her* in that destitution! If I was one who sat down and cried, sir, I could give way at this moment.'

Newman looked at her an instant. 'We mustn't cry, Mrs Bread, and still less must we sit down. We must stand right up and act. Please let them know.' And he took a forward step.

But she gently checked him. 'May I take another liberty? I'm told you were with poor Count Valentin, heaven forgive him, in his last hours, and I should bless you, sir, if you could tell me a word about him. He was my own dear boy, sir; for the first year of his life he was hardly out of my arms; I taught him the first words he spoke—and he spoke so beautifully, didn't he, sir? He always spoke well to his poor old Bread. When he grew up and took his pleasure he always had a kind word for me. And to die in that wild wrong way! They've a story that he fought with a wine-merchant. I can't believe *that* of him, sir! And was he in great pain?'

'You're a wise, kind old woman, Mrs Bread,' said Newman. 'I hoped I might see you with my own children in your arms. Perhaps I shall yet.' And he put out his hand. She looked for a moment at his open palm, and then, as if fascinated by the novelty of the gesture, extended her own ladylike member. Newman held it firmly and deliberately, fixing his eyes on her. 'You want to know all about the Count?'

'It would be a terrible pleasure, sir.'

'I can tell you everything. Can you sometimes leave this place?'

'The château, sir? I really don't know. I've never tried.'

'Try then; try hard. Try this evening at dusk. Come to me in the old ruin there on the hill, in the court before the church. I'll wait for you on that spot; I've something very important to tell you. A grand old woman like you can do as she pleases.'

She wondered with parted lips. 'Is it from the dear Count, sir?'

'From the dear Count—from his damnable deathbed.'

'I'll come, then. I'll be bold, for once, for *him*.'

She led Newman into the great drawing-room with which he had already made acquaintance, and retired to carry his message. He waited a long time; at last he was on the point of ringing and repeating his request. He was looking round him for a bell when the Marquis came in with his mother on his arm. It will be seen he had a logical mind when I say that he declared to himself, in perfect good faith, as a result of Valentin's supreme communication, that his adversaries looked grossly wicked and capable of the blackest evil. 'There's no mistake about it now,' he reflected as they advanced. 'They're a bad, bad lot; they've pulled off the varnished mask.' Madame de Bellegarde and her son certainly bore in their faces the signs of extreme perturbation; they were plainly people who had passed a sleepless night. Confronted, moreover, with an annoyance which they hoped they had disposed of, it was not natural they should meet their visitor with conciliatory looks. He stood before them, and of the coldest glare they could command he had the full benefit. He felt as if the door of a sepulchre had suddenly been opened and the damp darkness were exhaled.

'You see I've come back,' he said, however, with a tentative freshness. 'I've come to try again.'

'It would be ridiculous,' the Marquis returned, 'to pretend that we're glad to see you or that we don't question the taste of your visit.'

'Oh, don't talk about taste!'—and Newman permitted himself perhaps the harshest laugh into which he had ever broken; 'that would bring us round to yours! If I consulted my taste I certainly wouldn't come to see you. Besides, I'll make as short work as you please. Give me a guarantee that you'll raise the blockade—that you'll set Madame de Cintré at liberty—and I'll retire on the spot.'

'We hesitated as to whether we would see you,' said Madame de Bellegarde; 'and we were on the point of declining the honour. But it seemed to me we should act with civility, as we've always done, and I wished to have the satisfaction of informing you that there are certain weaknesses people of our way of feeling can be guilty of but once.'

'You may be weak but once, but you'll be audacious many times, madam,' Newman rang out. 'I didn't come, however, for conversational purposes. I came to say this simply: that if you'll write immediately to your daughter that you withdraw your opposition to our marriage I'll take care of the rest. You don't want to make of her a cloistered nun—you know more about the horrors of it than I do. Marrying a commercial person is better than being buried alive. Give me a letter to her, signed and sealed, saying you give way and that she may take me with your blessing, and I'll take it to her at her place of retreat and bring that retreat to an instant end. There's your chance—and I call them easy terms.'

'We look at the matter otherwise, you know. We call any terms that you can propose impossible,' Urbain declared. They had all remained standing stiffly in the middle of the room. 'I think my mother will tell you that she'd rather her daughter should become Sœur Catherine than Mrs Christopher Newman.'

But the old lady, with the serenity of supreme power, let her son make her epigrams for her. She only smiled, almost sweetly, shaking her head and repeating: 'But once, Mr Newman; but once!'

Nothing he had ever seen or heard gave him such a sense of polished marble hardness as this movement and the tone that accompanied it. 'Is there anything that would weigh with you?' he asked. 'Is there anything that would, as we say, squeeze you?' he continued.

'This language, sir,' said the Marquis, 'addressed to people in bereavement and grief, is beyond all qualification.'

'In most cases,' Newman answered, 'your objection would have some force, even admitting that Madame de Cintré's present intentions make time precious. But I've thought of what you speak of, and I've come here to-day without superfluous scruples simply because I regard your brother and you as very different parties. I see no connexion between you. Your brother was mortally ashamed of you both. Lying there wounded and dying, lying there confounded and disgusted, he formally apologised to me for your conduct. He apologised to me for that of his mother.'

For a moment the effect of these words was as if he had struck a physical blow. A quick flush leaped into the charged faces before him—it was like a jolt of full glasses, making them spill their wine. Urbain uttered two words which Newman but half heard, but of which the aftersense came to him in the reverberation of the sound. '*Le misérable!*'

'You show little respect for the afflicted living,' said Madame de Bellegarde, 'but you might at least respect the helpless dead. Don't profane—don't touch with your unholy hands—the memory of my innocent son.'

'I speak the simple sacred truth,' Newman now imperturbably proceeded, 'and, speaking it for a purpose, I desire you shall have no genuine doubt of it. You made Valentin's last hour an hour of anguish, and my friend's generous spirit repudiates your abominable act.'

Urbain de Bellegarde had, from whatever emotion, turned so pale that it might have been at the evoked spectre of his brother; but not for an appreciable instant did his mother lower her crest. 'You have *beau jeu*, as we say, before the silence of the grave, for every calumny and every insult. But I don't know,' she admirably wound up, 'that it in the least matters.'

'Ah, I don't know that poor Valentin's apology particularly does either,' Newman reflectively conceded. 'I pitied him certainly more for having to utter it than I felicitate myself even now for your having to hear it.'

The Marquise wrapt herself for a minute in a high aloofness so entire, so of her whole being, as he could feel, that she fairly appeared rather to contract than to expand with the intensity and dignity of it; and out of the heart of this withdrawn extravagance her final estimate of their case sounded clear. 'To have broken with you, sir, almost consoles me; and you can judge how much that says! Urbain, open the door.' She turned away with an imperious motion to her son and passed rapidly down the length of the room. The Marquis went with her and held the door open. Newman was left standing.

He lifted a finger as a sign to M. de Bellegarde, who closed the door behind his mother and stood waiting. Newman slowly advanced, more silent, for the moment, than life. The two men stood face to face. Then our friend had a singular sensation; he felt his sense of wrong almost brim over into gaiety. 'Come,' he said, 'you don't treat me well. At least admit that.'

M. de Bellegarde looked at him from head to foot and then spoke in the most delicate, best-bred voice. 'I execrate you personally.'

'That's the way I feel to *you*, but for politeness' sake I don't say it. It's singular I should want so much to be your brother-in-law, but I can't give it up. Let me try once more.' And Newman paused a moment. 'You've something on your mind and on your conscience, your mother and you—something in your life that you've kept as much as possible in the dark because it wouldn't look well in the light of day. You've a skeleton, as they say, in your closet.' M. de Bellegarde continued to look at him hard, but it was a question if his eyes betrayed anything; the expression of his eyes was always so strange. Newman paused again and then went on. 'You've done, between you, somehow and at some time, something still more base—wonderful as that may seem—than what you've done to me.' At this M. de Bellegarde's eyes certainly did change; they flickered like blown candles. Newman could feel him turn cold; but his form was still quite perfect.

'Continue,' he encouragingly said.

Newman lifted a finger and made it waver a little in the air. 'Need I continue? You know what I mean.'

'Pray, where did you obtain this interesting information?' M. de Bellegarde inordinately fluted.

'I shall be strictly accurate,' said Newman. 'I won't pretend to know more than I do. At present that's all I know. You've done something regularly nefarious, something that would ruin you if it were known, something that would disgrace the name you're so proud of. I don't know what it is, but I've reason to believe I can find out—though of course I had much rather not. Persist in your present course, however, and I *will* find out. Depart from that course, let your sister go in peace, and then fancy how I'll leave you alone. It's a bargain?'

Urbain's face looked to him now like a mirror, very smooth fine glass, breathed upon and blurred; but what he would have liked still better to see was a spreading, disfiguring crack. There was something of that, to be sure, in the grimace with which the Marquis brought out: 'My brother regaled you with this infamy?'

Newman scantly hesitated. 'Yes—it was a treat!'

The grimace, if anything, deepened. 'He raved at the last then so horribly?'

'He raved if I find nothing out. If I find—what you know I *may* find—he was beautifully inspired.'

M. de Bellegarde's shoulders declined even a shrug. 'Eh, sir, find what you "damn please"!'

'What I say has no weight with you?' Newman was thus reduced to asking.

'That's for you to judge.'

'No, it's for *you* to judge—at your leisure. Think it over; feel yourself all round; I'll give you an hour or two. I can't give you more, for how do we know how tight they mayn't be locking your sister up? Talk it over with your mother; let her judge what weight *she* attaches. She's constitutionally less accessible to pressure than you, I think; but *enfin*, as you say, you'll see. I'll go and wait in the village, at the inn, where I beg you to let me know as soon as possible. Say by three o'clock. A simple Yes or No on paper will do. That will refer to your attaching or not attaching what we call weight; or better still, to your consenting or refusing to take your hands off Madame de Cintré. Only you understand that if you do engage again I shall expect you this time to stick to your bargain.' And with this Newman opened the door to let himself out. The Marquis made no motion, and his guest paused but for a last emphasis. 'I can give you, let me add, no *more* than the time.' Then Newman turned away altogether and passed out of the house.

He felt greatly uplifted by what he had been doing, as it was inevitable some emotion should proceed for him from the evocation of the spectre of dishonour for a family a thousand years old. But he went back to the inn and contrived to wait there, deliberately, for the next two hours. He thought it more than probable Urbain would give no sign; since an answer to his challenge, in either case, would be a

recognition of his reference. What he most expected was silence—
in other words defiance. He prayed, however, that, as he imaged it,
his shot might bring them down. It did bring, by three o'clock, a
note, delivered by a footman; a note addressed in Urbain's handsome
English hand.

'I cannot deny myself the satisfaction of letting you know that I
return to Paris to-morrow, with my mother, in order that we may see
my sister and confirm her in the resolution which is the most effec-
tual reply to a delirium extravagant even as a result of your injury.—
HENRI-URBAIN DE BELLEGARDE.'

Newman put the letter into his pocket and continued his walk up
and down the inn parlour. He had spent most of his time, for the
past week, in walking up and down. He continued to measure the
length of the little *salle* of the Armes de France until the day began
to wane, when he went forth to keep his rendezvous with Mrs Bread.
The path leading up the hill to the ruin was easy to find, and he in
a short time had followed it to the top. He passed beneath the rugged
arch of the castle wall and looked about him in the early dusk for an
old woman in black. The castle yard was empty, but the door of the
church was open. He went into the little nave and of course found a
deeper dusk than without. A couple of tapers, however, twinkled on
the altar and just helped him to distinguish a figure seated by one of
the pillars. Closer inspection led him to recognise Mrs Bread, in spite
of the fact that she was dressed with unwonted splendour. She wore
a large black silk bonnet with imposing bows of crape, while an old
black satin gown disposed itself in vaguely lustrous folds about her
person. She had invoked for the occasion the highest dignity of dress.
She had been sitting with her eyes fixed upon the ground, but when
he passed before her she looked up at him and then rose.

'Are you of this awful faith, Mrs Bread?'

'No, indeed, sir; I'm a good Church of England woman—very
Low.* But I thought I should be safer in here than outside. I was
never out in the evening before, sir,' she added.

'We shall be safer,' he returned, 'where no one can hear us.' And
he led the way back into the castle court and then followed a path
beside the church, which he was sure must lead into another part of
the ruin. He was not deceived. It wandered along the crest of the hill
and terminated before a fragment of wall pierced by a rough aperture which had once been a door. Through this aperture Newman

passed, to find himself in a nook peculiarly favourable to quiet conversation, as probably many an earnest couple, otherwise assorted than our friends, had assured themselves. The hill sloped abruptly away, and on the remnant of its crest were scattered two or three fragments of stone. Beneath, over the plain, lay the gathered twilight, through which, in the near distance, gleamed two or three lights from the Fleurières. Mrs Bread rustled slowly after her guide, and Newman, satisfying himself that one of the fallen stones was steady, proposed to her to sit on it. She cautiously complied, and he placed himself near her on another.

XXII

'I'M very much obliged to you for coming,' he began with observing. 'I hope it won't get you into trouble.'

'I don't think I shall be missed. My lady, in these days, is not fond of having me about her.' This was said with a dry lucidity which added to his sense of having inspired his friend with confidence.

'From the first, you know,' he rejoined, 'you took an interest in my prospects. You were on my side. That gratified me, I assure you. And now that you know what they've done to me I'm sure you are with me all the more.'

'They've not done well—I must say it. But you mustn't blame the poor Countess; they pressed her cruelly hard.'

'I'd give a million of dollars,' he remarked, 'to know the secret of such successful pressure as that.'

Mrs Bread sat with a dull, oblique gaze fixed on the Fleurières lights. 'They worked on her sentiments, as they call 'em here; they knew that was the way. She's a delicate creature. They made her feel wicked. She's only too good.'

'Ah, they made her feel wicked,' said Newman, slowly; and then he repeated it. 'They made her feel wicked—they made her feel wicked.' The words represented to him for the moment, and quite as to the point of high interest, a wondrous triumph of infernal art.

'It was because she was so good that she gave up—poor sweet lady!' added Mrs Bread.

'But she was better to them than to me.'

'She was afraid,' said Mrs Bread very confidently; 'she has always been afraid, or at least for a long time. Her fear was there—it was always like a pit that yawned for her. That was the real trouble, sir. She was just a fair peach, I may say, with but one little speck. She had one little sad spot. You pushed her into the sunshine, sir, and it almost disappeared. Then they pulled her back into the shade, and in a moment it began to spread. Before we knew it she was gone. She was a delicate creature.'

This singular attestation of Madame de Cintré's delicacy, for all its singularity, set Newman's wound aching afresh. 'I see. She knew something bad about her mother.'

'No, sir, she knew nothing.' And Mrs Bread held her head very stiff and kept her watch on the glimmering windows of the residence.

'She guessed something then, or suspected it.'

'She was afraid to know,' said Mrs Bread.

'But *you* know, at any rate.'

She slowly turned her vague eyes on him, squeezing her hands together in her lap. 'You're not quite faithful, sir. I thought it was to tell me about the Count you asked me to come.'

'Oh, the more we talk of the Count the better,' he declared. 'That's exactly what I want. I was with him, as I told you, in his last hour. He was in a great deal of pain, but he was quite himself. You know what that means; he was bright and charming and clever.'

'Oh, he'd always be clever, sir,' said Mrs Bread. 'And did he know of your trouble?'

'Yes, he guessed it of himself.'

'And what did he say to it?'

'He said it was a disgrace to his name—but it was not the first.'

'Lord, Lord!' she murmured.

'He said his mother and his brother had once put their heads together to some still more odious effect.'

'You shouldn't have listened to that, sir.'

'Perhaps not. But I *did* listen, and I don't forget it. Now I want to know what it is they did.'

Mrs Bread gave a soft moan. 'And you've enticed me up into this strange place to tell you?'

'Don't be alarmed,' said Newman. 'I won't say a word that shall be disagreeable to you. Tell me as it suits you—and tell me *when* it suits you. Only remember that it was the Count's dying wish that you should.'

'Did he say that?'

'He said it with his last breath: "Tell Mrs Bread I told you to ask her."'

'Why didn't he tell you himself?'

'It was too long a story for a dying man; he was incapable of the effort and the pain. He could only say that he wanted me to know—that, wronged as I was, it was my right to know.'

'But how will it help you, sir?' she asked.

'That's for me to decide. The Count believed it would, and that's why he told me. Your name was almost the last word he spoke.'

This statement produced in her a sharp checked convulsion; she shook her clasped hands slowly up and down. 'Pardon me if I take a great liberty. Is it the solemn truth you're speaking? I *must* ask you that; don't you see that I must, sir?'

'There's no offence. It *is* the solemn truth; I solemnly swear it. The Count himself would certainly have told me more if he had been able.'

'Oh, sir, if he had known more!'

'Don't you suppose he did know?'

'There's no saying what he knew about anything,' she almost wailingly conceded. 'He was clever to that grand extent. He could make you believe he knew things he didn't, and that he didn't know others he had better not have known.'

'I suspect he knew something about his brother that made the Marquis mind his eye!' Newman propounded. 'He made the Marquis feel him pretty badly. What he wanted now was to put me in his place; he wanted to give me a chance to make the Marquis feel *me*.'

'Mercy on us,' cried the old waiting-woman, 'how malicious we all are, to be sure!'

'I don't know,' said Newman; 'some of us are malicious, certainly. I'm very angry, I'm very sore, and I'm very bitter, but I don't know that I'm malicious. I've been cruelly injured. They've hurt me and I want to hurt *them*. I don't deny that; on the contrary, I tell you plainly that that's the use I want to make of any information you're so good as to give me.'

Mrs Bread seemed to hold her breath. 'You want to publish them—you want to shame them?'

'I want to bring them down—down, down, down! I want to turn the tables on them—I want to mortify them as they mortified me. They took me up into a high place and made me stand there for all the world to see me, and then they stole behind me and pushed me into this bottomless pit where I lie howling and gnashing my teeth! I made a fool of myself before all their friends; but I shall make something worse of them.'

This passionate profession, which Newman uttered with the greater zeal that it was the first time he had felt the relief words at once as hard and as careful as hammer-taps could give his spirit, kindled two small sparks in Mrs Bread's fixed eyes. 'I suppose you've a right to your anger, sir; but think of the dishonour you'll draw down on the Countess.'

'If the Countess is to be buried alive,' he cried, 'what's honour or dishonour to her ever again? The door of the living tomb is at this moment closing behind her.'

'Yes, it's most awful,' Mrs Bread moaned.

'She has moved off, like her brother Valentin, to give me room to work. It's as if it were all done on purpose.'

'Surely,' said Mrs Bread, who seemed impressed by the ingenuity of this reflection. She was silent some moments; then she added: 'And would you bring my lady before the courts?'

'The courts care nothing for my lady,' Newman replied. 'If she has committed a crime she'll be nothing for the courts but a wicked old woman.'

'And will they hang her, sir?'

'That depends upon what she has done.' And Newman eyed his friend intently.

'It would break up the family most terribly, sir!'

'It's high time such a family *should* be broken up!' he outrageously declared.

'And me at my age out of place, sir!' sighed Mrs Bread.

'Oh, I'll take care of you! You shall come and live with me. You shall be my housekeeper or anything you like. You shall sit and be waited on and twiddle your thumbs. I'll pension you for life.'

'Dear, dear, sir, you think of everything.' And she seemed to fall a-brooding.

He watched her a while; then he said suddenly: 'Ah, Mrs Bread, you're too foolishly fond of my lady!'

She looked at him as quickly. 'I wouldn't have you say that, sir. I don't think it any part of my duty to be fond of my lady. I've served her faithfully this many a year; but if she were to die to-morrow I believe before heaven I shouldn't shed a tear for her.' Then after a pause, 'I've no such great reason to love her!' Mrs Bread added. 'The most she has done for me has been not to turn me out of the house.' Newman felt that decidedly his companion was more and more confidential—that, if luxury is corrupting, Mrs Bread's conservative habits were already relaxed by the spiritual comfort of this preconcerted interview, in an extraordinary place, with a free-spoken millionaire. All his native shrewdness admonished him that his part was simply to let her take her time—let the charm of the occasion work. So he said nothing; he only bent on her his large benevolence while she nursed her lean elbows. 'My lady once did me a great wrong,' she went on at last. 'She has a terrible tongue when she's put out. It was many a year ago, but I've never forgotten it. I've never mentioned it to a human creature; I've kept my grudge to myself. I dare say I've been wicked, but my grudge has grown old with me. It has grown good for nothing too, I dare say; but it has lived and lived, as I myself have lived. It will die when I die—not before!'

'And what is your grudge, Mrs Bread?' Newman blandly enquired.

Mrs Bread dropped her eyes and hesitated. 'If I were a foreigner, sir, I should make less of telling you; it comes harder to a decent Englishwoman. But I sometimes think I've picked up too many foreign ways. What I was telling you belongs to a time when I was much younger and of a quite different appearance altogether to what I am now. I had a very high colour, sir, if you can believe it; indeed I was a very smart lass. My lady was younger too, and the late Marquis was youngest of all—I mean in the way he went on, sir; he had a very high, bold spirit; he was a very grand gentleman. He was fond of his pleasure, like most foreigners, and it must be owned he sometimes went rather below him to take it. My lady was often jealous, and if you'll believe it, sir, she did me the honour to have an eye on *me*. One day I had a red ribbon in my cap, and she flew out at me and ordered me to take it off. She accused me of putting it on to make the Marquis look at me—look in the way he shouldn't. I don't know that I was impertinent, but I spoke up like an honest girl and didn't count my words. A red ribbon indeed! As if it was my ribbons the Marquis looked at! My lady knew afterwards that I was perfectly respectable, yet she never said a word to show she believed it. But the Marquis did—*he* knew the rights of me,' Mrs Bread presently added; 'and I took off my red ribbon and put it away in a drawer, where I have kept it to this day. It's faded now, it's a very pale pink; but there it lies. My grudge has faded too; the red has all gone out of it; but it lies here yet.' And Mrs Bread touched with old testifying knuckles her black satin bodice.

Newman listened with interest to this decent yet vivid narrative, which seemed to have opened up the deeps of memory to his companion. Then as she remained silent and seemed rather to lose herself in retrospective meditation on her perfect respectability, he ventured on a short cut to his goal. 'So Madame de Bellegarde was jealous; I see. And the Marquis admired pretty women without distinction of class. I suppose one mustn't be hard on him, for they probably didn't all behave so discreetly as you. But years afterwards it could hardly have been jealousy that turned his wife into a criminal.'

Mrs Bread gave a weary sigh. 'We're using dreadful words, sir, but I don't care now. I see you've your idea, and I've no will of my own. My will was the will of my children, as I called them; but I've lost my children now. They're dead and gone—I may say it of both of them; and what should I care for the living? What's any one in the house to me now—what am I to *them*? My lady objects to me—has objected to me these thirty years. I should have been glad to be something to young Madame Urbain, though I never was nurse to the present Marquis. When he was a baby I was too young; they wouldn't trust me with him. But his wife told her own maid, Mamselle Clarisse, the opinion she had of me. Perhaps you'd like to hear it, sir.'

'Oh, wouldn't I?' Newman almost panted.

'She said that if I'd sit in her children's schoolroom I should do very well for a penwiper! When things have come to that I don't think I need stand on ceremony.'

'I never heard of anything so vicious!' Newman rejoicingly declared. 'Go on, Mrs Bread.'

Mrs Bread, however, relapsed again into troubled reserve, and all he could do was to fold his arms and wait. But at last she appeared to have set her memories in order. 'It was when the late Marquis was an old man and his eldest son had been two years married. It was when the time came on for marrying Mademoiselle Claire; that's the way they talk of it here, you know, sir—as you might talk of sending a heifer to market. The Marquis's health was bad; he was sadly broken down. My lady had picked out M. de Cintré, for no good reason that I could see. But there are reasons, I very well know, that are beyond me, and you must be high in the world to catch all that's under and behind. Old M. de Cintré was very high, and my lady thought him almost as good as herself; that's saying as much as you please. Mr Urbain took sides with his mother, as he always did. The trouble, I believe, was that my lady would give very little money—

to go with the young lady; and all the other gentlemen wanted a bigger settlement. It was only M. de Cintré who was content. The Lord willed it he should have that one soft spot; it was the only one he had. He may have had very grand connexions, and he certainly made grand bows and speeches and flourishes; but that, I think, was all the measure of *his* honour. I think he was like what I've heard of comedians; not that I've ever seen one. But I know he painted his strange face. He might paint it all he would, he could never make me like it! The Marquis couldn't abide him, and declared that sooner than take such a husband as that, his daughter, whom he was so fond of, should stop as she was. He and my lady had a great scene; it came even to our ears in the servants' hall. It was not their first quarrel, if the truth must be told. They were not a loving couple, but they didn't often come to words, because after a while neither had them to waste; they had too much use for them elsewhere and otherwise. My lady had long ago got over "minding"—minding, I mean, the worst; for she had had plenty of assistance for throwing things off. In this, I must say, they were very well matched. The Marquis was one who would but too easily go as you please—he had the temper of the perfect gentleman. He got angry once a year—he kept to that; but then it was very bad. He always took to bed directly afterwards. This time I speak of he took to bed as usual, but he never got up again. I'm afraid he was paying for the free life he had led; isn't it true they mostly do, sir, when they get old and sad? My lady and Mr Urbain kept quiet, but I know my lady wrote letters to M. de Cintré. The Marquis got worse and the doctors gave him up. My lady gave him up too, and if the truth must be told she gave him up as I've seen her clap together—with a sound to make you jump—the covers of a book she has read enough of. When once he was out of the way she could do what she wished with her daughter, and it was all arranged that my poor child and treasure should be handed over to M. de Cintré. You don't know what Mademoiselle was in those days, sir; she was the sweetest, gentlest, fairest!—and guessed as little of what was going on around her as the lamb can guess the butcher. I used to nurse my unhappy master and was always in his room. It was here at Fleurières, in the autumn. We had a doctor from Paris, who came and stayed two or three weeks in the house. Then there came two others, and there was a consultation, and these two others, as I said, declared the Marquis couldn't come round. After this they went off, pocketing their fees, but the other one stopped over and did what he could. M. de Bellegarde himself kept crying out that he refused to be given up, that he insisted on getting better, that he would live and look after his daughter. Mademoiselle Claire and the Vicomte—that was Mr Valentin, you know—were both in the house. The doctor was a clever man—that I could see myself—and I think he believed the Marquis might recover with just the right things carefully done. We took good care of him, he and I, between us, and one day, when my lady had almost ordered her mourning, my patient suddenly began to mend. He took a better turn and came up so wonderfully that the doctor said he was out of danger. What was killing him was the dreadful fits of pain in his stomach. But little by little they stopped, and before I knew it he had begun again to have his joke at me. The doctor found something that gave him great comfort—some grand light-coloured mixture, a wonderful drug (I'm sure I forget the name) that we kept in a great bottle on the chimney-piece. I used to give it to him through a glass tube; it always made him easier. Presently the doctor went away, after telling me to keep on with the medicine whenever he was bad. After that there was a different sort of person from Poitiers—*he* came every day. So we were alone in the house—my lady and her poor husband and their three children. Madame Urbain had gone away, with her first small child, but a baby then, to her mother's. You know she's very lively, and her maid told me she didn't like to be where people were dying.' Mrs Bread had again a drop, but she went on soon and with the same quiet consistency: 'I think you've guessed, sir, that when the Marquis began to give hopes again my lady was disappointed.' And once more she paused, bending on Newman a face that seemed to grow whiter as the darkness settled down on them.

He had listened eagerly—with an eagerness greater even than that with which he had bent his ear to poor Valentin's weak lips. Every now and then, as his companion looked up at him, she reminded him of some old black cat, mild and sleek, protracting the enjoyment of a dish of rich milk. Even her triumph was measured and decorous; even her justice forbore to rattle the scales. 'Late one night,' she soon continued, 'I was sitting by the Marquis in his room, the great red room in the west tower. He had been complaining a little and I had given him a spoonful of the remedy that so seldom failed to ease him. My lady had been there in the early part of the evening; she sat for more than an hour by his bed. Then she went away and left me alone. After midnight she came back and Mr Urbain was with her. They went to the bed and looked at the Marquis, and my lady took hold of his hand. Then she turned to me and said he was not so well; I remember how the Marquis, without a word, lay staring at her. I can see his white face at this moment in the great black square between the bed-curtains. I said I didn't think he was very bad, and she told me to go to bed—she would sit a while with him. When he saw me going he gave a sound like a scared child and called out to me not to leave him; but Mr Urbain opened the door for me and pointed the way out. The present Marquis—perhaps you've noticed, sir—has a very high way of giving orders, and I was there to take orders. I went to my room, but I wasn't easy; I couldn't tell you why. I didn't undress; I sat there waiting and listening. For what would you have said, sir? I couldn't have told you, since surely a poor gentleman, however helpless, might be in safety at such a crisis with his wife and his son. It was as if I expected to hear his voice moan after me again. I listened, but I heard nothing. It was a very still night; I never knew a night so still. At last the very stillness itself seemed to frighten me, and I came out of my room and went very softly downstairs. In the anteroom, outside of where his father was, I found the Count, as he then was, walking up and down. He asked me what I wanted, and I said I had returned to relieve my lady. He said *he* would relieve my lady and ordered me back to bed; but as I stood there, unwilling to turn away, the door of the room opened and my lady herself came out. I noticed she was very pale; she was altogether extraordinary. She looked a moment at the Count and at me, and then held out her arms to the Count. He went to her and she fell upon him and hid her face. I brushed quickly past her into the room and came to the Marquis's bed. He was lying there very white and with his eyes shut; you could have taken him for a corpse. I took hold of his hand and spoke to him, but it was as if I had been dealing with the dead. Then I turned round; my lady and Mr Urbain were there. "My poor Bread," said my lady, "M. le Marquis is gone." Mr Urbain knelt down by the bed and said softly "*Mon père, mon père.*" I thought it most prodigious, and asked my lady what in the world had happened and why she hadn't called me. She said nothing had happened; that she had only been sitting there with him in perfect stillness. She had closed her eyes, thinking she might sleep, and she had slept she didn't know how long. When she woke up all was over. "It's surely death, my son, it's unmistakeably death," she said to the Count. Mr Urbain said they must have the doctor immediately from Poitiers, and that he would ride off and fetch him. He kissed his father's face—oh!— and then he kissed his mother and went away. My lady and I stood there at the bedside. As I looked at my poor master it came to me ever so sharply that he wasn't dead, that he was only in a stupor of weakness. And then my lady repeated "My poor Bread, it's death, it's just death"; and I said "Yes, my lady, it's certainly death." I said just the opposite to what I believed; it was my particular notion. Then my lady said we must wait for the doctor, and we sat there and waited. It was a long time; the poor Marquis neither stirred nor changed. "I've seen death before," said my lady, "and it's terribly like this." "Yes, please, my lady," said I; and I thought things I didn't say. The night wore away without the Count's coming back, and the Marquise began to be frightened. She was afraid he had had an accident in the dark or met with some prowling people. At last she got so restless that she went below to watch in the court for his return. I sat there alone and the Marquis never stirred.'

Here Mrs Bread paused again, and, for her listener, the most expert story-teller couldn't have been more thrilling. Newman made almost the motion of turning the page of a 'detective story'. 'So he *was* dead!' he exclaimed.

'Three days later he was in his grave,' said Mrs Bread sententiously. 'In a little while I went away to the front of the house and looked out into the court, and there, before long, I saw Mr Urbain ride in alone. I waited a bit to hear him come upstairs with his mother, but they stopped below and I returned to the other room. I went to the bed and held up the light to him, but I don't know why I didn't let the candlestick fall. The Marquis's eyes were open—open wide! they were staring at me. I knelt down beside him and took his hands and begged him to tell me, in the holy name of wonder, if he was truly alive or what or where he was. Still he looked at me a long time, and then made me a sign to put my ear close to him. "I'm dead, my dear," he said, "I'm dreadfully dead. The Marquise has killed me. Yes." I was all in a tremble. I didn't understand him. I didn't know what had become of him: it was so as if the dead had been speaking. "But you'll get well now, sir," I said. And then he whimpered again, ever so weak: "I wouldn't get well for a kingdom. I wouldn't be that woman's husband again." And then he said more; he said she had murdered him. I asked him what she had done to him and I remember his very words: "She has cruelly taken my life, as true as I lie here finished. And she'll do the same to my daughter," he said; "my poor unhappy child." And he begged me to prevent that, and then he said he was dying, he was "knowingly" dead. I was afraid to move or to leave him; I was almost as dead as himself. All of a sudden he asked me to get a pencil and write for him; and then I had to tell him I couldn't manage that sort of thing. He asked me to hold him up in bed while he wrote himself, and I said he could never, never trace a line. But he seemed to have a kind of terror that gave him strength. I found a pencil in the room and a piece of paper and a book, and I put the paper on the book and the pencil into his band, and I moved the candle near him. You'll think all this monstrous strange, sir—and I shall understand if you scarce believe me. But I must tell things as they happened to me—the rest is with Them that know all! Strangest of all was it, no doubt, that I believed it had somehow been done to him as he said and that I was eager to help him to write. I sat on the bed and put my arm round him and held him up. I felt very strong when it came to that; I believe I could have lifted him and carried him. It was a wonder how he wrote, but he did write, in a big scratching hand; he almost covered one side of the paper. It seemed a long time; I suppose it was three or four minutes. He was groaning terribly all the while, but at last he said it was ended, and I let him down upon his pillows, and he gave me the paper and told me to fold it and hide it, and to give it to those who'd act on it according to right. "Who do you mean?" I said. "Who are those who'll act on it?" But he made some sound for all answer; he couldn't speak—he was spent. In a few minutes he told me to go and look at the bottle on the chimney-piece. I knew the bottle he meant, the remedy we were never without and that we felt to be regularly precious. I went and looked at it, but it was empty of every drop, as if it had been turned upside down. When I came back his eyes were open—oh so pitifully!—and he was staring at me; but soon he closed them and he said no more. I hid the paper in my dress; I didn't look at what was written on it, though I can read very well, sir, if I haven't a hand for the pen. I sat down near the bed, but it was nearly half an hour before my lady and the Count came in. The Marquis looked as lost as when they had left him, and I never said a word of his having revived. Mr Urbain said the doctor had been called to a person in childbirth, but had promised to set out for Fleurières immediately. In another half-hour he arrived, and as soon as he had examined his patient he said we had had a false alarm. The poor gentleman was very low, but was still living. I watched my lady and her son, on that, to see if they looked at each other, and I'm obliged to admit they didn't. The doctor said there was no reason he should die; he had been going on so well. And then he wanted to know how he had suddenly taken such a turn; he had left him so quiet and natural. My lady told her little story again—what she had told Mr Urbain and me—and the doctor looked at her and said nothing. He stayed all the next day at the château, and hardly left the Marquis. I was always there, and I think I may assure you at least that I lost nothing. Mademoiselle and the Vicomte came and looked at their father, but he never stirred. It was a strange deathly stupor. My lady was always about; her face was as white as her husband's, and she looked very proud and hard, as I had seen her look when her orders or her wishes had been disobeyed. It was as if the poor Marquis had gone against her intention; and the way she took it from him made me afraid of her. The local apothecary kept him along through the day, and we waited for the gentleman from Paris, who, as I tell you, had already stayed here. They had telegraphed for him early in the morning, and in the evening he arrived. He talked a bit outside with the other one, and then they came in to see their *malade* together. I was with him, and so was Mr Urbain. My lady had been to receive the great man, and she didn't come back with him into the room. He sat down by the Marquis—I can see him there now with his hand on the Marquis's wrist and Mr Urbain watching them with a little looking-glass in his hand. "I'm sure he's better," said our country doctor; "I'm sure he'll come back." A few moments after he had spoken the Marquis opened his eyes, as if he were waking up, and looked from one of us to the other. I saw him look at me from very, very far off, and yet very hard indeed, as you might say. At the same moment my lady came in on tiptoe; she came up to the bed and put in her head between me and the Count. The Marquis saw her and gave a sound like the wail of a lost soul. He said something we couldn't understand and then a convulsion seemed to take him. He shook all over and closed his eyes, and the doctor jumped up and took hold of my lady. He held her for a moment harder than I've ever seen a gentleman hold a lady. The Marquis was stone dead—the sight of her had done for him. This time there were those there who knew.'

Newman felt as if he had been reading by starlight the report of highly important evidence in a great murder case. 'And the paper—the paper!' he said from a dry throat. 'What was written on it?'

'I can't tell you, sir,' Mrs Bread replied. 'I couldn't read it. It was French.'

'But could no one else read it?'

'I never asked a human creature.'

'No one has ever seen it?'

'If you do you'll be the first.'

Newman seized his companion's hand in both his own and pressed it almost with passion. 'I thank you as I've never thanked any one for anything. I want to be the first; I want it to be mine as this closed fist is mine. You're the wisest old woman in Europe. And what did you do with the blest thing?' Her information had made him feel extraordinarily strong. 'For God's sake, let me have it!'

Mrs Bread got up with a certain majesty. 'It's not so easy as that, sir. When you want great things you must wait for great things.'

'But waiting's horrible, you know,' he candidly smiled.

'I'm sure I've waited; I've waited these many years,' she quavered.

'That's very true. You have waited for *me*. I won't forget it. And yet how comes it you didn't do as M. de Bellegarde said—show the right people what you had got?'

'To whom should I show it and who were the right people?' she asked with high lucidity. 'It wasn't easy to know, and many's the night I have lain awake thinking of it. Six months afterwards, when they married Mademoiselle to the last person they ought to, I was very near bringing it out. I thought it my duty to do something with such a proof of what had happened, and yet I was terribly afraid. I didn't know what the Marquis had put there, nor how bad it might be, and there was no one I could trust enough to ask. And it seemed to me a cruel kindness to the person in the world I cared most for, letting her know her father had written her mother down so shamefully; for that's what he did, I suppose. I thought she would rather suffer from her husband than suffer from *them*. It was for her and for my dear Mr Valentin I kept quiet. Quiet I call it, yet it was a queer enough quietness. It worried me and changed me altogether. But for others

I held my tongue, and no one, to this hour, knows what had passed there between my poor prostrate master and his wife.'

'But evidently there were suspicions,' Newman urged. 'Where did Count Valentin get his ideas?'

'From our little local man—who has yet never been in the house, as you may imagine, since. He was very ill-satisfied and he didn't care who knew it. He had a very good opinion of his own sharpness, as Frenchmen mostly have, and coming to the house, as he did, day after day, he had more ideas—as a consequence—than he had had, before, any call to put about. And indeed the way the poor Marquis went off as soon as his eyes fell on my lady was a most shocking sight for any kind person. The great man from Paris may have known, after he had taken things in, what to think, but he also knew what not to say, and he hushed it up. But for all he could do the Vicomte and Mademoiselle heard something; they knew their father's death was somehow against nature. Of course they couldn't accuse their mother, and, as I tell you, I was as dumb as that stone. Mr Valentin used to look at me sometimes, and his eyes seemed to shine as if he were thinking of some question he could ask me. I was dreadfully afraid he would speak, and always looked away and went about my business. If I were to tell him I was sure he would hate me afterwards, which was what I could never have borne. Once I went up to him and took a great liberty; I kissed him as I had kissed him when he was a child. "You oughtn't to look so sad, sir," I said; "believe your poor decent old Bread. Such a gallant, handsome young man can have nothing to be sad about." And I think he understood me; he understood I was begging off and he made up his mind in his own way. He went about with his unasked question in his mind, as I did with my untold tale; we were both afraid of bringing disgrace on a great house. And it was the same with my dear young lady. She didn't know what had happened; she wouldn't hear of knowing. The Marquise and Mr Urbain asked me no questions, because they had no reason. I was as still as a stopped clock. When I was younger her ladyship thought me false, and now she thought me *bête*, as they say. How should I have any ideas?'

Newman turned it all gravely over. 'But you say that doctor made a talk. Did no one take it up?'

'I don't know how far they went. They're always talking scandal in these foreign countries—you may have noticed—and they must have had their stories about my lady. But after all what could they say? The Marquis had been ill and the Marquis had died; he had as good a right to die as any one. The doctor couldn't say he hadn't come honestly by what he suffered. The next year he left the place and bought a practice at Bordeaux, and if there had been ugly tales the worst of them were among ugly people. There couldn't have been any very bad ones that those who were respectable believed. My lady herself is so very respectable.'

Newman, at this last affirmation, broke into a resounding laugh. Mrs Bread had begun to move away from the spot where they were sitting, and he helped her through the aperture in the wall and along the homeward path. 'Yes, my lady's respectability's a treasure; I shall have a great deal of use for my lady's respectability.' They reached the empty space in front of the church, where they stopped a moment, looking at each other with something of closer fellowship, like a pair of sociable conspirators. 'But what was it,' Newman insisted, 'what was it she did to the miserable man? She didn't stab him or throttle him or poison him.'

'I don't know, sir. No one saw it.'

'Unless it was Mr Urbain,' he thoughtfully suggested. 'You say he was walking up and down outside the room. Perhaps he looked through the keyhole. But no; I think that with his mother he'd take it on trust.'

'You may be sure I've often thought of it,' Mrs Bread almost cheerfully returned. 'I'm sure she didn't touch him with her hands. I saw nothing on him anywhere. I believe it was in this way. He had a fit of his great pain, and he asked her for his medicine. Instead of giving it to him she went and poured it away, before his eyes, not speaking, only looking at him, so that he might have the scare and the shock and the horror of it. Then he saw what she meant and, weak and helpless, took fright, was terrified. "You want to kill me," he must have said—do you see? "Yes, M. le Marquis, I want to kill you," says my lady, and sits down and keeps her dreadful eyes on him. You know my lady's eyes, I think, sir; it was with that look of hers she killed him; it was with the terrible strong will and all the cruelty she put into it. It was as if she had pushed him out of her boat, fevered and sick, into the cold sea, and remained there to push him again should he try to scramble back; making him feel he was lost, by her intention, and watching him awfully sink and drown. It was enough indeed to take the heart out of him, and that, in his state, was enough for a death-stroke.'

Newman rendered this vivid image, which in truth did great honour to the old woman's haunted sensibility, the tribute of a comprehensive gasp. 'Well, you've got right hold of it—you make me see it and hate it and want to go for it. But I've got to keep tight hold of you too, you know.'

They had begun to descend the hill, and she said nothing till they reached the foot. He moved beside her as on air, his hands in his pockets, his head thrown back while he gazed at the stars: he seemed to himself to be riding his vengeance along the Milky Way. 'So you're serious about that?' she sighed.

'About your living with me? Why, you don't suppose I've turned you inside out this way not to want to get you into shape again. You're in no kind of shape for these people now—even if they were in any for you; after your seeing what they've done to me—and to *her*. You just give me the thing I'm after and then you move out.'

'I never thought I should have lived to take a new place—unless,' Mrs Bread made moan, 'I should have gone some day to Mr Valentin or, in her own establishment, to my young lady.'

'Come to me and you'll come to *her* establishment yet, I guess—you'll come at least to where both those names will be cherished and sacred.'

She considered a little and then replied: 'Oh, I shall like to pronounce them to *you*, sir! And if you're going to pull the house down,' she added, 'I had surely better be clear of it.'

'Ah,' said Newman almost with the gaiety of a dazzle of alternatives, 'it won't be quite my idea to appeal—if that's what you mean—to the police. The meanest and the damnedest things are always beyond their ken and out of their hands. Which has the merit in this case, however, that it leaves the whole story in mine. And to mine,' he declared, 'you've given power!'

'Ah, you're bolder than I ever was!' she resignedly sighed; and he felt himself now, to whatever end, possessed of her. He walked back with her to the château; the curfew—it couldn't have been anything but the curfew, he was sure—had tolled for the weary serfs and *villains* (as he could also quite have believed) and the small street of Fleurières was unlighted and empty. She promised he should have what he was after, as he had called it, in half an hour. Mrs Bread choosing not to go in by the great gate, they passed round by a winding lane to a door in the wall of the park, of which she had the key and which would enable her to re-enter the house from behind. Newman arranged with her that he should await outside the wall her return with his prize.

She went in, and his half-hour in the dusky lane seemed very long. But he had plenty to think about. At last the door in the wall opened and Mrs Bread stood there with one hand on the latch and the other holding out a scrap of white paper folded small and dearer to his sight than any love-token ever brought of old by bribed duenna to lurking cavalier. In a moment he was master of it and it had passed into his waistcoat pocket. 'Come and see me in Paris,' he said; 'we're to settle your future, you know; and I'll translate poor M. de Bellegarde's French to you.' Never had he felt so grateful as at this moment for M. Nioche's instructions.

Mrs Bread's eyes had followed the disappearance of her treasure, and she gave a heavy sigh. 'Well, you've done what you would with me, sir, and I suppose you'll do it again. You *must* take care of me now. You're a terribly positive gentleman.'

'Just now,' said Newman, 'I'm a terribly impatient one!' And he bade her good-night and walked rapidly back to the inn. He ordered his vehicle to be prepared for the return to Poitiers, and then he shut the door of the common *salle* and strode toward the solitary lamp on the chimney-piece. He pulled out the paper and quickly unfolded it. It was covered with pencil-marks, which at first, in the feeble light, seemed indistinct. But his fierce curiosity forced a meaning from the tremulous signs, the free English of which might have been, without the hopelessly obscure date:

'My wife has tried to kill me and has done it; I'm horribly, helplessly dying. It's in order to marry my beloved daughter to M. de Cintré and then go on herself all the same. With all my soul I protest—I forbid it. I'm not insane—ask the doctors, ask Mrs B. It was alone with me here to-night; she attacked me and put me to death. It's murder if murder ever was. Ask the doctors, tell every one, show every one this.

'HENRI-URBAIN DE BELLEGARDE.'

XXIII

NEWMAN returned to Paris the second day after his interview with Mrs Bread. The morrow he had spent at Poitiers, reading over and over again the signed warrant he had lodged in his pocket-book, persuading himself more and more that it had, as he put it to himself, a social value, and thinking what he would now do and how he would do it. He would not have said that Poitiers had much to hold him, yet the day seemed very short. Domiciled once more in the Boulevard Haussmann he walked over to the Rue de l'Université and enquired of Madame de Bellegarde's portress whether the Marquise had come back. The portress answered that she had arrived with M. le Marquis on the preceding day, and further informed him that should he wish to see them they were both at home. As she said these words the little white-faced old woman who peered out of the dusky gatehouse of the Hôtel de Bellegarde gave a small wicked smile—a smile that seemed to Newman to mean 'Go in if you dare!' She was evidently versed in the current domestic history; she was placed where she could feel the pulse of the house. He stood a moment twisting his moustache and looking at her; then he abruptly turned away. But this was not because he was afraid to go in—though he doubted whether, for all his courage, he should be able to make his way unchallenged into the presence of his adversaries. Confidence, excessive confidence perhaps, quite as much as timidity, prompted his retreat. He was nursing his thunderbolt; he loved it; he was unwilling to part with it. He felt himself hold it aloft in the rumbling, vaguely-flashing air, directly over the heads of his victims, and he fancied he could see their pale upturned faces. Few specimens of the human countenance had ever given him such pleasure as these, lighted in the lurid fashion I have hinted at, and he took his ease while he harboured the vindictive vision. It must be added too that he was at a loss to see exactly how he could arrange to witness the operation of his thunder. To send in his card to Madame de Bellegarde would be a waste of ceremony; she would certainly decline to receive him. On the other hand he couldn't force his way into her presence. He hated to see himself reduced to the blind satisfaction of writing her a letter; but he consoled himself in a measure with the thought that a letter might lead to an interview. He went home and, feeling rather tired—nursing a vengeance was, he had to confess, a fatiguing process; it took a good deal out of one—flung himself into one of his brocaded fauteuils, stretched his legs, thrust his hands into his pockets and, while he watched the reflected sunset fading from the ornate house-tops on the opposite side of the boulevard, began mentally to frame, as work for his pen, a few effective remarks. While he was so occupied his servant threw open the door and announced ceremoniously 'Madame Brett!'

He roused himself expectantly and in a few moments recognised on his threshold the worthy woman with whom he had conversed to such good purpose on the starlit hill-top of Fleurières. Mrs Bread had assumed for this visit the same dress as for her other effort, and he was struck with her fine antique appearance. His room was still lampless, and as her large grave face gazed at him through the clear dusk from under the shadow of her ample bonnet he felt the incongruity of her pretending to any servile stamp. He greeted her with high geniality, and bade her come in and sit down and make herself comfortable. There was something that might have touched the springs both of mirth and of melancholy in the spirit of formal accommodation with which she endeavoured to meet this new conception of her duty. She was not playing at being fluttered, which would have been simply ridiculous; she was doing her best to carry herself as a person so humble that, for her, even embarrassment would have been pretentious; but evidently she had never dreamed of its being in her horoscope to pay a visit at nightfall to a friendly single gentleman who lived in theatrical-looking rooms on one of the new boulevards.

'I truly hope I'm not forgetting my place, sir,' she anxiously pleaded.

'Forgetting your place? Why, you're remembering it as a good woman remembers her promise. This is your place, you know. You're already in my service; your wages as housekeeper began a fortnight ago. I can tell you my house wants keeping! Why don't you take off your bonnet and stay right now?'

'Take off my bonnet?'—she gave it her gravest consideration. 'Oh sir, I haven't my cap. And with your leave, sir, I couldn't keep house in my best gown.'

'Never mind your best gown,' said Newman cheerfully. 'You shall have a better gown than that.'

She stared solemnly and then stretched her hands over her lustreless satin skirt as if the perilous side of her situation might be flushing into view. 'Oh sir, I'm fond of my own clothes.'

'I hope you've left those wicked people, at any rate,' Newman went on.

'Well, sir, here I am! That's all I can tell you. Here I sit, poor Catherine Bread. It's a strange place for me to be. I don't know myself; I never supposed I was so bold. But indeed, sir, I've gone as far as my own strength will bear me.'

'Oh, come, Mrs Bread!' he returned almost caressingly; 'don't make yourself uncomfortable. Why, you're going to have now the time of your life.'

She began to speak again with a trembling voice. 'I think it would be more respectable if I could—if I could—!' But she quavered to a pause.

'If you could give up this sort of thing altogether?' said Newman kindly, trying to anticipate her meaning, which he supposed might be a wish to retire from service.

'If I could give up everything, sir! All I should ask is a decent Protestant burial.'

'Burial!' he cried with a burst of laughter. 'Why, to bury you now would be a sad piece of extravagance. It's only rascals who have to be buried to get respectable. Honest folks like you and me can live our time out—and live it together. Come! did you bring your baggage?'

'My two boxes are locked and corded; but I haven't yet spoken to my lady.'

'Speak to her then and have done with it. I should like to have your chance!' cried Newman.

'I would gladly give it you, sir. I've passed some weary hours in my lady's dressing-room; but this will be one of the longest. She'll tax me with base ingratitude.'

'Well,' said Newman, 'so long as you can tax her with murder—!'

'Oh sir, I can't; not I!' she pleaded.

'You don't mean to say anything about it? So much the better. Leave it all to me.'

'If she calls me a thankless old woman,' Mrs Bread went on, 'I shall have nothing to say. But it's better so,' she added with supreme mildness. 'She shall be my lady to the last. That will be more respectable.'

'And then you'll come to me and I shall be your gentleman,' said Newman. 'That will be more respectable still!'

She rose with lowered eyes and stood a moment; then, looking up, she rested her gaze upon Newman's face. The disordered proprieties were somehow settling to rest. She looked at her friend so long and so fixedly, with such a dull intense devotedness, that he himself might have had a pretext for embarrassment. At last she said gently: 'You've not your natural appearance, sir.'

'Why, Mrs Bread,' he answered, 'I've not my natural balance. If you mean I don't look sunny I guess I look as I feel. To be very indifferent and very fierce, very dull and very violent, very sick and very fine, all at once—well, it rather mixes one up.'

Mrs Bread gave a noiseless sigh. 'I can tell you something that will make you feel queerer still, if you want to feel all one way. About the poor Countess.'

'What can you tell me?' Newman quickly asked. 'Not that you've seen her?'

She shook her head. 'No indeed, sir, nor ever shall. That's the dead weight of it. Nor my lady. Nor M. de Bellegarde.'

'You mean she's kept so close?'

'The closest they keep any.'

These words for an instant seemed to check the beating of his heart. Leaning back in his chair he felt sick. 'They've tried to see her and she wouldn't—she couldn't?'

'She refused—for ever! I had it from my lady's own maid,' said Mrs Bread, 'who had it from my lady. To speak of it to such a person my lady must have felt the shock. The Countess declines to receive them now, and now's her only chance. A short while hence she'll have no choice.'

'You mean the other women—the mothers, the daughters, the sisters; what is it they call them?—won't let her?'

'It's what they call the rule of the house—or I believe of the order. There's no rule so strict as that of the Carmelites. The bad women in the reformatories are fine ladies to them. They wear old brown cloaks—so the *femme de chambre* told me—that you wouldn't use for a horse-blanket. And the poor Countess was so fond of soft-feeling dresses; she would never have anything stiff! They sleep on the ground,' Mrs Bread went on; 'they're no better, no better'—and she hesitated for a comparison—'they're no better than tinkers' wives. They give up everything, down to the very name their poor old nurses called them by. They give up father and mother, brother and sister—to say nothing of other persons,' Mrs Bread delicately added. 'They wear a shroud under their brown cloaks and a rope round their waists, and they get up on winter nights and go off into cold places to pray to the Virgin Mary. I hope it does *her* at least good!'

Newman's visitor, dwelling on these terrible facts, sat dry-eyed and pale, her hands convulsive but confined to her satin lap. He gave a melancholy groan and fell forward, burying his face and his pain. There was a long silence, broken only by the ticking of the great gilded clock on the chimney-piece. 'Where is the accursed place—where is the convent?' he asked at last, looking up.

'There are two houses,' said Mrs Bread. 'I found out; I thought you'd like to know—though it's cold comfort, I think. One's in the Avenue de Messine;* they've learned the Countess is there. The other's in the Rue d'Enfer.* That's a terrible name; I suppose you know what it means.'

He got up and walked away to the end of his long room. When he came back Mrs Bread had risen and stood by the fire with folded hands. 'Tell me this. Can I get near her—even if I don't see her? Can I look through a grating, or some such thing, at the place where she is?'

It is said that all women love a lover, and Mrs Bread's sense of the pre-established harmony which kept servants in their 'place', even as planets in their orbits (not that she had ever consciously likened herself to a planet), barely availed to temper the maternal melancholy with which she leaned her head on one side and gazed at her new employer. She probably felt for the moment as if, forty years before, she had held him also in her arms. 'That wouldn't help you, sir. It would only make her seem further away.'

'I want to go there, at all events,' he returned. 'The Avenue de Messine, you say? And what is it they call themselves?'

'Carmelites—whatever it means!' said Mrs Bread.

'I shall remember that.'

She hesitated a moment and then: 'It's my duty to tell you this—

that the convent has a chapel and that respectable persons are admitted on Sunday to the mass. You don't see the poor creatures in their
prison or their tomb, but I'm told you can hear them sing. It's a
wonder they have any heart for singing! Some Sunday I shall make
bold to go. It seems to me I should know *her* voice in fifty.'

Newman thanked her, while he held her hand, with a stare through
which he, for a good reason, failed to see her. 'If any one can get in
I will.' A moment later she proposed deferentially to retire, but he
checked her, pressing on her grasp a lighted candle.

'There are half a dozen rooms there I don't use;' and he pointed
through an open door. 'Go and look at them and take your choice.
You can live in the one you like best.' From this bewildering privilege she at first recoiled; but finally, yielding to her friend's almost
fraternal pat of reassurance, she wandered off into the dusk with her
tremulous taper. She remained absent a quarter of an hour, during
which Newman paced up and down, stopped occasionally to look out
of the window at the lights on the boulevard, and then resumed his
walk. Mrs Bread's interest in her opportunity apparently deepened
as she proceeded; but at last she reappeared and deposited her
candlestick on the chimney-piece.

'Well, have you picked one out?'

'A room, sir? They're all too fine for a dingy old body like me.
There isn't one that hasn't a bit of gilding.'

'It's only some shocking sham, Mrs Bread,' he answered. 'If you
stay there a while it will all peel off of itself.' And he gave a dismal
smile.

'Oh sir, there are things enough peeling off already!' she said with
a responsible head-shake. 'Since I was there I thought I'd look about
me. I don't believe you know, sir. The corners are most dreadful. You
do want a housekeeper, that you do; you want a tidy Englishwoman
that isn't above taking hold of a broom.'

Newman assured her that he suspected, if he had not measured,
his domestic abuses, and that to reform them was a mission worthy
of her powers. She held her candlestick aloft again and looked round
the salon with compassionate glances; then she intimated that she
accepted the mission and that its sacred character would sustain her
in her rupture with her old dread mistress. On this she curtsied
herself away.

She came back the next day with her worldly goods, and her

friend, going into his drawing-room, found her on her aged knees
before a divan, sewing up a piece of detached fringe. He questioned
her as to her leave-taking with her late mistress, and she said it had
proved easier than she feared. 'I was perfectly civil, sir, but the Lord
helped me to remember that a good woman has no call to tremble
before a bad one.'

'You must have been too lovely,' Newman frankly observed. 'But
does she know you've come to *me?*'

'She asked me where I was going, and I mentioned your name,'
Mrs Bread returned.

'What did she say to that?'

'She looked at me very hard, she turned very red. Then she bade
me leave her. I was all ready to go, and I had got the coachman, who's
an Englishman, thank goodness, to bring down my poor boxes and
to fetch me a cab. But when I went down myself to those terrible
great gates I found them closed. My lady had sent orders to the
porter not to let me pass, and by the same orders the porter's wife,
a dreadful sly old body, had gone out in a cab to fetch home M. de
Bellegarde from his club.'

Newman's face lighted almost with the candour of childhood. 'She
is scared! she *is* scared!'

'I was frightened too, sir,' said Mrs Bread, 'but I thank the powers
I felt my temper rise. I took it very high with the porter, and asked
him by what right he used violence to an honourable Anglaise who
had lived in the house for thirty years before he was heard of. Oh sir,
I was very grand—I brought the man down. He drew his bolts and
let me out, and I promised the cabman something handsome if he
would drive fast. But he was terribly slow; it seemed as if we should
never reach your blest door. I'm all of a tremble still; it took me five
minutes, just now, to thread my needle.'

Newman told her, in munificent mirth, that if she chose she might
have a little maid on purpose to thread her needles; and he went away
nursing this sketch of the scene in the Rue de l'Université and rejoicing in the belief that he had produced there what he might call the
impression of his life.

He had not shown Mrs Tristram the document he carried in his
pocket-book, but since his return to Paris he had seen her several
times, and she had not disguised from him that he struck her as in a
strange way—an even stranger way than his sad situation made

natural. Had his disappointment gone to his head? He looked like a man who was spoiling for some sickness, yet she had never seen him more restless and active. Some days he would hang his head and fold his brow and set his teeth, appear to wish to give out that he should never smile again; on others he would indulge in laughter that was almost rude and make jokes that were bad even for him. If he was trying to carry off his humiliation he went at such times really too far. She begged him of all things not to be 'strange'. Feeling in a measure answerable for the adventure that had turned out so ill for him, she could put up with anything but his strangeness. He might be tragic if he would, or he might be terribly touching and pierce her to the heart with silent sorrow; he might be violent and summon her to say why she had ever dared to meddle with his destiny: to this she would submit—for this she would make allowances. Only, if he loved her, let him not be incoherent. That would quite break down her nerves. It was like people talking in their sleep; they always awfully frightened her. And Mrs Tristram intimated that, taking very high ground as regards the moral obligation which events had laid upon her, she proposed not to rest quiet till she should have confronted him with the least inadequate substitute for his loss that the two hemispheres contained.

'Ah,' he replied to this, 'I think we're square now and we had better not open a new account! You may bury me some day, but you shall of a certainty never marry me. It's too rough, you see—it's worse than a free fight in Arkansaw.* I hope, at any rate,' he added, 'that there's nothing incoherent in this—that I want to go next Sunday to the Carmelite chapel in the Avenue de Messine. You know one of the Catholic clergymen—an abbé, is that it?—whom I've seen here with you, I think, on some errand for his poor; that motherly old gentleman with the big waistband. Please ask him if I need a special leave to go in, and if I do, beg him to obtain it for me.'

Mrs Tristram gave expression to the liveliest joy. 'I'm so glad you've asked me to do something! You shall get into the chapel if the abbé is disfrocked for his share in it.'

And two days afterwards she told him it was all arranged; the abbé was enchanted to serve him, and if he would present himself civilly at the convent gate there would be no obstacle.

XXIV

SUNDAY was as yet two days off; but meanwhile, to beguile his impatience, Newman took his way to the Avenue de Messine and got what comfort he could in staring at the blank outer wall of Madame de Cintré's present abode. The street in question, as some travellers will remember, adjoins the Parc Monceau,* which is one of the finest quarters of reconstructed Paris. It has an air of modern opulence and convenience that sounds a false note for any temple of sacrifice, and the impression made on his gloomily-irritated gaze by the fresh-looking, windowless expanse behind which the woman he loved was perhaps even then pledging herself to pass the rest of her days was less exasperating than he had feared. The place suggested a convent with the modern improvements—an asylum in which privacy, though unbroken, might be not quite identical with privation, and meditation, though monotonous, might be sufficiently placid. And yet he knew the case was other; only at present it was not a reality to him. It was too strange and too mocking to be real; it was like a page torn out of some superannuated unreadable book, with no context in his own experience.

On Sunday morning, at the hour Mrs Tristram had indicated, he rang at the gate in the blank wall. It instantly opened and admitted him into a clean, cold-looking court, beyond which a dull, plain edifice met his view in the manner of some blank stiff party to a formal introduction. A robust lay sister with a cheerful complexion emerged from a porter's lodge and, on his stating his errand, pointed to the open door of the chapel, an edifice which occupied the right side of the court and was preceded by a high flight of steps. Newman ascended the steps and immediately entered the open door. Service had not yet begun; the interior was dimly lighted and it was some moments before he could distinguish features. Then he saw the scene divided by a large close iron screen into two unequal parts. The altar was on the hither side of the screen, and between it and the entrance were disposed several benches and chairs. Three or four of these were occupied by vague, motionless figures—figures he presently perceived to be women deeply absorbed in their devotion. The place seemed to Newman very cold; the smell of the incense itself was

cold. Mixed with this impression was a twinkle of tapers and here
and there a glow of coloured glass. He seated himself; the praying
women kept still, kept their backs turned. He saw they were visitors
like himself, and he would have liked to see their faces; for he believed
that they were the mourning mothers and sisters of other women
who had had the same pitiless courage as the person in whom he was
interested. But they were better off than he, for they at least shared
the faith to which the others had sacrificed themselves. Three or four
persons came in, two of them gentlemen important and mature.
Every one was very quiet, with a perverse effect of studied submission. He fastened his eyes on the screen behind the altar. That was
the convent, the real convent, the place where she was. But he could
see nothing; no light came through the crevices. He got up and
approached the partition very gently, trying to look through. Behind
it was darkness, with no sign even of despair. He went back to his
place, and after that a priest and two altar-boys came in and began
to say mass.

Newman watched their genuflexions and gyrations with a grim,
still enmity; they seemed prompters and abettors of the wrong he
had suffered; they were mouthing and droning out their triumph.
The priest's long, dismal intonings acted upon his nerves and deepened his wrath; there was something defiant in his unintelligible
drawl—as if it had been meant for his very own swindled self. Suddenly there arose from the depths of the chapel, from behind the
inexorable grating, a sound that drew his attention from the altar—
the sound of a strange, lugubrious chant uttered by women's voices.
It began softly, but it presently grew louder, and as it increased it
became more of a wail and a dirge. It was the chant of the Carmelite
nuns, their only human utterance. It was their dirge over their buried
affections and over the vanity of earthly desires. At first he was bewildered, almost stunned, by the monstrous manifestation; then, as he
comprehended its meaning, he listened intently and his heart began
to throb. He listened for Madame de Cintré's voice, and in the very
heart of the tuneless harmony he imagined he made it out. We are
obliged to believe that he was wrong, since she had obviously not yet
had time to become a member of the invisible sisterhood; the chant,
at any rate, kept on, mechanical and monotonous, with dismal rep-
etitions and despairing cadences. It was hideous, it was horrible; as
it continued he felt he needed all his self-control. He was growing

more agitated, the tears were hot in his eyes. At last, as in its full
force the thought came over him that this confused, impersonal wail
was all that he or the world she had deserted were ever again to hear
of the breath of those lips of which his own held still the pressure,
he knew he could bear it no longer. He rose abruptly and made his
way out. On the threshold he paused, listened again to the dreary
strain, and then hastily descended into the court. As he did so he saw
that the good sister with the high-coloured cheeks and the fan-like
frill to her head-dress, who had admitted him, was in conference at
the gate with two persons who had just come in. A second glance
showed him that these visitors were Madame de Bellegarde and her
son, and that they were about to avail themselves of that method of
approach to their lost victim which he had found but a mockery of
consolation. As he crossed the court the Marquis recognised him; he
was on the way to the steps and was supporting his mother. From
Madame de Bellegarde he also received a look, and it resembled that
of Urbain. Both faces expressed a less guarded perturbation, something more akin to immediate dismay, than Newman had yet seen in
them. Evidently he was disconcerting, and neither mother nor son
had quite due presence of mind. Newman hurried past them, guided
only by the desire to get out of the convent walls and into the street.
The gate opened itself at his approach; he strode over the threshold
and it closed behind him. A carriage which appeared to have been
standing there was just turning away from the pavement. He looked
at it for a moment blankly; then he became conscious, through the
dusky mist that swam before his eyes, that a lady seated in it was
bowing to him. The vehicle had got into motion before he recognised
her; it was an ancient landau* with one half the cover lowered. The
lady's bow was very expressive and accompanied with a smile; a little
girl was seated beside her. He raised his hat, and then the lady bade
the coachman stop.

The carriage drew up again and she sat there and beckoned to
Newman—beckoned with the demonstrative grace of the Marquise
Urbain. Newman hesitated a moment before he obeyed her
summons; during this moment he had time to curse his stupidity for
letting the others escape him. He had been wondering how he could
get at them; fool that he was for not stopping them then and there!
What better place than beneath the very prison walls to which they
had consigned the promise of his joy? He had been too bewildered

publicly to fall on them, but now he felt ready to await them at the gate. Madame Urbain, with a certain attractive petulance, made a more emphatic sign, and this time he went over to the carriage. She leaned out and gave him her hand, looking at him kindly and smiling. 'Ah, monsieur, you don't include me in your wrath? I had nothing to do with it.'

'Oh, I don't suppose *you* could have prevented it!' he answered in a tone which was not that of studied gallantry.

'What you say is too true for me to resent the small account it makes of my influence. I forgive you, at any rate, because you look as if you had seen a ghost.'

'I *have* seen a ghost,' Newman darkly returned.

'I'm glad then I didn't go in with my *belle-mère* and my husband. You must have seen them, eh? Was the meeting affectionate? Did you hear the chanting? They say it's like the lamentations of the damned. I wouldn't go in: one's certain to hear that soon enough. Poor Claire—in a white shroud and a big brown cloak! That's the full dress of the Carmelites, you know. Well, she was always fond of long, loose things. But I mustn't speak of her to you; I must only say I'm very sorry for you, that if I could have helped you I would, and that I think every one has behaved infernally. I was afraid of it, you know; I felt it in the air for a fortnight before it came. When I saw you, at my mother-in-law's ball, take it all in such good faith I felt as if you were dancing on your grave. But what could I do? I wish you all the good I can think of. You'll say that isn't much! Yes; they've been abominable; I'm not a bit afraid to say it; I assure you every one thinks so. We're not all like that. I'm sorry I'm not going to see you again; you know I think you very good company. I'd prove it by asking you to get into the carriage and drive with me for the quarter of an hour that I shall wait for my mother-in-law. Only if we were seen—considering what has passed, and every one knows you've been *joué*—it might be thought I was going a little too far, even for me. But I shall see you sometimes—somewhere, eh? You know'—this was said in English—'we've a plan for a little amusement.'

Newman stood there with his hand on the carriage door, listening to this consolatory murmur with an unlighted eye. He hardly knew what Madame Urbain was saying; he was only conscious she was chattering ineffectively. But suddenly it occurred to him that, with her pretty professions, there was a way of making her effective; she might help him to get at the old woman and the Marquis. 'They're coming back soon—your companions? You're hanging about for them?'

'They'll hear the *office* out; there's nothing to keep them longer. Claire has refused to see them.'

'I want to speak to them,' Newman said; 'and you can help me, you can do me a favour. Delay your return for five minutes and give me a chance at them. I'll wait for them here.'

The young woman clasped her hands in sharp deprecation. 'My poor friend, what do you want to do to them? To beg them to come back to you? It will be wasted words. They'll never come back!'

'I want to speak to them all the same. Pray do what I ask you. Stay away and leave them to me for five minutes. You needn't be afraid; I shall not be violent; I'm very quiet.'

'Yes, you look very quiet! If they had *le cœur tendre* you'd move them. But don't count on them—you've had enough of that. However, I'll do better for you than what you propose. The understanding is not that I shall come back for them. I'm going into the Parc Monceau to give my little girl a walk, and my mother-in-law, who comes so rarely into this quarter, is to profit by the same opportunity to take the air. We're to wait for her in the park, where my husband is to join us with her. Follow me now; just within the gates I shall get out of my carriage. Sit down on a chair in some quiet corner and I'll bring them near you. There's devotion for you! *Le reste vous regarde.*'

This proposal Newman eagerly caught at; it revived his drooping spirit and he reflected that Madame Urbain was not quite the featherhead she seemed. He promised immediately to overtake her, and the carriage drove away.

The Parc Monceau is a very pretty piece of landscape-gardening, but Newman, passing into it, had little care for its elegant vegetation, which was full of the freshness of spring. He found the young Marquise promptly, seated in one of the quiet corners of which she had spoken, while before her in the alley her little girl, attended by the footman and the lap-dog, walked up and down as if to take a lesson in deportment. Newman seated himself by his friend, who began to chatter afresh, apparently with the design of convincing him that—if he would only see it—poor dear Claire didn't belong to the most pleasing type of woman. She was too long, too lean, too flat, too stiff, too cold; her mouth was too wide and her nose too narrow. She hadn't such a thing as a dimple, or even as a pretty curve—or call it really an obtuse angle—anywhere. And then she was eccentric, eccentric in cold blood; she was a furious Anglaise after all. Newman was very impatient; he was counting the minutes until his victims should reappear. He sat silent, leaning upon his cane, looking absently and insensibly at Madame Urbain. At last she said she would walk toward the gate of the park and meet her companions; but before she went she dropped her eyes and, after playing a moment with the lace of her sleeve, looked up again at her visitor.

'Do you remember the promise you made me three weeks ago?' And then as Newman, vainly consulting his memory, was obliged to confess that this vow had escaped it, she mentioned that he had made her at the time a very queer answer—an answer at which, viewing it in the light of the sequel, she had fair ground for taking offence. 'You promised to take me to Bullier's after your marriage. After your marriage—you made a great point of that. Three days after that your marriage was broken off. Do you know, when I heard the news, the first thing I said to myself? "Ah, *par exemple*, now he won't go with me to Bullier's!" And I really began to wonder if you hadn't been expecting the rupture.'

'Oh, my dear lady—!' he merely murmured, while he looked down the path to see if the others weren't coming.

'I shall be good-natured,' said his friend. 'One mustn't ask too much of a gentleman who's in love with a cloistered nun. Besides, I can't go to Bullier's while we're in mourning. But I haven't given it up for that. The *partie* is arranged; I have my cavalier—Lord Deepmere, if you please! He has gone back to his dear Dublin; but a few months hence I'm to name any evening, and he'll come over from Ireland on purpose. That's what I call really feeling for a woman.'

Shortly after this Madame Urbain walked away with her little girl. Newman sat in his place; the time seemed terribly long. He felt how fiercely his quarter of an hour in the chapel had raked over the glowing coals of his resentment. His accessory kept him waiting, but she proved as good as her word. Finally she reappeared at the end of the path with her little girl and her footman; beside her slowly walked her husband with his mother on his arm. They were a long time advancing, during which Newman sat unmoved. Aching as he fairly did now with his passion—the passion of his wrath at the impudence, on the part of such a pair, of an objection to *him* in the name of clean hands—it was extremely characteristic of him that he was able to moderate his expression of it very much as he would have turned down a flaring gas-jet. His native shrewdness, coolness, clearness, his lifelong submission to the sense that words were acts and acts were steps in life, and that in this matter of taking steps curveting and prancing were exclusively reserved for quadrupeds and foreigners—all this admonished him that rightful wrath had no connexion with being a fool and indulging in spectacular violence. So as he rose, when the elder lady and her son were close to him, he only felt very tall and unencumbered and alert. He had been sitting beside some shrubbery in such a way as not to be noticeable at a distance; but the Marquis, at hand, had quickly enough perceived him. The couple were then for holding their course; at sight of which Newman stepped so straight in front of them that they were obliged to pause. He lifted his hat slightly and looked at them hard; they were pale with amazement and disgust.

'Pardon my stopping you,' he dryly said; 'but I must profit by the occasion. I've ten words to say to you. Will you listen to them?'

The Marquis blinked, then turned to his mother. 'Can Mr Newman possibly have anything to say that is worth our listening to?'

'I assure you I've something,' Newman went on; 'besides, it's my duty to say it. It concerns you ever so closely.'

'Your duty?' said the Marquise, her small fine mouth contracting in its odd way as for a whistle. 'That's your affair, not ours.'

Madame Urbain meanwhile had seized her little girl by the hand, with a gesture of surprise and impatience which struck Newman, intent as he was on his own words, with its plausible extravagance. 'If Mr Newman's going to make a scene in public,' she exclaimed, 'I shall take my poor child out of the *mêlée*. She's too young to see such naughtiness!'—and she instantly resumed her walk.

'You had much better listen to me,' he persisted with his difficult ease. 'Whether you do or not your gain will be small; but at least perhaps you'll be prepared.'

'If you mean prepared for your preposterous threats,' the Marquis replied, 'there's nothing grotesque from you, certainly, for which we're not prepared, and of the idea of which you don't perfectly know what we think.'

'You think a great deal more than you yet admit. A moment,'

Newman added in reply to a sharp exclamation from Madame de Bellegarde. 'I don't at all forget that we're in a public place, and you see I'm very quiet. I'm not going to tell your secret to the passers-by; I shall keep it, to begin with, for certain picked listeners. Any one who observes us will think we're having a friendly chat and that I'm complimenting you, madam, on your venerable virtues.'

The Marquis gave a hiss that fairly evoked for our friend some vision of a hunched back, an erect tail and a pair of shining evil eyes. 'I demand of you to step out of our path!'

Newman instantly complied and his interlocutors proceeded. But he was still beside them and was still distinct. 'Half an hour hence Madame de Bellegarde will regret that she didn't learn exactly what I mean.'

The Marquise had taken a few steps, but at these words she pulled up again, as if not to have the appearance of not facing even monstrous possibilities—as monstrous, that is, as a monster of rudeness might make them. 'You're like a pedlar with something trumpery to sell,' she said; and she accompanied it with a strange, small, cold laugh—a demonstration so inconsequent that it meant nothing, Newman quickly felt, if it didn't mean a 'lovely' nervousness.

'Oh no, not to sell; I give it to you for nothing.' And he had never in his life, no matter under what occasion for it, spoken so completely and so gratefully to the point as now. 'You cruelly killed your help-less husband, you know; and I'm in possession of all the facts. That is you did your best, first, and failed; and then succeeded—by which I mean finished him—at a stroke and almost without trying.'

The Marquise closed her eyes and gave a small dry cough which, as a piece of dissimulation and of self-possession, seemed to her adversary consummate.

'Dear mother,' said Urbain as if she had been moved to hilarity, 'does this stuff amuse you so much?'

'The rest is more amusing,' Newman went on. 'You had better not lose it.'

The eyes she fixed on him might well have been, he recognised, those with which, according to Mrs Bread, she had done her husband to death; and they had somehow no connexion with the stifled shrill-ness of her spoken retort. 'Amusing? Have I killed some one else?'

'I don't count your daughter,' said Newman, 'though of course I might. Your husband knew what you were doing. I've a proof of it the existence of which you've never suspected.' And he turned to the Marquis, whose face was beyond any he had ever seen discomposed, decomposed—what did they call it? 'A paper written by the hand, and signed with the name of Henri-Urbain de Bellegarde. Written and dated after you, madam, had left him for dead, and while you, sir, had gone—not very fast—for the doctor.'

The Marquis turned to his mother; she moved a little at random, averting herself and looking vaguely round her. But her answer to his appeal fell, after an instant, rather short. 'I must sit down,' she simply said, and went back to the bench on which Newman had been posted.

'Couldn't you have spoken to me alone?' her companion then asked, all remarkably, of their pursuer, who wondered if it meant that there was suddenly, quite amazingly, a basis for discussion.

'Well, yes, if I could have been sure of speaking to your mother alone too,' Newman answered. 'But I've had to take you as I could get you, don't you see?'

Madame de Bellegarde, in a manner very eloquent of what he would have called her 'grit', her steel-cold pluck and her instinctive appeal to her own personal resources, seated herself on the bench with her head erect and her hands folded in her lap. The expression of her face was such that he fancied her at first inconceivably smiling, but on his drawing nearer felt this display to be strange and convulsive. He saw, however, equally, that she was resisting her agitation with all the rigour of her inflexible will, and there was nothing like either fear or submission in the fine front she presented. She had been upset, but she could intensely think. He felt the pang of a conviction that she would get the better of him still, and he wouldn't have been himself if he could wholly fail to be touched by the sight of a woman (criminal or other) in so tight a place. She gave a glance at her son which seemed tantamount to an injunction to be silent and leave her to her own devices. He stood beside her with his hands behind him, quite making up in attitude, as our observer noted, for what he failed of in utterance. It was to remain really a burden on Newman's mind to the end, this irritating, this perplexing illustration he afforded of the positive virtue and the incalculable force, even in the unholy, of attitude 'as such'. 'What paper is this you speak of?' the Marquise asked as if confessing to an interest in any possible contribution to the family archives.

'Exactly what I've told you. A paper written by your husband after you had left him that evening, for dead—written during the couple of hours before you returned. You see he had the time; you shouldn't have stayed away so long. It declares in the most convincing way his wife's murderous intent.'

'I should like to see it,' she observed as with the most natural concern for a manifesto so compromising to the—already in his day, alas, so painfully compromised—author of it.

'I thought you might,' said Newman, 'and I've taken a copy.' He drew from his waistcoat pocket a small folded sheet.

'Give it to my son,' she returned with decision; on which Newman handed it to the Marquis while she simply added 'Look at the thing.' M. de Bellegarde's eyes had a pale irrepressible eagerness; he took the paper in his light-gloved fingers and opened it. There was a silence during which he took it in. He had more than time to read it, but still he said nothing; he stood looking at it hard. 'Where's the original?' his mother meantime asked in a voice of the most disinterested curiosity.

'In a very safe place. Of course I can't show you *that*,' Newman went on—'a treasure the value of which makes it sacred to me. You might want to grab it,' he added with conscious quaintness, 'and I've too much other use for it. But this is a very correct copy—except of course the handwriting: I'll get it properly certified for you if you wish. That ought to suit you—its being properly certified.'

The Marquis at last raised a countenance deeply and undisguisedly flushed. 'It will require,' he nevertheless lightly remarked, 'a vast deal of certification!'

'Well,' Newman returned, 'we can always fall back on the original.'

'I'm speaking,' said the Marquis, 'of the original.'

'Ah, that, I think, will speak for itself. Still, we can easily get as many persons as possible—as many of those who knew the writer's hand—to speak for it. Think of the number it will interest—if I begin, myself, say, with the Duchess, that amiable, very stout lady whose name I forget, but who was pleasant to me at your party. She asked me to come to see her, and I've been thinking that in that case I shouldn't have much to say to her. But such a matter as this gives me plenty!'

'You had better, at this rate, keep what you have there, my son,' the old woman quavered with a strained irony.

'By all means,' Newman said—'keep it and show it to your mother when you get home.'

'And after enlisting the Duchess?' asked the Marquis, who folded the paper and put it away.

'Well, there are all the other people you had the cruelty to introduce me to in a character of which you were capable, at the next turn, of rudely divesting me. Many of them immediately afterwards left cards on me, so that I have their names correctly and shall know how to find them.'

For a moment, on this, neither of Newman's friends spoke; the Marquise sat looking down very hard, while her son's blanched pupils were fixed on her face. 'Is that all you have to say?' she finally asked.

'No, I want to say a few words more. I want to say that I hope you quite understand what I'm about. This is my vindication, you know, of my claim that I've been cruelly wronged. You've treated me before the world, convened for the express purpose, as if I were not good enough for you. I mean to show the world that, however bad I may be, you're not quite the people to say it.'

Madame de Bellegarde was silent again, and then, with a return of her power to face him, she dealt with his point. Her coolness continued to affect him as consummate; he wondered of what alarms, what effronteries, what suspicions and what precautions she had not had, from far back, to make her life. 'I needn't ask you who has been your accomplice in this clumsy fraud. Catherine Bread told me you had purchased her services.'

'Don't accuse Mrs Bread of venality,' Newman returned. 'She has kept your secret all these years. She has given you a long respite. It was beneath her eyes your husband wrote that paper; he put it into her hands with a solemn injunction that she was to make it public. You've had the benefit of her merciful delay.'

The Marquise appeared for an instant to hesitate, and then, 'My husband, for years, did what he—most remarkably!—liked with her,' she declared dryly enough. 'She was perhaps the meanest of his many mistresses.' This was the only concession to self-defence that she condescended to make.

'I very much doubt that,' said Newman. 'I believe in her decency.'

Madame de Bellegarde got up from her bench. 'It wasn't to your beliefs—however interesting in themselves—I undertook to listen; so that, if you've nothing left but *them* to tell me, this charming interview may terminate.' And turning to the Marquis she took his arm again. 'My son,' she then oddly resumed, 'say something!'

He looked down at her, passing his hand over his forehead to the positive displacement of his hat; with which, tenderly, caressingly, 'What shall I say?' he too uncertainly enquired.

'There's only one thing to say—that it was really not worth while, on such a showing, to have pulled us up in the street like a pair of pickpockets.'

But the Marquis thought he could surpass this. 'Your paper's of course the crudest of forgeries,' he said to Newman.

Newman shook his head all amusedly. 'M. de Bellegarde, your mother does better. She has done better all along, from the first of my knowing you. You're a mighty plucky woman, madam,' he continued. 'It's a great pity you've made me your enemy. I should have been one of your greatest admirers.'

'*Mon pauvre ami*,' she proceeded to her son, and as if she had not heard these words, 'you must take me immediately to my carriage.'

Newman stepped back and let them leave him; he watched them a moment and saw Madame Urbain, with her little girl, wander out of a by-path to meet them. The Marquise stooped and kissed her grandchild. 'Damn it, she *is* plucky!' he sighed; and he walked home with a sense of having been almost worsted. She was so quite heroically impenetrable. But on reflexion he decided that what he had witnessed was no real sense of security, still less a real innocence. It was only a very superior style of brazen assurance, of what M. Nioche called *l'usage du monde* and Mrs Tristram called the grand manner. 'Wait till she has seen how he puts it!' he said to himself; and he concluded that he should hear from her soon.

He heard sooner than he expected. The next morning, before midday, when he was about to give orders for his breakfast to be served, M. de Bellegarde's card was brought him. 'She *has* seen how he puts it and she has passed a bad night,' he promptly inferred. He instantly admitted his visitor, who came in with the air of the ambassador of a great power meeting the delegate of a barbarous tribe whom an absurd accident had enabled for the moment to be abominably annoying. The ambassador, at any rate, had also passed a bad night, and his faultlessly careful array only threw into relief the sick rancour of his eyes and those mottled spots on his fine skin that resembled, to his host's imagination, the hard finger-prints of fear. He stood there a moment, breathing quickly and painfully and shaking his forefinger curtly as Newman pointed to a chair.

'What I've come to say is soon said and can only be said without ceremony.'

'I'm good for as much or for as little as you desire.'

The Marquis looked round the room and then: 'On what terms will you part with what you call your original?'

'Ah, on none!' And while, with his head on one side and his hands behind him, he sounded his visitor's depth of detestation, Newman added: 'Certainly that's not worth sitting down about.'

M. de Bellegarde went on, however, as without having heard him. 'My mother and I, last evening, talked over your story. You'll be surprised to learn that we think your little document is—a'—and he held back his word a moment—'characteristic.'

Newman laughed out as it came. 'Of your mother and you, you mean?'

'Of my deplorable father.'

'You forget that with you I'm used to surprises!' Newman gaily pursued.

'The very scantest consideration we owe his memory', the Marquis continued, 'makes us desire he shouldn't be held up to the world as the author of an elaborately malignant attack on the reputation of a wife whose only fault was that she had been submissive to repeated outrage.'

'Oh, I see! It's for your father's sake!' And Newman laughed the laugh in which he indulged when he was, if not most amused, at any rate most pleased—an intimate noiseless laugh with closed lips.

But M. de Bellegarde's gravity held good. 'There are a few of his particular friends for whom the knowledge of so unfortunate an inspiration would be a real grief. Even say we firmly established by medical evidence the presumption of a mind disordered by fever, *il en resterait quelque chose*. At the best it would look ill in him. Very ill!'

'Don't try medical evidence,' said Newman. 'Don't touch the doctors and they won't touch you. I don't mind your knowing that I've not written to either of the gentlemen present at the event.'

He flattered himself he saw signs in his visitor's discoloured mask that this information was extremely pertinent. The Marquis remained, however, irreducibly argumentative. 'For instance Madame d'Outreville, of whom you spoke yesterday. I can imagine nothing that would shock her more.'

'Oh, I'm quite prepared to shock Madame d'Outreville. That's just what's the matter with me. I regularly *want* to shock people.'

M. de Bellegarde examined for a moment the fine white stitching on one of his black gloves. Then without looking up, 'We don't offer you money,' he said. 'That we suppose to be useless.'

Newman, turning away, took a few turns about the room and then came back. 'What *do* you offer me? By what I can make out the generosity is all to be on my side.'

The Marquis dropped his arms at his flanks and held his head a little higher. 'What we offer you is a chance—a chance a gentleman should appreciate. A chance to abstain from inflicting a terrible blot upon the memory of a man who certainly had his faults, but who, personally, had done you no wrong.'

'There are two things to say to that,' Newman returned. 'The first is, as regards appreciating your "chance", that you don't consider me a gentleman. That's your great point, you know. It's a poor rule that won't work both ways. The second is that—well, in a word, you're talking sad nonsense.'

In the midst of his bitterness he had kept well before his eyes, as I have noted, a certain ideal of saying nothing rude, and he felt a quick scruple for the too easy impatience of these words. But the Marquis took them more quietly than might have been expected. Sublime ambassador that he was, he continued the policy of ignoring what was disagreeable in his adversary's replies. He gazed at the gilded arabesques on the opposite wall and then transferred his glance to his host as if he too had been a large grotesque in a vulgar system of chamber-decoration. 'I suppose you know that, as regards yourself, a course so confessedly vindictive—vindictive in respect to your discomfiture—won't do at all.'

'How do you mean it won't do?'

'Why, of course you utterly damn yourself. But I suppose that's in your programme. You propose to throw at us this horrible *ordure* that you've raked together, and you believe, you hope, that some of it may stick. We know naturally it can't,' explained the Marquis in a tone of conscious lucidity; 'but you take the chance and are willing at any rate to show that you yourself have dirty hands.'

'That's a good comparison; at least half of it is,' said Newman. 'I take the chance of something sticking. But as regards my hands, they're clean. I've taken the awful thing up with my finger-tips.'

M. de Bellegarde looked a moment into his hat. 'All our friends are quite with us. They would have done exactly as we've done.'

'I shall believe that when I hear them say it. Meanwhile I shall think better of human nature.'

The Marquis looked into his hat again. 'My poor perverse sister was extremely fond of her father. If she knew of the existence of the few base words—at once mad and base—of which you propose to make this scandalous use, she would require of you, proudly, for his sake, to give them up to her, and she would destroy them on the spot.'

'Very possibly,' Newman rejoined. 'But it's exactly what she won't know. I was in that hideous place yesterday, and I know what *she's* doing. Lord of mercy! You can guess whether it made me feel forgiving!'

M. de Bellegarde appeared to have nothing more to suggest; but he continued to stand there, rigid and elegant, as a man who had believed his mere personal presence would have had an argumentative value. Newman watched him and, without yielding an inch on the main issue, felt an incongruously good-natured impulse to help him to retreat in good order. 'Your idea, you see—though ingenious in its way—doesn't work. You offer too little.'

'Propose something yourself,' the Marquis at last brought out.

'Give me back Madame de Cintré relieved of the blight and free of the poison that are all of your producing.'

M. de Bellegarde threw up his head and his flush darkly spread. 'Never!'

'You can't!'

'We wouldn't if we could! In the sentiment which led us to deprecate her marriage to you nothing is changed.'

' "Deprecate" is lovely!' cried Newman. 'It was hardly worth while to come here only to tell me that you're not ashamed of yourselves. I should have come to think of you perhaps as in your guilt-burdened hearts almost pitifully miserable.'

The Marquis slowly walked toward the door, and Newman, following, opened it for him. 'Your hawking that tatter about will be, on your part, the vulgarest proceeding conceivable, and, as having admitted you to our *intimité*, we shall proportionately wince for it. That we quite feel. But it won't otherwise incommode us.'

'Well,' said Newman after reflexion, 'I don't know that I want to do anything worse than make you regret your connexion with me. Only don't be sure you know yet,' he added, 'how very much you *may* regret it.'

M. de Bellegarde stood a moment looking on the ground, as if ransacking his brain to see what else he could do to save his father's reputation. Then, with a small cold sigh, he seemed to signify that he regretfully surrendered the late Marquis to the penalty of his turpitude. He gave a scant shrug, took his neat umbrella from the servant in the vestibule and, with his gentlemanly walk, passed out. Newman stood listening till he heard the door close; then for some minutes he moved to and fro with his hands in his pockets and a sound like the low hum of a jig proceeding from the back of his mouth.

XXV

HE called on the immense, the comical Duchess and found her at home. An old gentleman with a high nose and a gold-headed cane was just taking leave; he made Newman a protracted obeisance as he retired, and our hero supposed him one of the high personages with whom he had shaken hands at Madame de Bellegarde's party. The Duchess, in her armchair, from which she didn't move, with a great flower-pot on one side of her, a pile of pink-covered novels* on the other and a large piece of tapestry depending from her lap, presented an expansive and imposing front; but her aspect was in the highest degree gracious and there was nothing in her manner to check the effusion of his confidence. She talked to him of flowers and books, getting launched with marvellous promptitude; about the theatres, about the peculiar institutions of his native country, about the humidity of Paris, about the pretty complexions of the American ladies, about his impressions of France and his opinion of its female inhabitants. All this had a large free flow on the part of the Duchess, who like many of her countrywomen, was a person of an affirmative rather than an interrogative cast, who uttered 'good things' and put them herself into circulation, and who was apt to offer you a present of a convenient little opinion neatly enveloped in the gilt paper of a happy Gallicism. Newman had come to her with a grievance, but he found himself in an atmosphere in which apparently no cognisance was taken of such matters; an atmosphere into which the chill of discomfort had never penetrated and which seemed exclusively made up of mild, sweet, stale intellectual perfumes. The feeling with which he had watched Madame d'Outreville at the treacherous festival of the Bellegardes came back to him; she struck him as a wonderful old lady in some particularly 'high' comedy, thoroughly well up in her part. He noticed before long that she asked him no question about their common friends; she made no allusion to the circumstances under which he had been presented to her. She neither feigned ignorance of a change in these circumstances nor pretended to condole with him upon it; but she smiled and discoursed and compared the tender-tinted wools of her tapestry as if the Bellegardes and their wickedness were not of this world. 'She's fighting shy!' he said to himself; and, having drawn the inference, was curious to see, further, how, if this were a policy, she would carry it off. She did so in a masterly manner. There was not a gleam of disguised consciousness in the small, clear, demonstrative eyes which constituted her nearest claim to personal loveliness; there was not a symptom of apprehension he would trench on any ground she proposed to avoid. 'Upon my word, she does it very well,' he tacitly commented. 'They all hold together bravely, and, whether any one else can trust them or not, they can certainly trust each other.'

He fell at this juncture to admiring the Duchess for her fine manners. He felt, most accurately, that she was not a grain less urbane than she would have been if his marriage were still in prospect; but he was aware also that she led him on no single inch further. He had come, so reasoned this eminent lady—heaven knew why he had come after what had happened; and for the half-hour therefore she would be *charmante*. But she would never see him again. Finding no ready-made opportunity to tell his story, he pondered these things more dispassionately than might have been expected; he stretched his legs as usual and even chuckled a little quite appreciatively and noiselessly. And then as his hostess went on relating a *mot* with which her mother had, in extreme youth, snubbed the great Napoleon, it occurred to him that her evasion of a chapter of French history more interesting to himself might possibly be the result of an extreme consideration for his feelings. Perhaps it was delicacy rather than diplomacy. He was on the point of saying something himself, to make the chance he had determined to give her still better, when the servant announced another visitor. The Duchess on hearing the name—it was that of an Italian prince—gave a little imperceptible pout and said to him rapidly: 'I beg you to remain; I desire this visit to be short.' He wondered, at this, if they mightn't then after all get round to the Bellegardes.

The Prince was a short stout man, with a head disproportionately large. He had a dusky complexion and bushy eyebrows, beneath which glowed a fixed and somewhat defiant stare; he seemed to be challenging you to hint that he might be hydrocephalic. The Duchess, judging from her charge to our own friend, regarded him as a bore; but this was not apparent from the unchecked abundance of her speech. She caused it to frisk hither and yon as to some old rococo music and then pull up on a *mot* after the fashion in which a stage-dancer whirls, for breath and with arms arranged, into ecstatic equilibrium; she characterised with great felicity the Italian intellect and the taste of the figs at Sorrento, predicted the ultimate future of the Italian kingdom (disgust with the brutal Sardinian rule* and complete reversion, throughout the peninsula, to the mild sway of the Holy Father) and, finally, took up the heart-history of their friend *cette pauvre Princesse*, a lady unknown to Newman, who had notoriously so much heart. This record exposed itself to a considerable control from the Prince, who was evidently not related to the heroine in question otherwise than by an intimate familiarity with her annals; and having satisfied himself that Newman was in no laughing mood, either with regard to the size of his head or the authenticity of his facts, he entered into the controversy with an animation for which the Duchess, when she set him down as a bore, could not have been prepared. The often so oddly-directed passions of their friend led Newman's companions to a discussion of the *côté passionnel* of the Florentine nobility in general; the Duchess had lately spent several weeks in the very bosom of that body and gathered much information on the subject. This was merged, in turn, in an examination of the Italian heart *per se*. The Duchess, who had arrived at highly original conclusions, thought it the least susceptible organ of its kind that she had ever encountered, related examples of its Machiavellian power to calculate its perils and profits, and at last declared that for her the race were half arithmetic and half ice. The Prince became flame and rhetoric to refute her, and his visit really proved charming.

Newman was naturally out of the fray; he sat with his head a little on one side, watching the interlocutors. The Duchess, as she talked, frequently looked at him with a smile, as if to intimate, in the charming manner of her nation, that it lay only with him to say something very much to the point. But he said nothing at all, and at last his thoughts began to wander. A singular feeling came over him—a sudden sense of the folly of his errand. What under the sun had he after all to say to the Duchess? Wherein would it profit him to denounce the Bellegardes to her for traitors and the Marquise into the bargain for a murderess? He seemed morally to have turned a high somersault and to find things looking differently in consequence. He felt, as by the effect of some colder current of the air, his will stiffen in another direction and the mantle of his reserve draw closer. What in the world had he been thinking of when he fancied Madame d'Outreville could help him and that it would conduce to his comfort to make her think ill of the Bellegardes? What did her opinion of the Bellegardes matter to him? It was only a shade more important than the opinion the Bellegardes entertained of herself. The Duchess help him, that cold, stout, soft, artificial woman help him?—she who in the last twenty minutes had built up between them a wall of polite conversation in which she evidently flattered herself he would never find a gate? Had it come to this—that he was asking favours of false gods and appealing for sympathy where he had no sympathy to give? He rested his arms on his knees and sat for some minutes staring into his hat. As he did so his ears tingled—was he to have brayed like that animal whose ears are longest?* Whether or no the Duchess would hear his story he wouldn't tell it. Was he to sit there another half-hour for the sake of exposing the Bellegardes? The Bellegardes be deeply damned! He got up abruptly and advanced to shake hands with his hostess.

'You can't stay longer?' she graciously asked.

'If you'll pardon me, no.'

She hesitated, and then, 'I had an idea you had something particular to say to me,' she returned.

Newman met her eyes; he felt a little dizzy; for the moment he was conscious of the high—or at least the higher—air in which he performed gymnastic revolutions. The little Italian prince came to his help. 'Ah, madame, who has not that?' he richly sighed.

'Don't teach Mr Newman to say *fadaises*,' said the Duchess. 'It's his merit that he doesn't know how.'

'Yes, I don't know how to say *fadaises*,' Newman admitted, 'and I don't want to say anything unpleasant.'

'I'm sure you're very considerate,' Madame d'Outreville smiled; and she gave him a little nod for all good-bye, with which he took his departure.

Once in the street he stood for some time on the pavement, wondering if after all he had not been most an ass not to offer to the great lady's inhalation his nosegay of strange flowers. And then he decided, he quite had the sense of discovering, that he should simply hate to talk of the Bellegardes with any one. The thing he most wanted to do, it suddenly appeared, was to banish them from his mind and never think of them again. Indecision had, however, not hitherto

been one of his weaknesses, and in this case it was not of long dura-
tion. For three days he applied all his thought to not thinking—
thinking, that is, of the Marquise and her son. He dined with Mrs
Tristram and, on her mentioning their name, requested her almost
austerely to desist. This gave Tom Tristram a much-coveted opportunity to offer condolences.

He leaned forward, laying his hand on Newman's arm, compress-
ing his lips and shaking his head. 'The fact is, my dear fellow, you
see you ought never to have gone into it. It was not your doing, I
know—it was all my wife. If you want to come down on her I'll stand
off: I give you leave to hit her as hard as you like. You know she has
never had a flick of the whip from me in her life, and I do think she
wants to be a bit touched up. Why didn't you listen to *me*? You know
I didn't believe in the thing. I thought it at the best a high jump in
which you might bruise a shin. I don't profess to have been a tremendous *homme à femmes*, as they say here, but I've instincts about the
sex that, hang it, I've honestly come by. I've never mistrusted a
woman in my life that she has not turned out badly. I was not at all
deceived in Lizzie for instance; I always had my doubts about her.
Whatever you may think of my present situation I must at least admit
that I got into it with my eyes open. Now suppose you had got into
something like this box with your grand cold Countess. You may
depend upon it she'd have turned out a stiff one. And upon my word
I don't see where you could have found your comfort. Not from the
Marquis, my dear Newman; he wasn't a man you could go and talk
things over with in an easy and natural way. Did he ever seem to want
to have you on the premises? Did he ever try to see you alone? Did
he ever ask you to come and smoke a cigar with him of an evening
or step in, when you had been calling on the ladies, and take something? I don't think you'd have got much out of *him*. And as for that
daughter of a hundred earls his mother, she struck one as an uncommonly strong dose. They have a great expression here, you know;
they call any damned thing "sympathetic"*—that is when it isn't it
ought to be. Now Madame de Bellegarde's about as sympathetic as
that mustard-pot. They're a d—d stony-faced, cold-blooded lot
anyway; I felt it awfully at that ball of theirs. I felt as if I were walking
up and down the Armoury in the Tower of London—every one
cased in ancestral steel, every one perched up in a panoply.* My dear
boy, don't think me a vulgar brute for hinting it, but, you may depend

upon it, all they wanted was your money. I know something about
that; can tell when people want one's money. Why they stopped
wanting yours I don't know; I suppose because they could get some
one else's without working so hard for it. It isn't worth finding out.
It may be it was not with your Countess, Lizzie's and yours, that the
idea of chucking you originated; very likely the old woman put her
up to it. I suspect she and her mother are really as thick as thieves,
eh? You're well out of it, at any rate, old man; make up your mind
to that. If I express myself strongly it's all because I love you so
much; and from that point of view I may say I should as soon have
thought of making up to that piece of pale peculiarity as I should
have thought of wooing the Obelisk in the Place de la Concorde.'*

Newman sat gazing at Tristram during this harangue with a lack-
lustre eye; never yet had he seemed to himself to have outgrown so
completely the phase of equal comradeship with Tom Tristram. Mrs
Tristram's glance at her husband had more of a spark; she turned to
Newman with a slightly lurid smile. 'You must at least do justice,'
she said, 'to the felicity with which he repairs the indiscretions of a
too zealous wife.'

But even without the lash of his friend's loud tongue Newman
would have waked again into his bitterest consciousness. He could
keep it at bay only when he could cease to miss what he had lost,
and each day, for the present, but added a ton of weight to that quantity. In vain Mrs Tristram begged him to *se faire*, as she put it, *une
raison*; she assured him the sight of his countenance made her
wretched.

'How can I help it?' he demanded with a trembling voice—'how
can I help it when the sight of everything makes *me* so? I feel exactly
like a stunned widower—and a widower who has not even the consolation of going to stand beside the grave of his wife, one who has
not the right to wear so much mourning as a weed on his hat. I feel,'
he added in a moment, 'as if my wife had been murdered and her
assassins were still at large.'

Mrs Tristram made no immediate rejoinder, but at last she said
with a smile which, in so far as it was a forced one, was less successfully simulated than such smiles, on her lips, usually were: 'Are
you very sure that you'd have been happy?'

He stared, then shook his head. 'That's weak; that won't do.'

'Well,' she persisted as with an idea, 'I don't believe it would have really done.'

He gave a sound of irritation. 'Say then it would have damnably failed. Failure for failure I should have preferred that one to this.'

She took it in her musing way. 'I should have been curious to see; it would have been very strange.'

'Was it from curiosity that you urged me to put myself forward?'

'A little,' she still more boldly answered. Newman gave her the one angry look he had been destined ever to give her, turned away and took up his hat. She watched him a moment and then said: 'That sounds very cruel, but it's less so than it sounds. Curiosity has a share in almost everything I do. I wanted very much see, first, if such a union could actually come through; second, what would happen to it afterwards.'

'So you hadn't faith,' he said resentfully.

'Yes, I had faith—faith that it would take place, and that you'd be happy. Otherwise I should have been, among my speculations, a very heartless creature. *But*,' she continued, laying her hand on his arm and hazarding a grave smile, 'it was the highest flight ever taken by a tolerably rich imagination!'

Shortly after this she recommended him to leave Paris and travel for three months. Change of scene would do him good and he would forget his misfortune sooner in absence from the objects that had witnessed it. 'I really feel,' he concurred, 'as if to leave *you*, at least, would do me good—and cost me very little effort. You're growing cynical; you shock me and pain me.'

'Very well,' she said, good-naturedly or cynically, as may appear most credible. 'I shall certainly see you again.'

He was ready enough to get quite away; the brilliant streets he had walked through in his happier hours and which then seemed to wear a higher brilliancy in honour of his happiness, were now in the secret of his defeat and looked down on it in shining mockery. He would go somewhere, he cared little where; and he made his preparations. Then one morning at haphazard he drove to the train that would transport him to Calais and deposit him there for despatch to the shores of Britain. As he rolled along he asked himself what had become of his revenge, and he was able to think of it as provisionally pigeonholed in a very safe place. It would keep till called for.

He arrived in London in the midst of what is called 'the season',* and it seemed to him at first that he might here put himself in the way of being diverted from his heavy-heartedness. He knew no one in all England, but the spectacle of the vaster and duskier Babylon roused him somewhat from his apathy. Anything that was enormous usually found favour with him, and the multitudinous English energies and industries stirred in his spirit a dull vivacity of contemplation. It is on record that the weather, at that moment, was of the finest insular quality; he took long walks and explored London in every direction; he sat by the hour in Kensington Gardens and beside the adjoining Drive,* watching the people and the horses and the carriages; the rosy English beauties, the wonderful English dandies and the splendid flunkies. He went to the opera and found it better than in Paris; he went to the theatre and found a surprising charm in listening to dialogue the finest points of which came within the range of his comprehension. He made several excursions into the country, recommended by the waiter at his hotel, with whom, on this and similar points, he had established confidential relations. He watched the deer in Windsor Forest and admired the Thames from Richmond Hill; he ate whitebait and brown bread-and-butter at Greenwich; he strolled in the grassy shadow of the cathedral of Canterbury. He also visited the Tower of London and Madame Tussaud's exhibition.* One day he thought he would go to Sheffield, and then, thinking again, gave it up. Why the devil should he go to Sheffield? He had a feeling that the link which bound him to a possible interest in the manufacture of cutlery was broken. He had no desire for an 'inside view' of any successful enterprise whatever, and he wouldn't have given the smallest sum for the privilege of talking over the details of the most splendid business with the most original of managers.

One afternoon he had walked into the Park and was slowly threading his way through the human maze which fringes the Drive. This stream was no less dense, and Newman, as usual, marvelled at the strange dowdy figures he saw taking the air in some of the most shining conveyances. They reminded him of what he had read of Eastern and Southern countries, in which grotesque idols and fetiches were sometimes drawn out of their temples and carried abroad in golden chariots to be seen of the people. He noted a great many pretty cheeks beneath high-plumed hats as he squeezed his way through serried waves of crumpled muslin; and, sitting on little chairs at the base of the dull, massive English trees, he observed a number of quiet-eyed maidens who seemed only to remind him afresh that the magic of beauty had gone out of the world with the woman wrenched from him: to say nothing of other damsels whose eyes were not quiet and who struck him still more as a satire on possible consolation. He had been walking for some time when, directly in front of him, borne toward him by the summer breeze, he heard a few words uttered in the bright Parisian idiom his ears had begun to forget. The voice in which the words were spoken was a peculiar recall, and as he bent his eyes it lent an identity to the commonplace elegance of the back view of a young lady walking in the same direction as himself. Mademoiselle Nioche, seeking her fortune, had apparently thought she might find it faster in London, and another glance led him to wonder if she might now have lighted on it. A gentleman strolled beside her, lending an attentive ear to her conversation and too beguiled to open his lips. Newman caught no sound of him, but had the impression of English shoulders, an English 'fit',* an English silence. Mademoiselle Nioche was attracting attention: the ladies who passed her turned round as with a sense of the Parisian finish. A great cataract of flounces rolled down from the young lady's waist to Newman's feet; he had to step aside to avoid treading on them. He stepped aside indeed with a decision of movement that the occasion scarcely demanded; for even this imperfect glimpse of Miss Noémie had sharpened again his constant soreness. She seemed an odious blot on the face of nature; he wanted to put her out of his sight. He thought of Valentin de Bellegarde still green in the earth of his burial, his young life giving way to this flourishing impudence. The fragrance of the girl's bravery quite sickened him; he turned his head and tried to keep his distance; but the pressure of the crowd held him near her a minute longer, so that he heard what she was saying.

'Ah, I'm sure he'll miss me,' she murmured. 'It was very cruel of me to leave him; I'm afraid you'll think I've very little heart. He might perfectly have remained with us. I don't think he's very well,' she added; 'it seemed to me to-day he was rather down.'

Newman wondered whom she was talking about, but just then an opening among his neighbours enabled him to turn away, and he said to himself that she was probably paying a tribute to British propriety and feigning a tender solicitude about her parent. Was that miserable old man still treading the path of vice in her train? Was he still giving her the benefit of his experience of affairs, and had he crossed the sea to serve as her interpreter? Newman walked some distance further and then began to retrace his steps, taking care not to accompany again those of Mademoiselle Nioche. At last he looked for a chair under the trees, but he had some difficulty in finding an empty one. He was about to give up the search when he saw a gentleman rise from the seat he had been occupying, leaving our friend to take it without looking at his neighbours. Newman sat there for some time without heeding them; his attention was lost in the rage of his renewed vision of the little fatal *fact* of Noémie. But at the end of a quarter of an hour, dropping his eyes, he perceived a small pug-dog squatted on the path near his feet—a diminutive but very perfect specimen of its interesting species. The pug was sniffing at the fashionable world, as it passed him, with his little black muzzle, and was kept from extending his investigation by a large blue ribbon attached to his collar with an enormous rosette and held in the hand of a person seated next Newman. To this person our hero transferred his attention, and immediately found himself the object of all that of his neighbour, who was staring up at him from a pair of little fixed white eyes. These eyes he instantly recognised; he had been sitting for the last quarter of an hour beside M. Nioche. He had vaguely felt himself in range of some feeble fire. M. Nioche continued to stare; he appeared afraid to move even to the extent of saving by flight what might have been left of his honour.

'Good Lord!' said Newman; 'are you here too?' And he looked at his neighbour's helplessness more grimly than he knew. M. Nioche had a new hat and a pair of kid gloves; his clothes too seemed to belong to an eld less hoary than of yore. Over his arm was suspended a lady's mantilla—a light and brilliant tissue, fringed with white lace—which had apparently been committed to his keeping; and the little dog's blue ribbon was wound tightly round his hand. There was no hint of recognition in his face—nor of anything save a feeble fascinated dread. Newman looked at the pug and the lace mantilla and then met the old man's eyes again. 'You know me, I see,' he pursued. 'You might have spoken to me before.' M. Nioche still said nothing, but it seemed to his ex-patron that his eyes began faintly to water. 'I didn't expect,' the latter went on, 'to meet you so far from—from the Café de la Patrie.' He remained silent, but decidedly Newman had touched the source of tears. His neighbour sat staring and he added: 'What's the matter, M. Nioche? You used to talk, talk very—what did you call it?—very *gentiment*. Don't you remember you even gave lessons in conversation?'

At this M. Nioche decided to change his attitude. He stooped and picked up the pug, lifted it to his face and wiped his eyes on its little soft back. 'I'm afraid to speak to you,' he presently said, looking over the puppy's shoulder. 'I hoped you wouldn't notice me. I should have moved away, but I was afraid that if I moved it would strike you. So I sat very still.'

'I suspect you've a bad conscience, sir,' Newman pronounced.

The old man put down the little dog and held it carefully in his lap. Then he shook his head, his eyes still watering and pleading. 'No, Mr Newman, I've a good conscience,' he weakly wailed.

'Then why should you want to slink away from me?'

'Because—because you don't understand my position.'

'Oh, I think you once explained it to me,' said Newman. 'But it seems improved.'

'Improved!' his companion quavered. 'Do you call this improvement?' And he ruefully embraced the treasures in his arms.

'Why, you're on your travels,' Newman rejoined. 'A visit to London in the Season is certainly a sign of prosperity.'

M. Nioche, in answer to this superior dig, lifted the puppy up to his face again, peering at his critic from his small blank eye-holes. There was something inane in the movement, and Newman hardly knew if he were taking refuge in an affected failure of reason or whether he had in fact paid for his base accommodation by the loss of his wits. In the latter case, just now, he felt little more tenderly to the foolish old man than in the former. Responsible or not, he was equally an accomplice of his pestilent daughter. Newman was going to leave him abruptly when his face gave out a peculiar convulsion. 'Are you going away?' he appealed.

'Do you want me to stay?'

'I should have left you—from consideration. But my dignity suffers at your leaving *me*—that way.'

'Have you anything particular to say to me?'

M. Nioche looked round to see no one was listening, and then returned with mild portentousness: '*Je ne lui ai pas trouvé d'excuses.*'

Newman gave a short laugh, but the old man seemed for the moment not to heed; he was gazing away, absently, at some metaphysical image of his implacability. 'It doesn't much matter whether you have or not,' said Newman. 'There are other people who never will, I assure you.'

'What has she done?' M. Nioche vaguely enquired, turning round again. 'I don't know what she does, you know.'

'She has done a devilish mischief; it doesn't matter what. She's a public nuisance; she ought to be stopped.'

M. Nioche stealthily put out his hand and laid it on Newman's arm. 'Stopped, yes,' he concurred. 'That's it. Stopped short. She's running away—she must be stopped.' Then he paused and again looked round him. 'I mean to stop her,' he went on. 'I'm only waiting for my chance.'

'I see,' Newman dryly enough laughed. 'She's running away and you're running after her. You've run a long distance.'

But M. Nioche had a competent upward nod, 'Oh, I know what to do!'

He had hardly spoken when the crowd in front of them separated as if by the impulse to make way for an important personage. Presently, through the opening, advanced Mademoiselle Nioche, attended by the gentleman Newman had lately observed. His face being now presented to our hero, the latter recognised the irregular features and the hardly more composed expression of Lord Deepmere. Noémie, on finding herself suddenly confronted with Newman, who, like M. Nioche, had risen from his seat, faltered for a barely perceptible instant. She gave him a little nod, as if she had seen him yesterday, and then, without agitation, '*Tiens*, how we keep meeting!' she sweetly shrilled. She looked consummately pretty and the front of her dress was a wonderful work of art. She went up to her father, stretching out her hands for the little dog, which he submissively placed in them, and she began to kiss it and murmur over it: 'To think of leaving him all alone, *mon bichon*—what a horrid false friend he must believe me! He has been very unwell,' she added, turning and affecting to explain to Newman, a spark of infernal impudence, fine as a needle-point, lighted in each charming eye. 'I don't think the English climate does for him.'

'It seems to do wonderfully well for his mistress,' Newman said.

'Do you mean me? I've never been better, thank you,' Miss

Noémie declared. 'But with *milord*,' and she gave a shining shot at her late companion, 'how can one help being well?' She seated herself in the chair from which her father had risen and began to arrange the little dog's rosette.

Lord Deepmere carried off such embarrassment as might be incidental to this unexpected encounter with the inferior grace of a male and a Briton. He blushed a good deal and greeted his fellow-candidate in that recent remarkable competition by which each had so signally failed to profit with an awkward nod and a rapid ejaculation—an ejaculation to which Newman, who often found it hard to understand the speech of English people, was able to attach no meaning. Then he stood there with his hand on his hip and with a conscious grin, staring askance at the mistress of the invalid pug. Suddenly an idea seemed to strike him and he caught at the light. 'Oh, you know her?'

'Yes,' said Newman, 'I know her. I don't believe you do.'

'Oh dear, yes, I do!'—Lord Deepmere was sure of that. 'I knew her in Paris—by my late cousin Bellegarde, you know. He knew her, poor fellow, didn't he? It was she, you know, who was at the bottom of his affair. Awfully sad, wasn't it?' the young man continued, talking off his embarrassment as his simple nature permitted. 'They got up some story of its being for the Pope; of the other fellow having said something against the Pope's morals. They always do that, you know. They put it on the Pope because Bellegarde was once in the Zouaves. But it was about *her* morals—*she* was the Pope!' his lordship pursued, directing an eye illumined by this pleasantry toward Mademoiselle Nioche, who, bending gracefully over her lap-dog, was apparently absorbed in conversation with it. 'I dare say you think it rather odd that I should—a—keep up the acquaintance,' he resumed; 'but she couldn't help it, you know, and Bellegarde was only my twentieth cousin. I dare say you think it rather cheeky my showing with her in this place; but you see she isn't known yet and she's so remarkably, thoroughly nice—!' With which his attesting glance returned to the young lady.

Newman turned away; he was having too much of her niceness. M. Nioche had stepped aside on his daughter's approach, and he stood there, within a very small compass, looking down hard at the ground. It had decidedly never yet, as between him and his late protector, been so apposite to place on record that, for his vindication, he was only waiting to strike. As Newman turned off he felt himself held, and, seeing the old man, who had drawn so near, had something particular to say, bent his head an instant.

'You'll see it some day *dans les feuilles*.'

Our hero broke away, for impatience of the whole connexion, and to this day, though the newspapers form his principal reading, his eyes have not been arrested by any paragraph forming a sequel to this announcement.

XXVI

In that uninitiated observation of the great spectacle of English life on which I have touched, it might be supposed that he passed a great many dull days. But the dulness was as grateful as a warm, fragrant bath, and his melancholy, which was settling to a secondary stage, like a healing wound, had in it a certain acrid, palatable sweetness. He had the company of his thoughts and for the present wanted none other. He had no desire to make acquaintances and left untouched a couple of notes of introduction sent him by Tom Tristram. He mused a great deal on Madame de Cintré—sometimes with a dull despair that might have seemed a near neighbour to detachment. He lived over again the happiest hours he had known—that silver chain of numbered days in which his afternoon visits, strained so sensibly to the ideal end, had come to figure for him a flight of firm marble steps where the ascent from one to the other was a momentous and distinct occasion, giving a nearer view of the chamber of confidence at the top, a white tower that flushed more and more as with a light of dawn. He had yet held in his cheated arms, he felt, the full experience, and when he closed them together round the void that was all they now possessed, he might have been some solitary spare athlete practising restlessly in the corridor of the circus. He came back to reality indeed, after such reveries, with a shock somewhat muffled; he had begun to know the need of accepting the absolute. At other times, however, the truth was again an infamy and the actual a lie, and he could only pace and rage and remember till he was weary. Passion, in him, by habit, nevertheless, burned clear rather than thick, and in the clearness he saw things, even things not gross and close—having never the excuse that anything could make him blind. Without quite knowing it at first, he began to read a moral into his strange adventure. He asked himself in his quieter hours whether he perhaps *had* been more commercial than was decent. We know that it was in reaction against questions of the cruder avidity that he had come out to pick up for a while an intellectual, or otherwise a critical, living in Europe; it may therefore be understood that he was able to conceive of a votary of the mere greasy market smelling too strong for true good company. He was willing to grant in a given case that unpleasant effect, but he couldn't bring it home to himself that he had reeked. He believed there had been as few reflexions of his smugness caught during all those weeks in the high polish of surrounding surfaces as there were monuments of his meanness scattered about the world. No one had ever unprovokedly suffered by him—ah, provokedly was another matter: he liked to remember that, and to repeat it, and to defy himself to bring up a case.

If moreover there was any reason in the nature of things why his connexion with business should have cast a shadow on a connexion—even a connexion broken—with a woman justly proud, he was willing to sponge it out of his life for ever. The thing seemed a possibility; he couldn't feel it doubtless as keenly as some people, and it scarce struck him as worth while to flap his wings very hard to rise to the idea; but he could feel it enough to make any sacrifice that still remained to be made. As to what such sacrifice was now to be made to, here he stopped short before a blank wall over which there sometimes played strange shadows and confused signs. Was it a thinkable *plan*, that of carrying out his life as he would have directed had Madame de Cintré been left to him?—that of making it a religion to do nothing she would have disliked? In this certainly was no sacrifice; but there was a pale, oblique ray of inspiration. It would be lonely entertainment—a good deal like a man's talking to himself in the mirror for want of better company. Yet the idea yielded him several half-hours' dumb exaltation as he sat, his hands in his pockets and his legs outstretched, over the relics of an expensively bad dinner, in the undying English twilight. If, however, his financial imagination was dead he felt no contempt for the surviving actualities begotten by it. He was glad he had been prosperous and had been a great operator rather than a small; he was extremely glad he was rich. He felt no impulse to sell all he had and give to the poor, or to retire into meditative economy and asceticism. He was glad he was rich and tolerably young; if it was possible to have inhaled too fondly the reek of the market, it was yet a gain still to have time for experiments in other air. Come then, what air should it now be? Ah, again and again, he could taste but one sweetness; that came back to him and back; and as this happened, with a force which seemed physically to express itself in a sudden upward choking, he would lean forward, when the waiter had left the room, and, resting his arms on the table, bury his troubled face.

He remained in England till midsummer and spent a month in the country, wandering among cathedrals, hanging about castles and ruins. Several times, taking a walk from his inn across sweet field-paths and through ample parks, he stopped by a well-worn stile, looked across through the early evening at a grey church tower, with its dusky nimbus of thick-circling rooks, and remembered that such things might have been part of the intimacy of his honeymoon. He had never been so much alone nor indulged so little in chance talk. The period of recreation appointed by Mrs Tristram had at last expired and he asked himself what he should next do. She had written to propose he should join her in the Pyrenees, but he was not in the humour to return to France. The simplest thing was to repair to Liverpool and embark on the first American steamer. He proceeded accordingly to that seaport and secured his berth; and the night before sailing he sat in his room at the hotel and stared down vacantly and wearily at an open portmanteau. A number of papers lay upon it, which he had been meaning to look over; some of them might conveniently be destroyed. But he at last shuffled them roughly together and pushed them into a corner of the bag; they were business papers and he was in no humour for sorting them. Then he drew forth his pocket-book and took out a leaf of smaller size than those he had dismissed. He didn't unfold it; he simply sat looking at the back of it. If he had momentarily entertained the idea of destroying it this possibility at least quickly dropped. What the thing suggested was the feeling that lay in his innermost heart and that no reviving cheerfulness could long quench—the feeling that, after all and above all, he was a good fellow wronged. With it came a hope, as intense as a pang, that the Bellegardes were enjoying their suspense as to what he would do yet. The more it was prolonged the more they would enjoy it. He had hung fire once, yes; perhaps in his present queer state of mind he might hang fire again. But he restored the safe scrap to his pocket-book very tenderly and felt better for thinking of the suspense of the Bellegardes. He felt better every time he thought of it while he sailed the summer seas. He landed in New York and journeyed across the continent to San Francisco, and nothing he observed by the way contributed to mitigate his sense of being a good fellow wronged.

He saw a great many other good fellows—his old friends—but he told none of them of the trick that had been played him. He said simply that the lady he was to have married had changed her mind, and when asked if he had changed his own inscrutably answered, 'Suppose we change the subject.' He told his friends he had brought home no 'new ideas' from Europe, and his conduct probably struck them as an eloquent proof of failing invention. He took no interest in discussing business and showed no desire to go into anything whatever. He asked half a dozen questions which, like those of an eminent physician enquiring for particular symptoms, proved he was master of his subject; but he made no comments and gave no directions. He not only puzzled all the prominent men, but was himself surprised at the extent of his indifference. As it seemed only to increase he made an effort to combat it; he tried to take hold and to recover, as they said, his spring. But the ground was inelastic and the issues dead; do what he would he somehow couldn't believe in them. Sometimes he began to fear there was something the matter with him, that he had suffered, unwitting, some small horrid cerebral lesion or nervous accident, and that the end of his strong activities had come. This idea for a while hung about him and haunted him. A hopeless, helpless loafer, useful to no one and detestable to himself—this was what the treachery of the Bellegardes had made of him. In his anxious idleness he came back from San Francisco to New York, where he sat for three days in the lobby of his hotel and looked out through a huge wall of plate glass at the unceasing stream of pretty girls who wore their clothes as with the American accent and undulated past with little parcels nursed against their neat figures. At the end of three days he returned to San Francisco and, having arrived there, wished he had stayed away. He had nothing to do, his occupation had gone,* had simply strayed and lost itself in the great desert of life. He had nothing to do *here*, he sometimes said to himself; but there was something beyond the ocean he was still to do; something he had left undone experimentally and speculatively, to see if it could content itself to remain undone. Well, clearly, it couldn't content itself; it kept pulling at his heartstrings and thumping at his reason; it murmured in his ears and hovered perpetually before his eyes. It interposed between all new resolutions and their fulfilment; it was a stubborn ghost dumbly entreating to be laid. On the doing of that all other doing depended.

One day toward the end of the winter, after a long interval, he received a letter from Mrs Tristram, who appeared to have been moved by a charitable desire to amuse and distract her correspondent. She gave him much Paris gossip, talked of General Packard and Miss Kitty Upjohn, enumerated the new plays at the theatres and enclosed a note from her husband, who had gone down to spend a month at Nice. Then came her signature and after this her postscript. The latter consisted of these few lines: 'I heard three days since from my friend the Abbé Aubert that Claire de Cintré last week received the veil at the Carmelites. It was on her twenty-ninth birthday, and she took the name of her patroness, Saint Veronica.* Sœur Véronique has a lifetime before her!'

This letter reached him in the morning; in the evening he started for Paris. His wound began to ache with its first fierceness, and during his long bleak journey he had no company but the thought of the new Sister's 'lifetime'—every one's sister but his!—passed within walls on whose outer side only he might stand. Well, for that station* *he* would live, if it was to be spoken of as life; he would fix himself in Paris; he would wring a hard happiness from the knowledge that if she was not there at least the stony sepulchre that held her was. He descended, unannounced, on Mrs Bread, whom he found keeping lonely watch in his great empty saloons on the Boulevard Haussmann. They were as neat as a Dutch village; Mrs Bread's only occupation had been removing individual dust-particles. She made no complaint, however, of her solitude, for in her philosophy a servant was but a machine constructed for the benefit of some supreme patentee, and it would be as fantastic for a housekeeper to comment on a gentleman's absences as for a clock to remark on not being wound up. No particular clock, Mrs Bread supposed, kept all the time, and no particular servant could enjoy all the sunshine diffused by the career of a universal master. She ventured nevertheless to express a modest hope that Newman meant to remain a while in Paris. He laid his hand on hers and shook it gently. 'I mean to remain for ever.'

He went after this to see Mrs Tristram, to whom he had telegraphed and who expected him. She looked at him a moment and shook her head. 'This won't do,' she said; 'you've come back too soon.' He sat down and asked about her husband and her children, enquired even for news of Miss Dora Finch. In the midst of this, 'Do you know where she is?' he abruptly demanded.

Mrs Tristram hesitated; of course he couldn't mean Miss Dora

Finch. Then she answered properly: 'She has gone to the other house—in the Rue d'Enfer.' But after he had gloomed a little longer she went on: 'You're not so good a man as I thought. You're more—you're more—'

'More what?'

'More unreconciled.'

'Good God!' he cried; 'do you expect me to forgive?'

'No, not that. I've not forgiven, so of course you can't. But you might magnificently forget. You've a worse temper about it than I should have expected. You look wicked—you look dangerous.'

'I may be dangerous,' he said 'but I'm not wicked. No, I'm not wicked.' And he got up to go. She asked him to come back to dinner, but he answered that he couldn't face a convivial occasion, even as a solitary guest. Later in the evening, if he should be able, he would look in.

He walked away through the city, beside the Seine and over it, and took the direction of the Rue d'Enfer. The day had the softness of early spring, but the weather was grey and humid. He found himself in a part of Paris that he little knew—a region of convents and prisons, of streets bordered by long dead walls and traversed by few frequenters. At the intersection of two of these streets stood the house of the Carmelites—a dull, plain edifice with a blank, high-shouldered defence all round. From without he could see its upper windows, its steep roof and its chimneys. But these things revealed no symptoms of human life; the place looked dumb, deaf, inanimate. The pale, dead, discoloured wall stretched beneath it far down the empty side-street—a vista without a human figure. He stood there a long time; there were no passers; he was free to gaze his fill. This seemed the goal of his journey; it was all he had come for. It was a strange satisfaction too, and yet it was a satisfaction; the barren still-ness of the place represented somehow his own release from inef-fectual desire. It told him the woman within was lost beyond recall, and that the days and years of the future would pile themselves above her like the huge immoveable slab of a tomb. These days and years, on this spot, would always be just so grey and silent. Suddenly from the thought of their seeing him stand there again the charm utterly departed. He would never stand there again; it was a sacrifice as sterile as her own. He turned away with a heavy heart, yet more dis-burdened than he had come.

Everything was over and he too at last could rest. He walked back through narrow, winding streets to the edge of the Seine and there he saw, close above him, high and mild and grey, the twin towers of Notre Dame.* He crossed one of the bridges and paused in the voided space that makes the great front clear; then he went in beneath the grossly-imaged portals. He wandered some distance up the nave and sat down in the splendid dimness. He sat a long time; he heard far-away bells chiming off into space, at long intervals, the big bronze syllables of the Word. He was very tired, but such a place was a kingdom of rest. He said no prayers; he had no prayers to say. He had nothing to be thankful for and he had nothing to ask; nothing to ask because now he must take care of himself. But a great church offers a very various hospitality, and he kept his place because while he was there he was out of the world. The most unpleasant thing that had ever happened to him had reached its formal conclusion; he had learnt his lesson—not indeed that he the least understood it—and could put away the book. He leaned his head for a long time on the chair in front of him; when he took it up he felt he was himself again. Somewhere in his soul a tight constriction had loosened. He thought of the Bellegardes; he had almost forgotten them. He remembered them as people he had meant to do something to. He gave a groan as he remembered what he had meant to do; he was annoyed, and yet partly incredulous, at his having meant to do it: the bottom suddenly had fallen out of his revenge. Whether it was Christian charity or mere human weakness of will—what it was, in the background of his spirit—I don't pretend to say; but Newman's last thought was that of course he would let the Bellegardes go. If he had spoken it aloud he would have said he didn't want to hurt them. He was ashamed of having wanted to hurt them. He quite failed, of a sudden, to recognise the fact of his having cultivated any such link with them. It was a link for themselves perhaps, their having so hurt *him*; but that side of it was now not his affair. At last he got up and came out of the darkening church; not with the elastic step of a man who has won a victory or taken a resolve—rather to the quiet measure of a discreet escape, of a retreat with appearances preserved.

Going home, he said to Mrs Bread that he must trouble her to put back his things into the portmanteau she had unpacked the evening before. It was therefore as if she had looked at him on this, through bedimmed eyes, with the consciousness of a value, so far as she could see, quite extravagantly wasted. 'Dear me, sir, I thought you said you were going to stay for ever.'

'Well, I guess I omitted a word. I meant I'm going to stay *away* for ever,' he was obliged a little awkwardly to explain. And since his departure from Paris on the following day he has certainly not returned. The gilded apartments I have so often spoken of stand ready to receive him, but they serve only as a spacious setting for Mrs Bread's solitary straightness, which wanders eternally from room to room, adjusting the tassels of the curtains, and keeps its wages, which are regularly brought in by a banker's clerk, in a great pink Sèvres vase on the drawing-room mantel-shelf.

Late in the evening Newman went to Mrs Tristram's and found the more jovial member of the pair by the domestic fireside. 'I'm glad to see you back in Paris,' this gentleman declared, 'for, you know, it's really the only place for a white man to live.' Mr Tristram made his friend welcome according to his own rosy light, and repaired in five minutes, with a free tongue, the too visible and too innocent deficiencies in Newman's acquaintance with current history. Then, having caused him to gape with strange information—all as to what had been going on in '*notre monde à nous*, you know'—Tristram got up to go and renew his budget at the club.

To this Newman replied that Mrs Tristram was *his* club and that he had never wanted a better: a statement he felt the truth of when he was presently alone with her and even—or perhaps all the more—when she asked him what he had done on leaving her in the afternoon. 'Well,' he then replied, 'I worked it off.'

'Worked off the afternoon?'

'Yes, and a lot of other troublesome stuff.'

'You struck me,' she confessed, 'as a man filled with some rather uncanny idea. I wondered if I were right to leave you so the prey of it, and whether I oughtn't to have had you followed and watched.'

This appeared to strike him with surprise. 'Surely I didn't look as if I wanted to take life.'

'I might have feared, if I had let myself go a little, that you were thinking of taking your own.'

He breathed a long sigh of such apparent indifference to his own as would have ruled that out. 'Well,' he none the less after a moment went on, 'I *have* got rid of about nine tenths of something that had become the biggest part of me. But I did that only by walking over to the Rue d'Enfer.'

'You've been then,' she stared, 'at the Carmelites?' And as he only met her eyes: 'Trying to scale the wall?'

'Well, I thought of that—I measured the wall. I looked at it a long time. But it's too high—it's beyond me.'

'That's right,' she said. 'Give it up.'

'I *have* given it up. But on the spot there I took it all in.'

She rested now her kindest eyes on him. 'On the spot then you didn't happen to meet M. de Bellegarde—also taking it all in? I'm told his sister's course doesn't suit him the least little bit.'

Newman had a moment's gravity of silence. 'No, luckily—I didn't meet either of *them*. In that case I *might* have fired.'

'Ah, it isn't that they've not been keeping quiet,' she said; 'I mean in the country, at—what's the name of the place?—Fleurières. They returned there at the time you left Paris, and have been spending the year far from human eye. The little Marquise must enjoy it; I expect to hear she has eloped with her daughter's music-master!'

Newman had gazed at the light wood-fire, and he listened to this with an apparent admission of its relevance; but he spoke in another sense. 'I mean never to mention the name of those people again and I don't want to hear anything more about them.' Then he took out his pocket-book and drew forth a scrap of paper. He looked at it an instant, after which he got up and stood by the fire. 'I'm going to burn them up. I'm glad to have you as a witness. There they go!' And he tossed the paper into the flame.

Mrs Tristram sat with her embroidery-needle suspended. 'What in the world is that?'

Leaning against the chimney-piece he seemed to grasp its ledge with force and to draw his breath a while in pain.* But presently he said: 'I can tell you now. It was a proof of a great infamy on the part of the Bellegardes—something that would damn them if ever known.'

She dropped her work with a reproachful moan. 'Ah, why didn't you show it to me?'

'I thought of showing it to you—I thought of showing it to every one. I thought of paying my debt to them that way. So I told them, and I guess I made them squirm. If they've been lying low it's because they haven't known what may happen. But, as I say, I've given up my idea.'

Mrs Tristram began to take slow stitches again. 'Wholly renounced it?'

'Wholly renounced it.'

'But your "proof",' she went on after a moment, 'what was it a proof *of*?'

'Oh, of an abomination not otherwise known.'

'An abomination?'

'An abomination.'

She hesitated but briefly. 'Something too bad to tell me?'

He considered. 'Yes, not good enough now.'

'Well,' she said, 'I'm sorry to have lost it. Your document,' she smiled, 'didn't look like much, but I should have liked immensely to see it. They've wronged me too, you know, as your sponsor and guarantee, and it would have served my revenge as well! How did you come,' she then asked, 'into possession of your knowledge?'

'It's a long story. But honestly at any rate.'

'And they knew you were master of it?'

'Oh, but rather!'

'Dear me, how interesting!' cried Mrs Tristram. 'And you humbled them at your feet?'

Newman was silent a little. 'No, not at all. They pretended not to care—not to be afraid. But I know they did care—they *were* afraid.'

'Are you very sure?'

He looked at her hard. 'Why, they fairly turned blue.'

She resumed her slow stitches. 'They defied you, eh?'

'They took the only tone they could. But I didn't think they took it very well.'

'You tried by the threat of exposure to make them come round?' Mrs Tristram pursued.

'Yes, but they wouldn't. I gave them their choice, and they chose to take their chance of bluffing off the charge and convicting me of fraud, that is of having procured and paid for a forgery. Forgery was of course their easy word—but words didn't, and don't, matter. They're as sick as a pair of poisoned cats—and I don't want any more "revenge".'

'It's most provoking,' she returned, 'to hear you talk of the "charge" when the charge is burned up. Is it quite consumed?' she asked, glancing at the fire. He assured her there was nothing left of it, and at this, dropping her embroidery, she got up and came near him. 'I needn't tell you at this hour how I've felt for you. But I like you as you are,' she said.

'As I am—?'

'As you are.' She stood before him and put out her hand as for his own, which he a little blankly let her take. 'Just exactly as you are,' she repeated. With which, bending her head, she raised his hand and very tenderly and beautifully kissed it. Then, 'Ah, poor Claire!'* she sighed as she went back to her place. It drew from him, while his flushed face followed her, a strange inarticulate sound, and this made her but say again: 'Yes, a thousand times—poor, poor Claire!'

APPENDIX 1

THE STAGE VERSIONS

AT the end of 1888 James received an invitation from the actor-manager Edward Compton to dramatize *The American* for him and his company. James recalled that he had once dreamed 'of doing something for the stage, for fame's sake, and art's, and fortune's', but he had practically given it up, 'overcome by the vulgarity, the brutality, the baseness of the English-speaking theatre today'. Yet he could always do with the money. Imagine what it might buy him in 'time, leisure, independence for "real literature"'. As one reads this, it is hard not to think of the Bellegardes failing to swallow their pride before the lure of Newman's lucre, and of their author in turn trying to go one better, or worse. 'Oh, how it must not be too good and how very bad it must be!' He would seek inspiration from the French dramatists whose slick work he'd admired at the Comédie Française, not for the first time, while he'd been writing the novel in Paris. '*À moi*, Scribe; *à moi*, Sardou; *à moi*, Dennery!'[1]

The stage version of *The American* opened in Stockport on 3 January 1891 and had some twenty-five performances in the provinces before a run in London at the Opera Comique Theatre in the Strand from 26 September to 3 December 1891.[2] It had, as they say, a mixed reception, and James never saw the money he dreamed of. Compton kept it going as he toured the provinces, and James rewrote the last act for performance in Bristol in November 1892. All along he had tried his best to make the play as 'bad' as he could to cater for the supposedly base tastes of his audiences. He had assumed from the start that it would need the happy ending for which so many first readers of the novel had clamoured. The German translation had actually provided one, to James's disgust, but now he followed suit, letting Newman have his cake and eat it by renouncing revenge *and* getting a wife. He made a number of changes in the course of the London run, allowing Valentin to die on stage for example. But there was always a problem with the final act, which was just not happy enough. So James had a final go, after London, sparing Valentin from death and rewriting Act IV 'in a comedy-sense—heaven forgive me' (p. 241). This was still not enough to save the play.

---

[1] *The Complete Notebooks of Henry James*, ed. Leon Edel and Lyall H. Powers (New York, 1987), 52–3.

[2] See the Editor's Foreword(s) to the text(s) of the play in *The Complete Plays of Henry James*, ed. Leon Edel (New York, 1990), 179–91, 241–2. All page references are to this edition.

For readers now it is a mild curiosity. It shows James dumbing down as hard as he could by playing up the melodrama for all it was worth. The critics, Edel says, 'were generally unanimous that the play was more melo-dramatic than the novel had warranted'; the London correspondent of the *New York Times* pronounced it 'a mass of bold melodrama' (p. 188). The Marquise de Bellegarde now turns out to have been the lover of the old Marquis to whom she has married off her daughter. It is Claire herself who persuades Newman to let the bad Bellegardes off the hook. Over-come by his magnanimity she gives up the idea of the convent and sur-renders herself to him instead, just in time for the curtain. There are all sorts of economies practised on plot and character, such as involve the Nioches introducing Newman to the Bellegardes through Valentin's interest in Noémie (reversing the case in the novel), and Lord Deepmere becoming Valentin's rival for the scheming Noémie as well as Newman's for the seraphic Claire.

Newman himself becomes as broad as James dare make him. His opening line, in response to Noémie's painting, becomes a repeated gag: 'That's just what I wanted to see!' James tried to coach Compton in the required American accent, and indicated in the script that 'want' should be pronounced as 'wauhnt', 'long' as 'lawng', 'God' as 'Gawd', and so on. But the following extracts indicate something of the difficulty he had in finding an effective stage language for Newman. This is what he sounds like as he 'breaks out' to Claire in Act II:

Listen to me, trust me—*I'll* check you through! I know you've seen me, as yet, comparatively little—so little that there may even be, to your mind, a kind of failure of respect, or at least of ceremony, in my breaking out this way. That's my mis-fortune; for I could almost have done so the first time I saw you. The fact is, there was no first time. I had seen you before—I had seen you always, in imagination, in secret ambitions; you seemed an old friend! I felt like that dear old boy Columbus (you know I'm named after him: it's a good omen!) when the ascertained fact bore out his general conclusions and he sighted the New World. Like him I had exer-cised our national genius (he must have bequeathed it to us!)—I had *calculated*. (p. 207)

'The ascertained fact bore out his general conclusions'?

Here he is at the showdown with Mme de Bellegarde (the two of them are alone):

Call back here this instant the woman you've wrenched out of my arms, recant your incantations and reverse your spells, and your congruous darkness may close round you again, never again to be disturbed. (p. 235)

'Congruous darkness'?

There are occasional hints of the kind of play this might have become had James found a dramatic language for the symbolic dimensions of the

House of Bellegarde. As for instance when Valentin declares of Newman, that 'he seemed to fling open the windows of this temple of staleness and stagnation—he laid the irrepressible ghost' (p. 204). And when Newman wonders to himself why Claire is so scared of her family: 'What have they done to make her tread the world on tiptoe, as if she were passing and repassing a death-chamber?' (p. 208) And when Claire tries to tell him why she must take refuge in the convent: 'My reason is all the past—the inseparable, irreparable past. It calls for me (*raising her hands to her head*)— it closes round me!' (p. 229) In the London production Claire was played by Elizabeth Robins. James had wanted her for the role after seeing her perform in Ibsen's *A Doll's House* and *Hedda Gabler*. Not all the critics liked her as Claire, precisely because she reminded them of Ibsen—or as the writer in the *Atlantic Monthly* put it, 'the hysterical manners of Ibsen's morbid heroines' (p. 189). But James might have done better to put *more* Ibsen into his play rather than less, or to have learned more from the dramatist to whom he would refer, with admiration, irritation and envy, as 'the Northern Henry'.

Several weeks into the London run James was still contemplating, despite all the 'vulgarities and pains', a continued assault on the theatre. But his real creative life lay elsewhere. He reminded himself (and one notes his recourse to that Ibsenite phrase of the 1890s, 'the joy of life'):

The consolation, the dignity, the joy of life are that discouragements and lapses, depressions and darknesses come to one only as one stands *without*—I mean without the luminous paradise of art. As soon as I really re-enter it—cross the loved threshhold—stand in the high chamber, and the gardens divine—the whole realm widens out again before me and around me—the air of life fills my lungs— the light of achievement flushes over all the place, and I believe, I see, I *do*.[3]

The paradise of art, the true realm within: these were not, for James at least, to be found in the theatre.

[3] *Complete Notebooks*, 61.

APPENDIX 2

THE REVISED VERSION FOR THE NEW YORK EDITION

As described in the Note on the Text, *The American* exists in several different versions but two main states, early and late.[1] There is no general agreement about which is the superior. This reflects differences of opinion about the merits of the New York Edition as a whole, and about the relative merits of the late James, the 'difficult' author of *The Wings of the Dove* and *The Golden Bowl*, as against the more accessible virtues of the early *Daisy Miller* and *Washington Square* and *The Portrait of a Lady* (albeit the admirers of this last may unwittingly know it in its later, revised form).[2]

As regards the two *Americans* this is quite as it should be. The texts have their independent identities, their characteristic features, their 'values' (in the painterly sense of which James was so fond). To take some famous examples by way of comparison, one may think of the different versions of Shakespeare's *King Lear* and Wordsworth's *The Prelude*, or Titian's *The Rape of Lucrece* and Delacroix's *The Death of Sardanapalus* (the earlier version of which James saw in Paris when he was writing this novel.)[3] To shift the figure from art to life, the two texts are as like and unlike each other as brothers, or even more simply, the same person at different ages.

Nevertheless, for an edition such as this one must choose between them, and my judgement here is for the later version, which is, by a paradox that James himself enjoyed, at once older and newer. This is not to say that it is necessarily wiser and fresher, but it does entail an increase in weight, depth, reach, and complexity. There remain good reasons for admiring the novel in its earlier and nimbler state, particularly if one is looking to its position in time in the late 1870s, and reflecting on the history of fictional forms and their relation to the world around them. John Carlos Rowe for example has written illuminatingly on Newman's innocence of the French

---

[1] The texts referred to in this Appendix are those of the first English edition of 1879 by Macmillan and the New York Edition of 1907; these are abbreviated to 'M' and 'NYE'. Page numbers refer to the present edition.

[2] For concerted recent accounts of the New York Edition, see Philip Horne, *Henry James and Revision: The New York Edition* (Oxford, 1990), and David McWhirter (ed.), *Henry James's New York Edition: The Construction of Authorship* (Stanford, Calif., 1995).

[3] See note on p. 49. James's comments on the painting can be found in his letter to the *New York Tribune* of 19 February 1876, reprinted in *Parisian Sketches*, ed. Leon Edel and Ilse Dusoir Lind (London, 1958), 72–3.

political situation in the late 1860s, just before the demise of the Second Empire, the Franco-Prussian War and the Commune (1870–1).[4] The first readers of this novel were close enough in time to these historical events to enjoy the possibility of a more sharply ironic relation to Newman than would later be the case. Edwin Sill Fussell points out how vividly the disasters of 1870–1 are deplored in the pages of Baedeker and Galignani, the guidebooks with which the tourists of the 1870s would have armed themselves.[5] Rowe is doubtless right that what he calls the 'political allegory' is more clearly seen in the earlier version.

However there are other political considerations that affect a choice between the versions. In 1962 Leon Edel felt it necessary to declare that James's portrait of an American was 'so rich in national ambiguities that several generations of readers have seen him largely as an expansive generous warm-hearted hero without sufficiently noticing that he embodies also everything that Henry disliked in the United States'.[6] Those generations of innocent readers were soon to wither from the face of the earth. 'Dislike' is a mild word for what a new generation of readers has come to feel for Christopher Newman—and sometimes for his author for failing to dislike him enough.

Three decades after Edel, Lewis O. Saum reflects on the alteration in readerly attitudes towards 'The American', or as he might also be known, 'The Westerner'. In 1877 he was still a Man of the Future, and he could continue to presume on the sympathetic interest of readers until they began to feel uncomfortable at the thought of aligning themselves with a super-rich white western male chauvinist capitalist. To most academic readers at least, Newman seems now to be an object of calumny, for the reasons that Saum suggests when he concludes: 'From being a prominent energizer of the American dream, a de-mythified West now serves frequently as a dark focal point of the bad dream from which we seek to awake. O, tempora; O, mores. Goodbye, Christopher Newman.'[7]

No amount of retouching can wholly save Newman—from his own attitude to women, for example. His dream of a lovely being to perch on his pile, as he puts it, will strike the enlightened reader as at best deplorable. But revision attenuates and mitigates many of his obnoxious features when it does not entirely purge them, and he undoubtedly emerges less crass, brash, boorish, and shallow (and therefore of course, one might well say,

[4] John Carlos Rowe, 'The Politics of Innocence in Henry James' *The American*', in Martha Banta (ed.), *New Essays on the American* (Cambridge, 1987), 69–98.

[5] Edwin Sill Fussell, *The French Side of Henry James* (New York, 1990), 27–32.

[6] Leon Edel, *Henry James: The Conquest of London, 1870–1883* (London, 1962), 250.

[7] Lewis O. Saum, 'Henry James's Christopher Newman: "The American" as Westerner', *Henry James Review*, 15 (1994), 9.

more dangerous). He reflects more intelligently on the world around him, he is quicker on the uptake and slower to trust his first impulse, he imagines more actively how others may think of him and feel about him. It is hard to agree with William W. Stowe when he justifies his decision to use the later version—a choice he significantly calls 'eccentric'—on the grounds that 'James' perception of Newman as an inept interpreter is clearer in the 1907 New York Edition'.[8] Though this seems to me an eccentric judgement, Stowe's motive coincides with the dominant trend. Despite a claim that the 1907 text 'continues to have its champions', all five contributors to the important volume of *New Essays on the American*, edited by Martha Banta (Cambridge, 1987), choose the earlier version. To put it bluntly, literary critics now queue up to give Newman a good mugging for all sorts of ineptness and worse. They might do better to pit themselves, if a good fight is what they want, against the distinctly more substantial antagonist that is the later Newman.

The differences between the two versions are so considerable that it is here only feasible to offer a frankly tendentious account with some samples. The following summary of some salient features of the later version seeks to understand and explain what the revising James thought he was doing.

Of the general features of James's revision, one of the most important is the attention he gives to the quality of speech, its dramatic force and pitch and intonation. So that instead of the stiff little phrases 'he said' and 'she said', we get 'Newman's hostess wound up', or 'he patiently answered', or 'his friend sagaciously returned', or 'she safely enough risked'. These forms are sometimes dropped in favour of expressive physical gesture or posture, either introducing an utterance, as for instance 'Madame de Cintré turned on him again her soft lustre', or simply, 'Newman thought', or succeeding it, as in, 'She gave, still with her charming eyes on him, the slowest, gentlest headshake.'

We also find an immense number of little alterations to the identification of characters by name. There is a movement towards informality, most obviously in the relations between Newman and Valentin, who regularly becomes 'Valentin' rather than 'Bellegarde'. But there is also a consistent replacement of names by forms of words describing characters' relations to each other, so that 'Valentin' becomes 'his companion' or 'his guest', 'Madame de Bellegarde' turns into 'his hostess, if she might be so called', 'Newman' is amended to 'her generous patron' (that is, Noémie's). Instead of the 'Madame de Bellegarde' whom Mrs Bread goes back to see for her final rupture, it is 'her old dread mistress'. A related step is for characters to be identified simply by the pronouns 'he' and 'she' rather

[8] William W. Stowe, *Balzac, James, and the Realistic Novel* (Princeton, 1983), 182.

than by their proper names. When a novelist gives a character his or her formal name, we look at them from more of a distance, as if we might need to be reminded who they are. The substitution of pronouns assumes the reader's understanding of who is who, but it also serves to involve us in the illusion of live dramatic action, such as the recourse to names and titles—'the Marquise de Bellegarde', 'Christopher Newman'—inevitably tends to stiffen. This is a frequent move here in James's revision (as it is in his later novels more generally). It means that when he *does* then have recourse to a formal name, it has all the more sharp an effect of marking a distance between characters, or between reader and character.

There is a small number of revisions to what can be called matters of fact. Amongst these we should probably not count the 'roast dog' Newman claims to have eaten in a gold-digger's camp which turns into a 'boiled cat'. (James liked dogs.) It is more certain that Newman's age has crept up from 36 to 42 and a half, and Claire's from 25 to 28. One important consequence of Newman's new age is that he has now made his money *before* the Civil War. In 1879 he comes out of the war as penniless as he goes in, whereas now his interests are waiting for him (p. 33). By making Newman's money 'older', James alleviates some of the stigma associated with the quick fortunes made in the post-war years. There has been some predictable inflation. Newman was going to revenge himself on a business rival by thwarting him of $60,000 (M); this swells to 'a matter of half a million' (NYE, p. 36).

The later Newman is in all sorts of ways made more sensitive. 'I am not intellectual' (M) becomes 'I don't come up to my own standard of culture' (NYE, p. 45); and 'I am a highly civilised man' (M) becomes 'I have the instincts—have them deeply—if I haven't the forms of a high old civilisation' (NYE, p. 45). As he waits for Clàire the early Newman just takes up her books, while the later one does so with an added 'vibration of tact in his long and strong fingers' (NYE, p. 176). His hands also come into play when he takes his leave of the Bellegardes at the end of chapter 6. Instead of simply departing, he more civilly shakes hands all round before firmly marching away (NYE, p. 96). Shortly before this James cuts a substantial passage of dialogue in which Newman's eagerness gets the better of his manners, as he himself partly realizes:

'Mrs Tristram told you the literal truth,' he went on; 'I want very much to know you. I didn't come here simply to call to-day; I came in the hope that you might ask me to come again.'

'Oh, pray come often,' said Madame de Cintré.

'But will you be at home?' Newman insisted. Even to himself he seemed a trifle 'pushing', but he was, in truth, a trifle excited. (M)

His later manners are more delicate, hesitant, apprehensive. 'Anxious' and 'anxiety' are words with which he is frequently credited. When Claire admits that she knows she has done him great wrong in breaking her word, his response runs the risk of seeming superficial: ' "Oh, it's a great step forward!" said Newman, with a gracious smile of encouragement.' (M) In 1907 the smile changes more than his words, for he now replies 'with a fixed and ah—as he even himself felt—such an anxious smile of encouragement' (NYE, p. 278).

He is less confident in his innocence of the strange social world into which he has strayed. Compare these reactions to the Marquis de Bellegarde's announcement of his belief 'in the divine right of Henry of Bourbon, Fifth of his name, to the throne of France'.

Newman stared, and after this he ceased to talk politics with M. de Bellegarde. He was not horrified nor scandalised, he was not even amused; he felt as he should have felt if he had discovered in M. de Bellegarde a taste for certain oddities of diet; an appetite, for instance, for fishbones or nutshells. Under these circumstances, of course, he would never have broached dietary questions with him. (M)

This had in truth, upon Newman, as many successive distinct effects as the speaker could conceivably have desired. It made him in the first place look at the latter very hard, harder than he had ever done before; which had the appearance somehow of affording M. de Bellegarde another of the occasions he personally appreciated. It was as if he had never yet shown how he could return such a look; whereby, producing that weapon of his armoury, he made the demonstration brilliant. Then he reduced his guest, further, just to staring with a conscious, foolish failure of every resource, at one of the old portraits on the wall, out of which some dim light for him might in fact have presently glimmered. Lastly it determined on Newman's part a wise silence as to matters he didn't understand. He relapsed, to his own sense, into silence very much as he would have laid down, on consulting it by mistake, some flat-looking back-number or some superseded time-table. It might do for the 'collection' craze but wouldn't do for use. (NYE, p. 176)

Or consider the more complex sense of triumph with which he escorts Mrs Tristram through the Bellegardes' rooms, on the occasion of their grand party:

He led Mrs Tristram through all the rooms. There were a great many of them, and, decorated for the occasion and filled with a stately crowd, their somewhat tarnished nobleness recovered its lustre. Mrs Tristram, looking about her, dropped a series of softly-incisive comments upon her fellow-guests. But Newman made vague answers; he hardly heard her; his thoughts were elsewhere. They were lost in a cheerful sense of success, of attainment and victory. His momentary care as to whether he looked like a fool passed away, leaving him simply with a rich contentment. He had got what he wanted. The savour of success had always been highly agreeable to him, and it had been his fortune to know it often. But it had never before been so sweet, been associated with so much that was brilliant and suggestive and entertaining. The lights, the flowers, the music, the crowd, the splendid women, the jewels, the strangeness even of the universal murmur of a clever foreign tongue, were all a vivid symbol and assurance of his having grasped his purpose and forced along his groove. If Newman's smile was larger than usual, it was not tickled vanity that pulled the strings; he had no wish to be shown with the finger or to achieve a personal success. If he could have looked down at the scene, invisible, from a hole in the roof, he would have enjoyed it quite as much. It would have spoken to him about his own prosperity and deepened that easy feeling about life to which, sooner or later, he made all experience contribute. Just now the cup seemed full. (M)

He led Mrs Tristram from one room to another, where, scattering wide glances and soft, sharp comments, she reminded him of the pausing wayfarer who studies the contents of the confectioner's window, with platonic discriminations, through a firm plate of glass. But he made vague answers; he scarcely heard her; his thoughts were elsewhere. They were lost in the vastness of this attested truth of his having come out where he wanted. His momentary consciousness of perhaps too broad a grin passed away, and he felt, the next thing, almost solemnly quiet. Yes, he had 'got there', and now it was, all-powerfully, to stay. These prodigies of gain were in a general way familiar to him, but the sense of what he had 'made' by an anxious operation had never been so deep and sweet. The lights, the flowers, the music, the 'associations', vague and confused to him, yet hovering like some odour of dried spices, something faraway and, as he had hinted to the Marquis, Mongolian; the splendid women, the splendid jewels, the strangeness even of the universal sense of a tongue that seemed the language of society as Italian was the language of opera: these things were all a gage of his having worked, from the old first years, under some better star than he knew. Yet if he showed again and again so many of his fine strong teeth, it was not tickled vanity that pulled the exhibition-string: he had not wish to be pointed at with the finger or to be considered by these people for himself. If he could have looked down at the scene invisibly, as from a hole in the roof, he would have enjoyed it quite as much. It would have spoken to him of his energy and prosperity and deepened that view of his effective 'handling' of life to which, sooner or later, he made all

experience contribute. Just now the cup
seemed full. (NYE, pp. 223–4)

Newman is made generally quicker on the uptake. When M. Nioche
appeals to him to respect his daughter's 'innocence', both Newmans, we
are told, 'had wondered what was coming', but while one 'at this broke
into a laugh' (M), the other, fractionally swifter, 'had already burst into
mirth' (NYE, p. 64). Newman's French has advanced more rapidly, so that
instead of saying merely 'Come . . . let us begin', he can now playfully
invoke the opening words of the Marseillaise. He becomes generally
wittier. When Mrs Tristram hopes he'll cut the knot or untie it, instead
of simply avowing ' "I am sure I shall never fumble over it" ' (M), he more
sportively exclaims, ' "Oh, if ever there's a big knot", he returned—"and
they all seem knots of ribbon over here—I shall simply pull it off and wear
it!" ' (NYE, p. 46). He is given some more American colloquialisms, such
as 'Hang it then', 'Where are you hanging out?', and 'I really kind of pine
for a mate'.

Newman's antagonists, the old Marquise and her elder son Urbain, are
made even more formidable and sinister. The atmosphere in which the old
lady first receives Newman furtively darkens from 'The room was illumined' (M) to 'The dimness was diminished' (NYE, p. 133). In 1879 she
shakes his hand and in 1907 she refuses to do so, but on *both* occasions she
does so 'with a sort of British positiveness which reminded him that she
was the daughter of the Earl of St Dunstans' (p. 133). Newman thinks
that the Marquise resembles her daughter, 'and yet she was utterly unlike
her' (M), or rather, 'as an insect might resemble a flower' (NYE, p. 134).
Both Newmans are peculiarly repelled by her mouth, 'that conservative
orifice'. The early Newman only hears the word with which she refuses
his suit, but the later one takes in something more. This is a general truth
about the 1907 text, that we hear not just what people say but the way they
say it, so that much more than words seems to pass between them:

'Favour it?' Madame de Bellegarde | Madame de Bellegarde looked at him
looked at him a moment then shook his | hard and shook her head. Then her so
head. 'No!' she said softly. (M) | peculiarly little mouth rounded itself to
 | a 'No!' which she seemed to blow at him
 | as for a mortal chill. (NYE, p. 143)

The mortal chill induced by her elder son, Urbain, also gets more fully
registered. ' "He's the old woman at second-hand", Newman said to
himself, as he returned M. de Bellegarde's greeting.' (M) Newman's
thought is preserved, but the reflection is coloured by an additional
sense—'the sense of having his health drunk from an empty glass' (NYE,

p. 137). Or again, we are given an added little glimpse of the effect of Urbain's smile: 'and he went through that odd dim form of a smile that affected his guest as the scraping of a match that doesn't light' (NYE, p. 160). Such resourcefully comical figures of speech are new gifts in Newman—donated of course by author to character, but shared in the telling between them. Compare:

but the Marquis seemed neither more nor less frigidly grand than usual (M)	but if the Marquis had been ruffled he stepped all the more like some high-crested though distinctly domestic fowl who had always the alternative of the perch. (NYE, pp. 164–5).

Or this, of the Marquise, a moment later:

and in this position she stood a moment, holding her head high and biting her small under-lip. (M)	and in this position she stood a moment, bridling, almost quivering, causing her ornaments, her earrings and brooches and buckles, somehow doubly to twinkle, and pursing, as from simple force of character, her portentous little mouth. (NYE, p. 165)

James also gives more substance to the whole social order represented by the Bellegardes, and to Newman's correspondingly enriched but confused sense of it, as here for instance, in a description of some of the guests at the grand evening party:

They were elderly gentlemen, of what Valentin de Bellegarde had designated as the high-nosed category; two or three of them wore cordons and stars. They approached with measured alertness, and the marquise said that she wished to present them to Mr Newman, who was going to marry her daughter. (M)	They were elderly gentlemen with faces as marked and featured and filled-in, for some science of social topography, as, to Newman's whimsical sense, any of the little towered and battered old towns, on high eminences, that his tour of several countries during the previous summer had shown him; they were adorned with strange insignia, cordons and ribbons and orders, as if the old cities were flying flags and streamers and hanging out shields for a celebration, and they approached with measured alertness while the Marquise presented them the good friend of the family who was to marry her daughter. (NYE, p. 217)

Newman's ability to read the social text in front of him has developed new resources. But this text has deepened, and it still exceeds his grasp, as a further look at the Bellegardes' guests reveals:

It is a pity, nevertheless, that Newman had not been a physiognomist, for a great many of the faces were irregularly agreeable, expressive, and suggestive. (M)

It was a pity for our friend, nevertheless, that he had not been a physiognomist, for these mobile masks, much more a matter of wax than of bronze, were the picture of a world and the vivid translation, as might have seemed to him, of a text that had had otherwise its obscurities. (NYE, p. 219)

'Might have', we note—but did not. What had earlier been a brute deficiency in Newman becomes now more of a missed opportunity.

The revising James also took a lot of pains over the confrontations Newman has with the Bellegardes, at Fleurières and in the Parc Monceau. In the former the Bellegardes no longer flatly deny Newman's story that the dying Valentin denounced them, and the Marquise in particular behaves with even more formidable dignity:

The marquise gathered herself together majestically. 'This is too gross!' she cried. 'We decline to accept your story, sir—we repudiate it. Urbain, open the door.' (M)

The Marquise wrapt herself for a minute in a high aloofness so entire, so of her whole being, as he could feel, that she fairly appeared rather to contract than to expand with the intensity and dignity of it; and out of the heart of this withdrawn extravagance her final estimate of their case sounded clear. 'To have broken with you, sir, almost consoles me; and you can judge how much that says! Urbain, open the door.' (NYE, pp. 293–4)

Even more than the coldness of the Bellegardes, the revised version stresses their impenetrably smooth surfaces. When Urbain's composure trembles in the balance, James forgoes 'the breaking up of the ice in his handsome countenance' (M), in favour of this, which recalls amongst other things the 'dark oaken floor polished like a mirror', in the room that has just before witnessed Newman's last meeting with Claire: 'Urbain's face looked to him now like a mirror, very smooth fine glass, breathed upon and blurred; but what he would have liked still better to see was a spreading, disfiguring crack' (NYE, p. 295). He does see 'something of that', but it is a measure of Bellegarde's resistance that—like his mother—whereas in 1879 he 'gave a shrug', his shoulders now 'declined even a shrug' (NYE, p. 295).

There are comparable amendments to the dramatic confrontation in the Parc Monceau. James renews the 'Gothic' atmosphere created by Mrs Bread with a touch of Poe, when he makes the Marquis give 'a hiss that fairly evoked for our friend some vision of a hunched back, an erect tail and a pair of shining evil eyes' (NYE, p. 330). And instead of going 'fixed and dead' (M), the eyes of the old Marquise fasten on Newman, the eyes that 'might well have been, he recognised, those with which, according to Mrs Bread, she had done her husband to death' (NYE, p. 330). There is even more emphasis on Madame de Bellegarde's self-possession, but there is an added dimension to Newman's curiosity about its sources, his reluctant admiration for it, even perhaps envy.

Her self-possession continued to be extraordinary. (M)	Her coolness continued to affect him as consummate; he wondered of what alarms, what effronteries, what suspicions and what precautions she had not had, from far back, to make her life. (NYE, p. 333)

This is his last sight of her; the old lady, we note, is accorded the respect of her title.

The old lady stooped and kissed her grandchild. 'Damn it, she *is* plucky!' said Newman, and he walked home with a slight sense of being balked. She was so inexpressively defiant! (M)	The Marquise stooped and kissed her grandchild. 'Damn it, she *is* plucky!' he sighed; and he walked home with a sense of having been almost worsted. She was so quite heroically impenetrable. (NYE, p. 334)

Other eyes are important apart from those of the Medusa Marquise. Instead of being 'brilliant and mild' (M), Claire's eyes become, the narrator repeats talismanically, 'intense and mild' (NYE). The more intimate bond between narrator and character is confirmed by the later Newman's repetition of this phrase, as if one of them has overheard the other. When he asks Mrs Tristram about Claire, instead of 'And how were those eyes?' (M), his words are now 'And how were those intense mild eyes?' (NYE, p. 85). Revisions to the formal description of Claire diminish and destabilize the solidity of her independent existence; we see her more through the eyes and mind of the observing Newman.

Her clear gray eyes were strikingly expressive; they were both gentle and intelligent, and Newman liked them	Her wide grey eyes were like a brace of deputed and garlanded maidens waiting with a compliment at the gate

immensely; but they had not those depths of splendour—those many-coloured rays—which illumine the brow of famous beauties. Madame de Cintré was rather thin, and she looked younger than she probably was. In her whole person there was something both youthful and subdued, slender and yet ample, tranquil yet shy; a mixture of immaturity and repose, of innocence and dignity. (M)

of a city, but they failed of that lamp-like quality and those many-coloured fires that light up, as in a constant celebration of anniversaries, the fair front of the conquering type. Madame de Cintré was of attenuated substance and might pass for younger than she probably was. In her whole person was something still young and still passive, still uncertain and that seemed still to expect to depend, and which yet made, in its dignity, a presence withal, and almost represented, in its serenity, an assurance. (NYE, pp. 93–4)

There is very extensive revision to the passage at the start of chapter 13, which describes the state of Newman's mind and heart over the six weeks of his courtship. The 'intense all-consuming tenderness' he feels is unchanged and its object remains a woman 'extraordinarily graceful and delicate', but whereas she was once 'impressive' (M), she is now 'insidiously agitating' (NYE, p. 169). James carves out much more inner space for Newman, and fills it with more apprehension: 'He was in truth infinitely anxious, and, when he questioned his anxiety, knew it was not all for himself' (NYE, p. 169). This Newman tries to think of Claire and for her as well as for himself. The following is a representative kind of expansion:

She was a woman for the light, not for the shade; and her natural line was not picturesque reserve and mysterious melancholy, but frank, joyous, brilliant action, with just so much meditation as was necessary and not a grain more. To this, apparently, he had succeeded in bringing her back. He felt, himself, that he was an antidote to oppressive secrets; what he offered her was, in fact, above all things a vast sunny immunity from the need of having any. (M)

She was a creature for the sun and the air, for no sort of hereditary shade or equivocal gloom; and her natural line was neither imposed reserve nor mysterious melancholy, but positive life, the life of the great world—*his* great world, not the *grand monde* as there understood if he wasn't mistaken, which seemed squeezeable into a couple of rooms of that inconvenient and ill-warmed house: all with nothing worse to brood about, when necessary, than the mystery perhaps of the happiness that would so queerly have come to her. To some perception of his view and his judgement, and of the patience with which he was prepared to insist on them, he fondly believed himself to be day by day bringing her round. She mightn't, she couldn't yet, no doubt,

wholly fall in with them, but she saw, he
made out, that he had built a bridge
which would bear the very greatest
weight she would throw on it, and it was
for him often, all charmingly, as if she
were admiring from this side and that
the bold span of arch and the high line
of the parapet—as if indeed on occasion she stood straight there at the
spring, just watching him at *his* extremity and with nothing, when the hour
should strike, to prevent her crossing
with a rush. (NYE, pp. 172–3)

The bridge that Newman is here imagining reflects on the confession
James makes in his Preface, that as regards Claire, 'a light plank, too light
a plank is laid for the reader over a dark "psychological" abyss'. James
makes some efforts to reduce the implausibility, as he sees it, of Newman's
failure to spend more time with her after the 'engagement party'. To this
end he makes some extensive revisions to the interview Newman has with
Claire, just after she has seen her brother Valentin, though she doesn't
know it, for the last time. Again Newman is made prey to additional
'worry'.

In the afternoon Newman called upon
Madame de Cintré, but his visit was
brief. She was as gracious and sympathetic as he had ever found her, but she
was sad, and she confessed, on
Newman's charging her with her red
eyes, that she had been crying. . . .
Newman, of course, was perforce
tongue-tied about Valentin's projected
duel, and his dramatic talent was not
equal to satirising Madame de Cintré's
presentiment as pointedly as perfect
security demanded. (M)

In the afternoon Newman called on
Madame de Cintré for the single daily
hour of reinvoked and reasserted confidence—a solemnity but the more
exquisite with repetition—to which she
had, a little strangely, given him to
understand it was convenient, important, in fact vital to her, that their communion, for their strained interval,
should be restricted, even though this
reduced him for so many other recurrent hours, the hours of evening in particular, the worst of the probation, to
the state of a restless, prowling, time-
keeping ghost, a taker of long night-
walks through streets that affected him
at moments as the alleys of a great darkened bankrupt bazaar. But his visit to-
day had a worry to reckon with—all the
more that it had as well so much of one
to conceal. She shone upon him, as
always, with that light of her gentleness

which might have been figured, in the
heat-thickened air, by a sultry harvest-
moon; but she was visibly bedimmed,
and she confessed, on his charging her
with her red eyes, that she had been,
for a vague, vain reason, crying them
half out. . . . Newman was of course
tongue-tied on what he himself knew,
and, his power of simulation and his
general art of optimism breaking
down on this occasion as if some long
needle-point had suddenly passed, to
make him wince, through the sole
crevice of his armour, he could, to his
high chagrin, but cut his call short.
(NYE, pp. 244–5).

But in terms of Newman's relations with other characters it is the
quality of his friendship with Valentin that enjoys the most significant
rethinking. Early on a dry comment of Valentin's that is followed by 'murmured the young man' (M) modulates into 'the young man returned in a
tone that Newman thought lovely' (NYE, p. 95). This sets the tone for his
warmer appreciation of the young Count. Valentin's admiration for
Newman is also more fulsome. Compare these responses to Newman's
declaration that he never quarrels.

'Never? Sometimes it's a duty—or at
least it's a pleasure. Oh, I have had two
or three delicious quarrels in my day!'
and M. de Bellegarde's handsome smile
assumed, at the memory of these incidents, an almost voluptuous intensity.
(M)

'You mean you just shoot? Well, I notify
you that *till* I'm shot,' his visitor
declared, 'I shall have had a greater
sense of safety with you than I have
perhaps ever known in any relation of
life. And as a sense of danger is clearly
a thing impossible to *you*, we shall
therefore be all right.' (NYE, p. 101)

Both men are relieved of a certain complacency. The early Newman is at
times insufferably condescending towards the younger man. Instead of
telling Claire that 'He's a noble little fellow' (M), he roundly affirms 'I just
love him, you know, and I regard him as perfectly straight' (NYE, p. 124).
The obnoxious note struck by the following sentence simply disappears:
'Bellegarde did not in the least cause him to modify his needful premise
that all Frenchmen are of a frothy and imponderable substance; he simply
reminded him that light materials may be beaten up into a most agreeable
compound' (M). From the start the two men minister to much more than
each other's amusement. Valentin is less frothy and more ponderable, as

witness the disappearance of passages such as the following which depicts
his light-hearted reaction to Newman's plan to woo Claire.

'It will be more than amusing', said Bellegarde; 'it will be inspiring. I look at it
from my point of view, and you from yours. After all, anything for a change! And
only yesterday I was yawning so as to dislocate my jaw, and declaring that there
was nothing new under the sun! If it isn't new to see you come into the family as
a suitor, I am very much mistaken. Let me say that, my dear fellow; I won't call it
anything else, bad or good; I will simply call it *new*.' And overcome with a sense of
the novelty thus foreshadowed, Valentin de Bellegarde threw himself into a deep
armchair before the fire, and with a fixed intense smile, seemed to read a vision of
it in the flame of the logs. After a while he looked up. 'Go ahead, my boy; you have
my good wishes,' he said. (M)

The changes to Valentin are partly responsible for some changes to
Noémie Nioche. She too becomes less frivolous, less cheap. She is not so
often called 'young' and 'little', and generally suffers less condescension,
both from the characters and the narrator. This sort of sentence of
Valentin's gets cut: 'I see she is a vulgar little wretch, after all. But she is
as amusing as ever, and one *must* be amused' (M). Just as Valentin and
Newman become less simply amusing to each other, so too does Noémie
become, for both men, a more serious quantity, as James might have said.
The interest she incites in Valentin is still of course sexual, but the disappearance of this paragraph from the scene of their first meeting makes
it less crude:

Valentin took advantage of her downcast eyes to telegraph again to his companion.
He renewed his mysterious physiognomical play, making at the same time a tremu-
lous movement in the air with his fingers. He was evidently finding Mademoiselle
Noémie extremely interesting; the blue devils had departed, leaving the field clear.
(M)

Instead Valentin simply looks at Newman 'with eyes of rich meaning'
(NYE, p. 148), and again, when Noémie draws the red cross on her painting, instead of Valentin indulging 'in another flash of physiognomical eloquence' (M), we are more quietly told that 'The two men looked at each
other, Valentin as with vivid intelligence' (NYE, p. 149). Valentin's passion
is given more of an edge—or more teeth, one might say, as he thinks
himself, in a distinctly post-1890s' idiom, of 'a pretty panther who has
every one of her claws in your flesh and who's in the act of biting your
heart out' (NYE, p. 211). The early Valentin calls her 'a frightful little
monster!' (M); the later one, 'a beautiful little monster!' (NYE, p. 212).

The aftermath of his fatal first encounter with her entails some massive
additions to the end of chapter 11. There is a surge of interest on James's
part in the effect of Noémie on the relations between Newman and
Valentin—and an expansion of Newman's feelings about her father, M.

Nioche. The passage deals with Newman's desire to save both these men, and an idea of their honour. Here for example is a telling addition which tries to explain Newman's need to defend M. Nioche's honour from Valentin's imputations:

He was, to an extent he never fully revealed, a collector of impressions as romantically concrete, even when profane, as the blest images and sanctified relics of one of the systematically devout, and he at bottom liked as little to hear anything he had picked up with the hand of spirit pronounced unauthentic. (NYE, p. 151)

But it is Valentin who inspires a wholly new passage of dialogue, and of reflective, anxious, resigned emotions in Newman:

The grace of him, of Valentin, was all precious, the growth of him all fortunate, the quantity of him elsewhere all doubtless limited. 'I *might* perhaps have been a factor in that young lady's moral future,' Newman presently said—'but I don't come in now. And evidently,' he added, 'you've no room for me in yours.' (NYE, p. 153)

When Valentin tells Newman, at the end of chapter 12, that Noémie has left her father's protection and so given him licence to pursue her, the tone of the exchange between them is significantly altered.

'I suppose that now you will raise your protest?'

'My protest be hanged!' murmured Newman, disgustedly.

But his tone found no echo in that in which Valentin, with his hand on the door, to return to his mother's apartment, exclaimed: 'But I shall see her now! She is very remarkable—she is very remarkable!' (M)

'I suppose', he wound up, 'that I may now cease so elaborately to neglect her?'

Newman, struggling up out of intenser inward visions, listened as he could, and then, having listened, remained with his eyes on his friend's face. 'It would do you good to fall in love. You want it badly,' he at last remarked.

'Well, that's perhaps exactly what, according to my perpetual happy instinct, I'm now trying to do!'

'Oh hell!' said our hero impatiently as he broke away again. (NYE, p. 168)

Note that it is impatience now rather than disgust.

The disgust of the later Newman is roused rather by the duel into which Valentin is lured. There are very considerable differences in the dialogue the two men share the evening before Valentin's departure.

'Do you call this sort of thing satisfaction?' Newman asked.

'Does it satisfy you to receive a present of the carcass of that coarse fop? does it gratify you to make him a present

'Do you call this sort of thing satisfaction?' Newman groaned. 'Does it satisfy you to put yourself at the disposal of a bigger fool even than yourself? I'd see him somewhere first! Does

of yours? If a man hits you, hit him back; if a man libels you, haul him up.'

'Haul him up, into court? Oh, that is very nasty!' said Valentin.

'The nastiness is his—not yours. And for that matter, what you are doing is not particularly nice. You are too good for it. I don't say you are the most useful man in the world, or the cleverest, or the most amiable. But you are too good to go and get your throat cut for a prostitute.'

Valentin flushed a little, but he laughed. 'I shan't get my throat cut if I can help it. Moreover, one's honour hasn't two different measures. It only knows that it is hurt; it doesn't ask when, or how, or where.'

'The more fool it is!' said Newman.

Valentin ceased to laugh; he looked grave. 'I beg you not to say any more,' he said. 'If you do I shall almost fancy you don't care about—about—'—and he paused.

'About what?'

'About that matter—about one's honour.'

'Fancy what you please,' said Newman. 'Fancy while you are at it that I care about *you*—though you are not worth it. But come back without damage,' he added in a moment, 'and I will forgive you. And then,' he continued, as Valentin was going: 'I will ship you straight off to America.' 'Well,' answered Valentin, 'if I am to turn over a new page, this may figure as a tail-piece to the old.' And then he lit another cigar and departed.

'Blast that girl!' said Newman, as the door closed upon Valentin. (M)

it satisfy you that he should set up this ridiculous relation with *you*? I'd like to see him try anything of the sort with *me*! If a man has a bad intention on you it's his own affair till it takes effect; but when it does, give him one in the eye. If you don't know *how* to do that—straight—you're not fit to go round alone. But I'm talking of those who claim they *are*, and that they don't require some one to take care of them.'

'Well,' Valentin smiled, 'it would be interesting truly to go round with *you*. But to get the full good of that, alas, I should have begun earlier!'

Newman could scarcely bear even the possible pertinence of his 'alas'. 'See here,' he said at the last: 'if any one ever hurts you again—!'

'Well, *mon bon*?'—and Valentin, with his eyes on his friend's, might now have been much moved.

'Come straight to me about it. *I'll* go for him.'

'*Matamore!*' the young man laughed as they parted. (NYE, pp. 246–7)

Finally, as one might expect, Valentin's deathbed rouses in Newman a more plangent rhetoric. It is not clear whether he is thinking mainly of the loss of Claire when he reflects on 'his own situation', or of the loss, as now seems inevitable, of both the sister and brother. In 1907 the cumulative force of his love for Valentin makes the latter seem more likely.

What had happened to him seemed to have, in its violence and audacity, the force of a real calamity—the strength and insolence of Destiny herself. It was unnatural and monstrous, and he had no arms against it. (M)	What had happened to him was violent and insolent, like all great strokes of evil; unnatural and monstrous, it showed the hard hand of the Fate that rejoices in the groans and the blood of men, in the tears and the terrors of women, and he had no arms against it. (NYE, p. 265)

There is a good deal of revision in the final phase of the novel, as Newman takes stock of what he has been through. There are additions which characterize the sense of his loss: 'He had yet held in his cheated arms, he felt, the full experience, and when he closed them together round the void that was all they now possessed, he might have been some solitary spare athlete practising restlessly in the corridor of the circus' (NYE, p. 353). And he relives with a new sense of self-justification the impression he made on the Bellegardes who have left his arms empty.

If he had been too commercial, he was ready to forget it, for in being so he had done no man any wrong that might not be as easily forgotten. He reflected with sober placidity that at least there were no monuments of his 'meanness' scattered about the world. (M)	He believed there had been as few reflexions of his smugness caught during all those weeks in the high polish of surrounding surfaces as there were monuments of his meanness scattered about the world. (NYE, p. 354)

The narrator enriches an allusion which associates him with Othello's desolation (see note to p. 356):

He had nothing to do, his occupation was gone, and it seemed to him that he should never find it again. (M)	He had nothing to do, his occupation was gone, had simply strayed and lost itself in the great desert of life. (NYE, p. 356)

And the bells of Notre Dame say something more to him.

He sat a long time; he heard far-away bells, chiming off, at long intervals, to the rest of the world. He was very tired; this was the best place he could be in. (M)	He sat a long time; he heard far-away bells chiming off into space, at long intervals, the big bronze syllables of the Word. He was very tired, but such a place was a kingdom of rest. (NYE, p. 359)

He recognizes that now 'he could close the book and put it away' (M), or to make a nice distinction between learning a lesson and understanding it, 'he had learnt his lesson—not indeed that he the least understood it—and could put away the book' (NYE, p. 359). This is his own thought, be it noted, not the narrator's judgement on him. Meanwhile the narrator memorably refuses to say why exactly it is that Newman decides to let the Bellegardes go.

Whether it was Christian charity or unregenerate good nature—what it was, in the background of his soul—I don't pretend to say. (M)	Whether it was Christian charity or mere human weakness of will—what it was in the background of his spirit—I don't pretend to say. (NYE, p. 359)

The extensive revisions to the final scene with Mrs Tristram, in which Newman burns the incriminating paper, and in particular the closing paragraph, have attracted a good deal of attention. Here are the respective endings.

'Is it quite consumed?' she asked, glancing at the fire. Newman assured her that there was nothing left of it. 'Well then,' she said, 'I suppose there is no harm in saying that you probably did not make them so very uncomfortable. My impression would be that since, as you say, they defied you, it was because they believed that, after all, you would never really come to the point. Their confidence, after counsel taken of each other, was not in their innocence, nor in their talent for bluffing things off; it was in your remarkable good nature! You see they were right.' Newman instinctively turned to see if the little paper was in fact consumed; but there was nothing left of it. (M)	'Is it quite consumed?' she asked, glancing at the fire. He assured her there was nothing left of it, and at this, dropping her embroidery, she got up and came near him. 'I needn't tell you at this hour how I've felt for you. But I like you as you are,' she said. 'As I am—?' 'As you are.' She stood before him and put out her hand as for his own, which he a little blankly let her take. 'Just exactly as you are,' she repeated. With which, bending her head, she raised his hand and very tenderly and beautifully kissed it. Then, 'Ah, poor Claire!' she sighed as she went back to her place. It drew from him, while his flushed face followed her, a strange inarticulate sound, and this made her but say again: 'Yes, a thousand times—poor, poor Claire!' (NYE, pp. 362–3)

Readers and critics have been known to ask which ending is 'better', and many express a preference for the earlier one. It is indeed very good. But such judgements are meaningless when taken in isolation from the total narrative in its alternative guises. Each of the endings is entirely appropriate; these are different Newmans in two distinct novels.

EXPLANATORY NOTES

References to Baedeker are to *Paris and its Environs*, 6th edn. (Leipsig, 1878). Shakespearian references are to the Riverside Shakespeare, ed. G. Blakemore Evans (Boston, 1974). References to the early version of the novel are to the first English edition of 1879 by Macmillan.

3 *Thackeray's 'Denis Duval'... Mrs Gaskell's 'Wives and Daughters'... Stevenson's 'Weir of Hermiston'*: all unfinished at the time of their authors' deaths (Thackeray in 1863, Mrs Gaskell in 1865, and Stevenson—a good friend of James's—in 1894).

6 *Gray's beautiful Ode*: James is thinking of these lines from Thomas Gray's 'Ode on a Distant Prospect of Eton College' (1748):

> Alas, regardless of their doom,
> The little victims play!
> No sense have they of ills to come,
> Nor care beyond today: . . .

8 *Etretat*: James described his summer break at this resort on the Normandy coast in 'A French Watering Place' for the *New York Tribune*, 26 August 1876 (reprinted in *Parisian Sketches*, ed. Leon Edel and Ilse Dusoir Lind, (London, 1958)). He used it as the setting for a critical phase of his novel *Confidence* (1879), chs. 19–21 (see Introduction, n. 5).

Bayonne: half-an-hour's drive from Biarritz, near the Spanish border, James told his father, 'the prettiest little town in France; extremely picturesque, half Spanish in character' (*Letters*, ed. Leon Edel, vol. ii (London, 1975)). He spent a week here before returning to Paris in mid-September 1876.

Saint-Germain-en-Laye: James retreated to the Pavillon Louis XIV in this quiet town a short train-ride west of Paris. James had used it—including the famous view from its 'terrace'—as the setting for one of his finest early tales, 'Mme. De Mauves' (1874).

'Le Père Goriot': Honoré de Balzac's masterpiece of 1834, much admired by James.

9 *Robert Louis Stevenson ... in an admirable passage*: James probably has in mind the 'Letter to a Young Gentleman who Proposes to Embrace a Career of Art', first published in *Scribner's Magazine* (September 1888), and reprinted in *Across the Plains* (1892).

10 *Zola*: in one of his letters for the *New York Tribune* (13 May 1876) James had described Émile Zola (1840–1902), whom he had met in Flaubert's circle, as 'the most thorough-going of the little band of out-and-out realists' (*Parisian Sketches*). He delivered his mature judgement on Zola's achievement in an essay for the *Atlantic Monthly*, August 1903 (reprinted in *Notes on Novelists*, 1914).

11 *Flaubert's Madame Bovary*: title-character of the 1857 novel by Gustave Flaubert, about whom and which—character, author, and novel—James had mixed and unresolved feelings. He wrote on Flaubert in 1874, 1876, 1893, and 1902 (see *Literary Criticism*, vol. ii, in Select Bibliography).

12 *the thread of which . . . is not once exchanged . . . for any other thread*: in an important letter to Mrs Humphry Ward of 26 July 1899, James spoke of the technical variety displayed by his novels so far, as regards the possibility of 'going behind' the consciousness of his characters: 'I "go behind" right and left in "The Princess Casamassima", "The Bostonians", "The Tragic Muse", just as I do it but singly in "The American" and "Maisie", and just as I do it consistently *never at all* . . . in "The Awkward Age".' (*Letters*, ed. Leon Edel, vol. iv (Cambridge, Mass., 1984).)

17 *the year 1868*: James sets his novel in what would turn out to be the last years of the Second Empire, on the brink of the Franco-Prussian war (1870) and the Paris Commune (1871).

Salon Carré: this contained 'the gems of the collection', according to Baedeker (see below).

Murillo's beautiful moon-borne Madonna: Baedeker described the *Immaculate Conception* by the Spanish Bartolomé Esteban Murillo (1617–82) as 'pervaded with an intense sentiment of religious enthusiasm'. The Madonna is 'moon-borne' after the description in Revelation 12 : 1, of 'a woman clothed with the sun, and the moon under her feet, and upon her head a crown of twelve stars'.

Bädeker: Karl Baedeker's first *Handbook for Paris and Its Environs* was published in 1865, and thereafter regularly updated. Asterisks signalled 'marks of commendation' (the Murillo got two).

18 *muscular Christian*: devotee of the ethos of physical heartiness associated with the Christian socialism of Thomas Hughes and Charles Kingsley from the 1850s onwards. Edwin Sill Fussell points out an irony here: Kingsley was the vociferous antagonist of the man with whom Newman shares his name, 'the most famous Anglo-American Roman Catholic convert of the modern world', John Henry Newman (*The Catholic Side of Henry James* (Cambridge, 1993)).

Café Anglais: one of the expensive restaurants on the Boulevard des Italiens.

21 *Sèvres biscuit*: unglazed pottery from the town of Sèvres near Versailles.

22 *Noémie Nioche*: 'Noémie' is the first name of the American heroine of *L'Étrangère*, a play by Dumas *fils* which opened in 1876 starring Sarah Bernhardt. James wrote a scathing review for the *New York Tribune*, 25 March 1876 (reprinted in *Parisian Sketches*). For its possible influence on this novel see Oscar Cargill, *The Novels of Henry James* (New York, 1961). Along with 'Nioche', Noémie's name makes her sound more homey than she would wish, 'nioche' rhyming with *brioche* ('bread-roll') and *mioche* ('kid').

27 *Paul Veronese . . . the marriage-feast of Cana of Galilee*: Paolo Veronese (*c.*1528–88) completed his painting of Christ's first miracle (see John 2: 1–11) in 1562. It took up nearly the whole of the south wall of the Salon Carré; 'a perfect "symphony of colours"', Baedeker rhapsodized, awarding it another double asterisk.

29 *Palais Royal*: Baedeker warned readers about the 'tempting display of jewellery, and other "objets de luxe"', in the ground-floor shops in the square across the Rue de Rivoli, opposite the Louvre: 'These were once the best shops in Paris, but they are now greatly surpassed by those in the Boulevards and elsewhere.'

Avenue d'Iéna: one of the twelve avenues radiating from the Arc de Triomphe de l'Étoile, and the heart of the area known as the *Colonie Américaine*.

32 *Grand Hotel*: one of the three largest hotels in Paris, on the Boulevard des Capucines, 'managed somewhat in the same style as the large American hotels, and . . . replete with every comfort' (Baedeker).

33 *brevet*: rank.

34 *Dr Franklin . . . munching a penny loaf*: Benjamin Franklin's (1706–90) humble entrance into Philadelphia, as described in his unfinished *Autobiography*.

the golden stream: a reference to the shower of gold into which Zeus famously transformed himself to reach Danaë in the tower where her father had locked her.

more . . . than his philosophy had hitherto dreamt of: 'There are more things in heaven and earth, Horatio, | Than are dreamt of in your philosophy', says Hamlet, after seeing his father's ghost (*Hamlet*, I. v. 166–7). See note to p. 361 for a further allusion to *Hamlet*, added in revision.

36 *half a million*: $500,000 in 1907 would have been worth just over £100,000, figures which would need to be multiplied by a factor of nine or ten to get their modern-day equivalent. In the 1879 text the figure had been a mere $60,000.

37 *into the country*: as Brooklyn in 1868 would still have been.

38 *Bois de Boulogne*: converted after 1852 into an elegant public park (though about to be ravaged by the sieges of 1870–1).

Trouville: fashionable resort on the Normandy coast.

Newport: resort on Rhode Island.

39 *broad avenues distributed by Baron Haussmann*: Baron Georges-Eugène Haussmann (1809–91), responsible for the modernization of Paris under the Second Empire (1852–70), in the course of which, as Baedeker reported, 'Dense masses of houses and numbers of tortuous streets were replaced by broad boulevards, spacious squares, and palatial edifices.'

40 *furbelows*: showy ornaments, flounces, or trimming in a lady's dress.

42 *the iridescence of decay*: a 1907 addition which draws on a typically 'deca-dent' line of the previous decade, from Eugene Lee-Hamilton's 'Baude-laire' (1894), 'The gorgeous iridescence of decay'.

47 *as the French proverb puts it*: James cites it in French, in a letter of 28 May 1876, apologizing to his friend and editor W. D. Howells for his lack of news—' "*La plus belle fille du monde ne peut donner que ce qu'elle a.*" ' (*Letters*, ed. Leon Edel, vol. ii (London, 1975).)

49 *the heroes of the French romantic poets, Rolla and Fortunio*: Rolla was the eponymous hero of an 1833 poem by Alfred de Musset, and Fortunio of an 1837 tale by Théophile Gautier.

Circassian with a dagger in her baggy trousers: fair-skinned Circassian slaves on their way to Turkish harems caught the eye of nineteenth-century writers and painters from Byron onwards, in whose *Don Juan* 'Circas-sians' is rhymed with 'passions' (Canto IV, stanza 113).

Sardanapalus: Assyrian tyrant and voluptuary whose spectacular suicide was made famous by the poetic drama of Byron's named after him (1821), and the painting by Eugène Delacroix (1827), inspired by Byron, the earlier version of which James saw in Paris in 1876.

50 *the very top of the basket*: a literal translation of the common French phrase *le dessus du panier*, for which the equivalent English would be 'out of the top drawer'.

Rue de l'Université: one of the main streets in the aristocratic Faubourg St Germain, on the Left Bank. Baedeker warned tourists that 'the quarter presents a dull and deserted appearance especially on Sundays and holidays'.

Claire de Bellegarde: her first name associates her with light; later refer-ences will qualify this to suggest *clair de lune* or 'moonlight'. 'Bellegarde' tells us that she is 'well-guarded'.

51 *a Legitimist or an Ultramontane*: on the far right wing of French politics of the time, the Legitimists supported the claims of the Bourbons over-thrown in 1830, and specifically the claim to the throne of Henry Charles Ferdinand (1820–83) (see note to p. 176), while the Ultramontanists looked 'beyond the mountains' to the power of the papacy in all tem-poral as well as spiritual affairs.

Madame de Cintré: the name primarily suggests encirclement and con-striction, as in the English 'cincture' and 'cinct' from the same Latin root, but it also has the architectural sense of 'vaulted' or 'arched' (of a door, window, or roof), and heraldic associations with royalty. The ending in 'é' gives it an appropriately aristocratic ring, far removed from 'Nioche', for example.

55 *major-domo*: 'Butler' (as indeed it was in 1879).

57 *napoleons*: gold coins of the Second Empire named after Napoleon III.

58 *specie*: cash.

60 *Rue de Clichy*: a street in a working-class district of northern Paris.

Lamartine: Alphonse Lamartine (1790–1869), one of the major French Romantic poets.

Comédie: the Comédie Française or Théâtre Français, situated on the south-west side of the Palais-Royal, much admired by James for the high style of its acting and diction.

66 *a Marriage of Saint Catherine*: the *Betrothal of St Catherine*, painted by Antonio Correggio (1489–1534) in 1526–7, depicting Catherine's self-dedication to Christ.

Italian portrait of a lady: portrait known as the *Bella Nani*, painted by Veronese in 1555.

67 *Rubenses—the Marriage of Marie de Médicis*: celebration of the wedding in 1610 between Maria de' Medici and Henry IV of France, painted by Peter Paul Rubens (1577–1640).

69 '*What sort of a husband can you get for twelve thousand francs?*': adapted from an anecdote cited by James in one of his letters to the *New York Tribune* (19 February 1876), about the maidservant who was asked why she had spent the thirty crowns she had saved on marriage to a hunch-back: 'What sort of a husband can one get for thirty crowns?' (*Parisian Sketches*).

72 *cicerone*: tourist guide.

Counts Egmont and Horn: Dutch patriots executed in 1568 for their leading role in the resistance to Philip of Spain.

74 *Babcock . . . a young Unitarian minister*: William James wrote to his brother: 'Your second instalment of the American is prime. The morbid little clergyman is worthy of Ivan Sergeitch [i.e. Turgenev]. I was not a little amused to find some of my own attributes in him.—I think you found my "moral reaction" excessive when I was abroad' (*The Correspondence of William James*, vol. i, ed. Ignas K. Skrupskelis and Elizabeth M. Berkeley (Charlottesville, Va., 1992)). For an account of the brothers in Italy together in 1873–4, see Leon Edel, *The Conquest of London* (London, 1962) 146–56.

Graham bread and hominy: Babcock is a devotee of the vegetarian princi-ples advocated by Sylvester Graham (1794–1851); 'hominy' is maize or corn boiled with water or milk.

the table d'hôte system: fixed-price set menu.

75 *Mrs Jameson's volumes*: the once popular *Sacred and Legendary Art* (1848–60) by Anna Brownell Jameson (1794–1860)—now best known for her *Shakespeare's Heroines*—would have provided poor Babcock with some of the guidance for which he is looking.

76 *Goethe recommended*: in *Wilhelm Meister*, translated by Thomas Carlyle (1824, 1827).

77 *Simplon*: alpine pass between Switzerland and Italy.

78 *Luini*: Bernardino Luini (*c*.1485–1532) commended himself to the Victorians, especially Ruskin, for his sentimental treatment of religious subjects.

80 *Baden-Baden*: German spa-resort, setting for the opening scene of George Eliot's *Daniel Deronda*, which James was reading at the time of first writing in 1876, and used by James himself for a large part of *Confidence* (1879), chs. 3–15.

83 *Trebizond, Samarcand, Bokhara*: more exotic-sounding than the 'Medina and Mecca' of 1879 which they here replace.

   the joy of life: a phrase of the 1890s and after, derived from William Archer's translation of Ibsen's *livsglæde* (the whole sentence being a 1907 revision); cf. Appendix 1, p. 366.

85 *Boulevard Haussmann*: running east–west from the Arc de Triomphe in continuation with the Avenue de Friedland, named after the architect of modern Paris (see note to p. 39), and pronounced 'handsome' by Baedeker. Edwin Sill Fussell suggests (*The French Side of Henry James* (New York, 1990)) that the thick gilt of Newman's apartment may have been inspired by the new Opéra, which James described to readers of the *New York Tribune* as 'nothing but gold—gold upon gold: it has been gilded till it is dark with gold' (*Parisian Sketches*).

   church of Saint Sulpice: the 'richest and one of the most important of the churches on the left bank of the Seine' (Baedeker).

87 *The Morals of Murray Hill!*: a district on New York's Middle East Side below Grand Central Station, from 27th St on the south to 42nd St on the north, and from 6th Ave. east to 3rd Ave. (excluding 5th Ave.). It became an exclusive residential area in the post-Civil War period from 1870 onwards, attracting such wealthy families as the Belmonts, Rhinelanders, Tiffanys, and Havemeyers. (In 1879 Tristram exclaimed—'The Mysteries of the Fifth Avenue!')

91 *Louis-Quinze period*: Louis XV reigned 1715–74. (In 1879, 'the familiar rococo style of the last century'.)

   1627: John Carlos Rowe writes: 'At the very least, Newman ought to make some connection between this date and the early years of the Puritan Bay Colony, but even more important than this American connection are the historical events of the war waged between 1624 and 1629 by Cardinal Richelieu against the Huguenots. Richelieu attempted to exterminate the Huguenots not simply as the major Protestant opposition to Catholicism in seventeenth-century France but also as the religious basis for republican sympathies opposed to the monarchy.' ('The Politics of Innocence', in Martha Banta (ed.), *New Essays on The American* (Cambridge, 1987).) In 1627 France was invaded by English forces under the Duke of Buckingham.

103 *the Bonapartes*: descended from Napoleon Bonaparte, the Emperor in 1868—nearing the end of his time—was Napoleon III.

fight for the Pope: Valentin has fought with the French troops sent by Napoleon III to support Pope Pius IX (r. 1846–78) in his struggles against the Italian republicans.

Castelfidardo: on 18 September 1860 the papal forces were defeated by the Piedmontese at this small village on the Adriatic coast.

Heliogabalus: profligate Roman Emperor AD 218–22 (replacing the 'Caligula' of 1879).

castle of Saint Angelo: refuge of the Pope and his troops after the defeat at Castelfidardo until 1870.

105 *the Rue d'Anjou Saint Honoré*: short street running north–south from Boulevard Haussmann to the Rue du Faubourg St Honoré.

109 *Madame Dandelard*: not a dignified name, the first part might suggest *dandiner*, 'to waddle', and the second, *lard*, 'bacon' (or phonetically, *dent de lard*, 'bacon-tooth').

112 *Orestes and Electra*: the brother and sister who together avenged their father Agamemnon by killing his murderers, their mother Clytemnestra and her lover Aegisthus: an oddly disturbing allusion in its relation to the Bellegardes' family history, as it is eventually revealed.

113 *between two fires*: a literal translation of the French phrase *entre deux feux*, for which an English equivalent would be 'between the frying pan and the fire'.

115 *King Cophetua*: legendary King of Africa who fell in love with a beggar maid—the subject of a well-known painting by Edward Burne-Jones (1884).

117 *Samson . . . pulled down the temple*: as represented in Milton's *Samson Agonistes* (1671).

your quarterings: in heraldry, the division of a shield into quarters to produce a 'coat of arms'.

131 *abounding in her own sense*: a literal translation of the French phrase meaning 'to be in complete agreement' (*abonder dans votre sens*).

'a supersubtle Venetian': it is Iago who tries to sow the seeds of doubt in Othello's mind by so crediting or discrediting Desdemona (I. iii. 156). 'Supersubtle' is an epithet James became fond of applying to some of his own leading characters. For a further telling reference to *Othello*, see note to p. 356.

134 *Lady Emmeline Atheling*: the maiden name of the old Marquise connotes the dim and distant past, 'atheling' being derived from Old English to mean 'member of a noble family'.

Books of Beauty: fashion magazines of the 1830s.

140 *the Tuileries*: the public gardens of the Tuileries Palace (destroyed by the Communards in 1871). Baedeker described the sunny and sheltered west side as 'the paradise of nurse-maids and children, elderly persons, and invalids'.

145 *the long hall of the Italian masters*: the Grande Galerie.

146 *tulle*: fine silk net used for dresses, veils, and hats.

smaller apartment . . . on the left: known then as the 'Galerie des Sept Mètres', now the 'Salle des Primitifs Italiens'.

147 *expray, expray*: Newman's version of '*exprès, exprès*' ('specially, on purpose') allows us to hear what in 1879 had simply been reported as his 'bad French'.

151 *Virginius*: the story of the Roman father who killed his daughter Virginia to save her virtue from Appius, first told by Livy, was dramatized as *Virginius* in a popular play of 1820 by James Sheridan Knowles, and retold as 'Virginia' in one of Macaulay's *Lays of Ancient Rome* (1842).

154 *puff*: or, as it would normally now be spelt, 'pouf' or 'pouffe'.

156 *Sansovino*: Jacopo Tatti Sansovino (*c*.1486–1570), Venetian architect and sculptor, whose works include the Library of St Mark, with the adjoining Mint and Loggia of the Campanile.

158 *Corps Législatif*: lit. 'legislative body' (of the French government), first constituted as such under the Consulate of Napoleon Bonaparte in 1799.

163 *la Rochefidèle*: 'Loyal Rock'. Compare the declaration of the young Marquise a few lines later that she is *vieille roche*, literally 'old rock' (see Glossary).

the Empire: the young Marquise dissociates herself from the pro-Bourbon circle of the Bellegardes which 'pouts at' the Second Empire of Napoleon III, in power from 1852–70.

164 *your battles in the last century*: in the American War of Independence (1776–83).

The great Dr Franklin: in 1878 Benjamin Franklin secured France's support for the American revolutionaries, and stayed on in Paris until 1785. This means that M. de la Rochefidèle must now be in his mid-to-late 80s.

168 *Andromeda . . . Perseus*: Andromeda was fastened to a rock as a sacrifice to a sea-monster, and the hero Perseus rescued her.

176 *Henry of Bourbon, Fifth of his name*: legitimists such as the Bellegardes and their circle believed that the last true King of France had been Charles X (1824–30), and that the rightful claimant to the throne was his grandson Henri Charles Ferdinand, known to them as Henry V, but more generally as the Comte de Chambord. The elder line of the Bourbons was never to recover from the revolution of 1830. This saw the accession of Louis Philippe, of the younger line of the House of Orléans, overthrown in turn by the revolution of 1848. Newman remains oblivious to the enduring hostility between Legitimists and Orléanists, rival factions of the monarchist opposition to the Second Empire.

186 *the new Offenbach things . . . 'La Pomme de Paris'*: the light operas of Jacques Offenbach (1819–80) were at the height of their popularity in the

1860s with hits such as *La Belle Hélène* (1864) and *La Vie parisienne* (1867). If 'La Pomme de Paris' is in fact 'Pomme d'Api', then it was not one of them, but a lesser thing of 1873—and hence an anachronism here—when the mood of the times had changed against him.

'La Gazza Ladra': *The Thieving Magpie*, by Gioacchino Rossini (1817).

194 *falbalas*: original form of 'furbelows' (see note to p. 40).

197 *Madame Frezzolini*: the Italian soprano Erminia Frezzolini (1818–84) was by 1868 at the very end of her career.

200 *Rue Saint-Roch*: this runs north–south connecting the Rue de Rivoli and the Avenue de l'Opéra.

207 *Montmartre*: working-class district on the northern margin of the tourist route, distinguished by the Baedekers of the time only for its cemetery.

intaglio: a precious stone with a figure or design cut into its surface.

208 *tableaux vivants*: a form of charade in which paintings or scenes from plays were represented in still-life.

214 *green or yellow*: Newman is not to know that to sport a green bow was to signal yourself a prostitute.

216 *some historic figure painted by Vandyke*: Sir Anthony Van Dyck (1599–1641) painted portraits of the Genoese aristocracy in the 1620s, and spent his last years in England as court-painter to Charles I.

220 *a lady of monstrous proportions*: the Duchess is modelled on a princess of Saxe-Coburg whom James met, along with members of the Orléans family, at a reception at the Duc d'Aumale's; she gave him 'a realizing sense of what princesses are trained to' (Edel, *The Conquest of London*).

224 *Keats's 'Belle Dame Sans Merci'*: Keats's poem of 1820 tells the tale, all too ominously for Valentin, of a man enthralled and destroyed by a *femme fatale*, the Merciless Beauty of the title.

230 *'Don Giovanni'*: Mozart's opera of 1787, based on the legendary libertine of Seville, Don Juan.

Adelina Patti: the great Italian soprano (1843–1919) was in the 1860s still in the early years of her prime. She displaces the older 'Madame Alboni' of the 1879 text, the contralto Marietta Alboni (1823–94), whose heyday was past by 1868 (though she sang that year with Patti at Rossini's funeral).

roulades: a quick succession of notes.

233 *at night all cats are grey*: James was fond of this common French proverb, *La nuit, tous les chats sont gris*.

feuilleton in the Figaro: a serialized story in this newspaper, of which James had a low opinion—'a most detestable sheet', he told readers of his first *New York Tribune* letter, 22 November 1875 (*Parisian Sketches*).

Donna Elvira: seduced and abandoned by Don Giovanni, Donna Elvira's situation is indeed not much like Madame de Cintré's, but she shares her dignity and vows to end her days in a convent.

234 *Zerlina*: the country girl who just escapes the clutches of the seductive Don.

the Commander—the man of stone: the statue of the Commendatore, the father murdered by Don Giovanni while defending his daughter, Donna Anna.

235 *Poitiers*: where the Bellegardes have their country estate, Fleurières.

the Tuileries are dreadfully vulgar: the Palais des Tuileries was the official residence of the ruling Napoleon III and the 'clever Bonapartes', as it had been of their predecessors since the first Napoleon took up his quarters there in 1800. But the palace was about to be destroyed in the Commune of 1871.

the Latin Quarter: the Quartier Latin, on the Left Bank, a district dominated by University students and student life.

257 *the stony circle of Paris*: the city walls (in 1879, 'the *enceinte* of Paris'— which would have suggested an echo of *cintré*, 'girdled').

Auteuil: Newman has walked west to reach this wealthy district next to the Bois de Boulogne.

258 *Trocadéro*: terraced embankment south of the Arc de Triomphe overlooking the Pont d'Iéna, soon to be embellished with the Palais du Trocadéro (1878) and a full view of the Eiffel Tower (1889) on the Left Bank.

260 *the Jura*: mountain range on the border between France and Switzerland.

261 *canton*: name given to each of the states comprising the Swiss confederation.

264 *sabots*: wooden clogs.

265 *'Les Liaisons Dangereuses'*: the infamous epistolary novel of 1782 by Choderlos de Laclos (1741–1803). It supplanted, in the text of the first volume edition, the only slightly less shocking *Les Amours du Chevalier de Faublas* (1789–90) by Louvet de Couvray, which had featured in the *Atlantic Monthly* serial version.

268 *another Rothschild*: the family famously associated with banking and finance.

274 *his sacred vessel*: the Communion chalice.

276 *the reign of Henry III*: James based the Bellegardes' country-seat on a Château-Renard he saw when staying with the Edward Lee Childes at their own Varennes, near Montargis, in August 1876. In 1907 he pushed the origins of the château further back in time; in the early texts it had dated from the reign of Henry IV (1589–1610). The last monarch of the House of Valois, Henry of Anjou reigned as Henry III for fifteen war-torn years from 1574 until his assassination in 1589, when the crown passed to his remote cousin, Henry of Navarre, who became Henry IV, first monarch of the House of Bourbon.

a little Dutch-looking pavilion: these Dutch pavilions might suggest a promisingly Protestant element in the immense Catholic façade, or an historical possibility long lost in the religious conflicts of the sixteenth and seventeenth centuries. John Carlos Rowe points out that Holland was a refuge for many French Huguenots, and a stopping-place en route in due course to America ('The Politics of Innocence', in Banta (ed.), *New Essays on The American*). When Newman descends on Paris for the last time he finds that Mrs Bread has kept his rooms 'as neat as a Dutch village' (p. 357).

284 *Carmelite nun*: the strictness of the Carmelite order derives from the reforms made by St Teresa of Avila in 1562.

296 *very Low*: Low Church.

319 *Avenue de Messine*: just off the Boulevard Haussmann, where Newman has his apartment.

Rue d'Enfer: 'Hell Street'. At the time of the novel's setting there was not only a Rue d'Enfer, but a Boulevard, a Place, and a Passage, all d'Enfer, just to the east of the Montparnasse Cemetery. They have all been renamed. The Rue d'Enfer (now Rue Denfert-Rochereau and Rue Henri Barbusse) ran north-east from the Place d'Enfer (now Denfert-Rochereau) across the Avenue de l'Observatoire to link up with the Boulevard St Michel. Edwin Sill Fussell notes a 'Couvent de la Visitation' or 'Couvent des Dames Carmélites' marked on the 1872 Galignani map (*The French Side of Henry James* (New York, 1990)).

322 *Arkansaw*: evidently James's idea of a very rough place. In 1879 Newman's sentence had stopped at 'It's too rough.'

323 *Parc Monceau*: Baedeker declared this, recently converted into a public park, 'a pleasant and refreshing oasis in the midst of a well-peopled quarter of the city'.

325 *landau*: four-wheeled carriage with removable top.

339 *pink-covered novels*: an apparently anachronistic reference to the novels of George Sand, reissued in this distinctive form in the early 1870s.

341 *the brutal Sardinian rule*: a reference to Victor Emmanuel, now King of Italy.

342 *was he to have brayed like that animal whose ears are longest*: in 1879 Newman had more simply thought 'he had come very near being an ass'.

343 *'sympathetic'*: the French *sympathique* has more active associations of like-ability than its reactive English counterpart.

panoply: a complete suit of armour.

344 *Obelisk in the Place de la Concorde*: the Obelisk of Luxor, presented to Louis Philippe by the Pasha of Egypt and erected in 1836.

346 *'the season'*: the three months from May to July, when fashionable society gathered in London.

Kensington Gardens . . . the adjoining Drive: the Gardens are situated immediately to the west of Hyde Park, while 'the Drive' in the latter was patronized, especially during 'the season', by the carriages of everyone who was anyone.

346 *Windsor Forest . . . Madame Tussaud's exhibition*: Newman is again being a dutiful tourist visiting all the recommended sites, though Sheffield is certainly off the beaten track, a stray thought from his past existence in 'business'.

347 *'fit'*: to his clothes, presumably.

356 *his occupation had gone*: a reminiscence of Othello's great lament, in the grip of his belief that he has lost Desdemona for ever: 'Othello's occupation's' gone' (III. iii. 357). See also note to p. 131.

357 *Saint Veronica*: out of pity for Christ on the way to Calvary, she wiped his face with a cloth which is supposed to have retained the imprint of his features.

station: like a station of the Cross—an addition in 1907 which reinforces the religious associations of the 'stony sepulchre' in which he thinks of Claire being entombed.

359 *Notre Dame*: the cathedral on the Île de la Cité, the most ancient part of Paris, built over nearly 200 years from 1163 to 1345. It features again at critical moments of 'recognition' in *The Tragic Muse* (1890), Book Second, ch. 9, and *The Ambassadors* (1903), Book Seventh, ch. 1.

361 *draw his breath a while in pain*: a reminiscence of Hamlet's dying words to Horatio, added in 1907:

> If thou didst ever hold me in thy heart,
> Absent thee from felicity a while,
> And in this harsh world draw thy breath in pain
> To tell my story.
>
> (V. ii. 298–301)

In 1879 Newman merely 'drew a longer breath than usual'.

363 *'poor Claire'*: Edwin Sill Fussell points out that 'Poor Clares are the Second (Women's) Order of Franciscans'—vowed to poverty (*The Catholic Side of Henry James* (Cambridge, 1993)).

GLOSSARY OF FRENCH WORDS AND PHRASES

There is a good deal of French in this novel (more in the revised New York Edition than in its earlier forms), much of it simple enough, like the single word that initially constitutes the hero's vocabulary—*Combien?* Nevertheless readers may find this full glossary helpful, in which the translations offered apply to words and phrases *as they are encountered in the context of this novel*. Recurring French words and phrases are glossed here rather than in the Explanatory Notes. It seems unnecessary to notice words that have become domesticated in English, such as *finesse*, *casseroles*, *au revoir*, *papier-mâché*, *foyer*, and *crême de la crême* (*sic*, for *crème de la crème*), and words that differ minimally if at all between languages, such as *bourgeoisie*, *improbable*, *galant*, *légende*, *bizarre*, *parc*, *milord*, and so on. Nor need the reader puzzle over the English equivalents for such calculatedly French exclamations as *Heuh*, *Hein?*, and *Ouf!* There is a small number of cases in which it would be superfluous to compete with English versions supplied in the text by the speakers themselves, as for instance *râté* ('a dead failure'), *les gens forts* ('Strong people'), and '*Savoir vivre* ('knowing how to live').

abruti stupefied
à faire pleurer enough to make you weep
ah ça well really
ah vous, mon cher, vous en avez, vous, de toutes les couleurs! ah you, my dear, you have all the sorts there are, you do!
allons come on
allons, enfants de la patrie come, children of your native land (the first line of the 'Marseillaise')
anéantie exhausted
Anglaise Englishwoman
arrivez donc, messieurs! come on then, gentlemen!
au pas de charge at full speed (from military expression for advancing 'at the charge')
baignoire ground-floor box at the theatre

bavardé chattered
beaucoup, beaucoup a lot, a lot
beaucoup de cachet lots of style
beaucoup d'industrie a lot of hard work
beau jeu a free hand
beau jeune homme fine young man
beaux jours heyday
beaux noms good names
belle-mère mother-in-law
belle-sœur sister-in-law
bête silly, stupid
bien sûr! of course!
bonne maid
bureau de placement employment agency
cabinet study
cabinet de toilette bathroom
calèche barouche (four-wheeled carriage)
caprice de prince princely whim

ce que c'est que la gloire de race so much for the fame of ancestry

ces dames those, these, our women

c'est ça qui pose une femme! that's the thing to set a woman up!

c'est égal all the same

c'est le bel âge it's the best time of life

c'est plus qu'un Anglais, le cher homme—c'est un Anglomane! he's more than an Englishman, the dear fellow—he's an Anglomaniac!

c'est positif that's certain

c'est un beau choix it's a fine choice

cette pauvre Princesse this poor princess

charcutière pork butcher

charmante charming

chef de (la) famille head of (the) family

chère belle beautiful darling

cocottes loose women (from baby-language for 'hens' or 'chicks'), often used at the time of actresses

combien? how much?

commande order

comme il faut proper

commerçant tradesman, merchant

commode(s) easy

comprenez? do you understand?

contrat marriage-contract

côté passionnel inclination to passion

coulant easy-going

coup shot

coup de tête rash action

crever d'ennui die of boredom

Croix Helvétique Swiss Cross

cuisse de nymphe a shade of pale pink, after the so-named blush-pink variety of *Rosa alba* (lit. 'nymph's thigh')

dans le temps in time past

dame de compagnie lady's companion

dame, monsieur! why, sir!

dans le monde into society

dans le nôtre in our set

dans les feuilles in the papers

de grâce for goodness' sake

demi-tasse half-cup

de notre bord belonging to the same world as us

diable, diable, diable! devil take it!

disponible available

donnez! give it to me!

dot dowry

d'un sérieux! extremely serious!

embêter bother

en costume de ville in his suit

enfin after all

en prince like a prince

en somme all in all

en voilà du nouveau! there's a novelty!

éprouver experience

esprit wit

fadaises nonsense

faire la fête toujours still have a good time

fauteuils armchairs

femme de chambre maid

fête champêtre pastoral entertainment (as in the paintings of Antoine Watteau (1684–1721))

folichon, folichonne pleasant, exciting

franche coquette open flirt

gentil, gentille, gentils sweet, nice, kind

gentilhomme gentleman

gentiment nicely

grand monde great world

grande dame great lady

hélas [, oui!] sadly [, yes!]

homme à femmes ladies' man

homme de premier ordre first-rate man

homme d'esprit intelligent man

homme du monde man of distinction

hôtel mansion

hôtel garni rooming house

il en resterait quelque chose
something would still stick

incommodes difficult

intimité inner circle

je le veux bien! I don't mind
admitting it!

je ne lui ai pas trouvé d'excuses I
have found no grounds for excusing
her

joliment 'pretty' (colloquial)

joué duped

là-bas there

l'appétit vient en mangeant eating
gives you an appetite

le cœur tendre kindness,
susceptibility

le misérable! the wretch!

le reste vous regarde the rest is
your responsibility

liard farthing

loge aux Italiens opera box (at the
Théâtre des Italiens)

l'usage du monde the way of the
world

madère glass of madeira

ma bonne my dear

ma mère my mother

maîtres de café café-owners

malade patient

malaise discomfort

malheureux! you wretch!

matamore! you brave bully-boy!

mêlée fray

mieux causer be a better talker

mon bichon my little pet

mon bon my good man

monde social set

mon Dieu, oui my God, yes

mon pauvre ami my poor friend

mon père, mon père my father, my
father

monsieur mon frère my honourable
brother

mot(s) witticism(s)

notre monde à nous our own circle

office service

ordure filth

ouvreuse usherette

pardieu! by God!

par exemple good heavens

partie match

pas beaucoup? isn't that a lot?

pas de raisons! no excuses!

pas du tout aimable not at all
nice

pas insulté? You're not insulted?

petit bourg little town

petite noblesse gentry

plus fins causeurs cleverest
conversationalists

portière door-curtain

pour deux sous for two pence

pourtant nevertheless

procès-verbal oral statement

proprement decently

quartier neighbourhood

quelle folie! how silly!

quelle horreur! how dreadful!

qui se voit obvious

raffiné man of refinement

ranz-des-vaches Swiss rustic tunes
(often played by shepherds on their
traditional horns)

râté failure

rez-de-chaussée ground floor

roturière commoner

salle parlour

se faire une raison accept the
inevitable

sentimental sentimental person

seulement vous just you

soigné meticulous

tas d'ennuis load of troubles

tiens! well!

toilette dress

touchez-là shake hands on it

toupet nerve, cheek

tout craché spitting image

très-supérieure very high-class

valet(s) de place local servant(s)

venez donc come then

vieille roche the real thing (as of a diamond), or more generally, of the old, tried, and trusted (lit. 'old rock')

villains 'villains' or 'villeins' (in original sense of feudal serfs or tenants)

voilà! there!

votre serviteur yours truly

vous allez bien voir you'll see well enough

vous avez l'air bien honnête you look like a decent sort of man

vous m'imposez you impress me

vous ne doutez de rien! you've no doubts about yourself!

voyons come now

TROLLOPE IN   OXFORD WORLD'S CLASSICS

ANTHONY TROLLOPE   The American Senator

An Autobiography

Barchester Towers

Can You Forgive Her?

The Claverings

Cousin Henry

The Duke's Children

The Eustace Diamonds

Framley Parsonage

He Knew He Was Right

Lady Anna

Orley Farm

Phineas Finn

Phineas Redux

The Prime Minister

Rachel Ray

The Small House at Allington

The Warden

The Way We Live Now

ÉMILE ZOLA

L'Assommoir
The Attack on the Mill
La Bête humaine
La Débâcle
Germinal
The Kill
The Ladies' Paradise
The Masterpiece
Nana
Pot Luck
Thérèse Raquin

The Oxford World's Classics Website

www.oup.com/uk/worldsclassics

- Information about new titles
- Explore the full range of Oxford World's Classics
- Links to other literary sites and the main OUP webpage
- Imaginative competitions, with bookish prizes
- Articles by editors
- Extracts from Introductions
- Special information for teachers and lecturers

www.oup.com/uk/worldsclassics

American Literature

Authors in Context

British and Irish Literature

Children's Literature

Classics and Ancient Literature

Colonial Literature

Eastern Literature

European Literature

History

Medieval Literature

Oxford English Drama

Poetry

Philosophy

Politics

Religion

The Oxford Shakespeare

A complete list of Oxford World's Classics, including Authors in Context, Oxford English Drama, and the Oxford Shakespeare, is available in the UK from the Marketing Services Department, Oxford University Press, Great Clarendon Street, Oxford OX2 6DP, or visit the website at www.oup.com/uk/worldsclassics.

In the USA, visit www.oup.com/us/owc for a complete title list.

Oxford World's Classics are available from all good bookshops. In case of difficulty, customers in the UK should contact Oxford University Press Bookshop, 116 High Street, Oxford OX1 4BR.